Madapple

CHRISTINA MELDRUM

Madapple

Alfred A. Knopf
NEW YORK

THIS IS A BORZOI BOOK PUBLISHED BY ALFRED A. KNOPF

Visit us on the Web! www.randomhouse.com/teens

Educators and librarians, for a variety of teaching tools, visit us at www.randomhouse.com/teachers

Library of Congress Cataloging-in-Publication Data
Meldrum, Christina.
Madapple / Christina Meldrum. — 1st ed.
    p.   cm.
Summary: A girl who has been brought up in near isolation is thrown into a twisted web of family secrets and religious fundamentalism when her mother dies and she goes to live with relatives she never knew she had.
ISBN 978-0-375-85176-6 (trade) — ISBN 978-0-375-95176-3 (lib. bdg.)
[1. Miracles—Fiction. 2. Mothers and daughters—Fiction. 3. Trials (Murder)—Fiction.] I. Title.
PZ7.M515943Mad   2008
[Fic]—dc22
2007049653

The text of this book is set in 12-point Goudy.

Printed in the United States of America

May 2008

10 9 8 7 6

First Edition

For Doug, who believed,
and for our miracles, Jacob and Owen.
And for my mother,
who sees God in every mad apple.

GNAPHALIUM

Life Everlasting

Bethan, Maine
October 1987

*T*he women resemble schoolgirls with gangly limbs, ruddy cheeks, plaited flaxen hair; they walk holding hands. Yet the older of the two is pregnant; her unborn baby rides high and round. And the younger woman's left foot scratches a path through the leaves. She seems comfortable with her limp, accustomed to it.

A child darts before them, chasing leaves that swirl at her feet. Her dark hair, tied back in a scant tail, whips behind her. She stumbles, catches herself. *"Mor!"* she calls out. "Mommy!" Then she points at a bird perched high on a leafless branch, its plump breast berry-like against the low sky.

The older woman hesitates before she recalls the bird's name. "A robin. The bird is a robin. Soon it will fly south for the winter. It is too cold here in Maine."

"Men det er ikke koldt. But it is not cold." The child's words are malformed; she is not yet three.

1

"*Ikke for Danmark,*" the woman says. "Not for Denmark. And certainly not for you, but you are not a robin."

The robin jerks its head to the side, then back, before it takes flight.

"The robin was looking at you," the child says to the woman with the limp, not her mother. "He wanted to know your name."

"I'm *Moster* Maren, little Sanne. Aunt Maren. Have you already forgotten?"

"Yes!" The child laughs and sprints forward; her laugh is discordant, but the wind carries the sound away, and the woman, Maren, is grateful.

"Sanne reminds me of you when you were small," the child's mother says to Maren. "Do you recall what *Fader* called you? *Gnaphalium*, remember? That plant known at home as 'life everlasting.' You were so full of life."

Maren stops walking.

"What is it, Maren?"

"Don't go back to Denmark, Sara. Stay here with me. Please. Your marriage is ending—you know that. And with *Moder*'s death, there's little keeping you. And I can help you. We'll help each other."

Sara frees her hand from Maren's grip. "*Fader* is still in Denmark. And I told you before, I don't need your help."

"Yes, *Fader,*" Maren says. She reaches toward a plant and runs her index finger along a scar on the fleshy rhizome of the plant. "Solomon's seal. This plant's name is Solomon's seal. See, the mark here. It resembles the seal of King Solomon, the Star of David—the symbol Solomon used to cast away demons, summon angels."

2

Sara lifts Maren's hand from the stalk and turns Maren toward her. "Tell me what's wrong," Sara says. "This isn't about me. Why did you ask us to come? You said you were leaving Denmark to start a new life, but now you want to bring your life in Denmark with you here?"

"I want you here. And Sanne. And your new baby," Maren says.

"But why? What is wrong? Is it something about *Fader*?"

"Don't tell *Fader*."

"Don't tell *Fader* what, Maren?"

"I'm pregnant, too."

"*Mor!*" the little girl calls out. "*Løb efter mig, Mor!*" Sanne runs down the path; trampled leaves cling to her scarf and hair. "Chase after me, Mommy!"

"You are pregnant?" Sara says, but she looks at her daughter and the gray sky and the leaves.

"Don't be angry with me—" Maren says.

But Sara interrupts. "I didn't even know you knew about such things." She is fondling her own hands as her eyes search Sanne's hands, but Sanne's hands are a blur. "You're so young, Maren. Maybe you're mistaken."

"I'm a robin." Sanne's arms stretch wide. "I can fly!"

"I'm almost sixteen," Maren says. "I'm not that young."

"But you've been in the States for less than two months. How could this happen in such a short time?"

"I'm four months pregnant," Maren says. "Three months less than you. I was pregnant before I arrived."

"*Mor*," Sanne says. "I'm flying away. I'm flying south."

Sara wraps her arms around herself and begins walking again, toward Sanne. She can see Sanne's hands better now:

3

her fingers splayed, and those two webbed fingers not splayed. And she wonders. And then she says, "Before you arrived? But how can that be? I didn't even know you had a lover. I've been like a mother to you since *Moder* died. How could you have not told me?"

"I didn't know."

"Didn't know?"

"I didn't know I was pregnant. I found out the day I asked you to come."

"But you knew you'd been with someone. You had a lover, Maren. And you didn't tell me."

"I've flown away, *Mor*." Sanne has reached the end of the path. "I'm gone forever."

"But I didn't have a lover," Maren says. "I've never had a lover."

Solomon's Seal

2007

—Please state your name for the record.

—Aslaug.

—And your last name?

—I don't know.

—You don't know your last name?

—No.

—Your mother's name was Maren Hellig, was it not?

—Yes.

—You are Aslaug Hellig?

—Mother called me Aslaug Datter.

—So your last name is Datter?

—No. I mean, I don't know. *Datter* means "daughter" in Danish. I'm not sure it's my name.

—What was your father's name?

—I don't have a father.

—You don't know who your father is?

—I don't have a father, other than the one we share.

—You mean God in heaven?

—I never said God is in heaven.

—But you mean God, am I right?

—Yes.

—Well, I'm referring to your biological father. You don't know who he is?

—I don't have a biological father.

—Your Honor, the witness is being nonresponsive. She's being tried here for one count of attempted murder and two counts of murder in the first degree, and she's playing games—

—Do you have a birth certificate for the witness, Counsel? It seems that document may clarify this matter.

—She has no birth certificate, Your Honor. At least none we've found.

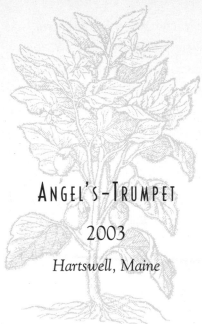

ANGEL'S-TRUMPET

2003

Hartswell, Maine

𝔪other crouches in the field, her body folded into itself as she uproots the salsify plants and lops off their purple heads. Our gathering baskets circle her like iced-over petals, their inert white handles conspicuous above the quiver of herbs and wildflowers. Her hands are gloved, should she encounter stinging nettle, she claims; its young shoots and upper leaves are worth collecting, she reminds me; we have eaten them as greens and in stew. Yet I know it is the jimsonweed, not the nettle, she is prepared to find: rank-smelling, rash-causing, poisonous jimsonweed. When I was growing up, Mother called the weed a variety of names. Madapple at times. Devil's apple at times. And green dragon and stinkwort and angel's-trumpet. No matter, her warning was always the same: deadly. Still, I know it is the jimsonweed she wants to-day. Her eyes pick through the flora, searching in vain for

7

the tall green plant with the prickly fruit and funnel flowers that look deceivingly benign.

For nearly two months now, I've found the weed's leaves and kidney-shaped seeds drying in the back porch sun, mingling as if innocent with the other berries, seeds and leaves. Perhaps Mother assumed I wouldn't notice the jimsonweed, subsumed in this mosaic of plant parts. Perhaps I wouldn't have noticed if it weren't for the weed's smell: like rot. But for much of this past week, I've smelled only its absence, and, as of today, absent it remains.

Despite the dearth of jimsonweed—perhaps because of it—our baskets are mostly brimming. I carry handfuls of yellow goatsbeard leaves to cook as greens for dinner, and I toss them into the basket on top of a mound of sweet clover. The vanilla scent of the clover hovers about the basket, obfuscating the stench of waste that lingers on my shoes and skirt. We spent our morning at the town dump, collecting the wild madder we use to curdle milk when making cheese. Had we found the jimsonweed then, we might have headed home. Instead, we've worked most of the afternoon in this field collecting far more of the other flowers than we need.

The basket containing the medicinal plants is overflowing, as if the whites and yellows of the blossoms were oozing free. And the mullein is so abundant; we'll have candles for a month at least. Only the basket for the plants Mother calls her *sapientia*, her wisdom, is not yet full, the Indian tobacco there making only a thin purple-green bed along the basket's base.

"Aslaug," Mother says. I watch her untangling as her back straightens and her clenched fingers ease just enough to release the salsify. "Those cinnamon ferns," she says, and she motions toward a gaggle of green bordering the woods we will pass through on our way home. "They have hundreds more chromosomes than you." I look to the ferns; even assuming her statement was meant as a slight, I can't quell my interest.

"I'm hurting," Mother says then, as if the ferns' genetic abundance has some bearing on her pain. I turn back to her, and I see it, the pain; it seems different suddenly; she wears it differently. Her lips are powder-dry and pursed. Her left eyelid is twitching, twitching, twitching, like an insect's pumping wings. I have the urge to press my fingers against it, hold it still.

"We've been out too long," I say, walking toward her. "We should go home." I say this, but I don't mean it: I don't want to go home. Our house sits outside the village of Hartswell, at the end of a dirt road, at what I imagine is the end of the earth. We have only one neighbor; the next closest house sits miles and miles away. Even so, Mother and I leave our house only to forage, less often to drive into Hartswell to collect the mail or to the college town, Bethan, to buy supplies. The outside world is my featherfoil plant, magnificent in its season, when it appears in abundance, but then it disappears, completely, for what seems years. Our drapes are thick as quilts, and tacked shut floor to ceiling, side to side, inch by inch by inch. We live in a cocoon, Mother and I, whether to keep the inside in or the outside out, I do not know.

"We can't go, Aslaug," Mother says. "I need help."

"I can help you walk."

"No. No. For the pain."

Mother is sick. She's been sick almost as far back as I can remember. Not terribly sick, but sick. I don't know the name of her illness; Mother's never mentioned its name, and I know not to ask. She's said only that her body is attacking itself like a tomcat that devours its progeny, the progeny being her cartilage and bone, and her muscles and ligaments and tendons. Her joints are red and swollen, and, day by day, little by little, she is becoming deformed.

I rip off a leaf of the Indian tobacco and lift it to her mouth. She chews it but shakes her head. "We have shinleaf at home," I say. "I'll make the leaf plaster for you, rub it on your knees and back. It will help."

"No," Mother says. "No shinleaf."

There's a feeling that wells in me I can't name. An instinct, it seems—an instinct that something is very wrong. "I found some scarlet pimpernel at the dump," I say. "Not a lot, but enough to make a poultice." Mother refers to pimpernel as adder's eyes—snake eyes. But she's taken it before; it's made her happier, nicer. I want to believe it will help her, but I know it won't, even before she answers.

"Adder's eyes?" Mother says. "Adder's eyes won't help."

"You want jimsonweed," I say, not meaning to, but the words come.

Mother looks at me like she doesn't know me; she doesn't ask how I know about the jimsonweed. "I make an ointment with it, Aslaug," she says, "for the pain. Like the shinleaf. I mix it with nightshade, and it helps. More than shinleaf."

"I'll find some," I say.

What I don't say is she is allergic to the touch of jimsonweed, as am I. This is something she knows, we both know;

10

each of us has been careless at times, brushed against the weed and endured its wrath. Mother has no intention of rubbing her skin with jimsonweed.

Nor do I say I've seen her make cigarettes from the weed's dried leaves and seeds. Her hands protected by gloves, she rolls the weed with hemp or Indian tobacco and smokes at night when she believes I am asleep. Sometimes she mixes the leaves with something flammable—potassium nitrate, maybe—and she burns them in a saucer and inhales their smoke deeply, and holds it. I watch from the top of the stairs, the jimsonweed burning in the distance like a neutron star, and the Kabbalah or Torah or Upanishads glowing faintly in its light. Although I don't know what the weed does for Mother, she seems transported in those moments, and sometimes for days, like she's entered another time and space. A time before me. A space without me—a space where the windows were open to the world. There is a softness about the way her mouth falls loose after she inhales, and in her eyes: their twitching and relentless blinking give way. She releases her hair at some point while she sits there, and it plunges to her waist like a flash of light.

I submit to sleep before she does, always, and I wake before she does, always. And I often find the remains of Mother's foray in the morning: her cigarette butts like magnified mouse droppings or the saucer like a diminutive swamp. Sometimes I pick up a butt with tweezers, lift it to my mouth, or I breathe hard from the saucer, trying to find that space Mother finds. But the power of the jimsonweed is dead for me; it takes me nowhere.

I run through the field now, moving far faster without

11

Mother. How easy it would be to run away from her. How easy; how impossible.

I find the jimsonweed at the far edge of the field, and I rip it down bare-handed, knowing even as I do I will suffer for this. I carry the weed back and throw it on top of the Indian tobacco. I expect Mother to seem relieved, even pleased with me, but she doesn't look up. She is watching a butterfly as it flutters across a bed of sweet clover. The butterfly is pale brown, almost gray, and from a distance it looks drab, but as I walk nearer, its delicate markings become apparent: the wings are speckled with darker spots ringed in white; a single blue splotch near the tail is flanked by patches of orange.

"An Edward's hairstreak," Mother says.

"It's beautiful—" I begin.

But Mother stops me. "It shouldn't be here. We're too far north." She jerks her hands into her pockets, and I wonder whether they are shaking, whether she is hiding them from me. She has the same look on her face as earlier this month when she saw the purple passionflower she says resembles a crown of thorns. Mother claims the flower doesn't grow in Maine, but there it was. When Mother saw the passion-flower, its showy blossom almost gaudy in the otherwise plain thicket, she crushed its fringed corona in one swoop like a bird of prey, and she tore it from the ground.

"We need to find some sneezeweed," Mother says now. The butterfly moves behind her, across the clover, and she turns away from me to follow it.

"You want sneezeweed?" We've never gathered sneeze-weed before; I assumed we never would. Mother told me her-self its only use is to purge the body of evil spirits, and

12

Mother claims she doesn't believe in spirits, evil or otherwise. On any other day, I would assume Mother is mocking me about the sneezeweed; today I'm not sure. I want to look at Mother's face again: at her eyes, to determine whether she is there with me or has escaped inside her mind; at the tilt of her mouth, to see whether her lips are tight in irony, or open in wonder. But Mother has her back to me now.

"Do you know atoms are comprised almost completely of empty space, Aslaug? Objects around us look solid, but they're not. The hairstreak is more not there than there. And yet we see it. It seems solid. The sneezeweed? You don't see the plant right now, but you know what it looks like— you have an image of it in your mind. That image has almost as much substance as the real thing."

"You want the sneezeweed for evil spirits?" I say, trying to draw Mother back. I want Mother to say yes; I want her to believe in spirits. Even evil spirits.

Mother continues as if I've said nothing. "Celtic people in the Middle Ages understood this about butterflies—they knew butterflies are ethereal, not really solid. They saw butterflies as souls. They believed women became pregnant by swallowing these butterfly souls." Mother removes a hand from her pocket and reaches toward the hairstreak; it flutters high for a moment, then descends again to the clover. "They believed each butterfly soul flew about in search of a new mother." She bends to the clover, grips a cluster and rips it from the ground. She turns and pushes the clover toward me, and I reach to take it. But she pulls it back. "Is that how you came to me, Aslaug Datter?" she says. "Did you come as a butterfly soul?"

13

I can feel her moist breath on my face—a fog of peppermint leaves and tobacco. "I don't know," I want to say. "You've never told me of my birth. You've never mentioned my father, not even his name. I don't know where I came from." But I don't say this. I've learned not to take Mother's bait.

"The words for *soul* and *butterfly* are the same in Greek," I say. "*Psyche*. It means both."

"So you've learned something I've taught you," Mother says. And I realize the butterfly is gone.

When we're not out foraging or doing chores, Mother teaches me Newton and Lyell and Darwin and Einstein and Dalton and Bohr and Heisenberg and Pauli. Newton's *Principia*, Lyell's *Principles of Geology*, Darwin's *On the Origin of Species* and Einstein's "Cosmological Considerations on the General Theory of Relativity."

And languages. I have no memory of learning Danish or English or Latin—as if they've always been mine. But I do recall Mother teaching me Greek before I could reach the kitchen sink. By the time I could hang clothes on the line, I was learning Hebrew and Arabic and Aramaic. And on the day of my first menses, Mother began with Sanskrit. Then other ancient languages: Coptic, and the runic alphabet, and a bit of the Celtic languages, Gaulish, Celtiberian and Lepontic.

Mother teaches me other subjects as well, but only because the state of Maine demands it. A man from the Department of Education came to our door two years ago—after our neighbor reported us, Mother claims—and now I learn language arts, social studies, health education,

14

library skills, fine arts. But of these subjects, Mother teaches me only what I need to pass the standardized test she's required to give me each year, and she blacks out passages from most every book I have to read. Although I'd never tell Mother, I'm grateful she has to teach me these subjects; otherwise, I'd have practically no understanding of the world outside our house, outside these woods, outside the microscopic, the scientific. I wouldn't know of poetry and fiction; I wouldn't know of art; I wouldn't understand democracy or taxes, or that human beings have sex for reasons other than procreation. And I wouldn't have this awareness of how much I'm missing—of how many passages Mother's blacked out.

Mother looks into the basket containing the jimsonweed and studies its contents. I notice Mother's expression, and I see what I'd wished to see before: relief, for certain; almost pleasure. She reaches behind her head and coils her pale fan of hair. "Madapple," she says, but not to me. And then, "You did well, Aslaug," as her eyes sift through the collected mound of jimsonweed. "You did very well."

She begins walking toward the woods in the direction of our home, carrying the basket of jimsonweed and tobacco, but she's struggling with the basket, still struggling with the pain. She seems to have forgotten the hairstreak butterfly.

"What about the sneezeweed?"

"You are ridiculous, Aslaug Datter," she says. "I was being facetious."

She says this, and yet I sense otherwise. She wanted the sneezeweed, I think; she *wants* the sneezeweed. I'm not sure whether to feel grateful or terrified. Mother scoffs at the mystical, the magical, the mythological, even if at times she slips into it, as with the hairstreak. And yet, the more Mother teaches me science, the more cracks I see, and the more cracks it seems Mother must see. Science describes the world; it doesn't explain it: it can describe the universe's formation, but it can't explain why such an event would have occurred, how something can come from nothing. That's the miracle. Mother ridicules me when I talk this way, but now she wants the sneezeweed.

I fumble behind Mother now, looping one basket around my forearm, gripping the other two. Juggling the baskets, I couldn't walk much faster than Mother if I tried, but I don't try; I wouldn't try. Our shadows, stretched before us, mingle like butterflies courting. A dance of searching souls, I think. That sense of insecurity—that something is amiss—still drags at me, so unlike gravity, so much stronger. I hear Mother in my head: "The force that keeps our universe from soaring off into the oblivion is astonishingly weak." The feeling I have now is anything but.

We approach the ferns Mother made reference to earlier. They look so simple, unadorned by flowers or fruit or extraneous color. Yet, they are more complex genetically than we humans, who seem to feel such need for adornment. I think of people I've seen in Bethan—of their painted toenails, fingernails, cheeks, lips and eyes.

This memory stirs my longing for bloodroot, for the blood of the root, that orange-red sap I've used in secret to dye my belly with the likeness of a spotted touch-me-not, as if somehow that golden flower with its splotches of burnt red could protect me from my mother: from her biting words, the stinging rod; her absence. Touch me not. And yet, I want her touch, and I want to hear her words—words that open small passages into the tunnels of her mind, and often seduce me with wonder.

I find myself looking beyond the ferns, into the moist woods. And I spot a withered bloodroot. Its leaves are collapsed and dried, but I know its rounded rootstock is still fleshy, and full, and waiting for me to release it from the ground, give it new life on me. Give me new life in its adornment.

I digress a bit from Mother as I move toward the bloodroot. There is a gully just before the woods, the water traveling almost indiscernibly, the ferns reflecting there like the trees of a submerged and miniature world. The impulse stops me: I put the baskets down and lean over the water, toward the ferns, and my face enters their world, but my reflection is obscured by my hair. I hear Mother behind me, first her voice calling my name, then her movement. I turn to see she is running toward me. Running. I didn't think she was capable of this. She grabs my hair before I think to get away; a hot splash of pain radiates across my scalp. She pulls me back from the gully, and I fall into the baskets; salsify and goatsbeard speckle the ground. Mother stands over me. "What were you doing?" Her hair has come loose, and it flails about her like wings. She is breathing erratically. I feel afraid of her, for her.

"I'm sorry, Mother," I say. "I'm so sorry." I don't ask her why she is angry, why I am sorry.

"What were you doing?" she says again.

"The cinnamon ferns," I say. "I was looking at them."

17

"The ferns?"

"You mentioned them earlier. Their chromosomes. You said they had more chromosomes . . ."

Mother doesn't move. She hangs over me like a willow, her hair, her arms, her clothing, suspended and caging. "You were looking at the ferns," she says; it is not a question. But her eyes challenge me.

Mother reaches into her pocket then and removes something. She tosses it onto my chest before moving away. I sit up, and the hairstreak tumbles into my lap.

"Is that what you were looking for, Aslaug Datter?" Mother says. She picks up the basket of jimsonweed and walks again.

I lift the lifeless body into my palm.

"It didn't belong here," she calls back.

I stand, still holding the butterfly; I can't bear to let it drop. I recall the story Mother told about the Celts. A butterfly soul. I lift the hairstreak, slip it inside my mouth and swallow.

SOLOMON'S SEAL

2007

—Please state your name for the record.

—Lens Grumset.

—What is your home address, Mr. Grumset?

—886 Bedrag Road, Hartswell, Maine.

—How long have you lived at this address?

—Thirty-one years.

—Do you know the defendant, the woman we are refer-ring to as Aslaug Hellig?

—I do. She and her ma lived next to me for about thir-teen years, until about four years ago.

—During the time Aslaug and her mother were living next to you, did you see them periodically?

—Well, I wouldn't say I seen them much. They kept to themselves, mostly. Kept their windows covered, for insula-tion I guessed at the time—but now that this is all come to light, well, who knows what the hell was going on.

—Objection, Your Honor. Move to strike. Speculation.

—I'll strike his last sentence only. Please just answer the question asked, Mr. Grumset.

—Yes, sir, Your Honor.

—Mr. Grumset, you said you didn't see Aslaug and her mother much. Did you ever see them?

—Sure I did. Mostly Aslaug. When she was a kid, I saw her now and then. She was quite a tomboy, that one. Racing round the yard like some wild animal, stomping through leaves and puddles, climbing trees. I always felt bad there weren't other youngsters round for her to play with. She was always alone. Makes kids strange spending so much time alone.

—Objection, Your Honor. Move to strike. The witness's conclusion is speculative and lacking foundation. Mr. Grumset is not an expert in child psychology.

—Sustained only as to Mr. Grumset's last sentence; otherwise, the objection is overruled.

—Did you see Aslaug during the months just prior to her mother's death, Mr. Grumset?

—No, not much. Aslaug didn't spend much time out of doors when she was a teenager. Lord knows what she was doing cooped up in that house of theirs. Although I would see her on their back porch hanging clothes and fiddling around. And she and her ma worked in the yard sometimes. And they also used to take these walks out in the woods. They'd come back with all manner of paraphernalia. Sometimes I wondered whether they was into witchcraft or the like.

—Objection. Move to strike Mr. Grumset's final sentence. Speculation.

—Sustained. Get to the point, Counsel.

—Mr. Grumset, did you observe Aslaug on the day of her mother's death?

—You bet I did.

—And what did you see?

—Well, I remember it happened on that day about four years ago when Aslaug pulled down all their curtains.

—Objection. Move to strike. Speculation. Lack of foundation. No one has testified Aslaug took down any curtains.

—Well, her ma sure as hell couldn't had done that—take down those big curtains, I mean. The woman was nearly crippled by then.

—Mr. Grumset, please. You are not permitted to speak when you haven't been asked a question. Your objection is sustained, Counsel. Strike Mr. Grumset's statements from the record.

—Sorry, Your Honor. Sorry.

—Mr. Grumset, please explain what you saw at the Helligs' house on the day of Maren Hellig's death.

—Well, like I was saying, about four years ago—the day those big curtains came down—I saw Aslaug dragging her ma's body to the backyard. She was going to bury it.

—Move to strike, Your Honor. Speculation.

—I'll strike that last statement. Please just describe what you saw, Mr. Grumset.

—Well, you see, I saw Aslaug dragging some large white thing out the back door of their house, into the yard. I couldn't see what the thing was at the time, but later, when the police got there, I saw it was her ma's body. Anyway, Aslaug was having trouble pulling it, and I wondered why on earth her ma wasn't helping her. Then I remembered her ma

21

was pretty much crippled. If I could've helped her, I probably would've gone over there, but I was in this damn wheelchair. When she finished pulling it out, she went and got a shovel and started digging. It was a couple hours before I appreciated the fact that the hole looked like a goddamned grave.

—What else, if anything, did you see the defendant doing while she was in the backyard?

—Well, I remember her rolling this big rock around. And I remember her doing something to that rock. Writing on it or something. I couldn't tell.

—What else, if anything, did you see the defendant doing?

—Nothing. She wasn't doing nothing else but digging, until the police got there.

—Let's back up a bit. Did you do anything when you realized the hole the defendant was digging looked like a grave?

—Well, I called the police. Not right away. I mean, the body was wrapped up in something white. A sheet, I think. I couldn't be sure what it was. But after another fifteen minutes or so, when I didn't see Aslaug's ma around, well, hell, I felt I had to call, especially 'cause I'd heard someone scream over there at their house earlier that day. In the morning.

—Objection. Move to strike. Nonresponsive.

—Overruled.

—You heard a scream coming from the Helligs' household that same morning?

—Yeah. At seven or eight that morning, I think. I'd not thought much of it when I first heard it. It could of been anything, I thought. But when I realized that goddamned

22

hole looked like a grave, well, Christ. I thought back on that scream, and I made the call to the cops. And it's a damn good thing I did. If I hadn't been watching the whole affair, Maren Hellig would probably be buried back there now. And I might be buried back there, too, if you know what I mean.

—Objection, Your Honor. Move to strike. Speculative. Narrative. Misleading. Counsel needs to get some control over his witness.

—Objection sustained. And I agree you need to rein your witness in, Counsel. Strike Mr. Grumset's last comments from the record, everything following his statement that he called the police.

—I apologize, Your Honor. I'll wrap things up here. Mr. Grumset, did the police arrive at the Helligs' house?

—They sure did. They came right away, and there was a whole bunch of them. They surrounded Aslaug, tried to take the shovel from her. But she started swinging at them with it. And she was kicking and cussing. I was shocked. I was damn well shocked. They had to handcuff her, you know, just to get her under control.

—Thank you, Mr. Grumset. I have no further questions, Your Honor.

Bittersweet

2003

We pass through the clearing, only minutes from our home now. The bloodroot bulges in my pocket; its blood pulses against my leg as I walk. I dug up its roots after Mother turned away, after I swallowed the hairstreak and it found its mother in me. I'll paint a butterfly on myself this time: the hairstreak will be reborn on me.

Clouds like gauze stretch low across the sky; it seems the whole world is enclosed by a rippled tarp. I can see the house: its exterior walls angle first to the left, then the right, as if behind warped glass. From the distance it seems impossible the house could be as imposing to me as it is. Lanky, its gables like antiquated hats, it stands like blue vervain gone dry: its broken shingles and peeling paint fold and crease; it seems the entire house could be uprooted and snapped.

Mother perches on a fallen log near a vine of nightshade;

her basket of *sapientia* rests on the ground. A stalk of canker-root juts from her lips; she chews it for the sores that speckle the interior of her mouth in mounds. She turns toward me, pulls the cankerroot from her mouth, tucks the soggy stalk in the hip pocket of her dress.

"Help me, girl," she says. She's removed her gloves and dropped them to the ground; green pulp hangs from her hands. I realize she's picking the nightshade berries. Trying to, her fingers no longer capable of subtlety.

"They're not ripe," I say. I lower the baskets, flatten the bloodroot deeper into my pocket. "We can't eat them."

"I know that, Aslaug," she says. Still, she tries to pick; her hands grab the berries in fistfuls and squash most.

I pick with her. The berries are cool and waxlike, firmer than I remember. Shiny and green. I imagine the taste of their juice, first bitter, then sweet. *Solanum dulcamara.* Bittersweet. Edible when ripe and red, poisonous when green. But not so poisonous, I think. I ate the unripe berries as a child, just three or four when Mother wasn't looking. If Mother weren't with me, I'd eat a handful; it's been a long time since breakfast.

"These are not the berries of *Atropa belladonna*," Mother says. "They won't kill you."

"*Atropa belladonna*," I say. "Deadly nightshade. It doesn't grow here."

"No," she says. But without conviction, it seems. "The name is Latin for 'beautiful woman'—have I told you? Women used to put drops of deadly nightshade in their eyes to dilate their pupils. They thought the enlarged pupils made them more beautiful."

"You told me before people first used belladonna because it's a hallucinogenic—it makes them feel like birds, like they're flying?" I say, but I think of dilated eyes. When Mother inhales the madapple, her pupils stay dilated for days. But now her pupils are pinpricks. Yet her eyes still look wild.

"You would remember that," Mother says. "Are you plotting to fly away?"

How is it that Mother knows my mind? When she'd first described deadly nightshade to me, I had wished the plant grew in Maine; I remember longing for that sense of flight.

"This is bittersweet nightshade," I say, and I turn my face to the bittersweet. "Not deadly nightshade. Why are we picking it? Why do you want it?"

Mother ignores me, keeps picking.

Jimsonweed is related to nightshade; they are in the same family, Solanaceae. I wonder if Mother plans to eat some bittersweet berries to see if they can do for her what the jimsonweed does while she waits for the jimsonweed to dry. I want to tell her not to bother, that the green berries give little: some momentary pleasure, yes; some nausea if one eats too many. But I can't tell Mother this. She'd forbidden my eating the unripe nightshade.

We strip the branches of their remaining fruit. Our swell of berries stains the *sapientia* basket, opposite the jimson-weed Mother's pushed to one side. Many of the berries are compressed to green jelly.

"We're done here," Mother says, nudging me off the log.

I step down, reach back to assist her. She lifts one hand

toward me; the pulp clings to her fingers like moss. I take her hand in mine and ease her down, and when I pull back my hand, the jelly strings between us.

"Have a taste, Aslaug Datter." Mother's arm remains stretched outward, her hand propped near me. I'm surprised she has energy to goad me. Her skin looks petal-thin, her feral eyes hollow. Still, I have the impulse to take her fingers in my mouth, shock her. Instead, I kneel to the ground and wipe my hands along the grass in two slick swipes. Then I stand and help Mother squat; I place her hands on the grass.

"Are you afraid tasting the berries might counter all the spells you've been putting on me?" Mother says.

I slide her still-curled hands along the ground. "You don't believe in witchcraft."

"That's never deterred you." Mother wiggles her hands from mine and attempts to wipe off the nightshade pulp herself, but she has difficulty flattening out her fingers and much of the pulp stays put. She motions for me to help her stand. "Don't tell me you've forgotten even this?" she says. "Bittersweet nightshade counteracts witchcraft."

"If only I did know witchcraft," I want to say. "Then I'd become a butterfly soul, find myself a new mother."

By the time we reach home, the mosquitoes circle. And stars show in the sky. Like seeds, I think, each star holding the possibility of life. I know I'm looking into the past when I look at the stars—that I'm seeing the universe as it existed years and years ago. I can't help but wish I could see into my past, into Mother's past. Into my father's life. I wish I could find a context for who I am.

We pass by our neighbor's house. He sits in the window that faces our yard watching us. His hands grip the wheels of his chair, his glasses sit askew and his few longish hairs dangle over his ear, having slipped free of his glossy scalp.

"Perverted old coot," Mother says when she sees him there, and she spits, at him or the ground, I can't tell. Then she smacks the deep vale of her collarbone, and the flattened mosquito sticks there, in the vale. "The old coot was waiting for us again. *En skefuld lort.* Spoonful of shit." But she says this with less ire than usual, it seems. Less contempt. Still, she glares at him.

She'll try to stare him down, I think. I take the opportunity to lower my baskets, lift a cluster of meadowsweet from the ground, drop the flowers onto the disheveled heap of plants.

Mother turns, sees me, and I see the mosquito hangs in a sketchy pool of red. "Why are you picking those?" she says. "You've got the runs?"

So like Mother to nearly rip my hair from my skull, then worry I have diarrhea. "Yes," I lie, but I speak to the abundance of meadowsweet stamens, not Mother. I lift the baskets from the ground, start walking.

"Wait," she says, and she drags herself and her *sapientia* to me. She presses her scaly palm against my cheek. "You're feverish," she says. "You feel feverish, Aslaug."

"I'm just hot from the trip back," I say. "Not feverish. I have some indigestion. It's nothing, *Moder.* Don't worry."

But she is worrying, and I feel a tinge of satisfaction in

seeing this. A tinge of relief. This is mother-love. This is my mother's love.

"Maybe I'm contagious," she says. "It's spreading from me. . . ."

"No," I say.

"Or an imprecation . . ."

"What are you talking about, *Moder*?"

"You're in pain?" she says.

"No, *Moder*. I'm not sick. Come. Come inside."

We walk again. Creep again. Our neighbor pushes his chair back just before we step from his sight; then he rolls himself to a side window of his house where he can see us trudge through our backyard, this landscape of doll-size peaks and valleys and muddy rivers, still sodden from yesterday's rain. The yard looks like the ceiling of my bedroom to me, where the cracking plaster forms similar mountains, where rain often slips through the roof and streams momentarily before dripping to the floor.

"Cursed beast," Mother says now, but not to the old man, not to me. She is looking at the oak tree that stands leafless near the house, its branches too still, too peaceful. Last season the oak's leaves fell early; this season its leaves didn't grow back. I'd loved this tree when I was a child: the tree had been wild-looking then, its emerald leaves jittery. I remember longing to climb it; I imagined sneaking outside, wrapping my small body against its grain, mounting higher and higher.

Mother spits again; this time she hits the tree, and cusses, *"En skefuld lort."* But I see the tree meant something to her, too. There's a tenderness in her voice despite her words, a fullness in her eyes. "What are you looking at?" she says to me, and her knotted hand swipes her vacant cheek, seems to vanish there. "Just get yourself inside."

She's weeping, I think. It feels like a caterpillar is slinking up the nape of my neck, and another layer crusts across the mystery that is my mother.

"I'm just waiting for you," I say, and I try to help her up the stairs, but she swats at me, shoos me away.

We enter through the back door, onto the back porch, where I'll sort and spread the jimsonweed. But first I'll separate out the salsify and goatsbeard for dinner. I expect Mother to move inside, settle in, but she remains still, staring at the jimsonweed.

"You want me to prepare it now?" I say, setting down the roots and leaves. "The jimsonweed?"

Mother looks from the weed to me. She shifts from her stronger leg to her weaker, winces, shifts back. She slumps against the counter, props herself there. Mother's changing before my eyes: she's growing so deformed, she's becoming something new.

"Lay it out to dry," she begins, but she stops herself. She can see in my eyes I know what to do: I saw what she'd done with the jimsonweed for months.

She leaves me, then; she turns and heads inside. But she doesn't pump water, wash in the porch sink, as she always does after we forage. And she forgets to remove her shoes. Mud from the backyard, still fresh, slips from her soles in purplish green smears. Her hands curl, but her arms hang open and limp. She walks hunching, as if her own weight's too much. I recall years and years back, to a time when Mother didn't hunch, when she towered above me like the goddess Artemis: proud and cruel, but still my protector.

"I'll bring up your dinner," I say. "And the adder's eyes. As soon as I finish here." I want to stop her, remove her shoes, help her wash. "And shinleaf," I say. "I'll make the paste."

I expect Mother to call back, remind me she doesn't want the adder's eyes, she doesn't want the paste. But she is silent as she climbs the stairs. One step, she waits. Another. She waits. She doesn't know I'm watching; she wouldn't want me to see her like this, and yet I can't turn away. I want to go to her, take her bony elbow in my palm, lift her like I did the hairstreak.

"*Moder*," I call to her. "What about the nightshade? You want those berries?" I'm surprised to hear myself offer this. They are poisonous, the berries; they won't help her.

"Are you trying to poison me, Aslaug Datter?" she calls back. "I told you, I gathered those berries to ward off your witchcraft."

Although Mother studies religious texts—the Torah and the Kabbalah, the Koran and the Bible, the Upanishads and the Bhagavad Gita, and Vedic writings and Tantric writings—as if each separate one were the key to our salvation, she claims she's an atheist. No gods. No spirits. No divine anything. No evil. And no witchcraft. But why does she scour these texts, then, searching for some illumination, some epiphany, some treasure buried beneath the yellow-oil glow of our claw-foot lamp? And why does she forbid my

31

looking at the texts, except when she's teaching me languages? Is it because she knows I'll find answers there that will make her less divine to me, empower me to leave her? Or is it because she's protecting me from the realization that there are no answers, even there?

Solomon's Seal

2007

—Cross-examination?

—Yes. Yes, Your Honor. Mr. Grumset, you live alone, isn't that right?

—Uh-huh.

—Please answer yes or no.

—Yes.

—You've lived alone since your wife died eighteen years ago, correct?

—Yes.

—And you've been confined to a wheelchair for approximately twenty years, correct?

—Yes.

—You've rarely received visitors since your **wife's** death, right?

—A nurse comes to the house a couple times a week,

and I get groceries delivered, and I get those damn sales-people and Jehovah's Witnesses.

—But no one else visits you regularly, is that right?

—That's right.

—In fact, no one else has visited you for years, correct?

—I don't know about that.

—When was the last time someone other than your nurse, a delivery person or a solicitor visited you at your house?

—I don't remember.

—Mr. Grumset, you mentioned you have groceries delivered to your house. In fact, since your wife died, you've had Soren's Grocery deliver supplies to your house once per week because you can't drive, isn't that right?

—Objection, Your Honor. What is the relevance of this?

—The objection is overruled for now, but please get to the point, Counsel. You may answer the question, Mr. Grumset.

—Yes.

—Isn't it true that Soren's Grocery has delivered a fifth of gin *and* a fifth of whiskey to you every week—*every single week*—for the past eighteen years?

—Objection, Your Honor. Mr. Grumset is not on trial here.

—But his credibility as a witness is, Your Honor.

—Objection overruled. Answer the question.

—How do you know that?

—Please just answer the question.

—I don't remember eighteen years ago.

—Do you remember even one week during the past

eighteen years when Soren's didn't deliver two fifths of hard alcohol to your house?

—I don't remember.

—And that would include the week when Maren Hellig died, isn't that right?

—Objection. Argumentative.

—Overruled.

—I don't remember.

—Thank you, Mr. Grumset. I have no further questions, Your Honor.

Daylily

2003

I untangle the crumpled roots from my pocket, stash them beneath the kitchen sink in the basket of soapwort leaves. Then I pump enough water for Mother to wash and pour it into a pot. Before I heat the water, I scoop out a jar for my meadowsweet, lower the stems into the water, then hide the jar under the sink. Next I heat the water, carry it upstairs and leave it in the bathroom, knowing Mother will see it there. And I head back down to the jimsonweed.

I separate the leaves and seeds and spread them to dry. Then I prepare the adder's eyes tincture, diluting alcohol and mixing it with the plant's fresh leaves. I make the shin-leaf plaster and start dinner, before I sort and store the remaining plants. It's close to nine by the time I walk upstairs with a tray for Mother, and I wonder what to do if she's asleep, knowing this is a possibility, although it's never happened before. Knowing she's especially unwell. Should I wake her if she's sleeping? Encourage her to eat? Or should I steal the chance to open the bloodroot, paint the hairstreak on me?

I reach the hallway; her door is open. I knock my foot against the doorframe, but barely; she doesn't answer. When I look inside, she's not there. I feel the weight of her in me, the weight of knowing I've no option of escaping her: she's awake. She must be in the bathroom, washing with the water I left for her, and rubbing her skin as she does each night with the bilelike sap of the celandine plant—the plant Mother calls her wartwort. It fades freckles, she claims; eliminates warts. But when I turn, I see her emerge from the green room, the room she refers to as our guest room— although we've never had guests. Mother stops when she sees me; she stops like she's been stopped. I know right then: there's something in that room, something she does not want me to see.

I've often stood in the green room and peered at the twin bed, the small green sofa, imagining someone visiting us, staying there in that room. Someone who might steal me away. The room's furnishings had always seemed illusory to me—as illusory as guests. Not now. Now my mind traverses each piece.

Is she hiding another book like she hid *The Scarlet Letter*? I wonder. That book was on my recommended reading list from the state, yet it never materialized. Never, that is, until I was changing the sheets on Mother's bed and, as I tucked, I struck it, mashed beneath her mattress and dog-eared. I realized she was reading it at night, behind her closed door. And none of the passages were blacked out.

I waited then, from Thursday to Sunday, until the hour of her bath. And I read. And I read again the following Wednesday as she bathed, and again the following Sunday. And I learned of Hester Prynne and Pearl and Reverend Dimmesdale and Chillingworth. And I found Mother in Hester Prynne, and Pearl in myself. But who, I wondered, is Dimmesdale? And now I wonder, Will this secret of hers in the green room reveal our Dimmesdale?

"Dinner's ready," I say. I try to steel my expression, to not let her read what I know. "I boiled the goatsbeard and salsify roots."

Mother lifts her hands and attaches her bent fingers like vines to the tray. She limps into her room but manages to turn toward me before she bumps her door shut. "Most of our universe is made up of dark matter, Aslaug." She speaks in a near whisper; she pants out the words. "No one knows what it is." I want to stop her, tell her I know about dark matter, she doesn't need to teach me right now. "You are not alone in that, you see?"

"It's okay, *Moder*," I say. She sways, the tray rocks; I fear she might fall. "Let me help you into your room. You should eat your dinner. Rest."

"But the old outhouse," she says, referring to the red shed we've never used that sits invisible at the rear of the property, overgrown and reeking with the rotting-carcass stink of the thorny carrion vine, and encircled in summer with metallic blowflies and flesh flies and midges. "There's a crack in the ceiling. The boards are loose."

38

"It doesn't matter, Moder," I say, but it does matter, I think: something's wrong, now, with her mind. "We don't use the outhouse—"

"You need to go there," she says. "Find it. It's hard to find."

I say, "It's overgrown, I know, but it doesn't matter—"

"You'll find it, won't you? And the ceiling, the crack in the ceiling. The boards—"

"I'll fix the ceiling, Moder. Don't worry."

I try to take the tray from her, but she pulls it back. "Why would you do that?" she says.

"I'm just trying to help, Moder. Carry the tray for you."

She shakes her head, leans into the doorway. I imagine her slipping into the narrow seams of the doorframe, disappearing there. "You are good to your mother, Aslaug Datter. My daughter. You have always been good to your mother," she says, and the door bangs closed. I stand there, looking at the door to her room, the door to the green room. I want to go into her room, show her I can be good—that I want to be good to her, even though I hate her at times. But I want to go into the green room more.

She's tired, I tell myself. We foraged the whole day. In the morning her mind will be fine. As fine as Mother's mind can be.

I walk down the stairs, letting my feet fall with weight, so Mother will hear my descent. I enter the kitchen; I have to force myself, now, to eat the greens, the roots. When I finish, I pump water and pour half into the sink; half I heat on the stove. I wash the dishes, clanging them together, then I carry the warmed water up the stairs, into the bathroom. I empty

39

the water into the tub, holding the pot high as I pour, so the sound of the splashing water carries to Mother. And I wash myself, slowly: my hair and nails and neck and ankles, once and again. All is normal, Mother, I'm trying to say. I'm in no hurry, Mother.

I towel off and dress, then I enter my bedroom, pull hard on the door; I want Mother to know I'm in my room, the door is closed. I climb into bed and push hard on the squealing springs. Then I lie quiet. And listen. I'm not surprised Mother isn't asleep: I hear her comforter rumple, her body settle. She's waiting for me to sleep; I expected this. So I pretend. I pass a half hour in silence before I hear her blow out her candle, watch the crack of dim light disappear. Gradually her breathing transforms from barely audible to audibly crisp.

Then I slip to the floor, to my knees, hands, stomach: I try to disperse my weight, hinder the creaking boards. I crawl down the hall like an insect; grit from the floor clings to my palms like pollen. I reach the green room, but I fear lighting a candle even though I've shut the door; I fear Mother might wake, notice the stealing tint of white light, so I search first in darkness, but my hands alone unearth nothing.

I strike a match and light a candle, and another, and another, until the room is almost bright, then I search with a fastidiousness that makes little sense. What do I think I might find? What epiphany could be tucked in the crevices of the sofa, the thick folds of the quilt? I look for close to fifteen minutes before I notice the framed poster of Tivoli: it depicts the Danish amusement park at night, from a distance, the city of Copenhagen sparkling around it. The poster has always been in this room, on this wall—as far back as I can remember. But now the poster hangs askew. I reach up and lift the frame from the wall, and I see Mother's secret just hanging there, no longer hidden by Tivoli.

I pull the cushions from the sofa, stack them. I stretch my skinny legs and torso high, and my hands lie flat against the wall; the sofa cushions beneath me cradle the balls of my feet.

The mirror I'm straining to reach is tiny—no larger than my outstretched hand—and I see from below that its glass is speckled, yellow and gray, as if diseased, like the infected skin of an animal turned hairless and crusted. But to me it is another world, hope of another world: it is beautiful.

I've never seen my face before, not in a mirror. There were no mirrors in this house as I grew up. And Mother destroyed the mirrors in the car long before I realized what those mirrors might have meant to me. I must have been little more than a toddler when I watched Mother crouch near the car's passenger door, rotate its mirror outward. I saw her grip the hammer like she did the switch used to punish me—praying hands, folded neatly, but separated, then stacked—and I was awash in the already-familiar deluge of incomprehension and dread. I closed my eyes: I saw neither the swing nor the slam. But I heard the high-pitched burst as the glass splintered, and the thump as the hammer dropped to the ground. I opened my eyes to discover Mother assessing the mirror, the absence of mirror: this mosaic of angled light. I was relieved. Confused, too, certainly, but more than anything I was relieved. She hadn't struck me. The mirror, yes. But what did that matter? I'd no appreciation then of what her conduct signified, of what it might portend.

Discreetly I stepped back from the car, from her, as she

41

collected the hammer from the dirt, opened the squealing door, slipped inside. She left the door ajar, and I could see her spider-like legs awkwardly curled beneath her. With effort, she repositioned the rearview mirror, angled it toward her. This time I watched as she whacked it, once and again, before she unraveled herself from the car.

I don't believe she'd intended initially to destroy the remaining mirror, the mirror on the driver's side. She'd ordered me back in the house and was following behind me, heading inside. But I paused, I glanced back at her. And it was as if someone behind had gripped the fabric of her gown. Her torso stiffened, pulled back, even as her neck stretched forward and her head plunged; her airborne foot slammed into the ground, stuttered.

I could almost feel her cold-ocean eyes scrutinizing: my young face, my wrinkled dress, my scrawny arms and legs. "*I huset,*" she said. "I told you, get in the house." Then she pivoted away, walked to the car. She struck the remaining mirror with too much force, too many times. Its base cracked, then broke, and it spilled to the ground.

I had a vague idea what I looked like before this moment in the green room. I'd seen a semblance of my face rippling in a muddy pool in the drive and in a sun-bathed window in Bethan and in a gully, as today. But the images I'd seen were fleeting and vague. I'd tried to find out; I'd tried to see myself. I'd studied my face in the curved bed of a spoon, the flat spread of a knife, the body of a pot, the base of a pan. But our utensils and cauldrons are tarnished; my image was barely decipherable. I was tempted to pull out a line of tacks, draw back a drape, find my face reflected in one of our hidden windows. But I never did—I never dared. Yet I would have if I thought Mother wouldn't find out. I would have done so in a breath.

Now I close my eyes before my face reaches the mirror's surface. I teeter on the cushions and wait: five seconds, ten. I count my breaths; I count the time. I know I should hurry— that every second I tarry risks Mother's wrath. But I want to savor the pulsing and pumping in my body, the rushing heat, the slippery vitality of my palms. How long have I awaited this moment?

Yet it is not my own reflection I've so longed to see.

It is my father's.

I feel certain I will open my eyes and he will be born there for me, in the features of my face. I've come to believe that Mother's fear of this—of my discovering Father in myself—is her rationale for preventing my seeing my reflection.

But when I open my eyes, I see Mother.

Mother.

In reality I'm certain I look far younger than Mother, but this difference is masked in the mirror's age. What I do see is colorless, almost translucent skin; her broad, high forehead; hair that frames the face like dangling shards of bone. And eyes that swirl in gray and green and the palest blue. The only aspect of my face that seems my own is the freckles that spot my nose and cheeks.

Then I remember the wartwort.

I want to scream, to obliterate Mother from my mind, from my face.

She'd not been hiding my father from me; she'd been

43

hiding herself. But why, I wonder. Why? I know the features of Mother's face, know them like I know the musty smell of our house, the creaking of the floorboards. Mother's face was an ever-present in my life, long before I saw that her face is mine.

I return to my bedroom and try to sleep, but it seems I hear the passing of every second, the mundane sticking, straining, ticking of the alarm clock's second hand. Ever since I'd learned about sex—since I'd learned someone had fathered me—I'd been buoyed by the knowledge there was part of me independent of Mother, part of me she could never touch. Each time Mother had punished me since then, and when she'd scorned me, I'd thought of Father. I imagined he loved in me all she hated, that he took pride in all she found alien, that each time she rejected me, he pulled me closer. But after seeing my reflection, I'm no longer certain of my separateness from Mother: I'm no longer certain Father exists. Intellectually, I understand that to have come into existence, I had to have had a father, but this knowledge no longer seems enough.

Is Mother like the short-lived daylily? I wonder. Capable of producing without fertile seed? Did I just sprout up from some piece of her that fell away? From a strand of her hair? A scrape of her skin? A torn nail?

I think back to a year or so earlier, to the one time I garnered courage to ask Mother about Father. I sat across from her, the morning light slipping through a gap in the drapes, stretching across the dining table like a diaphanous shield.

"You have no father, Aslaug."

She was lying. It seemed she was lying. Her ashen skin

44

transformed to scarlet, her limbs to tense cords. And her gray to green to blue eyes focused intently upon the white, the blank, of the wall.

At that moment I knew—I felt—that I did have a father. That I *had* had a father, for I sensed he was no longer alive. There was longing in Mother's face, and mourning. Her eyes, normally so dry she blinks almost incessantly, softened with moisture, as if waves had stirred those cold-ocean colors and warmed them. Her lips, usually tucked stingily, fell open and round, so I could almost imagine her kiss.

It had never before occurred to me Mother loved my father, lost him. I'd not known she had the capacity for this type of love.

Later that day I began to speculate how Father died. It became almost obsessive for me, this speculation: I imagined scenario after scenario. Eventually one overshadowed all others.

I could see my newborn body, tinged crimson and viscid, still throbbing with dry cold and fluorescent light, as if Mother had given birth to her own pumping heart. The doctor and nurses swarmed about me like gluttonous mosquitoes, sucking and sucking. Then wiping, for several seconds. Several seconds. More than enough time for his racing vehicle to lose control.

I envisioned Father driving a diminutive white car with burgundy interior. The traffic light before him turned yellow, then red, but he accelerated, desperate to reach the gasps and screams of the woman, his wife, my mother, as she labored. The truck that struck left little but rent steel, rent vinyl, stirred into a pinkish morass. Father's head lay like that of a dandelion, thrust from a child reciting a rhyme.

Had Father actually died this way, my life would make some sense. That Mother raised me as if I were a bastard would be unremarkable. That she locks me away like one would a psychopath might even be expected, for in a sense I'd be a no-conscience killer, my very existence bound with death. And her clothing, black and shapeless, her body buried there as if with his. What else might she wear? Her life would be one of mourning. Her brooding, tortured eyes watch me like an obsessed, obsessive lover because I'd be a reminder, a remnant, of what she had lost.

SOLOMON'S SEAL
2007

—Please state your name for the record.

—Detective Edith Fenris.

—Where do you work, Detective?

—I've worked for the Hartswell Police Department for nearly ten years.

—What do you do for the police department?

—I'm a forensic detective, but I also patrol, respond to calls.

—As a forensic detective, you investigate crime scenes?

—Yes.

—Were you or were you not on duty when Mr. Grumset made the 911 call concerning the situation at the Helligs' house?

—I was on duty. I was one of the investigators who went to the house after dispatch received the call from Mr. Grumset.

—Describe what you saw when you arrived at the Helligs' house.

—Well, it was four years ago. . . . I remember seeing a young woman in a nightgown in the backyard digging. There was something big wrapped up in a sheet lying next to her. Her hands and gown were soiled with what appeared to be blood, but . . .

—Do you see that woman you saw digging in this courtroom?

—Yes.

—Would you please point her out to the jury and describe how she's dressed.

—She's sitting next to defense counsel there, wearing a gray skirt, a gray blouse.

—May the record reflect the witness has identified the defendant, Aslaug Hellig?

—It may.

—Thank you, Your Honor. Did you examine the wrapped object, Detective?

—Yes.

—What was it?

—Maren Hellig's dead body.

—What, if anything, did you find unusual about the body?

—The body was naked, and there was an image painted on the torso.

—Please describe the image.

—It looked like a star, only upside down.

—When you say a star, do you mean a five-pointed star? A pentagram?

—I think so.

—So the image was an inverted pentagram?

—Yes.

—Thank you. Now, you said the defendant was digging. What was she digging?

—A hole.

—A grave?

—Objection. Leading.

—Sustained.

—Did you ask the defendant why she was digging a hole, Detective?

—I think so.

—What did she say?

—I don't think she answered. She was pretty messed up.

—What do you mean by "messed up"? Was she intoxicated?

—Objection. Leading.

—I'll withdraw that. What do you mean by "messed up"?

—She didn't seem to get why we were there. She seemed confused.

—How large was the hole?

—Pretty big.

—Big enough for a body?

—Objection. Leading.

—Sustained.

—How wide was the hole?

—A foot or so, I think.

—How long was it?

—Maybe five or six feet.

—What did the defendant do when you and the other investigators entered the yard?

—She stopped digging.

—And then what happened?

—Officer Halvard and I arrested her.

—Did the defendant offer any resistance?

—It was a long time ago. I really don't remember.

—Why did you arrest her?

—Because it looked like she was about to bury a corpse in the backyard of her house. It's a criminal offense to abuse a corpse—

—You suspected the defendant killed her mother, did you not?

—Objection. Leading. Argumentative.

—Sustained.

—Detective, did you discover anything on the premises indicating someone may have attempted to destroy evidence before you arrived at the scene?

—I don't remember.

—Would you say your memory is exhausted as to this point?

—Yes.

—Perhaps I can refresh your memory. I'd like you to review Exhibit E, the police report concerning the incident at the Hellig household. Are you familiar with this document?

—Yes.

—Who prepared the report?

—I did.

—Okay, please read the first two lines of the third paragraph on page five of the report.

—"Damp, washed-out nightgown found inside house. Deceased's body found cleansed postmortem."

—Does the report refresh your memory of finding the nightgown and cleansed corpse?

—Yes.

—In your experience, was finding a washed-out nightgown and a washed corpse consistent with an attempt to destroy evidence?

—I found it strange the girl may have washed out her mother's nightgown, if that's what you're getting at. I found it strange she'd washed the body.

—Objection. Move to strike. The detective's testimony lacks foundation. There's been no evidence submitted that Aslaug did either of these things. The officer is speculating.

—Sustained.

—Did you find any evidence indicating anyone other than the defendant and her mother had been in the Helligs' house, Detective?

—No.

—Did you find anything on the defendant's person indicating the defendant may have poisoned her mother?

—Objection. Leading. Argumentative.

—I'll rephrase. Detective, what, if anything, did you find on the defendant's person?

—The only thing we found on the defendant was a small jar containing a little liquid.

—Did you test the liquid to determine its contents?

—Yes.

—What was it composed of?

—It's in the report here. It was part alcohol, I remember. And the report here says it was part something called saponins, found in some local plants like—let's see—soapwort

and adder's eyes, which is another name for scarlet pimpernel, I guess.

—Was the liquid poisonous?

—Yes, it was, but only if someone were to take in a lot.

—So your answer is yes?

—Yes.

—Thank you. Detective Fenris, based on your professional experience, what else, if anything, did you find on the
Helligs' property that was inconsistent with Mrs. Hellig's
having died of natural causes?

—Objection. Relevance. Lack of foundation. There's no
evidence Mrs. Hellig died of anything but natural causes.

—Overruled. Counsel is trying to lay that foundation
right now, I believe. I'll allow the question.

—I don't remember. It was a long time ago.

—Why don't you look at the report for a minute? Refresh your memory again.

—Yes. Okay. It says here we found some nightshade. I
guess the berries can be poisonous. And adder's eyes, like I
said. We found some of that. Let me see. Some Indian tobacco. Some homemade wine. A few petals of meadowsweet
and some bloodroot, both of which can be poisonous, but
only in large doses. A cream that contained a plant called
shinleaf. And another cream that contained nightshade and
jimsonweed.

—Did you say jimsonweed?

—Yes.

—Is jimsonweed poisonous?

—Yes.

—Can it be deadly?

—Usually only children—

—Detective, please just answer yes or no. Can it be deadly?

—According to the *Field Guide to Poisonous Plants in North America*, it can, yes, but—

—Objection. Move to strike. The witness is not an expert on local flora.

—But she's a forensic detective, Counsel. Objection overruled.

—I have just a few more questions, Detective Fenris. You mention in your report that the defendant, Aslaug Hellig, had a rash on her arms and hands. Please describe that rash.

—I just remember it looked like her skin was irritated.

—How so?

—It was red. Inflamed. Had small blister-like spots, I think.

—Thank you. You also mention in your report that you found a large stone near the hole the defendant was digging. Please describe that stone.

—It was big. A rock, really.

—Did it look like it could be used as a gravestone?

—Objection. Leading. Calls for speculation.

—I'll withdraw that, Your Honor. Detective, you describe in your report some carvings in the stone. Please describe what you found carved in the stone.

—On one side there was an hourglass-type shape. On the other side there were carvings that looked somewhat like letters, but not exactly.

—Did those letters form a word?

—Objection. Speculation.

—Answer only what you know.

—I don't really know. I'd have to guess. Like I said, the carvings didn't look exactly like letters.

—Detective Fenris, please read page seven of the report to yourself. Does the report refresh your recollection of what you saw?

—Yes, but—

—Read the first sentence of the first full paragraph aloud, please.

—"Etching on rock appears to be the letters 'HCTIB'— that is, 'BITCH' spelled backward."

—Why did you write this in your report?

—At the time, that's what I thought it said.

—Thank you. I have no further questions.

DOLL'S-EYES

2003

*M*orning comes; I realize I've slept.

I step from my room; the weight of sleep still slows my thoughts. The hallway seems strange, its muted tones disturbed by a pinkish glow. I reach the stairwell: I can see too much. No candles light the passage, yet I see the nail in the third stair down that I'd pounded askew after ripping my heel, and the parallel, smoothed indentations from wear that mark the near center of each step, and the velvet-like paisleys of the wallpaper, hued the lightest eggshell blue, normally detectable only by feel.

"*Moder?*" I call out, but reluctantly. Mother always sleeps at this hour. I hate to wake her, but something is wrong. "*Moder?*" She doesn't answer. I start down the stairs. The pinkish glow transforms as I descend and bathes the base of the stairs in abrasive orange.

I step into the sitting room. Tacks speckle the table, and the oak tree stands barren against the morning sky.

The drapes lie heaped on the floor. Every one.

I find Mother in a corner of the sitting room, curled on the hardwood floor. She wears a dark cotton nightgown that's so faded and thinned, it seems intangible to me, like it's hovering there. Smoke or fog, hovering above her nakedness. I can see her pale legs beneath it, tucked tightly to her middle, their fullness shriveled, desiccated. Now weightless stalks. Her arms are sticklike, their skin wrinkled like bark; they embrace her legs and torso with fervor, as if she'd needed to enclose herself in this invisible package, a package that is too narrow, too meager, even for her. I can't see her face—her hair lies draped across it—but I see the cavity of her left eye, the hill of her nose, the sharp edges of her cheekbone and jaw. Her hair folds into these features like a butterfly's wing: the hairstreak's wing.

"*Moder?*" I say. But I know she won't move. I touch her. She's so cold. I'd gone to sleep just past eleven the night before. Was she dead then? Had she slipped from her bed in anguish while I scoured the green room? Descended the stairs and rolled herself into this ball? Or had she wakened in the night gasping? Then crawled to this spot? Intentionally encased herself here?

With effort I rotate her body. Her hair slips from her face, and I see her eyes are agape, their whites almost shiny, their pupils quiescent. Her eyes look like the fruit of the white baneberry plant, the berries Mother called doll's-eyes. For a moment I think she's still alive. I scream. Then I tug her hair and nudge my foot into her side, but she's still as the insect caught fast in the web. I know for certain, then. I know she's dead.

I feel cold. Scared. Numb. I'm barely conscious of collecting a bucket, filling it with water from the pump, warming it. I gather soapwort leaves from the basket beneath the kitchen sink, and I crush them into lather. I peel the gown from Mother's stiffened body. I've never seen my mother naked; I've never seen her body. I'm surprised at how small she is—how small and how human. I'd never fully appreciated Mother was human. She was a force in my life, more god to me than human. But here she is, small and wrinkled, and dead.

I've forgotten to bring a washcloth, so I wash her with the gown. I dip it into the bucket, drip the warm water upon her cold skin and scrub: first her neck, its cords thick and firm; then her collarbone and upper ribs; and then her breasts, which are no longer breasts but flaps of skin, tipped brown and pink. And I wonder if those breasts that are no longer breasts were ever heavy with milk for me.

I finish washing her body, and I lie next to her, I wrap myself around her. It's the only time I've ever embraced my mother; I half expect her to rise and rebuff me. She feels as I'd always expected she'd feel: stiff and hard and cold. Still, I hold her. And I tell her goodbye—I never said goodbye. So I say it now. I touch my lips against her hair and ear and I whisper it into her hair and ear, but even whispered, the goodbye seems too loud.

Mother and I communicated through ideas and symbols and words unsaid. "You have no choice but to think in words," Mother once told me. "The more languages you learn, the more free you will be in your thinking. But, no matter how many languages you know, never trust words to encompass you, to encompass your world. Words are like the physical objects around us that appear to be continuous and whole but are in fact composed of particles too small for the eye to see, for the brain to imagine. Words oversimplify reality. Break open a word, and it's like breaking a mold. The contents seep free, become something new. Be careful to see the contents, Aslaug. Be wary of confusing the contents with the mold."

I have to break the mold, I think now. Find another way to tell Mother goodbye. I close my eyes, and the bloodroot takes root in my mind.

I manage my way back into the kitchen: I stumble, bump into, knock over. And I exhume a bloodroot stalk from the soapwort leaves, lift some meadowsweet flowers from the jar, then carry the dripping flowers, a metal bowl and the root back to Mother. I crush the bloodroot over the bowl, feel its blood stain my hands, hear the gentle tap tap as the root's blood strikes the metal. I carry the drained root to the window, force the window open, toss it onto the ground, into the weeds below. And I look back to the dark bed of the bowl, where the blood of the root awaits me; my fingers encircle a tender meadowsweet, pull it free from the cluster. I lower a tip of the meadowsweet into the blood, the dye. And I begin to paint, thinking of Mother walking through the woods, cracking free a leafstalk from the plant she called Solomon's seal, showing me the scar that remained on the rhizome, telling me of its magic: "King

Solomon used this seal to cast away demons," she'd said, "call on angels." And so I cast away demons, call on angels: I paint the image onto her torso as I remember it to be. But I can't look at her face, into her doll's eyes, as I paint; I look only at the bloodroot, the meadowsweet. And now I think of Hester Prynne's blood-hued A on Dimmesdale's pale chest. Did he paint it there as a way to cast away his own demons?

When I finish, I lie with Mother again as I wait for the seal to dry. And I fall asleep. I dream I'm an infant and Mother is nursing me. She's swaddled my small torso in her bony fingers and pulled me close to her. I can feel the downy mounds of her small breasts and stomach; I can smell her scrubbed skin. She leans back into an armchair, softly, purposefully. And she holds me—she just holds me—like she wants to, like she wants me. And she strokes my hair, her spindly fingers caressing as tenderly as they can.

But when I wake, I smell the bloodroot and soapwort, and I see her, and I retch.

I run to Mother's room to pull the blanket from her bed; I see the tray I prepared for her the night before. The salsify roots and goatsbeard greens lie there untouched, grayish and dry. The shinleaf paste is crusted over and cracking. Only the adder's eyes tincture seems not aged, waiting at the bottom of the sealed glass jar. I unscrew the lid and dribble Mother's adder's eyes onto my tongue, hoping it will ease the weight bearing down on me.

I collect Mother's blanket and wrap her in it, enfolding her body again and again. Then I try to drag her outside, but the blanket is so laden with holes, it tears despite her weight.

I run back to Mother's room, pull the sheet from her bed and wrap her in that as well.

I dig for hours. And as I do, I imbibe the tincture drop by drop, and I pray. To whom, I cannot say. But I pray that I, too, will die. Mother is the beginning and end for me. I can't imagine living without her.

Solomon's Seal

2007

—Would you like to cross-examine Detective Fenris, Counsel?

—Yes, Your Honor. Detective Fenris, the pathologist's report indicates Maren Hellig died of natural causes, isn't that right?

—Objection. Hearsay.

—Overruled.

—Yes. She had cancer.

—And you have no information that disputes that finding?

—I don't.

—The fact that Mrs. Hellig's body may have been washed after she died does not change the result of the autopsy, does it?

—No, if the girl did wash the body, maybe she was trying

to show her mom some respect. Maybe she washed it out of kindness.

—Objection. Move to strike. Speculation.

—Sustained. Please disregard those last two statements— all but the word *no*.

—And the nightgown, Detective Fenris? Even if the nightgown had been washed out, that wouldn't change the result of the autopsy, would it?

—No. I don't think the nightgown's relevant.

—And what about the painted image? Regardless of what that image was, Maren Hellig died of cancer, correct?

—That's correct.

—You mentioned you found some potentially poisonous substances at the Helligs' house, right?

—Yes.

—You find poisonous substances at almost every household you investigate, don't you?

—Objection. Relevance.

—I'll allow it.

—Yes. Most houses are full of poisons. Any household cleaner pretty much could poison someone. So can alcohol and aspirin and a whole bunch of other everyday-type things.

—So, based on your professional experience, the presence of poisonous substances alone is not an indication that someone has been poisoned, is it?

—Objection. Relevance.

—Overruled.

—No. Not necessarily.

—You mentioned Aslaug's hands and clothes looked as

if they were stained with blood, but you didn't actually find any blood anywhere on Aslaug's body or clothes, did you?

—No. The discoloration on her hands and clothes came from plant dye, not blood.

—Okay, now, you mentioned in your report that you found a stone with some etchings in the backyard of the Helligs' house. You don't really know what the stone was for, do you?

—No, I don't.

—And you couldn't be sure what the etchings on the stone were, could you?

—No.

—In fact, even assuming those etchings were some sort of lettering, the letters didn't form a recognizable word when read from left to right, correct?

—That's correct.

—You regret having speculated in your report what those symbols on the stone may have meant, don't you?

—Objection. Argumentative.

—I'll allow it.

—I was just trying to do my job, but if I were to do it again, I wouldn't write the report the same way.

—You wouldn't speculate on the meaning of those symbols, would you?

—No. Mrs. Hellig died of natural causes. This stone— well, it's just a red herring.

—Objection. Move to strike. Calls for speculation.

—Overruled. She has a right to reevaluate her report.

—When you say the stone was a red herring, you mean

you don't think it was relevant to your investigation, correct?

—It's not relevant. It's misleading. The girl's mother died
of cancer, for God's sake.

—Thank you, Detective. I have no further questions.

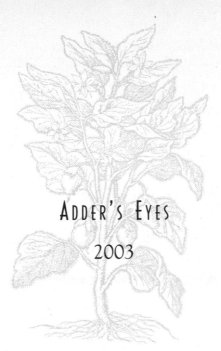

ADDER'S EYES

2003

Runestones were used in Scandinavia during the Middle Ages to protect the dead as they journeyed into the next life; placed over the buried bodies of the dead, the stones were inscribed with runic letters called runes. Mother told me of the runestones, not because she believed the stones had power to aid the dead but because she was interested in the runic language. "The runic alphabet is unusual," Mother told me. "Each letter is a word in the Germanic language and therefore holds meaning, over and above its sound." Mother taught me the twenty-four runes: *fehu*, meaning "cattle"; *uruz*, "wild ox"; *purisaz*, "giant"; *ansuz*, "god"; and so on. Mother taught me the runes, but she didn't teach me the secret of the runes; she couldn't.

Yet I knew the runes had a secret. The word *rune* itself comes from the Gothic word *runa*, meaning "a secret thing, a mystery." And according to Nordic mythology, the god Odin had to sacrifice one of his eyes to obtain the secret of the runes. So while Mother was drawn to the practical aspects of the runes, I was drawn to them because of their secret. I knew runes were used for divination and magic spells, and I loved that runes could turn the mundane act of writing into an act of magic.

I put the shovel down and wander the yard now, until I find a large stone and a small, sharp stone, then I spend the next hour etching. I etch *berkana*, the rune of femininity and healing, and *isa*, the rune of winter, to give Mother protection through the cold. I etch *tiwaz*, the rune for the god Tiw, who represents justice and truth. And *cen*, or *kaunaz*, the symbol of fire, to keep Mother warm. And last I give Mother *hagalaz*, the rune of hail and the rainbow and humor, because humor is something it seems Mother and I need. I write the symbols from right to left, the direction of runic writing. On the back side of the stone, I etch the rune *dagaz*, the rune of day; knowing Mother will be descending into the earth, I want to give her light. Then I roll the runestone near the side of the grave, and I dig again.

I'm nearly finished when I hear the sirens, but it doesn't occur to me the sirens have anything to do with me, that the police are seeking me. Not even when they enter the yard do I realize what's happening. I watch as their grayish uniforms crystallize to dark blue and the incandescent glow of their badges mellows as they pass toward me, into the shade. It's only when I see the next-door neighbor roll from behind his screen door, where his face has been pressed like salt to the tongue, bitter, biting, watching me, that I understand.

"You little witch," he calls. "You murderer."

There are five officers: four men, one woman. One of the men approaches me first, wraps his hand around my arm, stills it and the shovel.

I've never been so close to a man. He seems large to me—overwhelmingly large—and as he bends forward to ease the shovel from my grip, I can see the pink flesh of his scalp coursing through his cropped hair. I've never seen such short hair; it looks like fuzz to me, but more unyielding. Like remnants of cooked rice stuck to the base of a copper pan. He doesn't speak; he doesn't look at my face. Instead, he studies his fingers as they disentangle mine from the handle, as they envelop my wrist. His fingers are callused but warm. Alive. And his touch is firm and deliberate, but guarded, almost tender. The sensation startles me. I'm accustomed to the feel of the inanimate, not the animate. Not the tender.

The female officer approaches then. She runs her fingers up and down my body, pulls the jar of adder's eyes from my pocket. I try to grab it back from her, but she drops it into a plastic bag and hands it aside. She clutches the nape of my neck, steadies me. Her touch is more forceful, but also warm. Also alive. I don't understand at first I mean nothing to her—or him. Nothing more than a lurid story. For the initial moments they hold me, I trust them, I need them; I don't want them to let me go.

And they don't. Not even after the remaining officers unwrap Mother. The youngest holds the sheet and blanket while the others nudge her body, let it tumble. Nudge it again. Tumble. Nudge. Tumble. She spills out like hard plastic, a doll. The officer gripping the sheet gags when he sees

67

her; he turns away and heaves. But the other two seem un-
fazed. One takes out a camera, snaps pictures; the other en-
circles the yard with tape. A sixth person arrives and prods
Mother like a cut of meat. Then the officers gather Mother
onto a stretcher, pace to the ambulance, slip her in.

Only after the ambulance speeds away, only after its
sirens are almost inaudible, does the female officer detach
her fingers from my neck, the male officer my wrist. Together they handcuff me. He presses my hands against one
another, inserts them; she snaps the cuffs closed.

"You have the right to remain silent." The man is speaking, but he's looking at the shovel, the scattered soil, the
hole I'd dug. "If you do say anything, what you say can be
used against you in a court of law." He's speaking to me—I
know that—but his words are strange; I don't understand
what he means. "You have the right to consult with a lawyer
and have a lawyer present during questioning. If you cannot
afford a lawyer, one will be appointed for you, if you so desire. If you choose to talk to the police, you have the right to
stop the interview at any time."

The female officer leads me to the patrol car; she steers
with the cuffs—the short chain between the cuffs. She doesn't
touch me or speak. I don't care that she says nothing, but I
want her to touch me; I want again to feel the comfort of her
skin. But she tugs the chain and my arms extend toward
her, like stiffened reins. I stumble more than once; still, she
doesn't look back until we reach the car and she's opened
the door. Then she spins me around, backs me into the car. I
lose my balance, plummet to the seat. She lunges toward me;
her face is inches from mine.

I really see it now, her face: the large pores on her blushed cheeks, her too-narrow nose. She wears black liner around her eyes, rose on her lids. Her lashes are clumped and stiff. Snake eyes, I think: adder's eyes. I knew women wore makeup—I'd seen it from afar. Red lips, blue lids, lashes like black rays. It had seemed exotic to me before, but up close it looks absurd, dirty, like she's pressed her face into a bin of colored chalk. Even the smell is like chalk.

She slips in beside me, and her upper arm grazes mine; she jerks back, turns away, thrusts herself against the door. Then stares out the window at our unremarkable yard.

Still she says nothing. And neither does the pink-scalped officer as he drives the half hour into Bethan, then to the county jail. I'm a monster to them; I see this now. A freak. Someone outside of their world who will never understand the workings of their world; I doubt it ever occurs to them to explain to me what's happening. I smear my tears against the window, not wanting them to see. "You're the monsters," I want to say. "You're the freaks." But even I don't believe this.

I don't learn I'm to be incarcerated until an hour or so later. The sheriff informs me as he walks me to the cell. "Until a pathologist determines the cause of death," he says. He seems unconcerned whether I know what a pathologist is.

I do know.

It takes two days.

They've charged me with what they call abuse of a corpse. To clean Mother, bury her, bless her, was to abuse her, they tell me. And now they are cutting her up.

69

I sit on the cell's narrow cot, its scratchy sheets crinkling each time I move. The walls are gray cement with pores so large I feel impelled to scribble a prayer, stuff it in. My private Wailing Wall. But I have no paper, no pen. Other than the cot, a stained-basin sink and a toilet, there is nothing in the cell—nothing but a tattered copy of the King James Bible with Apocrypha the warden dropped through the bars after locking me in. I ignore the book for the first hour or two, but I can't endure myself, alone in this cell, alone with my thoughts, alone with the terror that pulses through me like crushed glass in my blood. How many times had I longed for Mother's death? How many times had I imagined poisoning her with blue flag or corn cockle or jimsonweed? And now she is finally dead. And I feel dead, because I loved her. And because I was Mother's marionette. Without her, what am I? Scraps of useless limbs and strings, with no one to hold me, direct my path.

So I read the creation stories and of the flood. Of Abraham and Sarah in Egypt, and of Ishmael and Isaac. I read of Jacob and his quest for Rachel. And of Joseph and Moses, and Samuel and Saul and David. Bathsheba and Solomon. And Micah. And I read through Matthew, Mark, Luke and John. And through parts of the Apocrypha, too. And I lose myself. But by morning I can't read more; I'm once again myself, imprisoned in my thoughts.

Until the sheriff unlocks the cell.

"You didn't kill her," he says. As if he knows I've been wondering.

It was cancer.

Hadn't I noticed Mother hadn't been eating? the pathologist asks via the sheriff. Hadn't I noticed she was weak?

"I can go?" I say, because I don't understand: I wasn't charged with killing Mother. And because I'm not sure I want to go: I've no idea how I'll survive once I leave, with no one pulling my strings.

"It's not up to me," the sheriff says, shrugs. "Charges are dropped."

A social worker has arranged a funeral and implores me to go. How can I refuse? I'm the only one there, excepting the social worker herself and a minister I've never seen before. Mother had no friends. None I knew of; none I can imagine. So I stand at her grave alone, and alone I see her coffin descend into the earth, after the minister shuts the lid on her plastic face, laboriously molded into sleeping eyes and a tight, toothless smile.

Solomon's Seal

2007

—Please state your name for the record.

—Dr. Arna Fiske.

—What is your profession, Dr. Fiske?

—I'm a professor at Bran College in the art history department. A specialist in iconology.

—What is iconology?

—It's the branch of art history dealing with the analysis and interpretation of iconic representations. Symbols.

—Okay. Are you familiar with the symbol of an inverted pentagram?

—Yes. The pentagram is a five-pointed star. It's significant in many religious traditions. It usually signifies the sacred in some way. But to invert the symbol changes its significance dramatically, and generally is a sign of relegating good to evil. The inverted pentagram is often used by

Satanists, for example, some of whom describe it as the devil's hoofprint.

—Thank you. I have no further questions, Your Honor.

—Would you like to cross-examine Dr. Fiske, Counsel?

—Yes, Your Honor. You mentioned the star most often represents the sacred in some way, correct?

—Yes.

—In Christianity, the star of the east is an example of this, correct?

—Yes.

—The star of the east symbolizes Christ's birth, right?

—But it wasn't inverted—

—And the Star of David, also known as Solomon's seal. The symbol initially was used as a means of protecting the bearer of the symbol against evil, right?

—But that's a six-point star. A hexagram. Not a pentagram. Not an inverted pentagram—

—Most of your students when they begin your class don't understand the symbolic difference between a hexagram and a pentagram and an inverted pentagram, do they?

—Some do.

—But many don't, isn't that right?

—Some don't.

—And we are talking about college students here, right? Not isolated fifteen-year-olds.

—Objection. Argumentative.

—Overruled.

—I teach college students.

—Thank you. I have no further questions, Your Honor.

WINDFLOWER

2003

*N*ight falls and the sepals of the wood anemones hug each other, their frailty forgotten in the fortification of company. Mother named the anemones her windflowers; by day they'd quiver in the breeze. I sit alone in Mother's house, the sepal that failed to close. Or the sepal ripped free by a gust. Free, I think. Free. I am free. All the minutes, hours—it seems years—I longed to open the curtains, run into the yard, run out of the yard. Read whatever I pleased. Experience whatever I pleased. And yet, it seems to me now freedom is its own sort of internment. I feel blown about, without roots, as if any decision I make could be altered by the next gust.

I'm scared to act; I'm scared to not act; I'm scared to fall asleep; I'm scared to wake to find myself alone with myself. I had so little responsibility for my actions before; my actions were chosen for me. Now I feel responsible for my choices, even as I realize the wind blows without regard for me.

The house is different: the officers tried to replace, re-plant, restore, return, reinstate, but I feel their presence. I know they were here when I was not, know they are part of my uprooting. I walk around the kitchen now, touching, adjusting, trying to undo their undoing. I slide the jar of dried peppermint leaves back to its home near Mother's now-chipped mug. I move the broom from one corner to the other, the mop from one corner to the other. The mop bucket belongs upside down, not right side up. The wash-cloth hangs to the right of the sink, not the left.

A loaf of bread sits unwrapped on the counter; the towel that had swathed it now straddles it in a heap. I remember Mother at the counter two days before her death, kneading and kneading. Dough clung to her gnarled hands; flung flour dusted her hair. She was so sick, I think. She was so sick when she made this bread. I lift the loaf to me, like a mother, a babe. It's stiff, the bread. Stale.

The world seems ugly to me in this moment as I open the cupboard beneath the sink to break the loaf into the compost. I see the basket of soapwort beneath the sink, next to the compost. Fewer leaves lie in the basket than before, and I see fewer stems of meadowsweet. I wonder what the officers wanted with the soapwort, the meadowsweet. I drop the bread, rummage through the basket, expecting to find the officers took the bloodroot as well. I find a small root, and I lift it and the remaining meadowsweet. I'll break the mold again, I think.

I put the root and flowers on the counter, blow out the candle so our neighbor, Mr. Grumset, can't see. I lift my gown over my head, toss it on top of a curtain mound. I feel night about my body: up my legs and torso, across my

75

shoulders, down my arms, and around my fingers as they pull free a meadowsweet stem. Again I crush the bloodroot into a bowl; again I paint. I feel the cool image as it takes form on my body; I see it barely. The wings of the hairstreak spread diagonally across my torso: one cascades across my left breast, encases the scar over my heart; the other descends. I recall the delicate beauty of the butterfly's markings. There is beauty, I tell myself. There is beauty in this world. And I mimic the beauty on me, hoping it will give me strength, guide me.

The hairstreak is barely dry when I hear a knock at the door. I expect it's old Grumset coming to accuse me, and I feel the welling fear. I slip the garment back over my head, light the candle. But before the visitor knocks again, I've looked to Grumset's house; I see him propped like a mannequin in the window, his head cocked. He is watching me, but he is watching someone else as well.

"Aslaug? Aslaug, are you there?"

The handle turns. I pick up the candlestick, prepare to hurl it. The door inches open. The social worker's face appears, and her eyes traverse the burning candle, the high ceiling, the scarlet walls, me. "You didn't answer," she says.

Her eyes seem an unnatural color, like imitation emerald, slightly transparent. And her ivory skin looks restless, hungry, so freckled it seems to be consuming itself.

"I was going to," I say, although I'm not sure that I was.

"Of course," she says. "I should have waited."

She does wait then, perched half in, half out. I realize I'm supposed to invite her in. And I do. But it feels a violation to have her enter our house; no stranger has ever entered this house, except those officers. And as much as I would never have admitted it to Mother—perhaps I wouldn't have admitted it to myself until now—there was something sacred about the sealed-off space Mother kept for us. Something exceptional.

"I'm Cecilia," the social worker says. "Remember? Cecilia Sture."

The colors of her clothing are so vibrant, they seem misplaced to me. They are the colors of an exotic bird or a poisonous frog or a jungle snake; I've seen them in books, rarely in life. She reaches toward me with her right hand, and I feel myself back away; my palms are stained with bloodroot, I think. I tuck my arms behind me. She drops her hand.

"I remember you," I say. "It was just today. . . ." I've talked to so few people in my life. How could I forget?

"Yes," she says. "But I wasn't sure. . . . Anyway, may I sit down?" And she does, before I answer. "Sit by me, here." She pats Mother's seat.

I shake my head. Why does she want me to sit near her? "Why are you here?"

"Why am I here?" she says, and it seems she's wondering herself. "I'm the social worker assigned to your case."

"But I thought the charges were dropped—"

"Not that kind of case. I mean, I'm here to help you—"

"I don't need any help," I say, but I'm not sure that's true. Yet how could I rely on this woman for help? How could I rely on anyone? Anyone but Mother?

"It's not your choice, Aslaug. You're the state's responsibility until you're eighteen, unless you have family to care for you."

"I am eighteen," I say, although I have no idea how old I am.

"No," she says. "That's not possible. I haven't been able to locate your birth certificate, but that newspaper article about your birth was written in '88, just fifteen years ago."

Newspaper article about my birth? Why would my birth be news? As with a seed buried beneath frozen earth and snow, only the person who plants it knows it's there. I was alive to Mother. To me. I was alive to no one else. Except perhaps a father. Except Grumset.

"Do you have your birth certificate?"

"I don't know," I say. I wouldn't even know what to look for. "What newspaper article?"

"The article wasn't much help. What about family? I haven't located any relatives. Do you still have family in the area? An aunt? Cousins?"

"Yes," I lie. "I'll get in touch with them. They'll take care of me." I'm not sure why I feel threatened by this woman; she looks almost a child with her full face and crooked-teeth smile. I'm not sure what I'm trying to preserve by lying to her, other than the freedom to be the torn sepal, to be blown about.

"I'll need to help you do that," she says. "I'll need their names, telephone numbers, addresses—"

"I don't know where Mother kept those things—"

"Well, you know their names, right? What city they live in. I can probably track them down."

I look out the window that faces the oak. I see the faint outline of the English ivy that scales the tree. The timothy grass and smooth aster show as a shaggy black carpet. The false violet Mother called robin runaway creeps low, around the edge of our moist yard and into the dark woods, and looks now like a shallow, inky wave. "Ivy," I say. "My aunt's name is Ivy."

She opens her bag, removes a pad of paper, a pen. "And her last name?"

"Aster."

"A-S-T-E-R?" she says. I nod. "You have cousins, too?" She writes, "Ivy Aster."

"Timothy and Robin," I say. "Also Aster."

"Great," she says. "They live in Hartswell?"

"Bethan."

"Okay, well, assuming I find them and they'll take you in, I'll still need to help you arrange it. And then there's the property. The house and all. Do you know if your mother made a will or some sort of trust? Because if she didn't, we'll have to go through probate. Eventually everything will go to you, unless your mother had other dependents, outstanding debts, that type of thing. Sorting through it all will take time, though. And some expense."

I want to tell her to get out—that she has no right. There was only Mother and me. Now there is only me. I belong to no one. Mother's things belong to no one.

"Do we have to do this right now?" I say. "I'm tired. Can't you come back?"

"You mean you want me to leave? You know I can't do that, Aslaug. I can't leave you on your own."

"You're going to stay here?"

"No . . . ," she says, and I see the heat that crawls from her blouse, up her chest and neck, and floods her freckles.

79

"You're taking me somewhere?" My scattered self begins to fall back together, jell: I'm not going anywhere with her.

She seems to sense this jelling, this hardening in me: her eyes shift to mine and away; her wide mouth shrinks. She tugs at the corner of one eye and narrows the eye, then strokes it; the skin around the eye reddens to the color of the flood, of her cheeks. "I understand it's been a hard day. It's been a hard several days. You must be exhausted." She laughs, sort of: like she thought to laugh, then changed her mind. "Even I'm exhausted." She stands up. "Okay, listen. I'll go. I'll come back tomorrow. I'm not supposed to do this, but it's probably better for you to stay here, given the options. I can't really see how letting you sleep at home tonight is going to hurt anything. Tomorrow we'll find those relatives." She walks to the door. "But let's just keep this between us, okay?" She opens the door. "Sleep in tomorrow morning. I'll come back around eleven or so, with lunch."

"Sure," I say.

She steps out, turns. "You'll be all right?"

"Yes."

"Don't let anyone in, okay?"

I nod.

"And don't go anywhere."

"I won't," I lie.

Solomon's Seal

2007

—What is your profession, Dr. Eira?

—I'm a forensic pathologist.

—How long have you worked as a forensic pathologist?

—I'm retired, actually. But I worked as a medical examiner for thirty-two years.

—Where were you employed prior to your retirement?

—I worked for the state, for the Office of the Chief Medical Examiner. I was there for eleven years, until two years ago.

—Dr. Eira, please take a moment to review this autopsy report.

—Yes. Okay.

—Are you familiar with the report?

—I prepared it after doing an autopsy on Maren Hellig, the defendant's mother.

—Dr. Eira, please turn to page seven of the report and read out loud, beginning with paragraph two.

—"Alkaloids atropine and scopolamine detected in toxicology screening."

—So, Maren Hellig had atropine and scopolamine in her bloodstream?

—That's right.

—Is atropine a poison?

—Objection. Leading.

—I'll rephrase, Your Honor. What is atropine?

—It's a psychoactive substance that can be toxic to humans.

—What is scopolamine?

—It's also a psychoactive substance that can be toxic to humans.

—Dr. Eira, during the course of your professional career, did you ever conduct an autopsy on another person who tested positive for both atropine and scopolamine?

—Objection. Leading. Relevance.

—Overruled. You may answer.

—Yes, twice. In both cases, the person died from consuming a local plant. *Datura stramonium*. Jimsonweed. The plant contains both atropine and scopolamine.

—Objection. Move to strike. Relevance.

—Overruled.

—You said jimsonweed?

—Yes.

—Did you find any dermatitis or other skin irritation anywhere on Maren Hellig's body?

—Objection. Leading.

—I'll allow it.

—No.

—What, if anything, unusual did you find on Maren Hellig's skin?

—Well, she had that star on her torso, painted on using sap extracted from a local plant. *Sanguinaria canadensis.* The common name of the plant is bloodroot.

—Thank you. I have no further questions.

ELDER TREE
2003

$\mathcal{M}$other used to make elderberry wine. She'd mix the berries with a bit of lemon juice. She'd add some yeast and boiling water. When the water cooled, she'd squeeze the berries to extract the juice. After a day or so, she'd add sugar, more yeast, and she'd cover the concoction and let it sit for several days. Then she'd strain it, add more sugar. And wait. For months. In the dark of our cellar, the berries would stew and ferment. When, finally, Mother thought the wine ready, we would go to the cellar and she would drink a glass. If she was satisfied, together we'd pour the clear liquid into dark green bottles, and she'd tell me stories about the elder tree, her hylantree.

"In Denmark," she'd say, "the dryad Hylde-Moder is believed to live in the hylantree. Cut down a hylantree and Hylde-Moder will haunt you." Or, "In Denmark, some say if you stand beneath the hylantree on the eve of the summer solstice, you'll see the king of Fairyland gallop past." Or, "In the ogham calendar—the Celtic tree calendar—the hylantree is the thirteenth tree, representing the end of the old year and the beginning of the new. It's the beginning in every end and the end in every beginning."

Mother rarely spoke to me of such things, but it seemed the elderberry wine had a magic about it that freed Mother's tongue. I always loved these stories. They intimated another world: a world of spirit and magic and the miraculous where rationality gave way, not to irrationality but to possibility. A world where berries could unlock the mind.

The food Mother and I usually prepared sustained our bodies, less our minds. Peppermint tea. Bearberry tea. Bee balm tea. Spicebush tea. We seasoned our stews with wild garlic, leek or basil, or the plant Mother called poor man's pepper, or with the pungent horseradish flavor of the sea rocket plant. Our starch came mainly from Mother's bread and porridge made of groundnut tubers, and from the chestnut-flavored tubers of the spring beauty plant and from salsify. We found protein in the nutlike green fruit of the American lotus and the seeds of the pickerelweed. And in madder-curdled milk. These foods satisfied the hunger in my body, but they couldn't satisfy the hunger of my mind.

I walk to the cellar and take another of the green bottles in my hands. It has what seems a warmth about it, despite the cool dampness of the cellar. The green bottle looks black in the dim light. The glass feels smooth in my hands. Smooth as a coffin lid, I think, but I stop myself.

Mother's hands touched this bottle; I remember her

holding the base of the bottle and the stem, the funnel propped on top, as I poured in the wine. I run my fingers around the base, up the stem.

She knew she was dying, I think. That's why she wanted the sneezeweed. That's why she was troubled by the hair-streak, the passionflower, our oak. They were omens to her, signs her world was off balance. For even though Mother ridiculed any interest I displayed in theology or witchcraft or the magical, it was Mother who scoured the sacred texts; it was Mother who told me stories of the elder tree.

I carry the bottle up the stairs, into the kitchen; I pour myself a glass. As I feel the wine's warmth run through me while I drink, I sense the inevitability of what I have to do. I'm making the choice to leave, of course. But it no longer feels like a choice. I've outgrown the shell, it seems. There's no going back. Yet even as I feel this, I wonder whether I'm fooling myself, telling myself it's destiny that I leave Mother's house so as to counteract the doubt and insecurity and foreboding that over and over again make me wonder whether I'm as crazy as that old man who lives next door seems convinced I am. I am Aslaug Datter, daughter of Maren. I am as much my mother as I am anything. And even I, despite my isolation, suspect Mother was not altogether sane. How can I be sure I am sane?

The neighbor is watching me again through the window of his house, through the window of mine—wheeling his chair about so as to get the best view—as if waiting for me to slip up, show my true self, so he can call the cops again, get rid of me for good.

"You don't need to get rid of me," I shout at him through

the glass; I can't see his expression, but I imagine his surprise. Grumset lifts his hand, grabs the cord of the shade. "I'm leaving, you old coot," I shout, and louder this time, wishing he could hear, but I know he can't. And the shade slices the space between us.

Solomon's Seal

2007

—Would you like to cross-examine Dr. Eira, Counsel?

—Yes, thank you, Your Honor. Dr. Eira, Aslaug's mother, Maren Hellig, did not die from jimsonweed poisoning, did she?

—No.

—In fact, Maren Hellig died of a rare form of spinal cancer that metastasized to her brain, isn't that right?

—That's right.

—You found Maren Hellig also suffered from severe rheumatoid arthritis, isn't that right?

—Yes, but that didn't kill her—

—Thank you. Please just answer my question. Mrs. Hellig was in a lot of pain before she died, wasn't she?

—Objection. Speculation.

—Sustained.

—Based on your professional experience, does the type of cancer Maren Hellig suffered from cause pain?

—Yes.

—Severe pain, right?

—Objection. Calls for speculation.

—I'm going to allow it.

—Yes, most likely.

—Based on your professional experience, wouldn't you say a person suffering from the type of rheumatoid arthritis Maren Hellig suffered from also would be in a great deal of pain?

—Objection. Speculation.

—Overruled.

—Without medication, yes.

—You found no evidence while conducting the autopsy that Maren Hellig was taking medication for pain, did you?

—No, I didn't—

—Except the jimsonweed, right?

—Jimsonweed is not a medication.

—Jimsonweed has narcotic properties, does it not?

—It does.

—It can dull the senses, correct?

—I suppose, yes.

—And it could make one care less about her pain, couldn't it?

—Objection. Speculation.

—Overruled.

—I suppose.

—Is that yes?

—Yes.

—It's possible, then, that Maren Hellig took the jimson-weed in an attempt to alleviate her pain, isn't it?

—Objection. Speculation.

—Overruled.

—It's possible.

—Given the degree to which Mrs. Hellig was suffering, it's even possible she took the jimsonweed in an attempt to take her own life, isn't that right?

—Objection. Speculation. Argumentative.

—That's going a bit far, Counsel. You've laid no founda-tion for that line of questioning. Objection sustained.

—Dr. Eira, you found no evidence during your autopsy of Maren Hellig indicating Aslaug played a role in her mother's death, did you?

—I found jimsonweed and also the bloodroot—

—But Mrs. Hellig did not die of jimsonweed poisoning, did she?

—No.

—And the bloodroot sap you found on the deceased's skin—bloodroot is not poisonous, is it?

—Not when applied to the skin. Taken orally, it can be poisonous in very large amounts. But—

—But there's no evidence of Maren Hellig's having in-gested bloodroot, correct?

—That's right.

—Just to be clear, you found absolutely no evidence dur-ing the autopsy indicating Aslaug had a role in her mother's death, right? Please just answer yes or no.

—No, I didn't—

—Thank you. I have no further questions.

CARRION FLOWER

2003

I walk through the house scanning each room, each object, as if somehow, through some transformation of a room or an object, or myself, it will become obvious what I can't live without, what I will need to live on my own, in some other place. It feels I'm seeing the house for the first time, as if it were someone else's house, already someone else's shell; as if all that is here has nothing whatsoever to do with me. I can still see strokes from Mother's paintbrush upon the crimson walls of the sitting room, from when she attempted to paint the walls years before. And I see the empty candleholder in the chandelier and the wax droplets on the carpet from when she'd forgotten to extinguish a candle just days before her death. Her quilt lies balled on her armchair, where strands of her hair cling serpent-like.

I lift Mother's jangle of keys from the hook in the

kitchen, and I unlock the drawers she kept locked, the closets she kept locked. And I realize as I search, what I'm looking for is Mother—for something that can reveal her to me.

It's odd to think there was someone in the world who had known Mother. Father. Was he as familiar with Mother as I? Her smell: like sweet lilacs left too long in a vase; the scent of her hair and her clothes and her bedclothes. When she would outuse a sweater or skirt or blouse and give it to me, then I stank her stink, until I could scrub it away. And her voice, the rounded vowels, the lilt. And her hands, as they malformed, until at last they were curled into balls. She liked her porridge overcooked and stuck in clumps, so when eaten, it clung to the mouth as if resisting its fate. And tea. She drank it so hot, it would scald her tongue, and she'd curse it, before taking a second drink.

And yet, she felt affection for me she couldn't hide. When she would brush my hair, and when she would struggle with her hands to fold my hair into a braid, I felt it. And sometimes at night when she thought I was asleep, she came into my room, and she watched me, and she touched my hair or my forehead; she lifted the covers to my shoulders; she whispered my name, "Aslaug Datter," not to wake me, just to say it.

I knew these things about Mother, but I didn't know my mother; it's almost unfathomable to me anyone could have understood Mother. Mother was the speed of light. Or dark matter, or gravity. "Gravity is powerless against the tug of even a tiny magnet," Mother would say. "And yet if gravity were stronger, our universe would collapse into itself. Sometimes there's strange power in frailty."

One drawer is stuffed with rubber bands, coiled in small

knots, tangled in large knots. Another is packed with canning lids and rims and small glass jars. The closets contain reams of fabric and cleaning supplies and flyswatters and mounds of rags. No photographs. No letters. No memorabilia from my childhood.

I'm missing something, I think as I cram contents back in and slam doors and drawers closed. Mother had secrets. I know she did: I found *The Scarlet Letter*; I found the mirror in the green room. And the look on her face when she stepped from the green room, I'd seen it before.

I fall asleep in Mother's armchair wrapped in her quilt, and in her sour-lilac smell, and I dream of Mother's switch. Again and again my mind replays the switch in her grip, the switch on my flesh, after she found me in the grips of Hester Prynne. On the third day of my reading the book, I neared the end and forgot the time. I turned the last page when Mother entered. "I just found it," I said when I saw her eyes on *The Scarlet Letter*, when I saw her scarlet face. "I was making the bed. . . ." She slipped the book from me, so calmly. She descended the stairs, so calmly. She returned upstairs without the book, with the switch, and she beat me.

I wake feeling the sting of the switch, and it comes to me: the outhouse. Mother mentioned the outhouse the night before she died. I thought she was so sick her mind was leaving her, but was she trying to tell me something? "There's a crack in the ceiling," she'd said. "The boards are loose. You need to go there. Find it."

I run through the house, to the porch, out the door. So strange, I think, to just run out the door. I stumble on the stairs as I descend, crash down, still foggy from elderberry wine and sleep. I lift myself, sit on the stairs, try to unravel the outhouse with my eyes, but the rear of the lot is far too overgrown. I can imagine the stench of the carrion flower, and the thorns of the carrion vine. I know the red house is out there, enveloped in stench and vine and flies. I stand up, let the swirling settle, and I walk now, into the snare of branches and thorns. It's been years since I've wandered into this morass, and I'm surprised to see a matted path of sorts, where branches have been snapped, leaves stripped, fallen leaves flattened. I push my way through; I snap more branches, strip and flatten more leaves. I smell the dead-animal scent of the carrion flower before I see the outhouse. But then I see it: its red door bright and free.

Someone cleared the brush, I think.

Mother cleared the brush.

But why? And when?

I near the door, touch the door. My heart fills my chest, pounds into my ears. I pull the door open: nothing. "A crack in the ceiling," she'd said. "The boards are loose." I walk inside, but it's dark. As I wait for my eyes to adjust, I climb on the seat, reach up, and I knock and push. A board slips; I push it aside, reach in. I finger something; I pull it down.

It's a suitcase—I carry it outside, into the light. It's brown leather and cracking, and I sense it's not empty. I try to open it, but it's locked. I race to the kitchen—I feel alert now, sharp—and I grab a large knife, carry it back. At first I try to use the knife to pry the case open, but I can't; the lock won't budge. When I jam the knife into the leather, I'm relieved Mr. Grumset can't see. The leather peels apart more easily than it seems it should, and the bills spill out.

94

Solomon's Seal

2007

—Please state your name.

—Cecilia Sture.

—What is your profession, Ms. Sture?

—I'm a graduate student right now. But I was a social worker before going back to school.

—When did you work as a social worker?

—Beginning about five years ago.

—For whom did you work?

—For the Department of Health and Human Services.

—How long did you work as a social worker?

—Two and a half years.

—Ms. Sture, have you met the defendant, this woman, Aslaug Hellig?

—Yes.

—When?

—Right after her mother's death. I was the social worker on her case.

—How would you describe Ms. Hellig's state of mind after her mother's death?

—Objection. Vague. Speculation.

—Overruled.

—It's hard to say. She seemed overwhelmed. I think she was intoxicated the last time I saw her. She was standoffish with me for the most part. She misled me about the names of her relatives. And then she just disappeared.

—Objection. Move to strike. Nonresponsive. Speculation. Hearsay.

—Overruled. Please proceed, Counsel.

—When you say she misled you about names, what do you mean?

—She told me she had an aunt and some cousins in Bethan. She said her aunt's name was Ivy Aster. Her cousins, she said, were Timothy and Robin Aster. I wrote it all down.

—Objection. Move to strike. Hearsay.

—Overruled.

—How do you know the names were false?

—Bethan's not a very big place. There's no one at all in Bethan with the last name Aster. As far as I can tell, there never has been.

—Okay, now, when you say Aslaug disappeared, what do you mean?

—I mean just that. She disappeared. One day she was there, the next day she was gone. I didn't see her again until now. I tried to locate her, but I had a big caseload. I couldn't devote endless hours to finding her, you know. Honestly, her situation was a lot less critical than many of the cases I was dealing with. She was nearly an adult at the time her mother died. I had kids as young as six months without parents.

—Did it occur to you when the defendant "disappeared," as you say, that she may have had something to do with her mother's death?

—Objection. Leading. Argumentative.

—Sustained.

—I'll rephrase. Did you ever determine the reason for Aslaug's disappearance?

—No. I wondered if she had something to do with her mother's death—that crossed my mind for sure. But I couldn't dwell on Aslaug's disappearing. I had a lot on my plate. I figured it was up to people in the legal system to pursue a case against her if they thought it was appropriate. I told that police detective, though. Detective Fenris? I told her Aslaug took off.

—Objection. Move to strike, Your Honor. Speculation.

—Sustained.

—Ms. Sture, did you or did you not discover any legitimate reason for Aslaug's disappearance?

—I did not.

—Thank you. I have no further questions.

EVENING STAR

2003

The evening primrose blooms at night; between six and seven in the evening, it opens, and it remains open throughout the night, while the hawk moth flies and pollinates; by noon the next day, the primrose is closed, and the hawk moth rests. I will be gone before the primrose closes, I tell myself. Before the hawk moth rests, I will be gone.

Mother called the primrose her evening star. "She's like me," Mother would say. "The evening star's like me." I wondered whether she said this because the primrose seeks darkness, or because it's surrounded by hawk moths that suck it dry. Regardless, I sensed she admired the flower's quirky tastes. And, for this, I loved the primrose. Mother's evening star showed me a side of her I otherwise might not have seen. A side I liked.

The suitcase was full of money. Although I have little

sense of money, it seems like a lot. Some of the money remained sealed in envelopes Mother never bothered to open, postmarked in Bethan, just miles away. Mother never permitted my retrieving the mail. When we would go to the post office in Hartswell, she would produce a key from her pocket, unlock the box, then dump the mail into a bag and it would disappear; I'd never see it again.

Now I understand why: it's my father who sent the money; I feel sure of this. All these years he's been absent, he sent money to care for me. He's alive after all. The money is evidence of his existence, and of his love. Evidence he wants me to find him.

I think back to the November ten months before Mother's death. I remember the sky hung wide and blue; I'd seen it when I'd stepped onto the porch to hang clothes.

"Strange for Hartswell," Mother had remarked when I'd passed by her on my way back inside. She was talking about the sky, stealing my thoughts. Or had I stolen hers?

It was strange. The sky of Hartswell is usually gray and confining from early October through mid-April. But on this day it was huge, brilliant, tempting.

Yet in all other ways the afternoon, then evening, seemed ordinary. I retreated to the sitting room, purportedly to study, while Mother took her Wednesday evening bath. I sat with an opened book in my lap and three or four more books sprawled on the table before me. But I wasn't studying. Mother bathed just twice a week—on Wednesday and Sunday evenings—from half past five to half past six. These hours were precious to me.

I was observing a twine of light. Formed by the irregular gap between the drawn drapes, it had originally appeared golden—a shimmering snake—but as night hastened, it grew more and more faint.

And I was thinking of girls. Girls I'd seen in Hartswell and Bethan. Girls with mothers. Girls with boys. Girls with girls with girls. What is it like to be these girls? I'd wondered then, as I often did, as I often do. What would I be like if I were one of these girls? Would I have friends? A boyfriend? Would I dangle beads from my ears? Would I have read books Mother's forbidden me to read, passages she's blackened? Would I wear underwear that rides higher than my slacks and that seems little more than a confluence of threads? Would I know the feel of a real boy's skin, or the smell of his skin? Would I have traveled to Europe or Asia or Africa, and know with my body, not just my mind, these places exist? Would I still be Aslaug Datter, only broader, richer? Or would the breadth of me thin me out, make me as shallow as Mother has intimated these girls I admire must be?

"Get your coat, Aslaug. We're going out."

I remember hearing Mother's voice and disentangling myself from the girls. And I remember seeing the snake had muted—that it was nearly indecipherable. Nearly. Not completely. Because Mother had finished early: it was only six-fifteen.

"We're going out?" We never went out in the evenings; I couldn't imagine why we would.

"*Er du døv, barn? Kom nu for Satan.* Are you deaf, child? Come on, for Satan."

100

"But—"

Mother lifted her hand, tried to spread it before me to stop my speaking; her palm flattened, but her fingers curled into themselves.

I rose to go for my coat but stopped to put away my books, knowing Mother might punish my slovenliness. I was fumbling with the books when Mother slammed her fist against the table. "*Du ku braek en kniv i en lort.* You could break a knife in shit. I said get your coat, Aslaug. How much more clear can I be?"

"Yes. Yes, Mother." I was afraid, suddenly. Not that I wasn't accustomed to fear, but the fear I knew was contained, familiar. It was fear of disappointing Mother: fear of her words, or the switch. The fear I felt then: it was wild fear. Mother's and my life was predictable. We were so accustomed to our routines—to our churning—that we passed each day as if sentenced. Sentenced to the clutter of waking, eating, cleaning, bathing, studying. Mother determined what and when we ate, what and when we studied, when we slept, and when, if ever, we left the house. Every aspect of my existence was foreordained: my every move; at times it seemed my every thought. But leaving the house at night didn't fit the pattern of our life. Like with the hairstreak, the passionflower, the order of my world was shifting.

I scrambled down the hallway and nearly tripped on the rug. I pulled my jacket from the hall closet, slipped it on, then followed Mother's halting figure as it passed outside, across the blades of dying grass and mush of fallen leaves, into the driveway, where the car was parked. It had already snowed once, and melted. The sticky mud of the driveway clung to the soles of my shoes. I dropped to the seat of the car but hung my feet out the door. Then I beat my shoes against one another and felt the heavy clumps release.

We drove in silence.

Mother pulled into the local high school and turned immediately to the right, as if she knew where she was going, as if she'd been there before. But I knew she hadn't, because I'd not.

There were ten to fifteen cars in the lot, and scattered windows of the school emitted light. I could see through the main doors, into the main hall, where a stream of fluorescent lights spanned the ceiling, illuminating patches of orange and green and blue lockers. A man sat near the entrance, reading a thin pamphlet, his bald head refulgent in the fluorescent light.

Mother parked the car, released her door; I released mine. She climbed out cussing, *"Lort, lort."* Then paced around the car. I was garnering courage to question Mother, to ask her why we were at the school, whether we were there to see the man in the window; I wondered if the man was my father.

"Get in," Mother said.

"Get in?" I'd just gotten out.

"In the driver's seat," she said. "I'm going to teach you to drive."

And she did, in less than an hour. I didn't have to ask Mother why she was teaching me. I knew. Mother's limbs were failing her; it was not clear how much longer she would be able to drive.

When Mother instructed me to drive out of the parking

lot, into Bethan, it was nearly dark. "Turn right here," she said. "And then here." It seemed she was directing me someplace. And I sensed, even before we arrived, that what we were doing was significant. Rare. This was Mother's small whorled pogonia, that orchid that lies dormant underground for ten years between bloomings: Mother was flowering, showing me part of herself—of her life—I'd never seen before.

She instructed me to pull through a gate, part of which was obscured by a flowering witch hazel tree, its petals curled into buds to endure the night's chill. We stopped in front of a stone building, its yard overgrown, its roof shingled in a sporadic array of brown and gray. Yet it had a dignity about it, a majesty; at one time it had been grand. I thought of the elderly women I'd seen when I'd been out with Mother in Bethan: their striking white hair, wound and piled on their heads; their diamonds polished; their matching purses and shoes, colored peach or beige. Yet their lipstick quivered above their lips in pinkish smears, and stains marked their blouses, having evaded their farsighted eyes.

"Turn off the engine," Mother said.

We sat there, then, Mother and I. We sat in front of this place—a place I knew had some relevance to Mother's life, to my life. Mother didn't speak; she looked out the window for what seemed hours, although it may have been minutes. Her left eye was twitching, and she was biting her bottom lip. Her hands were tangled in the front of her skirt like she was hiding something there, finding it, hiding it again. In my memory her eyes were glistening, but I couldn't have seen this in the dark. What I know I did see, as the darkness thickened and the interior of the building came more and more to life, were people moving about inside: a woman, maybe two; a man.

It's that building that beckons me now; it's that man I know I must find.

SOLOMON'S SEAL

2007

—Cross-examination?

—Yes. Ms. Sture, what are you studying in graduate school?

—Art history.

—Art history?

—Yes.

—You said you worked as a social worker for the state of Maine for two and a half years, isn't that right?

—Yes, for the Department of Health and Human Services.

—Where were you employed before that?

—Before I worked as a social worker for the state? I wasn't employed. I was in school.

—So it sounds like you were sort of training on the job when you worked for the state, is that right?

—Well, no. I mean, I had to do some clinical work while in school in order to get my degree.

—Ms. Sture, you had been employed as a social worker for less than a year when you took on Aslaug's case, isn't that right?

—Yes, I think that's right.

—And yet, you say Aslaug's case was one of your less critical cases?

—That's right.

—Isn't it true, prior to Aslaug's case, you had never dealt with a situation during your course of employment in which a teenage girl's mother died?

—Objection. Relevance.

—Overruled.

—I believe that's true.

—And you certainly hadn't dealt with a situation in which the teenage girl who lost her mother had no siblings or known father, isn't that right?

—I hadn't encountered that situation before meeting Aslaug.

—So, it's fair to say you were sort of learning on the job when it came to Aslaug's situation?

—I'd been trained to deal with all sorts of situations.

—But you hadn't dealt with this type of situation in the field, correct?

—That's right.

—You yourself described Aslaug as standoffish. You had a difficult time relating to Aslaug, didn't you?

—She was standoffish.

—With you?

—Yes.

—Did it ever cross your mind you failed Aslaug?

—Objection. Vague. Relevance.

—I'm going to allow the question.

—I don't understand.

—Did it ever cross your mind Aslaug may have left because you frightened her?

—Objection, Your Honor. Argumentative.

—Sustained.

—Ms. Sture, you threatened to send Aslaug away from the only house she'd ever known just hours after she watched her mother being buried, isn't that right?

—I told her we would try to find relatives to take her in.

—But that would have been at another house, right?

—Yes.

—You were unable to locate any relatives, correct?

—Like I said, Aslaug said she had some relatives. I knew there'd been an aunt.

—But you weren't able to locate any of Aslaug's relatives, correct?

—I hadn't found any by that point in time.

—So you weren't able to assure Aslaug she would be placed with relatives, correct?

—That's right, but she misled me about her relatives—

—Ms. Sture, you are aware, are you not, that Aslaug did in fact have relatives in Bethan?

—I found that out because of the trial.

—In fact, Aslaug had an aunt and cousins in Bethan, just like she said, and she went to live with them, right?

—Obviously she had them. . . . But the actual people had different names than she said.

—It's possible, isn't it, that you just got the relatives' names wrong?

—No. I wrote them down.

—I have that piece of paper here, in fact. Is this the piece of paper on which you wrote down the names?

—Yes.

—I'd like to submit this as Exhibit N. This paper is not dated, is it, Ms. Sture?

—No.

—And it has no case file number on it, does it?

—No.

—In fact, it has no identifying information at all on it, does it, other than the names of the Asters?

—It doesn't, but—

—Thank you, Ms. Sture. Now, without this paper, you would not have remembered the names Aslaug supposedly gave you, would you? Because this happened four years ago.

—I wouldn't have remembered.

—So it's possible that you're mistaken about the names, isn't it?

—No. Like I said, I wrote them down.

—But, Ms. Sture, there is absolutely no identifying information on this piece of paper that would connect it to Aslaug Hellig.

—But I remember—

—I thought you said you wouldn't have remembered the names absent the paper?

—Objection. Argumentative.

108

—I'll overrule the objection, but I think it's time to move on, Counsel.

—Okay, Your Honor. I'll withdraw the question. Ms. Sture, you told Aslaug that all her family possessions would be controlled by the probate system, isn't that correct?

—I told her if her mother hadn't made provisions prior to her death, probate would get involved, yes.

—And you told her this just hours after Aslaug had attended her mother's funeral?

—I talked to Aslaug the evening of the funeral.

—Is that a yes?

—Yes.

—But it hasn't occurred to you that you might have scared Aslaug away? She was gone by the next morning, isn't that right? You were her last memory at that house.

—Objection. Compound and argumentative.

—Sustained.

—Ms. Sture, it was against regulation for you to leave Aslaug alone after her mother died, wasn't it?

—It was only supposed to be for one night.

—Please answer my question. You were not supposed to leave Aslaug alone after she was released from jail, were you? Because she was under eighteen?

—I wasn't supposed to leave her.

—And yet you went ahead and left her all alone anyway, didn't you? Even though you described her as seeming overwhelmed and possibly intoxicated.

—Yes, but—

—You're trying to cover up your own failings by blaming Aslaug, aren't you, Ms. Sture?

—Objection. Argumentative.

—Sustained.

—You have regrets about how you handled Aslaug's case, don't you, Ms. Sture?

—I try to learn from every situation.

—You have regrets related to your handling of Aslaug's case, isn't that true? Please answer with a yes or no.

—Yes.

—And you have regrets in part because you did not follow regulations in your handling of Aslaug's case, isn't that right?

—I wanted what was best for Aslaug. I may have made mistakes, but I wanted what was best for her.

—Is that why you're blaming Aslaug for your own failings?

—Objection. Argumentative.

—Sustained.

—Thank you, Ms. Sture. I have no further questions, Your Honor.

LOW SWEET BLUEBERRY

2003

There is a hill behind our house that rises in a hump. From a distance it looks like a showy hat. The base is decorated in a splattering of trees, but quickly the ground stretches smooth and sparse. Standing on our back porch, I can't see the blueberry bushes, their branches heavy now, kneeling low with plump fruit. But I know the bushes are there near the top of the hill, and the sweet berries are there, speckling the hat like sapphire suns. And I know the pink-edged sulphur is there, too, the yellow butterfly with the pink fringe that lays its pitcher-shaped eggs on the flat green of the blueberry plant's leaves.

The pink-edged sulphur will die soon. But its descendants will live on. The yellow-green caterpillars will cling to the blueberry bushes, gain nourishment from their leaves. And in the spring, each caterpillar will bind itself to the blueberry plant in a silk cradle. Only when the new butter-flies emerge will they leave the blueberry plant, feeding instead on milkweed and knapweed, hawkweed and fireweed.

I return inside the house to gather clothing, a hairbrush, a toothbrush, some books. And I wonder as I assemble these things, What do I have that is mine? My clothes are Mother's; my books are Mother's; even my hairbrush is one that we shared; my head is full of Mother's ideas; my face is her face. I wish I knew if it was possible to emerge anew. Will the young sulphur know its past? Will it know at one time it couldn't fly?

After the young sulphur has visited the milkweed, after she's tasted the sweet nectar of the knapweed, after she's carried away pollen from the hawkweed and fireweed, she mates. Then she does return to the blueberry plant. It is there she lays her eggs, and the process of egg to caterpillar to chrysalis begins again, as if the sulphur does know, does sense, her history; instinctively she's drawn to her blueberry home.

I patch up the suitcase with masking tape. Fill a jug with water. I put all these things in the car. And I leave. I just drive away, looking back at the house only once, so I know I've seen it absent Mother's eyes. The gravel beneath me is loose and loud. I turn onto the road; it seems too smooth, the dividing line too close. A car is approaching in the opposite lane. I veer right and nearly run off the road.

I can't see behind me without mirrors, but I hear the police car there. First the sirens, then, "Pull to the side of the road." The sound vibrates around me. Grumset, I think; that mean old man called the police again. "Pull over to the side of the road."

By the time the officer walks up to the car, my hands are wet on the wheel. The car window is rolled down, and I look up to see the police officer who arrested me. The woman. She takes off her hat and rests it on the car roof; she bends to the window. Her hair is pulled tight to her scalp, her roots a dark halo. "Ass-log?" she says. She wipes the back of her hand across her brow, flips her hand, wipes again. Her fingernails are cardinal red and long, like tubular petals. Like the petals of scarlet lobelia. "It's Ass-log, right?"

I nod.

"I'm one of the cops who came to your house when your mother died."

I nod again.

"Where you going?"

I pause, consider lying, but I can't think where else to say. "Bethan."

"Why?"

"Family. I have family there."

"You do?" she says. "Right." She looks at the taped suitcase lying on the seat next to me. "What's in there?" She doesn't wait for a reply; she walks around to the passenger side and opens the door. "You're driving with no rearview mirrors, Ass-log. That's not safe. And it's illegal." She lifts the case and sets it on the ground. She tries to open it, but it's locked. "Where's the key?"

"I don't have it."

"That why it's taped like this? You cut it open?" She claws at the tape, snaps a nail. "Damn," she says, and she sucks the nail. "You have no license?" But she knows I don't. She claws at the tape again, frees it this time. Then she peels back the leather. "Holy Christ." She looks up at me with her adder's eyes. "What the hell you up to, Ass-log?"

"I found it after Mother died. I think my father sent it for me. To take care of me."

"Your father, huh?" she says, and her lips stretch thin, as if she's smiling, but she's not smiling. "How come we didn't find this when we searched the house?"

"It wasn't in the house. It was out back, in the outhouse."

"What outhouse?" she says. "There wasn't any out-house."

I try to explain, but she cuts me off. "I like you, Ass-log. I don't want you to get in trouble. This doesn't look good, though. I'm not saying you've done anything you shouldn't have done. You've had some hard knocks for someone so damn young. But I can't just let you run off like this, not with all this money."

"You can have the money," I say. "I don't care about the money."

She releases the leather and it flaps back down. "God-damn, Ass-log," she says, and she shakes her head. "You sure are a hard nut to crack. If you don't care about the money, what the hell you running off for?"

"I'm not running off," I say, but she lifts her hand and fans it before me.

"Don't," she says. "Don't lie to me. I said I like you, but I could change my mind." She motions toward the backseat. "I see your belongings back there." Then she looks back down at the case. "How much?"

"Money?" I say. "I don't know—I didn't count it." The amount would have meant little to me.

She wipes her brow again, then lifts the suitcase from the ground like it's alive. "Wait here." She walks to the patrol car and pushes the suitcase across the seat before she climbs in. I can't see what she's doing, although I've turned around and I'm trying to see.

Within minutes she comes back and drops the suitcase next to me; it's taped again, but the tape looks curdled, and the strip's end, where she broke her nail, curls up and sticks to itself. I think of our house after the officers came and went: I think of their undoing, and their futile attempts to replace and restore.

"You've enough in there to last you a long while," she says. She walks around to the driver's side and collects her hat from the roof of my car. She puts the hat back on and begins to walk away, but then she stops, turns around. "I'm sorry about your mother. I thought you killed her when I was at your house. I thought you were some psycho, especially when I saw that paint on your ma's stomach, and that rock. But for some reason I sure as hell can't figure out, I felt sorry for you. And then I read the path report. It said cancer." She pauses. "Did you kill her, Ass-log? Did you kill her for that money?"

"I told you, you can have the money. You can have all of it. I wouldn't kill my mother for money."

"You wouldn't," she says. "I believe that. That's why I'm letting you go today. But I want you to go home, hide that suitcase wherever it was hidden before, and wait for that social worker to come."

"Okay," I lie, but it's not as easy this time.

"Let her help you, that social worker. She'll help you find

115

relatives if that's what you want. Don't tell her about seeing me, though. Don't tell anyone about seeing me, or about that money. It'll complicate things. Just keep the money hidden. Take out only what you need. You understand?"

"Yes."

"I have a daughter about your age," she says then. She looks away, behind our cars, and her broken nail outlines her badge. "She's sick. Got cancer, like your ma had."

"I'm sorry," I say.

"Her doctors say she'll die."

I feel I should say something, but I don't know what to say. And now I want to tell her I was lying to her. I want to tell her the truth.

"There's this treatment. It's experimental. And damn expensive. But what choice do I have? Shit," she says then, but not to me. She pulls a pink handkerchief from her pocket, holds it to her nose and trumpets. Then she walks back to the patrol car, gets in. I hear her engine bellow, hear her wheels roll, feel my lungs draw in air, realize I'd barely been breathing—that my head feels light. Her car stops when it's parallel with mine. She rolls down the passenger-side window. I see her eyes are smudges, her cheeks zebra-striped. "Did you see me today, Ass-log?"

"No," I say.

"Good girl."

Solomon's Seal

2007

—Ms. Hellig, you claim your mother used jimsonweed fairly regularly, isn't that right?

—During the months just prior to her death she did, yes.

—And you claim she smoked dried jimsonweed, right?

—Yes.

—Or she would inhale from a mixture made from dried jimsonweed and some chemical compound that would ignite easily, correct?

—Yes.

—Ms. Hellig, you claim you and your mother went out foraging in the woods for wildflowers the day before you discovered her dead, isn't that right?

—Yes.

—And you claim your primary reason for foraging that day was your mother's desire to find jimsonweed, right?

117

—Objection. Calls for speculation.

—Objection overruled, but answer only what you know.

—Mother wanted jimsonweed. There was none left at the house.

—None at all?

—None.

—In fact, you claim there had not been any jimsonweed in the house for approximately one week before your mother and you went out looking for it the day before her death, is that right?

—That's right.

—So your mother hadn't used jimsonweed during that week before her death, correct?

—Objection. Speculation.

—Overruled. But, again, answer only what you know.

—She couldn't have used any. We didn't have any. Until we went out foraging—

—Okay. So the day before your mother died, when she was supposedly in so much pain, she managed to go walking in the woods looking for jimsonweed?

—Objection. Argumentative.

—Sustained.

—Ms. Hellig, you claim you found your mother dead approximately twelve hours after the two of you returned from gathering the jimsonweed, right?

—About twelve hours, yes.

—Ms. Hellig, in order for your mother to smoke or otherwise inhale jimsonweed, it would first have to be dried, correct?

—Yes.

—It takes jimsonweed more than a day to dry out, doesn't it?

—Objection. Relevance. Speculation.

—Overruled.

—Yes.

—But, Ms. Hellig, your mother could not have used the jimsonweed you claim you picked for her the day before her death, could she, because the jimsonweed would not yet have been dried?

—I-I hadn't realized that. It doesn't make sense.

—No, it doesn't, Ms. Hellig. It doesn't make any sense at all.

—Objection. Move to strike. Argumentative.

—Sustained.

—Ms. Hellig, you washed your mother's body after she died, didn't you?

—Yes.

—But you don't have an explanation as to why you did that, do you?

—It just seemed right—

—And you painted the inverted pentagram on her body with bloodroot sap after she was dead, didn't you?

—I was painting the seal of Solomon—

—Solomon's seal is a hexagram, Ms. Hellig. The Star of David. What you painted was an inverted pentagram.

—Objection. Narrative. Argumentative.

—Sustained. Move on, Counsel.

Eve's Cups

2003

*A*s I drive through Bethan, through its one-way streets, I have an idea where I want to go, but the streets seem to choose my path for me. Again and again I pass the same squarish homes, white painted wood with black shutters or brick with black shutters, with double chimneys like insect antennae. And the Bran College campus, adorning the spread of green grass in its regal brown-red. I see all of this, yet I don't; it seems merged in my fear, as if my fear is the frail gravity that holds it all in place.

I find myself driving down Irnan Street for the third time, and I feel like an insect slipping into eve's cups, that carnivorous pitcher plant that lures insects with its beauty, then traps them, devours them. I stop myself: I'm being histrionic, I think; Mother hated when I acted like this. I'm not going to be devoured; I'm just driving. This town's not alive. The streets are not alive.

I pull to the side of the road, turn off the engine, roll up the window, look out. Mother didn't bring me to this part of Bethan, except when she taught me to drive, and that was night: everything looked so different. It's ninety degrees in the afternoon, extraordinary for Maine. There are so many people, standing in conversation, huddled on the grass, moving along sidewalks in clusters of undulating color. Phones nest in hands and dangle from hips. Earphones plug ears, and heads bob. It's like looking out into a field of the strangest flowers—flowers without roots that can change shape, change location, make sound. Many of the women are barely clothed, wearing short pants that expose their upper thighs and shirts without sleeves. Some of the men have no shirts at all. And there are children with soft bellies and plump arms, sitting atop shoulders. Skin upon skin next to skin.

"Hey there."

I turn to see a man standing outside the driver's-side door. I think he's a man—he's big enough to be. He leans down, rests his forearms on the car, nearly presses his nose against the window. His hair is the color of ash, after the hot coals fade. He wears a necklace with what looks like a shark tooth; the tooth dangles beneath his Adam's apple, dips into the hair on his arm. "You lost?" he says.

I hadn't heard him approach, and for a second I can't take in he's talking to me. I realize I felt invisible here, like I'm such an outsider, I couldn't be seen. I struggle to roll down the window; I feel sweat beading along my upper lip.

"You lost?" he says again. "You sure look lost. And you must be damn hot in that dress."

I wipe the sweat from my lip, try to push the sleeves of the dress up, but my skin's sticky. "I'm trying to find this

121

building I saw a few months ago." I realize I have little to say; I know almost nothing about the place. "It's around here, I'm just not sure where." I've never spoken to a man before. Or a boy. Except those officers and the sheriff. Except Grumset. But I'd wanted to. I'd seen a teenage boy in Bethan with auburn hair and cider eyes, and cheekbones sharp and high, and deep underlying vales. And I'd imagined his voice, his laugh. And I'd imagined my fingers over his cheekbones, into the vales: the feel of his textured skin. And the scent of that skin, like the ocean.

"You have an address?" the boy-man says now, and he stands upright. He smells like spice and dirt; the smell's strong. His T-shirt looks several sizes too small: it squeezes his upper arms and rides up his stomach. His pants hang low, and a phone hangs from them; the tips of his hipbones spike above the pants' waist. And a small spurt of yellowish brown hair forms a line to his belly button, as if he'd tucked a furry anther of sweet vernal grass behind the pants' snap.

Sweat beads sprout above my upper lip again, and on my forehead; I imagine the red shine on my cheeks, like I'd seen on Mother's so many times: that translucent, bright red of the redberry elder, a fruit so loved by birds, so distasteful to humans. "No," I say, "I don't." I avert my eyes from the path up his middle. "I saw it in the dark." I look up, into his face, and I see he's pulled his mouth to one side, like he's trying not to smile, or forcing a smile.

He leans back down, peers into the back of the car and at the suitcase. "You looking for somewhere to hang?" he says.

"To what?"

"You running away?"

"No," I say, but the officer thought I was running away, and this boy-man does, too: I feel transparent. Yet I wasn't meaning to run away; I was meaning to find my father. "I'm just trying to find some people. I don't know them, but I think they may be important to me."

He nods, like what I said made sense. "You have a vision or something?" he says. "This some kind of New Age thing?"

"New what?"

"You're not from around here, are you?" he says.

I shake my head. And then I stop. "Actually, I am." But it doesn't feel like I am. I think of the passionflower Mother saw those weeks ago, and of the hairstreak. Neither belonged here and yet they were here. Did they feel out of place? I wonder. Did they realize this wasn't their home? Or did they feel more at home because they'd chosen their habitat, not accepted their fate?

"You don't talk like you're from around here," he says. "You a student?"

"No."

"I didn't think so. I hadn't seen you before, and I've been a student here for what seems like my whole goddamned life." He laughs, but I'm not sure why he's laughing, and I don't laugh. He stops laughing. "You don't act like a student either," he says. "And you sure as hell don't look like a student—let's just say that attire ain't exactly local fashion."

Why am I talking to this person? I think. Why am I telling him about myself? Mother would ridicule me, call me an idiot, him an imbecile.

"I have to get going," I say. I don't feel invisible anymore, but I wish I did. I start to roll up the window, but he grabs my arm.

"Don't get me wrong," he says. "I'm not into all this conformity shit. To each his own, I say. That's my goddamned motto anyway."

I don't know what he's talking about.

"I could help you for a little cash," he says. "Help you find what you're looking for." I wiggle my arm, but he holds fast. "I know this area like the back of my frickin' hand." The back of his hand is just inches from my face, and I think about sinking my teeth into it. "My parents are a bit stingy when it comes to entertainment money, if you know what I mean. So I'm happy to help for a little com-pen-sa-tion."

I remember Mother's warning about people: "Human beings are like poison ivy," she'd said. "They vary in form. Upright at times, climbing at times, trailing at times. And sometimes appealing, attractive. Colorful. But come in contact with them and chances are you'll blister."

"I appreciate it," I say. "Your offer. But my dad knows his way around." I look over into the field, between buildings. "That's him, there."

He releases my arm, pivots: no one's there.

I turn the key and gun the car forward. I jerk the wheel and barely avoid smashing into a parked car.

The boy-man pounds on my car's rear as I pull away. "I'll see you around," he calls.

I want to turn back, go home; I want Mother to be alive again; I want to climb back into our cocoon. My hands drip with sweat, splotch the lap of my dress. I need to be smarter, I think. More careful.

I drive again; I course through the tangle of streets. I'm on Irnan Street a fourth time when I see what looks like the road I want—the road where the building is—but I'm driving the wrong way; I can't reach it. I pull to the side again, try to back into a parking space, thinking I'll walk, but the horns of the cars behind are shrieking like birds, like the blue jays of Hartswell. I give up, just as the car in the space ahead pulls away, just before I realize I can drive straight in.

I do, then turn off the engine, but I don't move from the car. From within this chrysalis, the universe outside is the aberration; if I exit, the aberration will be me. But after two or three minutes, the heat is intolerable.

I climb out. The pale green of my dress is spotted beneath my arms and breasts, and I feel it clinging to my buttocks and upper thighs. I'm not accustomed to what the past year has done to my body: the softer, more fleshy feel of my arms and legs, and the subtle mounds of breasts, of rounded bottom. The breasts, the bottom, look ridiculous on me, I think. Unnatural. Hanging from my scrawny frame like gaudy jewelry.

My hands tremble as I separate the dress from my skin, as I try again to push the sleeves high up my arms. I reach to pull the suitcase from the car. I'll have to carry it; I have no key for the car's lock. I'm surprised, for a moment, at how much lighter the suitcase is. Then I'm not surprised: I told the officer she could take the money; at least she didn't take it all.

There's a library near where I've parked that seems too great for the small space allotted it, as if it's a growth—a mutation—of the earth itself, especially given its color. It's cow's-eye brown, like fertile soil—soil that has sprouted,

125

mutated, become elegant. I focus on the structure, as if I'd come there to study it, as if it is my purpose for being there. As if it's the reason I ignore—try to ignore—the people passing by me and the sounds all around me. I need time to adjust to this new world, accept my presence here, stop shaking. But the people and sounds are like pungent odors; no matter my effort to seal them out, they slip in, as if I need them. The tapping, thumping, clanking of shoes against pavement: this orchestra of soles. And the voices that mingle like songs of riotous birds, converging pitch with pitch, rhythm with rhythm, pitch with rhythm. And the unfamiliar but somehow familiar clamor of engine after engine, the subtle but distinctive variations of the same grating purr. The occasional horn. A car alarm. And the abrupt emptiness when a car finds parking, when the grating purr ceases.

And the music. It comes suddenly, first the guitar strumming, then the song. The voice is that of a man, yet it sounds frail to me, diluted, as if at one time there had been more to it, but it's degenerated like Mother's scant hair or her emaciated body. Its emergence makes me feel more confident, although I can't say why. It enables me to turn back toward Irnan Street, toward the sound of the song.

It's at that moment that I see her.

She's standing near the corner of Brollachan and Irnan streets, dressed in the same kind of formless dress she always wore, except the dress is not black, it's brilliantly white, and her hair is tied and wrapped. She looks different dressed in white. Her skin seems to meld into the gown, rendering her less substantial somehow, even thinner. Yet I know it is Mother, the ghost of her. Without thinking, I rush toward her lugging the suitcase. She turns and walks down Brollachan Street, like she's a real person. I can't see around the building there, a building called Cyhreath House. I reach the corner, round it, stumble over the guitar case of the man I'd heard singing.

Mother is nowhere.

I stand near the street performer thinking of Mother: she's haunting me. I'm not all that surprised by this. In many ways I suppose I'd been expecting it—waiting for her spirit to reveal itself to me. It was almost unfathomable to me she would leave me entirely.

The street performer glances up at me, seemingly curious as to why I've stopped; no one else has. I walk away, then. Down Brollachan to Cleona Street to Fianat Street.

There's no trace of Mother.

I continue walking carrying the case, following a robin flitting. The building I'm looking for is somewhere nearby—I'm sure of this. Without intending to, I arrive back at the corner of Irnan and Brollachan, and I look toward my car, to where my car should be, and I see it is gone. Vanished, as if to demonstrate how unreal my world has become.

I'm stunned—for a moment I feel unbearably confused—but then I let it go. I just let it slip away, and I'm relieved in a way. Another remnant of the past eradicated from my life.

Solomon's Seal

2007

—Please state your name.

—Officer Emil Regin.

—Have you ever seen the defendant before today?

—Once.

—When?

—A little over a year ago.

—Would you describe what she looked like the day you saw her?

—She looked like she'd been through the wringer. She had soot on her cheeks and clothes. Her hair was scorched in one spot. She had what looked like some burns on her hands, and some on her face, I think. And I remember there was this—I don't know—this wild look about her.

—Objection, Your Honor. Move to strike. This is irrelevant.

—I'll strike just that last statement. Everything else is relevant. Just the facts, please, Officer. You may proceed, Counsel.

—Where did you see her?

—Down where we impound towed vehicles. She was asking about a car she said had been stolen years before. She said she left the keys in the car by accident, that she thought it was stolen by some guy she described as looking like just about every male twenty-year-old around here. But she didn't have a driver's license with her, and she didn't know the license plate number.

—Objection, Your Honor. Move to strike. What's the relevance of this?

—The defendant was trying to get away, Your Honor. After she poisoned her aunt and cousin last year, after she set that church on fire, she was trying to get her hands on a car. Shows her state of mind.

—Objection. Move to strike Counsel's comment from the record, Your Honor. It's misleading. And lacks foundation. The prosecution has provided no evidence Aslaug poisoned anyone or that she set any fire.

—Objection sustained. Any more of those types of monologues and you'll be sanctioned, Counsel.

—My apologies, Your Honor.

—You may proceed with your questioning about the vehicle, Counsel.

—Thank you. Officer Regin, did you find her car?

—No. I don't imagine she'd ever had a car stolen. It was just a charade she was putting on, trying to get a car. We see it all the time.

—Objection, Your Honor. Move to strike. Speculative. Argumentative.

—Sustained. Please strike all but the word *no*.

—Thank you, Officer. I have no further questions, Your Honor.

WITCH HAZEL

2003

The witch hazel is not yet blooming, but even absent its spidery flowers, it's unmistakable: the limbs and twigs of the witch hazel are crooked, but smooth as skin. When Mother and I would dowse for water, each gripping the fork of a witch hazel branch, I could feel the witch hazel's power in my hand, every time the branch would bend toward the earth, toward the water beneath the earth. I was a good dowser, even better than Mother was; I thought it was because I was more open to the spirit realm, more sensitive. Mother would have no part of such talk. Dowsing was not magic, according to Mother; dowsing had nothing to do with spirit, nothing to do with sensitivity. Dowsing worked because of electromagnetic radiation, or the direction of the gravitational field, or ultrasonic waves. It seemed Mother always had a different explanation when the topic arose, and each explanation was no more convincing than the last. Not even to her. I could see the surprise and wonder in her eyes each time I found water, each time she found water; I could see the way she looked at the witch hazel as if it held a secret she longed to own.

The building stands twenty yards or so beyond the witch hazel, beyond the gate; it looks different by day. Still, I recognize it, this genteel old woman with the stained blouse and smeared mouth. I walk to the end of the driveway, not sure what I'm planning to do, knowing only that my head feels full and my mouth dry. Unlike the night I came here with Mother, daylight seals off the interior from me: I can see nothing there. But I can see a sign propped near the porch—one I hadn't noticed when we were here before. It's large and white with removable letters, like the sign outside Soren's Grocery. The sign reads: "Charisma Pentecostal Church, Pastor Sara Lerner, Sunday Services 11:00 a.m. and 6:00 p.m., Tuesday Prayer Meeting 7:00 p.m., Wednesday Healing Service 7:00 p.m." I hear music playing inside, the type of jarring music I've heard blaring from passing cars. And I hear singing, too, but the voices are barely audible over the music.

I walk up the steps, peer through the window on the door. Twenty or so people stand with their backs to me, many with their hands above their heads, their fingers spread.

I wonder, is my Dimmesdale among them?

Most of the people move to the music: some sway with the rhythm, some jump up and down. A woman wearing army fatigues runs circles around the group waving a purple flag. Another woman spins, her skirt an umbrella about her; she shakes a tambourine high above her head. A teenage boy stands in front on a low stage, facing me, playing an electric guitar, and to his far left a young woman plays drums, next to a poster of haloed Jesus in a ruby robe. An adolescent girl stands between the guitar player and the drummer, singing into a microphone, her free hand stroking the air. But even her magnified voice is difficult to discern, the accompanying music is so loud. At the rear of the stage hangs a large screen with words. An overhead projector sits beneath the screen next to a boy, his hair a dusting the color of persimmon. The boy yawns, looks at the ceiling, then the screen; he doesn't sing.

"We are God's soldiers," the screen says, "the Chosen Ones. We will fight the battle, till Glory is won." The words slip away, and new words appear; the boy looks back at the ceiling. "We are God's children, we believe in God's Son, Jesus the Savior, in Him Glory is won."

The music stops and the singing stops.

"God is great," the girl holding the microphone says. "I feel His presence here tonight." She's like a painting, this girl. Like a painting of an angel in the margin of one of Mother's old books. Peach-flesh hair curling down her sides and periwinkle eyes. And yet, there is a weight about her— not a physical weight. She's slight. But I feel a drawing down when I look into her eyes.

The music starts again; new words slide in and the angel girl starts to sing, and then everyone but the orange-haired boy sings. But the music is quiet now, and the people sway almost in unison; their hands rock like branches in a breeze.

"Praise you, Jesus," a man calls out. "Yes, yes, yes," a woman says.

Then the woman in army fatigues starts to shout what sounds to me like nonsense, like she's imitating Hebrew. Occasionally I think I hear her say "Adonai," but otherwise I can make sense of nothing she's saying. She still swings the purple flag—the faint light leaps from its fabric in silvery bursts—but no one in the room even looks at the woman, except the man to her right.

"That's right, sister," he says, as if what the woman is saying has meaning to him. "Uh-huh. That's right."

As soon as the army woman's outburst fades, the man to her right speaks. "Our sister said there's a darkness in our midst tonight. Tho the light of God's grace is free to us, we all at times face an alley of darkness. And that alley is like a snake making a road into our souls. We must stamp out that snake, fill that alley with light."

"Amen," someone says. And then several people say, "Amen" and "Praise God" and "Praise Jesus."

The guitar player and drummer fumble with their instruments before they move to the rear pew. The angel girl hands the microphone to the woman with the tambourine; then she joins the drummer, the guitar player.

The tambourine woman is alone onstage now. She turns to face the group, and I see she's an older woman, much older than Mother was, and yet she holds herself so differently, more comfortably. She wears a suit jacket and a wide skirt, and her hair is tied tight. And when she speaks, I feel needles up my spine. She has an accent, a familiar accent: it's Mother's accent, my accent, but stronger. "The holy spirit is with us tonight. Thank you, Jesus, for blessing our sister with the gift of tongues." She nods at the woman with the flag. "And for her joy in Christ." She looks at the man who'd just spoken. "And thank you for our brother's gift of interpretation. We are blessed with the gifts of the spirit tonight."

"Amen," someone says. "Hallelujah."

"And we are blessed with you, Pastor," the man says. There is another round of "Amens" and "Hallelujahs," and I realize the woman with the tambourine is the preacher.

"Anyone needing to be blessed tonight," the preacher says, "anyone needing the alley to their soul to be filled with light, come forward. Let God's light fill you, heal you. Heal your body and soul."

People from the pews stream forward and form a line along the stage. The preacher walks from one to the next, lifting each person's hands to the air. They look like a belt of ferns, these people, with their arms making V's to the sky. I think of the ferns parallel to the gully, the ones Mother pointed out the day before she died. I think of that image of me in the gully, veiled by my hair, and the sound of Mother's moving feet, one slapping the ground, one dragging the ground. And I remember the sensation of Mother's grip; I remember hearing the hair strands tear, and I remember the look in Mother's eyes.

The preacher grips a small bottle containing a yellowish liquid. She pours a bit of the liquid onto the tips of her fingers. She again walks the line of people; she dabs the liquid on each person's forehead, then lays her palm over the dabbed oil. She speaks quietly—I can't understand her words—but within moments every person she touches drops to the ground, as if the preacher's words or her touch or that liquid she's holding were imbued with some strange power. Two men stand behind waiting, easing the people down as they fall. And the men throw swatches of thin red fabric over the legs of the sprawling women, some of whom have skirts now bunched up past their knees. And soon everyone who stepped forward lies on the floor—some still, some quivering, their bodies like leeches in salt. The preacher and the two men assisting her walk among the fallen, gingerly stepping over one person's legs, another's torso. The preacher's mouth moves as she walks—I still can't make out her words. She kneels by one woman and yanks the red fabric farther down the woman's legs; then she places her hands on the woman's shoulders, and the woman starts to writhe. The preacher is thin, yet I see strength in her body as she holds the writhing woman down. The preacher's face reddens, and then her words become audible; her voice sounds different, deeper. "In the name of Jesus," she says, "I cast out the demon that has hold on this woman, that has tainted her seed. This spirit of illness and depression is cast out, because the devil is a coward when faced with the might of the Lord."

The drummer, guitar player and angel girl had been huddled on the back pew, whispering. But when the woman started writhing, and the preacher's voice changed, the drummer rose from her seat. And now, when the preacher falls quiet again, the drummer turns toward the door, toward me.

SOLOMON'S SEAL

2007

—Cross-examination?

—Yes, just a brief one. Officer Regin, you described Aslaug as looking like—and I'm quoting here—"she'd been through the wringer." But you didn't ask her what happened to her, did you?

—I figured if she wanted to tell me, she would. I mean, we see all sorts.

—But as an officer of the law and a community servant, isn't it your duty to help if you spot someone in trouble?

—I didn't say she looked like she was in trouble.

—Well, let me tell you what you did say. You said Aslaug had soot and burns on her clothes and face and body. Doesn't that sound like someone in trouble to you?

—Listen, I'm not a social worker, all right? Or a medical professional. I'm an officer of the law. When I met Ms. Hellig, it didn't look like anyone had broken any laws—although it sure looked like Ms. Hellig here may have been trying to break one, trying to get a car that wasn't hers.

—But you don't really know whether Aslaug had a car that had been stolen, do you, Officer Regin?

—No, I—

—Thank you, Officer. A simple yes or no is fine. And you don't really know whether her car had been impounded, do you?

—No.

—And you certainly don't know why she was looking for her car at that time, do you?

—Well, the timing doesn't look good—

—But you don't know, do you? Your answer is no, isn't that right?

—No, I don't know.

—Thank you. I've no more questions.

LILY

2003

I'm standing plain in the yard, like a blue pickerelweed in the starkness of a marsh, when the door opens. The drummer steps onto the porch; at first she doesn't see me. But I see her, better than when she was inside. She passes down the stairs, then from the stairs into the soft light of the low sun, and I realize she's the apparition—the apparition of Mother. Except she is no apparition, and she's not Mother. She's the person I saw earlier, the one I thought was Mother—the ghost of Mother. The coincidence seems too much, too strange, and I wonder if I'm dreaming now, or if I was dreaming then when I thought I saw Mother's ghost. The days and nights since Mother's death blur in my mind; it's hard for me to be sure what's real.

I set the suitcase on the ground and sit down on it, aiming to make myself smaller, less visible, as I try to make sense of the sign, the music, this woman, that preacher. As I try to find some moisture in my mouth. I feel the masking tape wrinkle beneath me and stick to my dress; I feel the tickle of the warm grass on my calves. I'm not dreaming, I think: this woman is real.

She's older than I am—I see this in her body—but not much older. And while she shares some traits with Mother—the pale skin, the delicate frame—she's different, too. Taller. Her movements less erratic. Her eyes larger, her lips fuller.

Still, she reminds me of Mother. She wears a loose white garment that rides high up her neck, reaches to her ankles, extends to her wrists despite the heat; it billows as she descends the stairs, and it seems for a moment the air alone could lift her. A dandelion gone to seed.

Fallen apples speckle the yard like sores on the grass, and she begins to collect them; she bundles the front of her gown and drops them in—as if to weigh herself down. Mother often referred to apples using the Celtic word for "apple," *abal*, the foundation of the word *Avalon*, the mythical isle of apples. She said the apple symbolizes the life inside a mother's womb. *Abal* connotes fertility, immortality.

Minutes pass, and I start to think it possible the woman won't notice me—she seems absorbed in the gathering, in the arranging of each *abal* within her gown. I feel my jaw ease, feel the familiar ache that follows the unclenching of my teeth. She'll go back inside, I tell myself. And I'll slip away, watch the church from a distance, look for my Dimmesdale from where I can't be seen. But then the woman jerks to a stop and looks directly at me. I expect she knew I was there all along.

Her cheekbones roll creamy white; her fair skin is fairer than mine. Yet her lips are full, and their color so vivid, they seem too lavish, almost clownish. Her eyes are those of the black-eyed Susan, that daisy-like flower with light rays eclipsed by a black-moon core.

The kerchief she wears slips, and some of her hair falls loose, and I see it's a menagerie of pink and black and reddish gold. I wonder how she painted her hair that way. And I wonder whether her hair is her hairstreak.

"You caught me scavenging," she says, and she laughs a laugh that's scratchy and high-pitched. "I hate letting the apples go to waste. *Gudinden* gets annoyed when I do this. She says they're full of vermin."

"*Gudinden?*" I say. But I understood her words. *Gudinde* means "goddess" in Danish. I've never heard anyone but Mother speak Danish.

"The pastor," she says, but she doesn't explain. She collects another apple from the ground, holds it toward me. "They're not bad."

I stand and the masking tape holds me, then gives way. I walk toward her, take the apple—it's wet in my hand—and I notice two of her fingers are webbed. I sense I should look away, but I don't. Her eyes follow the path of my eyes but then quickly move on to the suitcase behind me.

"The service is still going on. You can just head in," she says, but to the suitcase.

"I'm not here for the service."

"Lucky you." She looks back at me. "You selling something?"

A moment passes before I realize what she means. "No, I'm not. I'm just—"

"You looking for someone?"

"Yes. I mean, I guess I am. There's this man, I thought he lived here. . . ."

She tucks her bottom lip in her mouth, holds it there, rounding her narrow chin, making it bulge like a bullfrog's. I can hear Mother's taunting voice in my mind—what she'd say if I were to make such a face. "Goddamn you, Rune," she says after she's freed her lip. And then, "Hold on. I'll see if I can get his attention. They've all been slain in there. I shouldn't have much trouble."

"Wait," I say as she pivots; she turns back. "They've been slain?"

She laughs that laugh. "In the spirit," she says. "Nobody's dead."

I don't have any idea what she's talking about. "I don't know Rune," I say then. But I know the name, I think; I know runes.

"You don't?" She blows a strand of pink hair from her face. And she becomes in this moment one of the girls I admired, one of the girls I saw in Bethan, one of the girls I imagined being.

"I came here months ago with my mother," I say. "She brought me here, my mother—she didn't say why. We just sat outside. Looked. There were people inside. A man. I think this place meant something to my mother. That that man meant something to her. She died, my mother. I didn't expect her to die. . . . I just wondered if that man knew her."

"She went to church here?" The apples slip from her grip, tumble to the ground. She looks at them like she's not sure how they got there. She makes no effort to pick them up.

I shake my head, squat to gather the apples.

142

"Don't," she says. I look up from the apples and see she's looking at me in a different way, like I might look at a plant I'd never seen before. "Leave them."

I do. I stand.

She bends and picks up one of the apples, pulls a penknife from her pocket, slices the apple through its middle. She holds out one half toward me, but it trembles; her hand trembles. "When an apple's cut like this, through its center," she says, "each half makes a pentagram."

I see the pentagram, each point on the star containing a seed, but I can't focus on what she's saying. Not with her hand shaking like it's dangling on a string.

"Sometimes *Gudinden* calls the pentagram the star of Bethlehem," she says. "Sometimes she calls it the Three Kings' star. But her favorite is five wounds of Christ. You know, like the five points, here, represent Christ's wounds. Two in his ankles, two in his wrists, one in his side." She bites into an apple half, into Christ's ankle or his wrist or his side. "That make sense to you?"

"I don't know," I say. I don't want to talk about the star of Bethlehem or Christ. I want to talk about the trembling I hear in her voice, the trembling I see in her webbed hand.

"It's bullshit," she says. "The Christians co-opt everything. The pentagram first symbolized the pagan goddess Kore. The apple was sacred to Kore. People across Europe— even in Egypt—worshiped Kore, long before they worshiped Christ. The Christians even took Kore's festival, turned it into the Feast of the Epiphany."

"Isn't this church Christian?" I think of the music. The Jesus poster.

"Yeah," she says. "So?"

143

The door to the building opens, and noise from inside spreads outside. The woman grabs my hand with her webbed one and pulls me toward the bushes.

"What are you doing?" I say, and I remember Mother's words: poison ivy.

She grabs the suitcase as she yanks me across the yard. "Get down." She pushes me and I crouch behind a bush, beside her. "Trust me," she says, "or you'll be another sheep to the slaughter." She yanks her dress up, sits cross-legged. I see her upper calf is painted, like her hair: that pale skin of hers is no longer pale, but hued in reddish strands and flecks. I can't see enough to discern an image. I want to ask whether there is an image there, like Mother's Solomon's seal, or my touch-me-not, or my hairstreak. But she sees my looking, pulls at her garment, tucks it around her calves. Then she unearths a small box from under the bush, opens it and removes a square of what looks to me like hemp-fiber paper, the same as Mother would use to fold her cigarettes. She rifles through the box, pulls out a small bag, pinches out a tablespoon or so of some dried plant—I can't see what—and arranges it in a loose line along the paper. She lifts the paper with her forefingers and thumbs, and she rocks it, until the plant pile becomes cylindrical. She rolls the cigarette, then, as Mother would; she licks it, lights it. And I smell Mother.

People trickle out the door of the church, and I watch them now as she smokes and sways. I see the woman in army fatigues, her purple flag pocketed. And an older woman with pink shoes. A man steps out behind them; he stands too upright, his neck hugged by an oversize ring that's white and stiff. The fatigues-wearing woman takes one of his arms, the pink-shoed lady the other, and together they descend the stairs as if negotiating ice. They chatter as they walk from the yard, about lobster rolls.

The angel girl appears then, and the guitar player, and they walk down the stairs together. The girl dissects a strand of hair: she rolls it like that cigarette, pulls at its tip, rips its tip. Then she drops it, starts on another. The boy tugs his hands from his pockets, looks at them as if he'd just happened upon them, seems unsure what to do with them, pushes them back inside his pockets. The angel girl kicks at the apples as she passes through the yard; she arranges them in a line of sorts, leaves a trail of sorts.

When the two disappear behind the church, the drummer says, "She's screwed."

"What did you say?" I know what she said, not what she meant.

"Literally," she says. I see her eyes are dilated, like Mother's would be, and pink as those shoes. She looks out toward the apple trail. "Did you see that girl, the one that just passed?"

"The one who was singing before?" I say. "With the long hair, the light eyes?"

She turns those black-eyed-Susan eyes on me: I'm inverted in their pool. And I realize I shouldn't have said what I just said. How did I know the girl was singing?

"Yup, her," she says. It seems the cigarette's changed her. "She's pregnant, that girl. She just told me tonight. She's only fifteen. About your age. And it wasn't a holy union, if you know what I mean. It's going to be interesting. Her parents are as stodgy as you can get in a church like this, and that's saying a lot. They probably think she doesn't even know about sex. And *Gudinden* thinks she's some sort of goddamned saint. Welcome to the real world." She rolls backward on the grass, lifts her feet in the air, drops them back down. "You smoke?" she says, still lying on her back. She holds the cigarette between her webbed fingers and a free one. She lifts her head; I shake my head. I've never smoked, but I've wondered where Mother went when she smoked. And I wonder where the drummer has gone. I wonder if I could go there, too.

"What was your mother's name?"

"My mother?" I'm surprised she's asking this; it seemed her thoughts had moved on. "Maren."

"What's your name?"

"Aslaug."

"'Consecrated to God.'"

"Pardon me?"

"Pardon me?" she says, and she laughs again, but this time it sounds forced. "The name, Aslaug. It means 'consecrated to God.'"

"You know me?"

"Do you know what *consecrated* means? It means 'dedicated,' right? But it also means 'to make sacred.' Like you can just choose to make something sacred. To make someone holy."

"You know who I am?" I say again.

"Like changing bread and wine into Christ's body and blood. Consecrate some bread and wine, and voilà, you've got your Savior. The mundane becomes the hallowed."

"How do you know my name?"

146

"You told me your name."

"But you knew my name—"

"It's a Scandinavian name. I said I knew the name. I didn't say I know you." She lifts up farther, props herself on her elbow. "What are you doing here, Aslaug?"

"I told you—"

But she shakes her head, peels grit from her tongue. "You didn't tell me squat."

I feel blood pulse to my head, flush my face; I feel sweat creep up my spine and into the pits of my arms; and I feel the swirling in my head, the scattering of my thoughts, that always aggravated Mother. But I also feel exhilaration, a sense that life might not always be as it's been, that there may be more to my existence, that I might belong somewhere. There's nothing mundane about this, nothing familiar.

"You knew her," I say, like I know it's true. "You knew my mother."

"I'm Susanne," the woman says then, as if this should mean something to me. "I'm Sara's daughter."

The name Susanne comes from the Hebrew word *shoshannah*, meaning "lily." The biblical story of Susanna is a tale of a bathing woman who is propositioned by two men. She refuses them, and in response they claim they witnessed her committing adultery. Susanna is condemned to death, but then Daniel, inspired with the wisdom of God, interviews her accusers separately. Daniel asks each man to name the tree under which he saw Susanna and her lover. The first man says a mastic tree, the second says an evergreen oak. Their inconsistent testimony indicates Susanna is innocent. Susanna is freed, and the two elders are stoned.

147

Mother assigned me to read two versions of this story, one from the original Septuagint translation, and the other in the Greek version of Theodotion. Mother never discussed the actual story with me, only the language. She pointed out that the Greek word for *mastic tree* is similar to the Greek word for *cut,* and the Greek word for *evergreen oak* is similar to that for *split.* The use of these particular trees in the story was satirical wordplay, according to Mother. But I was captivated less by the language and irony, more by the story of Susanna, the lily of the garden, saved by the difference between the mastic tree and the oak.

I'm still holding the apple she gave me. It's rotted on one side; I see this now. I let it drop. "I don't know who Sara is," I say.

SOLOMON'S SEAL

2007

—*P*lease state your name.

—Dr. George Florens.

—What is your profession, Dr. Florens?

—I'm a medical doctor and a botanist. I've been employed for seven years as a professor at Bran College, in the
biology department.

—Are you familiar with the plant jimsonweed?

—*Datura stramonium?* Yes, I'm quite familiar with the
poisonous plant. It has several common names, including
jimsonweed. It's also at times referred to as thorn apple,
madapple, angel's-trumpet. . . .

—You said the plant is poisonous. How so?

—Well, the plant contains the alkaloids hyoscyamine,
atropine and hyoscine, also known as scopolamine. These
are toxins. Atropine, in particular, is quite deadly.

—What part of the jimsonweed plant is poisonous?

—The entire plant—although the seeds are the most poisonous.

—Does boiling or drying the plant alter its poisonous properties?

—Objection. Leading.

—Overruled.

—No. The plant is just as poisonous if it's consumed fresh or if it's dried or boiled before it's used. Some people have a reaction on their skin to just touching the plant.

—What kind of reaction?

—They get a rash. The rash isn't fatal, of course, but it can be unpleasant.

—So if someone were to handle jimsonweed, the person might develop a rash on her skin in the area where the person came in contact with the weed?

—Objection. Leading.

—Overruled. You can answer.

—Yes.

—Thank you.

ZARA

2003

*T*he biblical Sarah was the half sister of Abraham, and the wife of Abraham. She was once called Sarai, then Sarah, which means "princess" in Hebrew; she also may have been called Iscah. The Arabic form of Sarah is Zara, or "flower." Sarah was a prophet who heard directly from God. She gave birth to a child, Isaac, when she was an old woman, then nursed strangers' children to prove Isaac was her own. She committed adultery with an Egyptian pharaoh and compelled Abraham to cast his other son, Ishmael, into the wilderness. Sarah's son, Isaac, fathered Jacob, who became the patriarch of the twelve tribes of Israel.

I hear the door open again, and the preacher steps onto the porch, then off the porch. "Sanne?" she says. And she walks directly toward us, like she knows where we are.

I expect Susanne to extinguish the cigarette, hide it, but

151

she doesn't. She stands up before the preacher reaches us. "How did you know where I was?"

"Don't I always know?" the preacher says, the smoke a screen around her. She is tall, the preacher, with elongated features, and the line of her nose is distractingly straight; its tip seems honed. Her skin hangs in crisp folds, especially around her eyes, which sit snug against the bridge of her nose, and slightly too close to the expanse of her brow.

"She was in the yard," Susanne says. She holds her hands flat against the air, and the diminished cigarette juts. "She was just out here in the yard."

The preacher sees me huddled. My heart thumps in my ears, and when I stand up, I feel I might drop again, and I wonder if it's the preacher's power coming down on me.

"Maren," the preacher says. Then again, "Maren." And I think she believes I'm my mother. But then she says, "You look just like her." She walks around the bush, nudging Susanne to the side. Then she lifts her hand to my hair, then my cheek, my mouth. She takes my hand, holds it in hers, seems to study it. Then she lets it drop, pushes my hair behind my ears, stands in front of me, holds my face toward her, looks at me straight on.

Mother taught me much can be gleaned about objects by the light the objects emit. When heated, chemical elements emit distinctively hued lights: sodium emits a yellow light; helium, orange. A compound of copper and chlorine produces blue; strontium and carbon form a hot bright red. Some elements emit light not visible to humans—as do flowers. Flowers often highlight the location of their nectar using ultraviolet light that bugs can see, humans cannot. The evening primrose appears yellow to humans, but a bee sees an ultraviolet halo around the flower's periphery that serves as a guidepost for the bee, directing the bee to the nectar and the pollen. Watching this woman study me, I wonder what it is she sees, whether she sees something in me I can't see myself.

And I wonder about what I see in her: the darkening blood-vessel rays about her nose; the rising gloss on her forehead and cheeks; the expanding and collapsing as her breathing thins out, accelerates; the green tunnel of her eyes clouding over.

"I'm Aslaug," I say again, but this time I say it as if it matters, as if I need to convince her of something.

"Aslaug," the preacher says. "Aslaug." And then, "I'm Sara."

Susanne's mother.

This should have been obvious to me; the two are the same person at different stages of life. The wrinkles and weight of age had masked this from me, as winter's tree. But their stalks are the same, and their limbs, and the structure of their faces, the shape of their lips. Only Susanne's hair betrays them, and her webbed fingers. And her eyes: they are almost black. But the preacher's are the yellow-green of wild leek—a color pearls would be if God were a child.

"Maren sent you to us?" the preacher says.

"No," I say, although I nearly say yes. "Maren—my mother—she died."

"I hadn't realized she was so sick," the preacher says. "I wish you would have come to us before."

"I couldn't have come to you," I say. "I didn't know of you."

"But you did come, Aslaug," Susanne says. "You're here,

153

aren't you?" And I'm reminded of how different she seems compared to when I first arrived; how misplaced. And I think of the mastic—symbolic of the biblical Susanna. The mastic could never flourish in Maine. Accustomed to warmth, it would suffer here, and its lemon white resin would slowly dry up.

Solomon's Seal

2007

—Cross-examination?

—Yes. Dr. Florens, the alkaloids in jimsonweed make the plant narcotic, correct?

—Yes.

—And the plant is narcotic whether consumed fresh or dried, right?

—Yes.

—People do, at times, consume the plant fresh for its narcotic properties, correct?

—Yes, but it's unwise.

—It's unwise because the plant is also poisonous, correct?

—Yes.

—It is possible, isn't it, that Mrs. Hellig was using fresh jimsonweed as a narcotic?

—Objection. Speculation.

—Sustained. The jury can make its own inferences.

—Dr. Florens, not everyone who touches jimsonweed develops a skin rash, isn't that right?

—That's right.

—In fact, many people can handle jimsonweed and show no physical signs of having touched the plant, correct?

—That's right. The people who develop a rash after contact with jimsonweed are having an allergic reaction to the plant. Not everyone is allergic to the plant in this way.

—Thank you, Doctor.

GREAT ASH TREE

2003

In Norse mythology, the universe consists of nine worlds, all contained in the great ash tree, Yggdrasil. The upper level of Yggdrasil houses three worlds: Asgard, land of gods; Alfheim, land of elves; and Vanaheim, land of Vanir gods and goddesses. In the middle of the tree are the worlds of Midgard, land of humans; Jotunheim, land of giants; Svartalfheim, land of dark elves; and Nidavellir, land of dwarves. The lower level of Yggdrasil holds the worlds of Muspelheim, land of fire; and Niflheim, land of cold and ice. Three old crones reside in the roots of Yggdrasil—Urd, crone of fate; Skuld, crone of necessity; and Verdandi, crone of being—where they weave the "tapestry of fates." Each person's life represents a thread in their loom, and the length of the thread corresponds with the length of the life.

Mother knew I loved the story of Yggdrasil, of its nine

worlds and three old crones. She told me the story once when I was a child, and I never forgot. I imagined the crones weaving my fate, and sometimes at night I would talk to them, as if they were real, and I would ask them to give me a glimmer of my fate, an idea of my place in the world. But then one day when Mother and I were out foraging, we came upon a great ash tree, Yggdrasil; I couldn't help but venture toward it, touch it.

"Yggdrasil is not invincible," Mother called to me. "One day the dragon Nidhogg gnaws its roots to shreds, and the entire universe comes crashing down."

I stopped myself from thinking of Yggdrasil after that day; I stopped myself from looking to the crones for comfort or guidance. They were imaginary, I told myself. A fantastic fabrication. They couldn't be destroyed, because they weren't real—they didn't exist. But now, at this moment, Urd, Skuld and Verdandi feel alive to me again. And I want to tell Susanne and the preacher that Mother's string came to an end; that in the "tapestry of fates," Mother's string no longer reached the loom. I want to tell them that I couldn't have told them Mother was dying because I didn't know myself; I couldn't have known. Only the old crones knew Mother's fate.

But I don't say this. Instead, I speak again of the night Mother taught me to drive, the night I first saw this building I now realize is a church. I tell them I don't know who they are—the preacher and Susanne. That I don't really know who I am. I am here to find my father, I say. I show them the suitcase of dwindled money, and I tell them he sent it to my mother. And I ask them, "Do you know my father? Do you know where he is?"

The preacher doesn't answer my question, but she does answer. "I'm your aunt. Your mother's sister."

What does the monarch feel when it emerges from its chrysalis to find itself in a sea of monarchs? Or the spring beauty flower when it bursts into bloom, awakening in an ocean of pink? I'm not alone. The Yggdrasil crones are binding me to similar strings. We look alike, the preacher and Susanne and I; we are drawn from the same cloth. Yet I don't know this older woman, this younger woman: they are strangers to me. I feel the pull of fate, though. Fate has chosen them for me and bound us together.

Until Yggdrasil crashes down.

"Why didn't Mother tell me about you?" I say to Sara, this stranger, my aunt, the preacher. "She never told me I had family close by. She never told me I had family at all. Did you know we lived so near to you?" The questions burst forth like buds, all at once. I've been waiting so long for answers, like my entire life has been winter. "And my father?" I ask again. "Do you know him? Do you know who he is?"

Solomon's Seal

2007

—Ms. Hellig, in your experience, handling jimsonweed gives you a rash on your skin in the area where you come in contact with the weed, isn't that right?

—Yes.

—And when your mother touched jimsonweed, she would get a skin rash, too, wouldn't she?

—Objection. Speculation.

—Only answer what you know.

—She'd get a rash if she touched the weed, just like I would. She—

—Thank you, Ms. Hellig. Now, it's true, isn't it, that the hole you were digging in your backyard was intended to be a grave for your mother?

—Yes—

—Thank you. And the stone that was near the grave, that was supposed to be a gravestone, isn't that right?

160

—A runestone.

—A runestone is a gravestone, is it not? Please just answer yes or no.

—Yes.

—I'd like to mark for identification a picture of this so-called runestone. Ms. Hellig, is this a fair and accurate representation of the object you are describing as a runestone?

—The picture shows one side of the stone.

—Okay. Please mark the picture as Exhibit R. Ms. Hellig, the etchings shown here on the stone, you made them, right?

—Yes.

—And you intended to put the stone over your mother's grave, correct?

—Yes.

—Ms. Hellig, please read the word you etched into the stone, from right to left.

—I didn't intend to write a word. I was writing Scandinavian runes. Symbols. They were supposed to be gifts to Mother. Protection for her.

—Ms. Hellig, assuming only for the sake of argument that these images here are runes, runes are letters, are they not?

—Yes, but—

—And letters are used to spell out words, are they not?

—Runes are also symbols.

—Please answer my question. Letters are used to spell out words, right? Just answer yes or no.

—Yes.

—Even if the letters here are runes, the word they spell is *bitch* backward, isn't that right?

—It's not what I intended.

—Ms. Hellig, answer the question. Even assuming the letters here are so-called runes, they spell the word *bitch* backward, don't they?

—I know it appears that way—

—Thank you. Just a few more questions on this topic. You are aware, are you not, that the earliest Scandinavian runes, known as the Elder Futhark runes, may well have their origin in the Etruscan system of writing?

—Yes, Mother taught me—

—And you are also aware, are you not, that Etruscan usually was written right to left, like Arabic and Hebrew?

—Yes.

—It seems reasonable to assume, does it not, that Scandinavian runes would be read from right to left, then?

—Mother thought so—

—In other words, from the perspective of a reader of English, the runic language would appear backward, correct?

—Objection. Calls for speculation.

—She can read English. I don't think she needs to speculate on this. I'll allow it.

—Yes.

—Thank you.

SANGUISORBA

To Drink Up Blood

2003

The preacher and I sit on the steps of the church, this building that seems to reach into the roots of Yggdrasil, to house
my fate. We look out toward the witch hazel, a web in the
faded light. Sitting next to the preacher feels strange, awkward, too intimate. I can see her in my mind at the front of
the church, spinning with her tambourine, touching the
parishioners, watching them crumple. And I realize I still
think of her as the preacher, even though I now know she's
my aunt: those images of her are seared in me.

I reach up, touch my scar. Seared in me. Like the butt of
Mother's cigarette pressed onto my chest. I imagine Mother
now as she was the day I started to bleed: she had tobacco on
her lip, her cigarette burned low. She unbuttoned my blouse,
dragged. The cigarette pounced from her lips to my chest,
and I felt the sizzling, the smoldering. The pain. "The blood

comes just a few days a month. But it's with you every day. Like this scar. Never forget that, Aslaug." Then she cleaned the wound, disinfected it, bandaged it. And I thought she might hug me or kiss me or caress me. But she didn't. Not with her body. But her eyes did. Her face did. And I realized her intention was not just to hurt me. That, in her eyes, she was teaching me. Giving me a gift. If only I'd understood the gift.

The mosquitoes move in clouds now; they insert their proboscis swords, drink our blood. I watch the preacher kill one after another. "*Fader* said Maren was born on the eve of the midnight sun," the preacher says, and I assume she is referring to the summer solstice, when at midnight the Scandinavian sun still burns faintly in the sky. The preacher sent Susanne inside the church before she offered to tell me the story of my mother: of Mother's birth and her childhood; and of Mother's father, my grandfather, a man named Edvard Jokum; and of my grandmother, named Janne. "*Moder* claimed it wasn't true," the preacher says. "She swore Maren was born in the bright light of day, but *Fader* insisted. His beautiful flower Maren was born on Midsummer Eve, when, according to *Fader*, the herbs and flowers and spices are at their peak, making the air replete with magic, and with evil."

It seems so fitting to me, this story of Mother's birth. And yet, it seems too fitting in a way. My experience of Mother is tangled with herbs and flowers. And magic. And evil.

"I didn't believe in any of that, even then. But I remember *Fader* telling me he lit a bonfire the night Maren was born," the preacher says, "to protect his new daughter from witches and evil. For *Fader* insisted the witches are out on Midsummer Eve picking ingredients for their magic brews.

"I was nearly sixteen when your mother was born." The preacher rocks to and fro and stares out at the day as it journeys to night. Her hands lie open and free on her lap, and I remember Mother's hands long ago. "But I can't recall whether Maren was born by day or night. I do recall a fire burning on Midsummer Eve, though, its flames orange and hungry, making night seem day. And I recall Maren's alert eyes, their blue so deep when she was first born. *Fader* called her his *Gnaphalium*, because her hair was golden yellow, and, as she aged, her eyes grew lighter and almost iridescent—like shimmering pollen, *Fader* said. *Fader* loved Maren. He loved her in a way that changed him."

I watch the preacher's face now; I watch her eyes as she speaks, watch them traverse the muted colors of grass and sky and witch hazel. And I wonder if she has any sense what it's like for me to hear this story of my mother, and of my grandfather and my grandmother; I wonder if she knows she is giving them life—that until now, I knew nothing of their lives.

"I wasn't jealous of *Fader*'s love for Maren," the preacher says. "I was older, not so needy of *Fader*'s love—and I couldn't really relate to *Fader*. He was a botanist and mythologist, interested in what he thought was the interweaving of nature and the divine."

I'm like my grandfather, I think. This Edvard Jokum. I'm not sure what to make of this; it makes me feel more connected to him, to Mother and to life. Yet I feel violated in a way, usurped, as if even the small bit of freedom I'd thought I'd preserved despite Mother was a farce.

"I never shared *Fader*'s interests," the preacher says. "I had a calling on my life—a calling by God. I knew it even as a child. And I knew *Fader*'s beliefs were misguided. It was a strange place to be for a child, a teenager. Knowing your father is lost. I tried to pretend when I was younger. I tried to pretend I was interested in his theories, that I didn't feel sorry for him, didn't judge him. But he knew my interest wasn't genuine. He'd hear *Moder* and me talk sometimes about God, about the calling on my life, about his soul. We were Lutheran, back then, *Moder* and I. In reality, even we were lost—that's clear to me now. Yet, still, *Fader* seemed such a heathen."

I feel the impulse to defend my grandfather, or myself— I'm not sure which. It's hard to believe this woman is related to my mother. The preacher seems satiated, as if she knows all there is worth knowing. If Mother was anything, she was curious; she wanted to understand everything. It made her seem scrawny and ravenous at times, like she'd eat others alive if she'd the energy to, just to take in their minds.

"But Maren, she was just like *Fader*," the preacher says. "She scoffed at Christianity, refused to go to church almost as soon as she could talk, wanted to run around the forest with *Fader* collecting specimens on the Sabbath. You can't imagine how grateful *Fader* was to have Maren—to have a child who not only didn't judge him but who loved what he loved. He doted on her, took her everywhere, taught her everything he knew. And Maren thrived, on the surface, but her soul was rotting, and this was awful for *Moder*. She and

Fader started fighting about Maren. Then *Moder* became ill. She just seemed to wither away. And she died, in midsummer, the year Maren was fifteen."

I've found my grandmother, only to lose her within minutes. I wish the preacher would have taken more time telling me about her. I wish she would have described what Janne looked like and smelled like and felt like; I wish she'd told me my grandmother's favorite season, her favorite food, what she liked to read, before she took her away.

"I was married then," she says. "I married Mikkel several years before *Moder*'s death, against her wishes. Mikkel was Jewish. I'd tried to convince *Moder* it didn't matter that he was Jewish. I was so taken with him. He'd been my philosophy professor at Københavns Universitet. We started dating after I finished university. A month before I was supposed to leave for seminary, he called me, asked me to dinner. We were married six months later. I never left for seminary. But I was so happy. I felt so lucky. Mikkel was brilliant, and he made me laugh. . . ." And suddenly she becomes Mother, as Mother sat at the breakfast table beyond that shield of light. I see the longing, the mourning: the wave of moisture across those eyes, and the kiss.

"I know now God was testing me. Tempting me with Mikkel to test my commitment to Him. And I failed. Mikkel became my god. It wasn't until I'd given birth to Sanne, and I was pregnant again, that this became clear to me. I'd made such a mistake. I felt I had no purpose in life. I had Sanne, of course, and I was pregnant . . . but I felt I'd failed God. Then *Moder* died, and Maren became so needy. Sanne was just a toddler, but I mothered Maren more than Sanne in the months following *Moder's* death. Maren became sullen, withdrawn, so unlike herself. And she developed arthritis. She moved in with Mikkel and me. Our marriage was already suffering. It couldn't bear the additional strain of Maren living with us. Mikkel moved out. And shortly after that Maren said she was leaving, not only our house but Denmark. She was going to the United States. She'd been accepted at a college here in Maine. Bran. She was not yet sixteen, but she was gifted. I knew that. I encouraged her to go.

"She was in the States for less than two months when she begged me to visit. I agreed. I could tell by the sound of her voice that something had happened—that she needed me."

"Tell me what's wrong," Sara says. "This isn't about me. Why did you ask us to come? You said you were leaving Denmark to start a new life, but now you want to bring your life in Denmark with you here?"

"I want you here. And Sanne. And your new baby," Maren says.

"But why? What is wrong? Is it something about Fader?"

"Don't tell Fader."

"Don't tell Fader what, Maren?"

"I'm pregnant, too."

"Mor!" the little girl calls out. "Løb efter mig, Mor!" Sanne runs down the path; trampled leaves cling to her scarf and hair. "Chase after me, Mommy!"

"You are pregnant?" Sara says, but she looks at her daughter and the gray sky and the leaves.

"Don't be angry with me—" Maren says.

But Sara interrupts. "I didn't even know you knew about such things." She is fondling her own hands as her eyes search Sanne's hands, but Sanne's hands are a blur. "You're so young, Maren. Maybe you're mistaken."

"I'm a robin." Sanne's arms stretch wide. "I can fly!"

"I'm almost sixteen," Maren says. "I'm not that young."

"But you've been in the States for less than two months. How could this happen in such a short time?"

"I'm four months pregnant," Maren says. "Three months less than you. I was pregnant before I arrived."

"Mor," Sanne says. "I'm flying away. I'm flying south."

Sara wraps her arms around herself and begins walking again, toward Sanne. She can see Sanne's hands better now: her fingers splayed, and those two webbed fingers not splayed. And she wonders. And then she says, "Before you arrived? But how can that be? I didn't even know you had a lover. I've been like a mother to you since Moder died. How could you have not told me?"

"I didn't know."

"Didn't know?"

"I didn't know I was pregnant. I found out the day I asked you to come."

"But you knew you'd been with someone. You had a lover, Maren. And you didn't tell me."

"I've flown away, Mor." Sanne has reached the end of the path. "I'm gone forever."

"But I didn't have a lover," Maren says. "I've never had a lover."

*   *   *

"I thought it was a miracle," the preacher says. "I thought she'd been blessed by God. I'd been praying to God for direction, for a sign. I so wanted to know what God's plan was for my life. *Fader* had become depressed; we barely spoke. And with my marriage falling apart and *Moder* dead and Maren gone, I felt abandoned by God. But I still believed in my heart God had a plan for me. So when Maren said she was pregnant, that she'd never had a lover, I convinced myself she was carrying the Christ child, the Messiah—that Jesus was returning to earth. I told myself God had chosen Maren rather than me because He was punishing my disobedience. It's hard for me to understand, now, how I ever believed this. Why would God choose Maren—a young Scandinavian woman who didn't even believe in Christ—to carry the Messiah? Perhaps I knew even then, but I couldn't face the truth."

"What truth?" I say.

But she talks over me. "I agreed to stay with Maren. I told her I would help her come to an understanding as to why she'd been chosen in this way. I told her I would help her raise the child. I was financially secure—*Moder* had assured that before she died. She didn't want me to be dependent on Mikkel. So I bought this building, this church, for us. It had been a monastery. We could live here. It seemed so perfect.

"Maren never disputed my belief she'd been touched by God—that she was carrying some miraculous child. It was a way out of her having to face the truth. And she didn't want me to leave her. She even permitted my talking to a reporter from the local paper, telling him Maren was carrying the

Christ child. That was the beginning of the end. The reporter wrote an article making fun of us. And then you were born. You were no Jesus. You were a girl—just an average girl."

I can barely make sense of what she's saying. It seems impossible she's talking about Mother, about me.

"Things were difficult between me and Maren," the preacher says. "She started coming up with bizarre theories about your birth. She started teaching herself all these old languages, studying all this nonsense. And then, one day, I was watching you and Rune, my son—I was watching the two of you play—and I knew, I knew it in my bones. Mikkel fathered you. On the surface there were reasons to doubt it, but down deep I knew. And I realized why Maren was so desperate to come up with some theory about your birth. She didn't want me to figure out the truth."

Mikkel? Your husband is my father? "No," I want to say. "No." I feel Yggdrasil is falling fast. Father was the light, to me, that slipped through the slit in the drapes—that reminded me of possibility. He was the whisper of wind forging its way that Mother never seemed to notice but that was a symphony to me; he was the bursting of spring and the fermenting of fall; he was the sensation of a cool petal in my palm. Father was the beauty that soaked me, that ran beneath Mother's feet. "Don't take him from me," I want to say to her. "Don't lock me in an even smaller room, a more narrow world."

"I confronted Maren about Mikkel," the preacher says. Either she's oblivious to the impact of her words on me, or she's pretending to be. "She denied she'd had relations with

171

Mikkel, but she left just the same. And I knew it was true, then. When she took you and left, I knew it was true. You were two years old the last time I saw you. And Maren? She wasn't even nineteen.

"Looking back, I know I shouldn't have been angry with Maren. I know I shouldn't have blamed her. She was just a girl herself—it's awful what Mikkel did to her. But at the time I didn't see it that way. I couldn't bear to be around her. I couldn't bear to see her. And yet, I couldn't go back to Denmark either, be near Mikkel. Besides, it was better for my children to stay in the States. Sanne was nearly six by that time and had started school. Rune was only two, but he was born here. This was their home.

"So I stayed here with Sanne and Rune. I made a life for us here. I began homeschooling the children. First Rune, then Sanne." She lifts her face to the sky now, as if talking to this God she's convinced is real. "When the children were old enough to be left alone, I went to seminary. I became a minister. And now I'm fulfilling God's call on my life. But I never forgot you, Aslaug. I never forgot Maren. I'm the one who sent the money, not Mikkel. I found where you were living—I found your address—and I sent it.

"*Fader* had died a year after you were born, a year before you and Maren left us, and he'd willed the rest of *Moder's* estate to Maren and me. Maren had received some of her inheritance by the time she left—I knew she had enough to settle somewhere, live for a while. But *Fader* had made me the executor of his will. Maren was to receive her inheritance over the course of fifteen years, because of her age. Month by month. And so I sent it to her month by month. I sent cash—I wasn't sure Maren would cash a check. But I never tried to contact you beyond sending the money. I couldn't, even after time passed—even after I'd come to blame Mikkel, not Maren. I'd moved on with my life. I'd formed my church. God was blessing people through me. It seemed I'd be going backward if I were to get involved with Maren again. It would have been a disservice to my children, my congregation.

"My children grew up knowing little about you and Maren. They certainly didn't know Mikkel was your father. Sanne did remember Maren, and when she became a teenager, she started rummaging through Maren's things as a way to be rebellious. She knew it made me uncomfortable. But, even then, I told her and Rune only what I thought they needed to know. I didn't tell them about Mikkel. Until recently. Until we learned Maren died." She looks at my face now, but the sun has nearly set and her eyes are shadows; I can't make out her expression, and I know she can't make out mine. "There was an article in the paper about her death, your birth. It referred to the earlier article about your birth. Sanne read it, told Rune. I didn't have a choice, then—I had to tell them."

I sense Mother's rage in me. I'd never understood it before; I'd never understood the rage that would well up in her. But now I think: Of course Mother had rage. How could she not have? Of course her rage spilled into me.

"Rune pressed me to find you," the preacher says. "He wanted to help you—he claims he remembers you, although I don't know how he could. But Sanne, it shook her world. She's had some contact with Mikkel over the years. Not a

173

lot, but more so than Rune. She didn't want to accept what Mikkel did. I don't know that she has accepted it. She challenged me. Wanted to know how I could have known—claims I couldn't have known. I stopped trying to convince her—I didn't see the point—and we stopped talking about it. But now you're here."

The Latin name for the Canadian burnet is *Sanguisorba,* meaning "to drink up blood." The plant is so rare in Maine, I've seen it only twice. Yet I think of the burnet now; I try to remember what it looks like, is like. I remember the burnet is dense, its flower white. That it stands erect, daring. I can't remember its smell or the way it felt in my hands. But I remember Mother showing me its milky sap. "The burnet's blood," Mother said, referring to the plant's sap, "is the coagulant. The plant is called *Sanguisorba* because of the sap. It is the sap that drinks up blood. Put the sap over a bleeding wound, and the wound dries up." I wish I understood whether this story of my birth, my father, my mother's life, is the sap that stops the blood, or the wound itself.

"How could you have abandoned us like that?" I say, still trying to sort out what I feel. "Do you have any idea what it was like for my mother? What it was like for me growing up, knowing nothing about my family or my father? How could you have turned on her? Rejected me?"

"It wasn't like that," the preacher says. She hadn't expected this outburst, it seems. But how could she have not expected it? Did she think I would hear this account of Mother's life—of my life—and feel nothing? "Your mother left on her own," she says. "I didn't ask her to leave."

"But you blamed her. She was fifteen when she became

pregnant." I can feel the heat in my face I know she can't see. "She was just a girl, younger than your Susanne."

"Don't bring Sanne into this," the preacher says. "My children have nothing to do with this."

"They have as much to do with this as I do." I feel I'm losing control of my voice, my words. "They have as much to do with it as my mother did. None of us chose this, including her. You're more culpable than any of us—you married the man." I wouldn't have spoken like this to Mother, but Mother spoke like this to me—and I realize I learned from the way she treated me: I learned fury. I expect the preacher to meet my fury; I expect her thin body to bulge in her power.

I don't expect her to collapse into her lap. I don't expect her to bury her head under her arms. At first I'm not sure what she's doing—the noises she's making sound barely human. Then I realize she's crying.

She sits up and pulls me to her. My head is beneath her moist chin, and my cheek presses into her breasts. I feel myself being comforted—although I don't want to be comforted by her.

"I'm sorry, Aslaug." She tries to run her fingers through my hair, but they get tangled; her touch feels nothing like Mother's. "I should have protected Maren. I should have . . ." She pushes my body back, looks at my face. "Let me make it up to you, Aslaug. Stay with us. Come live with us."

SOLOMON'S SEAL

2007

—Please state your name.

—Detective Jordan Ignis.

—What's your profession, Detective Ignis?

—I'm an investigator for the Bethan police and fire departments.

—Please take a moment to look at this photograph. Do you recognize the image in the photo?

—Yes. It shows the remains of the Charisma Pentecostal Church.

—The old monastery on Kettil Street?

—Yes, the monastery was most recently used as a church. The picture here shows the building after the fire that occurred there last year. I was the lead investigator on that fire.

—Okay. So you'd say the photo is a fair and accurate representation of the building after the fire?

—Yes.

—The photo is submitted as Exhibit U. Detective Ignis, at the conclusion of your investigation, were you able to determine what caused the fire?

—Yes.

—What did you conclude was the cause?

—Arson.

—You mean someone intentionally set fire to the building?

—Yes.

—How did you come to conclude the cause was arson?

—We found remnants of kerosene-soaked rags lining the interior eastern wall. It was pretty clear-cut. There's no question those rags were the source of the fire.

—During the course of your investigation, did you determine whether anyone was hurt in the fire?

—We recovered the bodies of two women.

—What, if anything, did you find unusual about the women's bodies?

—Well, the younger woman was unclothed. We found some clothing remnants lying near her. But how and when she became undressed, we don't know. We do know she was not wearing clothing at the time of the fire.

—Thank you, Detective.

DEVIL'S-BITE

2003

The roots of the Indian poke plant, false hellebore, are poisonous, the foliage lethal. Devil's-bite, Mother called the plant. "The person chosen as chief," Mother had said when explaining how some Native tribes used the plant, "was the one who could swallow the juice of the root of the devil and tolerate its bite the longest." I feel I'm being tested now, and I'm failing: the devil's-bite is killing me. I've found my family, only to find they don't want me. I've found my father, only to find I don't want him. And I've found my mother—parts of her—only to find I knew her even less well than I thought. And I miss her more.

And despite the gnawing sense I should leave this place, I stay. I agree to go in, spend the night. I tell myself it will only be for one night—that I'm not wanted here. That I don't want to be here. Yet it's hard for me to decipher what it is I want.

Darkness lies heavy across the yard now, and heavier inside; when the preacher swings open the door, I see only blackness. She takes the suitcase from me, walks in. I hesitate in the doorway, thinking of our house in Hartswell, dark even in the day, until Mother died, until the curtains came down. And for a moment I fear I'm stepping into another place like Mother's place: another world within the world, but apart from the world, shielded from the world; another cocoon. I watch the preacher meld into the darkness; her light-colored clothes and hair transform into a subtle, pulsing gray.

"Sanne!" she says, then turns toward me; the porch light passes through the door and illuminates her face, but her eyes look hollow. "Sanne?" she says again.

I see a glowing point of orange floating to the left of the door, and Susanne's face emerges.

"Put that out," the preacher says, and the room lights up.

Susanne stands near the light switch, a newly rolled cigarette draped between her fingers, its ashes piled and hanging. She puts the cigarette in her mouth, pulls hard, then drops it onto the stone floor, grinds it with her heel. The preacher waves her hand through the air, swirling the scent, the smoke. She lifts the cigarette from the floor. "Not in God's house," she says, and she walks into the sanctuary, carrying the suitcase in one hand, the cigarette in the other.

I look around, past the pews and stage and projector and white screen, and I feel God, or at least the sense of something vast and unknowable. The building is magnificent in a way I thought only nature could be. The walls are smooth stone forming arched vaults along the nave, the ceiling stretches high, and the stone floor is patterned in geometric

179

designs that seem elevating in a way, like the floor is rising, and lifting me.

"She was lying to you," Susanne says. She's standing behind me; I turn to see her arms crossed over her chest, one hip jutting to the side. Her potpourri hair is loose now, and it curls about her: a thousand of Mother's hands. "I was listening through the door. *Gudinden* told you a boatload of lies."

"She was lying?" I say.

"Her own father chose Maren, and then her heavenly father did, too."

"I don't understand—"

Susanne nods inward, and I see the preacher is heading back.

"We need to make a bed for Aslaug, Sanne," the preacher says when she nears us; she no longer carries the suitcase or cigarette. "She's going to stay with us tonight."

"Great," Susanne says, without exclamation. She grips my hand hard—hers is cold, and as clammy as mine—and she directs me through the nave, past the pews and screen and stage. She compresses my fingers too much. I waggle them, and the cage shrinks.

"What are you doing?" the preacher says. "I said we need to get a bed together." The preacher walks up behind us and takes Susanne's arm, but Susanne shakes her off like Mother might a blowfly or a flesh fly, or the caudal sucker of a leech. And unlike the flies, unlike the leech, the preacher falls away easily. And stays away. She follows us still, but at some distance now. And I'm fascinated: a daughter who patently defies, a mother who retreats, and the world does not end.

Susanne leads me inside one of the vaults and barricades the exit with her body. She releases my hand, and I feel my fingers swell into place.

The floor of the vault is peppered with rugs and mosaics. A thin table stands in the center, and behind it sit bookshelves jammed with books, binders, folders, stacks of paper. Some of the books and binders have titles in Hebrew, some in Greek, some in runes. One is entitled Chester Beatty Papyri. I don't recognize the name. Several others are prefaced with the name Nag Hammadi, including the Gospel of Thomas and the Secret Book of James.

"This was where your mother worked," Susanne says. She looks at my right hand as it massages my left.

I drop my hands. "My mother?" A rush of warmth moves through me. I feel the impulse to touch the table, the books. I try to imagine Mother as she would have been then: her bone-hair draped toward a notebook on the table; her lean back hunched; her water eyes hidden by the hair, the hunching; her hands still able; her written word still legible. "What was she working on?"

"A lot of these were hers." Susanne motions toward the shelves. "Some of them are mine." She removes a gray binder from the shelf, and I see Mother's hand on the binder in my mind. But it is the preacher's hand, not Mother's. The preacher pulls at the binder; Susanne pulls back; the preacher does not fall away this time.

"What are you doing, Sanne?" the preacher says. "What the devil is this?" And I think of the writhing woman; I feel a tightening in my chest, expecting another barrage about demons and devils and hell.

181

The binder bridges Susanne and the preacher, and I remember Mother's words: "There's a bridge. The Cobwork Bridge. It connects Bailey and Orrs islands. It's a hump-backed bridge of granite rocks held together only by cleverness, by the stacking. The tides come and go, and the bridge holds tight. Some things stay together because they fit, Aslaug. Not because they're forced." I wondered then whether we fit, Mother and I. Or whether we stayed from force. And I wonder now of these women: is it fit or force?

"*Mor* used to keep her stash in here," Susanne says to me, as if the preacher were not at the other end of this paper bridge. "Told her parishioners this vault was off-limits. That it was the house of blasphemy. That the only reason she kept all these devil books was that they didn't belong to her—she had no choice. She was able to slip in and out of here in a jiffy. Get a fix. Get back to damning others to hell. It's no wonder she was pissed when I started spending time in here. She had to find a new hiding place, a new house of blasphemy."

"I'd never damn anyone to hell," the preacher says, and the bridge breaks.

Susanne looks down at the binder, now in only her hands. "Sorry, *Mor*," she says. "I know that. I know you think Maren was making it all up. But you don't know for sure. I just want to see . . ." She walks to the table, lays the binder on it, then reaches beneath it and pulls out three hassocks upholstered in burgundy cloth, so worn in the center the burgundy has given way to pale pink. I imagine Mother's twiglike legs pressed into this cloth. And I wonder, Was her body so less scarce then, she could make an imprint independent of her mind?

Susanne motions for me and the preacher to kneel beside her, and she opens the binder, puts it on the table. "Can you read this?" she says to me.

I lower my own knees to the thinned cloth. I hunch over the binder. My own bone-hair drapes toward the binder and shields my eyes from Susanne, but I see the preacher: she doesn't kneel; she doesn't move. Yet I feel a connection between her and Susanne—their entanglement. Even though the bridge fell away. Like the mysterious quantum particles Mother taught me about, so entwined, if one spins, the other spins, no matter that a universe spans between them.

"I thought I could trust you," the preacher says.

"Aslaug's not one of your sheep, *Mor*. No harm done." Susanne looks to me. "Can you read this?"

The old crones' weaving has gone awry, I think: I don't belong in this moment, woven into this private space. "'The Pharisees and the scholars have taken the keys of knowledge and have hidden them,'" I read. "'They have not entered, nor have they allowed those who want to enter to do so. As for you, be sly as snakes and simple as doves.'"

"You know how to read Greek," Susanne says.

"Mother taught me."

"And other languages?"

I nod.

"You've read this passage before?"

"No."

"It's not from the Gospel of Thomas," she says, as if this should mean something to me. "At least not from the contemporary version. It's a transcription of some sayings by Jesus found on papyrus fragments in the late eighteen hundreds.

183

The fragments are probably more representative of the original version of Thomas."

"I don't know the Gospel of Thomas," I say. I try to place it in the Bible or the Apocrypha, but I can't. "Mother studied material like this, but she didn't teach it to me."

"Your mother studied this?" Susanne says.

"Documents like this. I never understood why, though. She said religion's nonsense."

"She didn't believe that," Susanne says. She looks at the preacher. "Maren kept studying, *Mor*. Searching. After she left. She still believed."

"Believed what?" I say.

"Maren told Aslaug religion is nonsense," the preacher says to Susanne. "That's what she believed. You have to give this up, Sanne. You have to let it go. Aslaug's father was Mikkel. You have to accept that. It's the truth."

"It's not the truth," Susanne says. "Look at her."

I hear a door open, and close. I hear steps on the stone getting louder and louder and stopping. I turn to see the guitar player. He stands at the entrance to the vault, spinning a paintbrush in one hand. His skin is the color of Mother's wheat bread, and his eyes remind me of the blackberries hanging heavy and tempting along the back roads of Hartswell.

"'The sounds of mourning do not suit a house which serves the Muse. They are not wanted here,'" he says. He stops the spinning, bends as if bowing, kisses the preacher's cheek. He has a mole on his own cheek that looks nearly alive and a deep cleft in his chin. But the groove between his nose and upper lip is almost nonexistent, as is his upper lip, which stretches long and thin. The glasses he's wearing seem too large for his face; when he stands, they teeter halfway down the bridge of his nose.

"That's Sappho," Susanne says. "You're a plagiarist, Rune."

"And hello to you, Muse," he says. His hair is mop-thick and dark as the mole, and it hangs into his glasses now and obscures his eyes. "Would you prefer Emily Dickinson?" He pushes the glasses up, but they slip back down. "'I felt a funeral in my brain,'" he says, feigning an accent, "'and mourners to and fro, kept treading, treading, till it seemed that sense was breaking through. And when they all were seated, a service, like a drum, kept beating, beating, till I thought my mind was going numb.'" He turns to the preacher. "Why the morose tone when I walked in? Who are you burying now?"

The preacher presses her thumbs into the inner corners of her eyes.

"Aslaug, meet Rune," Susanne says, "my dear brother, who is never a show-off, and who is interminably gracious."

Rune looks at Susanne, the preacher, me.

The preacher lowers her thumbs. "It's Aslaug, Rune. Your wish came true."

"Be careful what you wish for," Susanne says.

"Are you worried she'll steal your show?" Rune is speaking to Susanne, I know, but he's looking at me. He kneels down close to me. He lifts his right hand, and I notice his two fingers are webbed, like Susanne's. "I'm sorry, Aslaug. I'm sorry about your mother. We read about it . . . I didn't know . . . I didn't mean . . ."

He reaches for my hand. There's a tingling in the tips of my fingers where he touches me, a prickling coldness that starts there, then rushes up my arms, through my shoulders, into my chest, where it settles, becomes heavy. There is a fluttering in my belly. Butterflies? I'd read this analogy, butterflies in the stomach. Except the butterflies are unruly: they escape into my spine, surge up my neck.

"You were my first friend," he says. "I really loved you."

"I don't remember," I say. Yet I feel so strange—so much emotion—maybe I do.

"Can we get more light in here?" he says. "I'd like to see her." Although the building has electricity, unlike my Hartswell home, the church is old—clearly older than electricity—and there is no electric light in the vault, only a kerosene lamp.

The preacher carries over the lamp and sets it on the table. Sanne removes the chimney, rotates the wick upward, lights the wick, replaces the chimney, and the vault brightens.

"My God, Aslaug," Rune says. "It's so strange to see you as a woman. You're beautiful."

A woman? I think. I've never thought of myself as a woman. I've certainly never thought of myself as beautiful. Flowers are beautiful. Butterflies.

"You don't remember anything?" he says to me. "You don't remember anything about our time together?"

I shake my head.

"Your mother would be poring over her books, trying to uncover the great mystery of your birth. *Mor*, here, would be reprimanding her, telling Maren that God was going to condemn her lost soul. Sanne would be running from Maren to *Mor*, and back again, trying to figure out which one of them was right. And you and I? We were artists. We knew even as toddlers God can't be understood but through art. So we colored in Maren's magnificent books. Tore pages from Mor's Bible to make collages. They thought we were wreaking havoc, but we knew we were speaking with God."

"You don't remember that," Susanne says. "You only know what I told you I remember. And I don't remember that."

"Of course you don't, Queen of Sheba. You were too busy asking Maren questions. Tugging on Mor's clothes, seeking King Solomon's wisdom. Even as a six-year-old, you were an insufferable bore." Rune stands and puts his arms around Susanne; she makes a halfhearted effort to push him away.

"So what were you discussing when I walked up?" he says, poking Susanne's waist. "Aslaug's miraculous birth, yet again?" He looks at me. "Sanne doesn't want to believe our father was a lecher and a child molester."

"Stop it, Rune," Susanne says, and now she does push him away.

"We're a nuclear family and an extended family all wrapped up in one."

"That's really enough, Rune," the preacher says.

"I don't see the point in not facing the truth," Rune says. "I've had to face reality since I was a kid, right, Mor? Would it have been better if I'd buried my head in the proverbial sand?"

"It's not the truth," Susanne says. "Mor knows it's not the truth. Look at Aslaug's eyes, Rune. And her hands—no syndactyly. And her hair. Where's Mikkel?"

Rune lifts my hand with his webbed one. Then he looks at my eyes. "She just got lucky."

"No," Susanne says. "She has Maren's eyes. She has Maren's everything. There would be some part of Mikkel in her, but there's none." She looks at the preacher. "How do you explain it, *Mor*?"

"I don't have to explain anything, Sanne. There's no other explanation."

"Maren thought there was another explanation." Susanne opens her hands, her arms. "Do you see all these books, Aslaug? Do you know why they're here? Because your mother thought they would explain the mystery of your birth. No matter what lies *Mor*'s told you, your birth was a mystery to Maren. Mikkel's not your father."

"I didn't tell her any lies—" the preacher says.

"Bullshit," Susanne says.

"That's enough, Sanne," the preacher says.

"Leave *Mor* alone," Rune says.

But Susanne seems undeterred. "Why did Maren study all these old texts, *Mor*? Because she was trying to understand the mystery of Aslaug's birth."

"It was just a charade," the preacher says. "Maren was just trying to divert attention from the truth."

"*Mor* knows all about charades," Susanne says to me.

The preacher stole my dreams. But now Susanne has handed them back: she's given me back the mystery of my father, the mystery of me. And Rune? He's stirred my dreams up.

So I stay. I stay for more than one night. And then many nights. I stay to learn more about my birth, my mother's past; I want to understand what my mother herself believed about my life; I want to understand what was driving her to keep us

188

isolated the way she did, to study the way she did. She was looking for something—trying to understand something. And I have a glimmer, it seems, as to what that something was.

But I also stay because of Susanne, because of Rune. As much as I sense the preacher's ambivalence, I sense Susanne's interest. And from Rune, I sense a kind of affection I've never felt from anyone else, ever.

The old crones are pleased, I think: I'm finding my fate.

Solomon's Seal

2007

—Cross-examination?

—Yes, Your Honor. Detective Ignis, you were not able to conclude who set fire to the Charisma Church, the former monastery, were you?

—No.

—In fact, you found no physical evidence whatsoever linking Aslaug Hellig to this crime, did you?

—No physical evidence, no. Other than she was at the scene of the crime, and she was the only one there who seems to have lived through the fire.

—But that doesn't indicate she started the fire, does it?

—No.

—Other than the two bodies, what, if anything, did you recover from the fire?

—Well, the building was stone, so much of the structure

itself remained intact, but most everything inside was destroyed. We didn't recover much, really. Some kitchen items, candlesticks, tools, that kind of thing.

—What about books?

—Objection. Leading.

—Sustained.

—What else, if anything, did you find?

—We did find a few pages from books and notebooks. Some remnants of what looked like paintings. And some personal items, like a comb, some hair clips. . . .

—You mentioned finding some pages from books and notebooks. What kind of books?

—Objection. Relevance.

—I'll allow the question, but please get to the point, Counsel. Go ahead and answer.

—I don't know what the books were, but the odd thing about all the pages we found is that they were written in foreign languages.

—Which languages?

—Greek. Hebrew. There was one we couldn't figure out. Come to find out, it was this ancient language. Something like runic, I think.

—Did you say "runic"?

—Yeah.

—Thank you. Now, regarding the body you recovered that was not clothed. You have no way of knowing why the woman was not wearing clothes, do you?

—No.

—And there is no way to determine how she became undressed, right?

—That's true.

—She herself could have removed her own clothing before the fire, correct?

—She could have, yes.

—You found no evidence suggesting Aslaug removed the woman's clothing, did you?

—Well, there aren't many options—

—But you have no evidence to suggest the victim didn't remove her own clothing, correct?

—I have no evidence either way. I can't say how the woman came to be undressed. All I know is that during the fire, the woman wasn't wearing clothing. Whether Aslaug removed the woman's clothing, or the woman removed her own clothing, or the woman had sworn off clothing, I just can't say.

—Okay, Detective. I have no further questions, Your Honor.

KING'S CROWN

2003

It's Thursday morning, two days after I arrived at this church and began scaling this family tree: these overlying branches of irony and cruelty and strength and warmth and wonder. And I wonder: On which of these branches was I birthed? What of these traits will grow in me?

I sit up and dab sleep from my eyes, look around the tiny room. The bedroom I'm using sits beneath the sanctuary, near the bedrooms of Susanne, Rune and the preacher. There is little here but a bed and a bureau and a toilet, and a basin for washing, and a mirror of Mother's haunting face. Some paper. A pen. And a nightstand made from a wooden box. The ceiling is low; the walls are stone. There are no windows in the room, except a diminutive one in the door leading to the hall; the hall light shinnies through the window, into the room.

I've not had opportunity to question Susanne about her theories of my birth, her theories of my mother. I've not had opportunity to question Rune. The preacher ushered me away that first night. She took me to this room, prepared my bed, spoke only of practicalities. And yesterday was a day of electricity and running water and telephones. It's not as if I'd not known of these things. I'd seen lights in stores, and tele-phones; I'd read about how each worked. I'd seen water sprinkling lawns, and fountains spewing. And, once, I'd used a public bathroom when Mother and I were in Bethan. I stood there, flushing the toilet again and again, and turning off and on the spout, until Mother pounded on the door.

But now no one pounds on the door.

I reach to the left of the bed, to the switch, and I turn on the light. I envision the excited electrons, the liberated light photons, the wavelength of the emitted light. Mother knew of electricity, too, of course—she taught me of it. But she never seemed to long for it, as I did. She behaved as if her knowing of it was enough—as if the reality of electricity, the sensation of it, was superfluous.

I turn off the light and climb from the covers, stand on the bed, unscrew the warm lightbulb, look at its glass mound, its filament. I climb down, lay the bulb on the floor, slip on one clog. I crunch the glass gently with my heel, and I imagine the argon gas's release. I wait several minutes while the metals cool before I disassemble the wires and filament. Then I uncoil the filament; it's nearly impossible to uncoil it, it's so thin—a hundredth of an inch, maybe. I stretch it; it spans longer than I do. I know the electrons zip along through it, bump into the atoms that make up the filament, heat the atoms up. I scribble an image of the bulb on the paper near the bed, make notes of what I've learned through this disassembly to ensure I'll remember.

I've piled the glass shards and metal scraps on the floor and I've just removed the cover to the back of the toilet when I hear the sound. It's a rustling of sorts. A scurrying. Maybe a mouse. I ignore it. I lay the cover on the seat, push the flusher, watch the valve lift, the water drain, the valve fall, the water fill. Then I hear it again, the sound. It comes from the hall.

I realize someone might walk in. I replace the cover. I scoop up the pile of shards and metal and dump them into a corner of the bureau drawer. I lift out a dress from the drawer. Susanne gave me clothes to wear—mine were lost in the car. But she's taller than I am. I take off the nightgown, pull the dress over my head; its sleeves hang to my knuckles and its skirt tangles my legs.

I unlatch the door. Rune stands there, his glasses cock-eyed. He takes a step back, opens his mouth as if to speak. Says nothing. Then starts laughing.

"What?" I say.

"Lovely style. You'll fit right in in Bethan. I think that look is called grunge."

"What look?" I look down at my clothes: the dress is on backward.

He reaches up and flattens my hair. "Ever heard of a mirror?"

"It never occurred to me to look in it," I say. And I feel myself laugh. And I think, What a strange thing, laughter. This breathy release. It's weightless, and yet it lifts weight

195

away. Like the gas that seeped from that broken bulb, invisible but essential. Its presence changes everything, it seems. Yet I've lived my life without it.

"I made pancakes," Rune says. He adjusts his glasses now, rakes his fingers through his hair. "Blueberry. I picked them."

I can't help but think of the blueberry hill behind our house, and of the pink-edged sulphur. I can't help but wonder if I've found my blueberry home.

"I wasn't sure if you were awake . . . ," he says. "I thought you might want some."

Listening to his voice now, I think of the night before. I watched as he and Susanne rehearsed their songs, before I attended the evening service. His singing voice is full and rich, and fertile, it seems, like it settles in and just keeps growing. I could feel it inside my body, even after his voice went silent. And when I closed my eyes, it seemed I could see his voice in color, swirling and stretching itself around me.

Only a handful of people came to the service last night, far fewer than the evening before, yet participating in the service made me feel part of something far bigger than myself. Much of what happened during the service was foreign to me—much of the preacher's message I found confusing—and yet being there felt expanding, like my world was opening up. Like the preacher was opening my world up.

Rune slathers butter on the pancakes and dribbles warmed maple syrup. He looks up at me as he pours, and the dribble grows: he drenches the stack. The wet pancakes sit in a brown-blue pool, but Rune doesn't seem to notice. He slides a purplish red jam across the wet pancake.

"What is that?" I say, pointing to the jam.

"Jam? Don't tell me you've not heard of that either." He folds a napkin, unfolds it. His fingers are lean and long; his wrists narrow. And his arms are lean and long. And his neck. There's a beauty about his body, the way he holds it, moves it. A beauty in its lines. A sort of graceful power. Like lightning to the earth: defined and luminous, yet still ethereal. "I'm starting to think you truly did come from another planet. That's Sanne's most recent theory, have you heard?"

"No," I say, and again I laugh. And again it seems some ingredient fundamental to me has only now switched on. "I've heard of jam. But what's in the jam?"

The jam looks just like jam Mother would make from highbush cranberry. She'd call it her king's crown jam, because it was bitter, smelled disagreeable. "The king is tolerable," she'd say, "only when he's so sweetened, he's barely recognizable."

"Berries?" he says. He touches my lips with his webbed fingers but pulls his hand away fast. Too fast, it seems. Is he uncomfortable because he touched me? I wonder. Or because he touched me with his webbed fingers? "Be quiet now, and eat. I slaved away and here my masterpiece is getting cold."

He watches as I cut the pancakes, as I take a bite into my mouth. It is king's crown jam—the taste is like nothing else. I wonder where he got the berries. I didn't expect anyone but Mother and I collected these berries for jam. The taste of it, mixed with sweet syrup and still-warm pancakes, confounds me: I didn't know food could taste like this.

"So I guess this means you like it?" Rune uses the napkin to dab jam or syrup or berries from my lips. And this time he

197

doesn't jerk away. "You can slow down. I promise, I won't steal your plate."

"Sorry," I say. "It's delicious." I can imagine the grin on my face—what Mother would say. But for the first time I can remember, I don't care. At least not as much. I take another bite.

"I have a surprise for you," he says, but he doesn't rise; he doesn't explain.

I finish chewing. "Are you going to show me?"

"What?" he says.

"The surprise?"

"Oh, right." He reaches over and takes the fork from my hand. He stabs a sloppy mound of pancake and lifts it to his mouth. He stabs another mound, lifts it to mine. Then he reaches beneath the table and picks up a small trunk from the floor.

"What's in there?" I say through the sticky mouthful of syrup and king's crown and pancake. I motion toward the trunk, trying to distract him from whatever is welling in me. The butterflies again? Or just one butterfly, with windlike wings.

He pushes away my plate, sets the trunk on the table next to me. "Why don't you look?"

The trunk is a dirty white with brown leather straps. It's as old as Mother's suitcase of money. The money, I think. Where is it?

I unlatch the case and lift the lid. The case is full of photographs, and childish drawings and paintings. I expect I know what the photos are, and part of me wants to slam shut the lid, not because I don't want to see them but because I so want to see them.

Rune lifts a picture of a teenage girl and hands it to me. She stands in a thicket, the girl, with her arms spread wide. Her head is back and her mouth is open, and I know she is howling with laughter. The girl could be me, I think. But she's not me.

"My mother?" I say, but I know it's my mother.

Rune nods. "She's a looker. The real reason Mor kicked Maren out had nothing to do with you, you know. Nothing to do with Mikkel. Mor was just jealous of Maren's great beauty. . . ."

But I shake my head. I don't want him to joke about this. My whole history is sitting on this table, in a box. It's so strange, I think, the way a life can be summed up. Anyone who went through this case would have known more about me than I knew myself.

I lift another picture, this one of a younger Sara wearing a dress that puddles about her, holding the hand of a man with Rune's eyes. I find myself looking to the man's hands, finding the web.

There's another berry Mother would make into jam. The clammy ground-cherry. Mother and I would gather the yellow tomato-like berries, unwrap each berry from its papery balloon, then Mother would cook them and sweeten them and seal them away. But I never longed for the taste of the ground-cherry, never relished it, as I did the king's crown, because I knew the berry's past: ground-cherry fruit, before it ripens, is poisonous, like bittersweet nightshade. So when I would spread the jam across a thick slice of Mother's bread, I always would wonder: Were they ripe enough? Or am I painting the bread with poison?

It seems to me now as I look at my past, as I learn more

199

about my past, that perhaps it would be better if I didn't know. If I'd never learned of the ground-cherry's history, I would have been more able to enjoy the ground-cherry for what it had become. But now, it seems, I'll always wonder whether my bread was painted with poison, whether it poisoned me.

Rune takes the picture of Sara and Mikkel from me. "You lived the first fifteen years of your life as Aslaug, not Mikkel's daughter. You're still Aslaug. He can't take that from you."

I've not lived my life as Aslaug, I think. I've lived as Aslaug Datter, the daughter of Maren. "So you believe it?" I say. "That Mikkel fathered me?" I don't want him to believe this. I don't want to believe this. I want him to believe in Mother. In other possibilities. I want to believe in Mother.

"I believe it doesn't matter," he says. "We all have a cross, you know. We all have some cross to bear. Maybe this not knowing is yours. You can carry the burden around with you, let it drag you down, but that's all it does. Drag you down." He lifts a stack of the photos, slides the one of Sara and Mikkel deep into the trunk, lets the stack drop.

As if that could do it, I think. As if burying Mikkel in a mound of memories could erase him from my life. And then I think of jail, of reading the story of Jesus carrying his own cross. "What's your cross? You said the other day you've had to face reality since you were young. What did you mean?"

"That's called prying, Aslaug," he says. "But I suppose on the planet you come from, social graces are different than ours here on Earth."

"Sorry," I say.

"I don't mind. But I thought maybe I could impress you a bit with my wit and creativity, and my remarkable ability to cook, before I told you I can't read."

"What?"

"Well, I can, but not well. I see the same words you see, but my brain jumbles the letters up. Scrambles them. I have to decode every word."

"But you know poetry. . . . You recited that poetry."

"I have a good memory. My saving grace. I hear it once and I don't forget. I've been able to fool a lot of people because of it. Most people don't know. Except *Mor* and Sanne, of course. And the people who broke the news to *Mor* when I was six. And this girl in the church, Rebekka. Sanne used to read to me, but she won't do it anymore. Now Rebekka does. *Mor* pays her. . . ."

"I'm sorry." I can't imagine not being able to read. I can't imagine living without books.

"Relax, Aslaug," he says, and I realize he sees what I feel. "I have some learning challenges, is all, I'm not going to die. Besides, I'm dumping that cross. You don't know Sanne and *Mor* well, but living with them and not being able to read, I may as well have been a leper. It used to really get to me. But I'm not going to let it get to me anymore."

Rune hands me a picture of a man with young Maren. The man holds her on his lap; he kisses her cheek. Her head bends into him and her eyes smile. She looks so confident, so carefree. It's Mother, I know, but it's not Mother, too: some part of this girl died long before Mother did.

"That's *Bedstefar*," Rune says. "*Mor*'s dad, Maren's dad."

"I know," I say.

"You do?"

I see he wonders how I know. But how could I not know? This man is Mother; he's me.

"Look at this," Rune says.

The picture he hands me is of two babies, each with flesh-ringed thighs, each toothless, each grinning. And each gripping a handful of the other's ringed flesh. The quality of the picture is poor, but I see one baby is nearly bald and November-snow pale. The other has hair of brown mounds and skin of bronzed mounds.

"It's us," Rune says. "It's how I knew we were tight."

"Tight?" I say.

"Friends. Fond of each other."

I've never seen a picture of me before. "Are you sure this is me?"

"You are Aslaug, right? We've established that? Not Mikkel's daughter, but Aslaug?"

He smiles, takes back the photo, flips it. "Aslaug and Rune," it says, "1988."

Rune lays the photo back in the pile, pulls out a painting. It's a smear of orange and purple and turquoise blue. He points to a penciled name and date: "Aslaug, 1989."

My hands are on the paint, its texture. And on the penciled name.

"And look at this one," he says. "It's mine."

But I can't look. The painting before me is so childlike. So innocent. So not self-conscious. So free. I didn't recognize the grinning baby with plump thighs, and I don't recognize the girl who painted this. Are they trapped inside me somewhere? Or am I like a butterfly that metamorphosed in reverse: began in flight, entered a chrysalis, lost its wings?

"Are you okay, Aslaug?" Rune says. But he knows I'm not okay. His arms are suddenly around me; my face is in his neck. I feel his strength, his warmth.

"Hey." It is Susanne's voice; Rune's arms fall away. "What's going on?" Susanne stands just steps away; her arms are stiff and still; her hands rest on her hips.

"I was showing Aslaug these old photos, her old artwork," Rune says. "It's hard for her to see. . . ."

"Rebekka called," Susanne says, like she's lost interest in her own question.

"She's coming to rehearse for Sunday?" Rune says, and now I realize Rebekka is the angel girl.

"I don't know." Susanne sits down and rifles through the trunk, but she doesn't look long at anything. "Rebekka's going through hell right now."

"Is she?" Rune says.

"Don't worry, though," Susanne says, and she closes the trunk. "If Rebekka's parents don't kill her, she should be just fine."

Solomon's Seal

2007

—Please state your name.

—Dr. Oda Lennart.

—What type of doctor are you, Dr. Lennart?

—A forensic pathologist.

—How long have you been practicing forensic pathology?

—Seventeen years.

—Where are you currently employed?

—I'm a medical examiner for the state of Maine. For the Office of the Chief Medical Examiner. I've been in this position for almost two years.

—Are you familiar with the fire that occurred at the church on Kettil Street in Bethan?

—Yes. I conducted the autopsies on the two female corpses retrieved from that fire.

—Could you determine their approximate ages?

—One was midforties to early fifties. One was in her twenties.

—Were you able to positively identify them?

—Yes, through dental records.

—And who were they?

—Sara Lerner. The woman who had pastored the Charisma Church. And Sara Lerner's daughter, Susanne.

—Could you determine the cause of death for either?

—Sara and Susanne were poisoned.

—Objection. Move to strike. The doctor cannot know if someone poisoned these women. She can only know if they did or did not have poison in their systems.

—Objection sustained. Please strike that testimony.

—I'll ask that again, Doctor. What did you determine was the cause of death?

—Both women died from poison.

—So they didn't die from smoke inhalation?

—No. They were both dead before the fire.

—What kind of poison killed them?

—Both had toxic amounts of atropine and scopolamine in their bloodstreams.

—Atropine and scopolamine, the alkaloids found in jimsonweed?

—Objection. Leading.

—Others have already testified to this. Objection overruled.

—Yes.

—Is it your opinion these women both died from jimsonweed poisoning?

—Objection. Leading.

—I'm going to allow it.

—Yes.

—Why?

—Well, when I conducted the autopsy on Sara Lerner, I expected to find evidence she died of suffocation from smoke inhalation. I didn't find this. It appeared she was dead before the fire. So I ran a toxicology screen. There was scopolamine in her system, and enough atropine in her to kill a cow. I found the same situation with the young woman, Susanne. The only other times I've seen this situation is when people consumed jimsonweed.

—What, if anything, else did you find unusual about the bodies?

—The younger woman had remnants of plant dye on her skin. It looked as if her skin had been painted at some point before the fire. We couldn't decipher any image. Her body was too burnt. But we were able to determine that the dye came from the plant *Sanguinaria canadensis*. Bloodroot.

—Thank you, Dr. Lennart. I have no further questions.

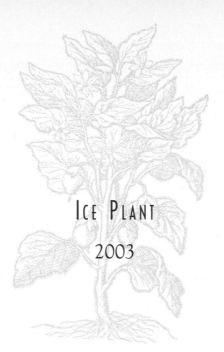

ICE PLANT

2003

*T*he sound pulses through me.

I've been in this church for only five days, and yet the sound is familiar enough to be comforting, this jarring, rage-like music that blares about soldiers and the enemy, God and Jesus, the Way, the Truth and the Light.

It is Sunday morning, and upstairs Rune and Susanne are preparing for the service. I imagine them now as I saw them Wednesday evening: Susanne sitting at the drums, her mess of hair wrapped in a bud, or flowering down her neck and shoulders; her hands gripping the sticks, the blue veins riding her arms; her white dress splayed across her wide knees. And I imagine Rune's hips waving, and his glasses slipping and his fingers stroking the strings. I see him close his black-berry eyes, disappear somewhere inside the music, or in the beauty of the church, or in some version of God. He opens his eyes, kneads his hair. His glasses skim up, skate down. Then up. Before his hands again find the strings.

In my mind, the preacher scurries. Her face is lined with excitement. Her pale hair is shining and knotted, her suit jacket lean; her wide skirt is pressed and prepared to spin and fly with the tambourine. She plants one glass of water on the podium, then another. And the bottle of yellowish liquid, which I now know is anointing oil, she exhumes from some sticky drawer and fixes on the center of the podium, pushing the water to one side. She passes through the pews, checking for hugging gum and stuffed wrappers and torn fingernails from the service before. And she collects these donations in a brown paper bag without uttering a word. Somewhere, behind one of the many closed doors, she disposes of the bag, and reappears with the excitement etched deeper: the time is approaching. Soon the parishioners will stomp in and limp in and roll in and stroll in; soon the buzz of their voices will echo from the stone walls and floor; soon the preacher will be respected among those who are her family in Christ. And Susanne and Rune will become the children she wishes they were, if only for these hours: pious and obedient and in awe of the preacher's power.

I hoist my body from the warm sheets, feel my toes enfold the stone, wrap Susanne's robe around me, wash my face and neck. The room smells stale and is hot, but the water splattering my skin is stinging cold, and when I look into the mirror expecting to see Mother's face, I see cheeks made cherry by the cold, and youth: I see Aslaug.

"Aslaug?"

I realize the music has given way to plodding feet and a

pounding on my door. Susanne's face is framed in the door's window. I towel my skin, open the door.

"*Gudinden* will have your head," she says, "if you don't get your ass in gear."

"Get my what?" This is the first time I've been alone with Susanne since meeting her outside.

"Maren may have taught you every language under the sun, Aslaug, but speaking to you in slang is like speaking to a walrus." She shakes out a rolled cigarette from her wide sleeve. "God forbid one of *Mor's* sheep learns I smoke." She tugs a book of matches from her shoe, drapes the cigarette from the corner of her mouth while she lights the match. But she doesn't light the cigarette; she frees it from her mouth.

"How you feeling?" she says. "You seem out of it."

"I'm okay," I say. "I've been hoping we could talk. . . ."

"You need to get dressed, *for Christ's sake*." And she laughs that laugh. "It's the Lord's day. The flock will be arriving within the hour, and *Gudinden* will want to announce the return of her long-lost niece to those who haven't yet heard, so they all can baa and whinny in praise of God's miraculous hand that guided you here."

"Why do you go to the services?" I say. "Why do you play the music? You seem to have such contempt for it all." I did what Mother told me because she was the law of my universe. Disobeying Mother was akin to leaping from a cliff and expecting to fly. But Susanne leaped long ago, it seems.

"Do you think I have a choice? As long as I live here, I go, I play, and around the sheep, I act the part. But that doesn't mean I believe."

"Well, I don't think Sara believes God guided me here." I think of the annoyance carved around the preacher's leek-like eyes. She's said little to me since that first night—but her eyes speak.

"Yeah, well. If she doesn't want you here, she sure talks about you enough. You'd think you were the Blessed Virgin the way she and Rune go on." She puts the cigarette in her mouth, jerks back the pink strand of hair that seems lured by her eyes, then tries to light the cigarette, but the match has burned low and sears her. "Damn," she says. "No surprise why the ancients worshiped fire." She drops the match on the floor, lights another. I feel the urge to pick up the match, but I see Susanne expects me to pick it up, so I leave it there.

"Do you think Sara would prefer I just stay downstairs? Not go to the service?"

"Are you kidding?" Susanne lights the cigarette now; the smoke snakes to the ceiling, swells into a cloud; I try not to cough, but I cough. "*Gudinden* would never pass up the opportunity to attribute some fortuitous accident to God's grace." And the laugh strikes. "I know I'm hard on her, but you need to give her a chance. You two just might grow on each other."

I rummage through the clothes in the bureau drawer. They look like Indian pipe blossoms: white on white on top of white. Mother called the Indian pipe "ice plants" because the plants have no chlorophyll. "Sunlight nourishes the ice plants as much as it nourishes ice," Mother said. "Not at all."

"Why are all these clothes of yours the same?" I say. "They're all white."

"To drive *Gudinden* mad," she says. But knowing I don't understand, she adds, "There was this ancient religious sect called the Essenes that Maren studied. Some of the scholar-ship about them theorizes they wore only white, so Maren did, too, when she lived here, because of them. I just like to remind *Mor* she's not omnipotent."

But Mother never wore white, I think.

"Why do you so want to goad her?" I say. Yet in a sense, I know. I would have loved to prickle Mother at times. Watch her squirm the way she watched me.

"Why not?" she says. "Seriously, though, I never got to be a kid. That's why. I'm nearly nineteen years old, but I was never a kid. And now I'm not sure what the hell I am. I spent my childhood hearing how this life is just a precursor for the eternal life. That the only point of this life is to not get damned to hell. I was scared shitless by all the devil-talk as a child. And convinced I'd burn. I've never had a friend outside the simpletons who come to this church. I've never played a sport, seen a movie, gone to a dance. Hell, I've never been in the ocean, and we live miles away. What's the point, right? It's all meaningless at best, and almost certain to corrupt. So there you have it."

"I never did any of those things either," I say. But I didn't know anyone who did; I guess in a way it was easier for me. Besides, Mother's mind was a minefield. And the woods were Eden. And our house was a prison, but a palace, too: at times it spiraled deep into the earth, and deep into the sky, depending on Mother's mood. I see that now. Life was a revolving mystery, sometimes terrifying, sometimes maddening. But always provocative. Interesting. And al-though its meaning seemed beyond my grasp, it never seemed meaningless.

"If I'd been a freak like Maren or a screwup like Rune, maybe things would have worked out better for me. Instead, I had no behavioral issues. No learning issues. In fact, I was 'gifted,' whatever the hell that means. What did it get me? Ignored. My needs were not pressing, right? I'd do fine no matter what, right? I got yanked from my father because of Maren's needs. Yanked from school because of Rune's needs. Shut up in this hellhole because of Mor's needs. And left to be fucking bored out of my mind.

"Mor's not a bad person," Susanne says then, as if I'd asked. "A guilt-ridden person, yes. A fucked-up person, yes. An egomaniac at times. Absolutely. But she didn't mean me any harm. She just didn't mean me . . . anything. Anyway," she says, "about the clothes, maybe the Essenes and Maren were onto something."

"Why did the Essenes wear white? Did the clothes represent something?" I ask, but I'm thinking about Susanne's rant, not the Essenes: she called Mother a freak.

"The masculine and feminine in the soul. The union of the two."

"The masculine and feminine in the soul?" Susanne's like different people to me. She's the man I first met when I drove into Bethan; she's the preacher; she's Mother. "How do you know what the Essenes believed? What my mother believed? What she read? You were so young when she was here." I'm holding the ice plant dress in my hands, waiting for Susanne to leave before I disrobe, and thinking, Does she mean Mother was as crazy as I sometimes feared?

"A lot I don't remember, but I've learned," Susanne

says. "Again, mostly to goad *Mor*." I expect the laugh, but it doesn't come this time. "I'm partly joking." But it doesn't seem she's joking. "It's true in the beginning I was motivated by that—I knew it would drive *Mor* crazy if I started looking through Maren's things. It was little different than smoking or dyeing my hair or cussing. Satisfying because it got *Mor* riled. I found some of Maren's notes. That got me started. And I realized Maren wasn't quite the person *Mor* had made her out to be. And the stuff Maren wrote about, some of it blew me away. Finally something for my brain to do. Finally the world started to make some goddamned sense."

"So you don't think Mother was crazy?"

"Crazy? No. Maren was the sanest thing around. But in the world of the insane, it's the sane who seem insane."

"What about her notes?" I feel some relief. "You mentioned notes." I rearrange the dress in my hands. I know I need to put the dress on, but I'm not accustomed to seeing my own breasts, my own fuller rear; I don't want to undress in front of Susanne.

"Yeah," Susanne says. "She wrote a lot about botany. I guess that's why Maren was in the States to begin with. To study botany at Bran. It's all really interesting, actually. The botany. There's some crazy shit even in the sane world. Who knew? But after she got pregnant, she started keeping notes about the Essenes and the Gnostics and pagan mythology." She tugs the belt of my robe, unties it; my hands are tangled in the dress and I can't stop the robe from falling open; I feel the touch of air on my breasts, my stomach.

"What the hell?" she says. She pulls the robe from my shoulders, lets it drop to the floor. "What is this?"

I look down and see the hairstreak. Its lines have faded, but it's there.

"It's just a painting," I say. "Like a tattoo. Like you have—"

"I don't have any tattoos," she says.

"But I—"

"You don't seem the type to tattoo yourself at all, let alone with a snake."

"It's not a snake. It's a butterfly."

"Right," Susanne says. "It's a butterfly. It's easy to mistake a butterfly for a snake. Especially a butterfly with a very large, very out-of-place eye."

I see she's looking at my scar. "That's just an old wound. I was burned."

"The eye of the fire."

"I don't know anything about the Essenes"—I try to divert her attention from the heat coloring my face, and from my body, the painting, the eye—"or the Gnostics, or much about the pagans."

"Well, it's no wonder." She drags from the cigarette, her eyes fixed on me. "Hardly anyone knows. Or what they do 'know' is based on misinformation." She pauses. "But I'd have thought Maren would have explained this to you. It was all in her notes."

I shake my head.

She opens the top drawer of the bureau, pulls out a bra, tosses it at me. "Strange, don't you think?"

"What? What's strange?" I want to turn away from her, put the bra on without her watching, but I don't. I drop the dress on the bed, hook the bra, lift it over my breasts. The bra's too big on me and curdles.

"That I seem to know more about your mother than you do."

It's true, I think. My loss has been Susanne's gain. Like the parasitic broomrape, Susanne's been nourished by other plants' roots: Mother is my root; Mother's ideas are my roots.

Susanne heaves a pair of underwear toward me and nearly strikes my face. "According to Maren's notes," she says, "Christians beginning around the third century CE used the term *pagan* to describe people who subscribed to religions other than Christianity and Judaism, particularly the ancient mystery religions."

"The what?"

"The mystery religions. The secret religions prevalent in areas surrounding the Mediterranean before and after Christ. Many of the great philosophers and scientists of that time participated in these religions, including Pythagoras, Socrates, Plato, Sappho. . . ."

I pull the dress over my head and feel myself relax some as the dress drapes my breasts and stomach and folds into my legs. "So the Gnostics and Essenes were members of mystery religions?"

"No," Susanne says. "The Essenes were Jewish. The Gnostics were Christian—the earliest Christians. At least that's what Maren believed. But the Essenes and the Gnostics both incorporated aspects of various mystery religions and pagan philosophy."

"I still don't understand why Mother was interested in any of this," I say, but I'm thinking less about Mother now, more about my body, all goose-bumped and pale.

"Because Gnostic Christianity is extremely different from modern Christianity, and Maren believed Gnostic

215

Christianity was the true Christianity. The Gnostics were mystical, far less literal. The Gnostic gospels—"

"I've read the Gospels—"

"In the Bible?"

I nod.

But Susanne shakes her head. "Uh-uh," she says. "The Gnostic gospels were excluded from the Bible, but the Gnostic texts are the oldest Christian texts, according to Maren. The original Christian texts. Don't suggest that to *Mor*, though—"

"So my mother and Sara disagreed about this?"

"This and everything else. Maren insisted Jesus was an Essene at some point between the ages of twelve and thirty, for example," Susanne says. "And that Mary, Jesus's mother, may also have been an Essene. A lot of modern scholars would disagree with this—"

"But why does it matter? Why would Sara care if Jesus and Mary were Essenes?"

"Because Maren thought the Essenes' teachings, although mainly Jewish, drew on many faiths—including the many mystery religions of the time, as well as the Vedas, the Upanishads and Brahmanism. She believed the Essenes considered different religions to be different aspects of one divine revelation. In other words, the Essenes didn't think any single faith had all the answers. According to Maren, the Essenes believed they had a duty to understand principles common to many religions. In fact, a basic tenet of the Essene faith, the Essene tree of life, is comparable to the tree of the knowledge of good and evil, and the Buddhist bodhi tree and the Tibetan wheel of life."

216

And Yggdrasil?

I recall Mother reading through the Upanishads, the Vedas, her lips silently working the words, her fingers petting each page. "I'd like to see Mother's notes," I say.

"Until I found her notes, I had no idea about any of this," Sanne says. She glances at the paper and pen on the nightstand and at my lightbulb scrawl, seeing I'm a note taker, like Mother. I'm grateful when she doesn't ask about what's written there—grateful I don't have to explain. "Imagine how duped I felt. Although I'll admit the notes didn't come as a complete surprise. Even as kids, Rune and I could see the hypocrisy in this church. There's so much pressure for people in the congregation to receive the baptism of the Holy Spirit, people fake it. They pretend to speak in tongues. They fake being slain in the spirit."

"What is the baptism of the Holy Spirit?"

"Those people who fall down when *Mor* prays for them? Supposedly it's the spirit of God that knocks them down, but *Mor* half pushes them down. I've had her do it to me. She raises your hands in the air so you can't control your balance, and then she lays her hand on your forehead, and suddenly you're on your ass." She stops. "There's something to it, though, you know? *Gudinden*'s tapped into something. It's not all horseshit. In a lot of ways, the evangelicals are more like the Gnostics than other Christian sects. *Mor* can heal people, did you know that?"

"She heals people?"

"Sheep actually. Or so the sheep say. That's why Rune and I call her *Gudinden*." Susanne takes hold of my shoulders, seats me on the bed. She grabs a brush from near the sink and manages to yank it through my hair. "It's to tease her, for sure. But we sort of mean it."

"The first day I was here, you mentioned her keeping a stash of something. . . ."

"Don't get me wrong about Mor. Just because I think she may be onto something doesn't mean she's not a hypocrite, and full of shit to a large degree. Evangelicals may be closer to Gnostics, but that's not saying much. Christianity as it's practiced today doesn't have a leg up on any other faith—although it sure does piss on every other faith, doesn't it? Christ wasn't *Christian*, for Christ's sake. Christ has a hell of a lot more in common with pagan gods than he does with what the modern Christians suggest he stands for. I mean, look at Dionysus, Mithra, Adonis, Attis. Christ is just another in a long line of gods."

Solomon's Seal

2007

—Cross-examination?

—Yes. Dr. Lennart, you know of no evidence linking Aslaug Hellig to the bloodroot you found on Susanne Lerner's body, correct?

—No.

—Regardless, the bloodroot didn't kill or otherwise harm Susanne Lerner, did it?

—No, bloodroot's not poisonous when used as a dye—

—Thank you. You found Aslaug also tested positive for atropine and scopolamine, isn't that right?

—Yes.

—It's your belief, then, that Aslaug also ingested jimsonweed, correct?

—Yes.

—You're a medical examiner—meaning you usually work on corpses. But you know that Aslaug tested positive for jimsonweed because you asked that a toxicology screen be run on her, right?

—Yes.

—And you asked that the screen be run because you thought it would show Aslaug had *not* consumed jimsonweed, right?

—Objection. Argumentative.

—Overruled.

—I thought her test would come back negative.

—So you were surprised when you received the positive result?

—Objection. Relevance. Argumentative.

—Overruled. Please answer.

—Yes.

—And you were surprised because the test indicates Aslaug didn't poison anyone—that she herself was poisoned—isn't that right?

—Objection. Argumentative. Calls for speculation.

—Sustained. Move on, Counsel.

—Dr. Lennart, is it your professional opinion that Aslaug was also poisoned?

—Objection. Speculation.

—I'll allow it.

—She may have taken the jimsonweed herself.

—Just like Maren Hellig. And the two women in the fire. They all may have taken the jimsonweed because they *wanted* to take it.

—Objection. Argumentative.

—Sustained.

—I have no further questions.

FALSE NETTLE

2003

"Dionysus was a god-man," Susanne says. "He was worshiped in Greece six centuries before Christ. His mother was a mortal—and a virgin. Semele. His father was the god Zeus. He was born around the time of the winter solstice. Late December. Many of the stories about him describe him sleeping in a manger after his birth. As an adult, he was a teacher who performed miracles. He encouraged his followers to liberate themselves from society's rules and promised them new life. Sound familiar?"

"It's the story of Jesus, with a different virgin, a different God." I hear stirring above me—the muffled footsteps, the muffled voices, the occasional twang of Rune's guitar. The congregation is arriving; the service is about to start. I expect the preacher wonders where we are, but Susanne no longer seems concerned about the service, or the preacher.

"Or maybe the story of Jesus is the story of Dionysus?" she says. "With a different virgin, a different God? Ever heard of the wedding feast at Cana? When Jesus made water into wine?"

"I read it in one of the Gospels," I say. "John?" The preacher's voice is audible now, in spurts. Not her words, just the lilt. She's greeting people, I think; we need to head up there.

But Susanne seems to be settling in. "Well, Jesus wasn't the first to perform this miracle. Dionysus did it long before Christ supposedly did. At a celebration in Sidon. But that's the least of it. Dionysus also rose from the dead and was called the 'Only Begotten Son,' 'King of Kings,' 'Alpha and Omega,' and 'Savior.' Names all later attributed to Christ. And Dionysus was associated with the ram and the lamb, before Christ."

Susanne's left foot taps the stone, along with the beat from above. She hears it, too, I think. The music. She knows we're late.

"Maybe it's just a coincidence," I say.

"And maybe I'm Mother Teresa."

"Who?"

"It's no coincidence, Aslaug," she says. "Because Attis was also a god-man, worshiped in Asia Minor two hundred years before Christ. He also was born in late December, and his mother also was a virgin. Nana. His followers ate bread that supposedly symbolized his body. He's been described as a 'savior sacrificed for the sake of mankind.' Coincidence? He was crucified and traveled deep into the so-called underworld. Hell? After three days—three days—he rose again. Followers referred to him as the Divine Son and the Father."

222

"Like Jesus," I say. I stand, walk to the door, grip the handle.

"And there's more." Susanne makes no move to follow me. "Mithra was a god-man, too. Worshiped in Persia during the first century before Christ. He also was born of a virgin—big surprise?—at the end of December. He was visited by gift-toting shepherds shortly after his birth. Remember the shepherds and wise men in the Christ story? Mithra had twelve confidants. Twelve disciples? He promised his followers immortality and performed miracles. *Three days after being buried in a tomb, he rose from the dead.* His followers celebrated his resurrection, and they also ate a sacred meal of bread and water and drank a wine they believed possessed miraculous power. Just like Jesus, he was referred to as 'Messiah,' 'Good Shepherd' and 'the Way, the Truth and the Light.' He was associated with the lamb and lion, like Christ."

Suddenly I realize what she's saying, realize what it means; I'd been only partially paying attention before, distracted first by my body, then by the noise from above. But Western civilization revolves around the Jesus story; even I know this. I let go of the handle. "And Adonis?" I say. "You mentioned Adonis earlier. What about him?"

"A god-man, of course," she says. "From Syria. Born of the virgin Myrrh. His devotees celebrated him by referring to the dawning of the 'Star of Salvation' in the east. Even the star of the east wasn't new. Adonis was crucified and was resurrected, also on the third day. Witnesses watched his ascent to heaven. He was associated with the symbol of the fish—a symbol *Mor* is convinced uniquely represents Christ."

223

"If that's all true, why don't people know? I mean, if Mother could figure it out—"

"People did know. In fact, during the first few hundred years after Christ's birth, even followers of Christianity wrote about the similarities between pagan faiths and Christianity. Some tried to explain away the similarities by claiming the devil had anticipated the story of Jesus and mimicked it, before Jesus was born—if you can believe that."

"But what about now? If people knew of the similarities before, why not now?"

"Some people do know. It's not just Maren. But the early Roman church destroyed a lot of pagan writings. The masses could more easily be united under one all-encompassing faith, et cetera."

"So what does it all mean? That the stories of Jesus and the others all are just myths?"

"That's one way to look at it. But I think it's more complicated. I think there's something to these stories. The stories all involve virgin births, right? And there are other, similar stories as well. For instance, Aion's mother was the virgin Kore. Maybe the virgin birth is God's way of showing the world whom He has chosen to be the next prophet."

"But aren't some of those gods just that, gods? Not people."

"Maybe. Or maybe they were actual people, like Jesus, and the stories about them turned them into gods. Like Jesus."

"But what does any of this have to do with the Essenes or the Gnostics or the mystery religions you spoke about?"

"Like I said before, Maren believed that the Essenes and Gnostics and pagans recognized the wisdom in other faiths—that they studied other faiths. Modern Christianity scoffs at other faiths. Maybe it's time for someone to set the record straight."

"You're talking about a person?"

"According to Maren, the Essenes believed in 'consecrated human beings.' People they believed God chose to be 'custodians of the divine on earth.' That's who Maren believed Jesus was. And Dionysus and Attis . . ."

I've been drawn in by Susanne's ideas. The picture I saw of Mikkel, we look nothing alike, he and I. And the syndactyly, I have no trace of it. At times I'm convinced Mikkel's not my father. But then I question myself: I don't want him to be my father, and that desire is a film that distorts what I see—I know this.

"These god-men," Susanne says, "many of them didn't begin their ministries until they were in their thirties. You're still in your teens. You have time. I think that's why God sent you back to us. God wants us to work with you. Study with you, prepare you."

You're kidding, I think. You've got to be kidding. You're supposed to prepare me to be a prophet? Like one of these god-men you described?

"Until you showed up," Susanne says, "I thought maybe God had chosen me. I started looking through Maren's books and folders and notes, and I thought God had directed me to them. That I was supposed to be this 'custodian of the divine.' But now that you're here, well, it's got to be you, right? Yours was the virgin birth."

I feel like I should want to laugh, but I don't want to. "So you believe in a God who intervenes in our lives? Who sends prophets to earth?"

"It's hard not to. Look around. Look at *Mor*. It's harder

for me not to believe. But that doesn't mean I believe in the Judeo-Christian God. Like I said, Socrates and Plato and Pythagoras all believed in God long before Jesus showed up, and their God was not the Jewish God. When Jesus supposedly started preaching some revolutionary spirituality, all he was really doing was meshing the values of pagan mythology with Judaism."

"Mother taught me science," I say. "Not theology. I'm not sure she would have believed any of this." And she wore black most every day, I think. Not white like the Essenes— like when she lived here.

Susanne takes one more drag on the sloppy stub of cigarette. "The great pagan philosophers, like Pythagoras and Socrates, didn't separate science from God. They believed the natural world was a reflection of God. In trying to understand science, maybe Maren was trying to understand God, trying to understand what happened to her. She kept looking, that's clear. She kept searching."

False nettle has no stinging hairs. It looks like stinging nettle with its wide, flat leaves and berry-like clusters of moss green flowers. But if one were to touch the plant, or pull a stalk from the ground, no needle-like hairs would puncture the skin; there would be no burning, no irritation. For false nettle is a mimicker. It capitalizes on stinging nettle's reputation, warning animals not to touch or eat. It's a charlatan, this plant, as am I. For as I listen to this, I don't tell Susanne what I believe is true: I was not chosen by God. Although I don't know how I came to be, I expect it had little, if anything, to do with Susanne's theories. Perhaps I say nothing because I wish it were true, that my life were somehow blessed; perhaps because I need something to cling to, even if I know that something is false.

Or perhaps my silence is because of Rune.

"Hop to." I hear Rune's voice in the hall. "Hop to." He pounds on the door. "The herd is stampeding."

"I spoke to Mikkel, my dad," Susanne says, as if this has something to do with Rune, or the herd. Rune pounds again, then moos and neighs and whinnies. "I told him what *Mor* said about you. About him and Maren. He called *Mor* a vindictive bitch. Said she's full of shit."

SOLOMON'S SEAL

2007

—*Y*our Honor, I'd like to ask Dr. Lennart a few additional questions.

—You're permitted redirect, Counsel.

—Thank you, Your Honor. Dr. Lennart, you said Aslaug Hellig also tested positive for atropine and scopolamine. How much of these toxins did she have in her system compared to the two women who died?

—The toxicology screen indicated Ms. Hellig had less of both toxins in her bloodstream. Obviously, her levels were not fatal.

—Dr. Lennart, in your professional opinion, is it possible Aslaug Hellig poisoned the two women, then took a much smaller amount of jimsonweed herself in order to deflect attention from herself?

—Objection. Leading and argumentative. And calls for speculation.

—Sustained.

—Dr. Lennart, do you have any way of knowing whether Aslaug Hellig voluntarily took the jimsonweed or whether it was given to her without her knowledge?

—No.

—So she could have taken it voluntarily?

—Yes.

—Thank you. I have no further questions.

HERB OF GRACE

2003

When we enter the sanctuary, only ten people, or fewer, sit in the pews. I realize the music I heard was from a recording, not from Rune. We're not late; Susanne hasn't been missed.

Rune stands, now, like a prop beneath the projector screen, near a vase of blue vervain. Mother called the vervain *herba sancta*, meaning "sacred herb" or "herb of grace." Rune bends toward the vervain and smells it, but *herba sancta* has no smell. Its spiking plum-hued flowers are beautiful, but scentless—although they taste bitter, astringent. Mother made me eat the vervain for headaches and fever. And once when I was bitten by a snake in the woods, she sucked out the wound, then tied a stalk of blue vervain around my neck, like a charm.

Mother herself took the vervain for everything, it

seemed, from bladder infections to stomach discomfort to pain in her bowels—even to calm the twitch of her eye. She'd take it as a poultice and it would flush her cheeks a splotchy red, like she'd tried to apply blusher but layered too much, missed patches. She called it *herba sancta*, she said, because it was her herb of grace, a cure-all.

I was fascinated by the vervain as a child because Mother seemed in awe of it. I remember the evening after she'd wrapped the vervain around me, to charm me. I scoured her botany books during the hour she bathed. And I found what Mother didn't tell me: that, by legend, *herba sancta* was first discovered on the Mount of Calvary, where it staunched the crucified Christ's wounds; that priests used it for sacrifices, and sorcerers used it for all sorts of incantations. And that, to some, the herb is named *herba veneris*, referring to the goddess Venus: it's an aphrodisiac, the vervain. I remember this fact as my eyes travel the arch of Rune's shoulders, his slender neck. And I feel the vervain staining my cheeks.

I look away, at the preacher, and I see her smile is colossal today, but easy, too; she seems in genuine enjoyment, still standing at the entrance, still welcoming. She wears her hair loose, unlike in my mind, and it makes her look younger. She is dressed in the suit jacket and flowing skirt, but her pale lips are brightened. She hugs and kisses and pats, and the parishioners reciprocate. Some whisper through her hair—which seems Mother's hair—into her veiled ear. Children pull at her skirt, and she envelops them before they squeal and run.

Susanne walks onto the stage and approaches the boy who controls the projector. I sit near them, in a corner of the first pew, where the preacher directed me, and I hear Susanne refer to the boy as Hagen, and I hear the edge in her voice despite the rumble of other voices around me. And then the angel girl—Rebekka—joins them. She bends her slight body nearer the boy's—she doesn't look pregnant, I think—and strands of her hair twist onto the projector and are magnified like snakes on the screen. The boy laughs, points to the snakes, and Rebekka sees and slithers them. Then Susanne tousles the boy's persimmon-hued hair, making it stand erect. He glowers at Susanne, but Rebekka shakes her head, whispers in his ear; the boy shrugs, nods.

They settle into place then—Susanne and Rebekka and the boy. Susanne moves to the circle of drums, the boy adjusts his seat below the now-snake-free screen. And Rebekka deposits herself at center stage. She shakes her head and enlivens the snake-strands that rise up, then fall to her shoulders and over her breasts.

Rune tugs free his glasses, swipes his eyes, and when he replaces the glasses, his eyes are focused on Rebekka, or just beyond her. Rebekka turns to him, as if she feels his gaze, and nods. Then she nods to Susanne. And the words slide up on the screen.

The music assaults the room. The preacher bounces down the aisle; her skirt flounces; the tambourine rattles not quite to the beat. The children stand motionless, on the pews or floor, or they hang from mothers' hips, their mouths wide but silent. But the adults move, and I feel myself moving. The music liberates my body, it seems; paralyzes my mind.

Rune, Rebekka and Susanne are a triangle, aware of each other, affected by each other. When Rebekka's voice dips,

232

Rune softens his touch, or hardens it, depending. I can see Susanne thinking, adjusting; her hands quicken or slow or change direction. I feel a yearning inside of me, a desire to be part of their web.

Rebekka launches a new song; Hagen scrambles, slides the words. People from the congregation join the preacher near the stage now; they jiggle their bodies in ways they do and don't intend. The woman in army fatigues is back, still in fatigues, without the purple flag. Her hips pulsate, and her shoulders counter-pulsate, and her head does something in between. The preacher approaches her, embraces her, and the woman starts to laugh, and her laughter swells. And soon the preacher laughs, then the children laugh, and I find myself laughing, although I'm not sure why.

"Praise Jesus," the preacher says when the song ends; she wipes tears from her eyes. "Oh yes," she says. "Praise Jesus. Do you know what just happened here? We were all a little drunk in the spirit. Acts, chapter two, says on the day of Pentecost, God so filled the people with the Holy Ghost, they were thought to be drunk. Amen?"

"Amen, sister. Amen."

"We don't need wine," the preacher says. "We have the holy wine. We have the spirit."

"Oh yes, sister. Amen."

Elderberry wine, I think. That's what I feel like right now, like it's dousing my veins, my brain. I'm glad for this. My brain felt distended with all Susanne told me; it feels good to let it slip free.

"You had a healing, sister?" the preacher says to the woman in army fatigues.

"Praise God," the woman says. "Oh, glory be to God."

"What was it, sister?" the preacher says. "How were you healed?"

"My tooth was aching so much—I couldn't bear it," the woman says. "But when you touched me, Pastor, the pain just washed away." And now she weeps, this woman. And others weep. And then they sing again, and dance again. The singing goes on and on, and the dancing, too. And when the music slows and the congregation sways in rhythm, I realize well over an hour has passed. The song service ends, and Rune yanks the guitar strap over his head; Susanne circles back around the drums. They walk with Rebekka offstage, then past me to the rear pew, and I feel exposed suddenly—although I've been sitting in this pew, alone, from the start.

"Good morning," the preacher says. "Thank you for coming today. God is happy you're here. Praise God. I have a special announcement." I remember Susanne's forewarning. "For all of you who couldn't be here on Wednesday night, we are blessed to have my niece visiting. Would you stand, Aslaug?"

I feel my legs sweating against the cotton of my dress; I worry the dress will cling to my legs when I stand. So I wave up and down fast.

"Thank you, Aslaug," the preacher says, but she doesn't elaborate, embellish the situation in some self-aggrandizing way, as Susanne intimated she would.

The preacher then discusses what she calls administrative matters, and I find myself thinking of Rune. He can barely read, but he makes me think, like Mother did, and yet not like Mother at all. Mother roused me with her abundance, her knowledge; Rune strips away, finds the core.

"Now," the preacher says, "the Holy Spirit is moving me to talk about the difference between the soul and the spirit. Amen?"

"Amen, Pastor."

I'm aware, suddenly, of the preacher's God-pearl eyes.

"The soul comprises the mind, the will and the emotions," she says. "Amen? But when the Holy Spirit fills you, God's not filling your soul. When we receive the baptism in the Holy Ghost, we don't experience the baptism in our minds. Amen? And it's not about our will. It's not even about our emotions, although it sure feels good."

I feel Susanne in my head critiquing the preacher's words, mocking her. I push the voice from my mind—as I'm learning to do with Mother's voice.

"When God bathes us in His Holy Spirit, it's our spirit that gets filled up. Amen?" the preacher says. "Our spirit is that void in all of us. That hollow space that can only be filled up with God's Spirit. Now, that void is in all of us, but it's different in each and every one of us, because even though we are each made in the image and likeness of God, we are individuals. We are individual incarnations of God, each one of us a fingerprint of God."

Unless you're me, I think. I'm a fingerprint of Mother. But then I stop myself. I remember seeing my face this morning, all shining and fresh as dew. Maybe she's right. Maybe everybody feels an emptiness, a void. Until they get filled up. Maybe I'm starting to get filled up.

"But we have to be careful," the preacher says. "We have to let the right spirit fill us. There is darkness in this world, don't be fooled. We all have to make a choice whether to let in the light or to fill up with darkness. When God falls on you, fills you, His is an enabling presence. It may knock you off your feet, but when you get back up, the Holy Spirit will have nourished you, refreshed you. But the darkness, it is provocative. There's no question about that. It can seem so appealing. And when it fills you, it may feel so good. But it will leave you hungry. It will leave you so hungry.

"So, people," the preacher says, "are you hungry? We all get hungry at times, because there is a void there, in all of us. We need to keep that void filled up with the *Holy Spirit.* Amen?"

A piano sits to the left of the stage, and Rebekka, the angel, sits there now; her fingers fondle the keys. People in the pews stand, move forward, flow toward the stage. I feel myself join the river. The preacher meets me, lifts my hands in the air; I sense the thick moisture of the anointing oil, and the flat coolness of the preacher's palm on my brow.

It would be so much easier to lie down, I think. I'd just like to lie down.

Solomon's Seal

2007

—Please state your name.

—Detective Gar Hoder.

—Where do you work, Detective?

—For the Bethan Police Department.

—Have you ever met the defendant, Aslaug Hellig?

—I arrested her last year.

—Please describe the circumstances of her arrest.

—Well, we got the call about the fire at the old monastery on Kettil Street, and when we arrived, she was just standing there in the yard, watching the building burn down. I thought at first she was a neighbor, somebody not involved. Normally people are screaming bloody murder if they have loved ones inside. But she was just watching it all. She didn't even tell anyone there were people inside. We figured that out on our own.

—How?

—We went in. But it was too late. The two women were dead.

—Okay. Then what happened?

—Well, the defendant stood and watched us remove the bodies. We'd placed them on stretchers and were bringing them out, putting them in the ambulance. Anyway, she started going ballistic at that point. One of the officers restrained her.

—When you say "going ballistic," what do you mean exactly?

—It was almost like she didn't want us to take them away. She was screaming at us to stop. She gave me a good lash on my face with her nails.

—Okay, and then?

—We tried to calm her down, talk to her. But she wouldn't answer any questions. It was obvious enough she was connected to the fire in some way, though. I felt we had probable cause to search her. So I told my officers to do it— search her. But she was like a wild animal. She got away.

—What do you mean, "she got away"?

—She took off running. We lost her.

—And then what happened?

—We ended up picking her up later. She came back to the church, tried to get inside. Said someone in the church had taken her money. We arrested her.

—And then?

—We had her examined by a doctor, to make sure she hadn't been hurt in the fire. She wasn't cooperative.

—Had she been hurt?

—She had some bruises and small burns. Nothing much to speak of.

—What, if anything, else happened?

—Well, we tried to question her again, and she started telling this cockamamy story about a virgin birth. I don't remember exactly all she said. It was clear, though, she wasn't right in the head.

—Objection. Move to strike. Speculation.

—Sustained. Strike everything following his statement that he tried to question the defendant.

—Okay. Then what?

—The pathologist said we should do a tox screen on her, so I ordered that done. We got a search warrant. She fought tooth and nail when they were trying to get her blood. They had to strap her down. After that we didn't even try to talk to her. It was two days or so, I'd say, before she calmed down. By that time we'd charged her. We'd found the fire was arson, and we'd learned the women died of poison. There weren't any other suspects. But we never really got to question her after that. She was assigned an attorney. You know the drill.

Amphicarpaea

Seed at Both Ends

2003

The genus name for the hog peanut plant is *Amphicarpaea*, meaning "seed at both ends." The hog peanut's butterfly-shaped flowers are common in woodlands, its white-purple blossoms easily discovered by pilfering insects able to transfer the pollen from hog peanut to hog peanut. Yet along the lower, creeping branches of the vine hang additional flowers, strange flowers—flowers without petals. Flowers with no need to entice hungry insects: they are self-sufficient, these flowers, able to self-fertilize. Mother explained this to me as we gathered the plant's underground fruit to boil and eat.

"But why does the plant bother with cross-pollination," I'd asked her, "if the lower flowers can fertilize themselves?"

"Inbreeding produces degenerate offspring, Aslaug Datter," Mother had said. "Why would the hog peanut rely on inbreeding alone?"

I think back on that conversation now as I sit in Mother's vault watching Rune across the nave. I've told myself my feelings for Rune are not inappropriate—that I'm drawn to him because of our shared history, because I share history with almost no one. But then I look at him and the hog peanut grows in my mind. I'm just confused, I tell myself. I've never been around boys, men. Humans are animals, too. I know what it means to enter puberty—I've read of it in physiology books. My body is changing; there are hormones. It's all natural. It doesn't mean my spirit is filling with darkness.

The Sunday morning service is over, and the evening one, too. And although Susanne would ridicule me if she knew, I enjoyed the services. I woke up at the morning service in a prairie of bodies, the red modesty cloth riding my thighs. Although I'm not sure whether I lay down or whether I was "slain in the spirit," as Susanne would say, I felt refreshed. I felt good.

Rune is writing now; I wonder what. Knowing he has difficulty reading, I'm not surprised to see he scribbles, scratches, scribbles. His hand rests as his eyes traverse the page. Then he scratches and scratches again, until it seems little legible could remain. His glasses slip down his nose; he nudges them up, fingers the cleft in his chin.

The telephone rings. At first I'm not sure what it is, then I remember, and I think, How odd people choose to let the outside world enter their private world so shrilly, and without invitation. I expect Rune to stop working, stop the ringing, as I've seen him and Susanne and the preacher do: scramble to the receiver with what seems urgency, lift

241

it, welcome the world. But he doesn't seem to hear the call. The phone rings again. Where is Susanne? I think. Where is the preacher? I look down at the work spread before me: Susanne asked that I translate the Gospel of the Holy Twelve, the Essene Gospels of Peace, the Sophia of Jesus and the Book of Enoch. But I can't think with the ringing. The phone has rung nine times, ten times, eleven, twelve. I stand and walk toward the noise. Toward the door hiding the phone, not the noise. And I open the door to a closet of sorts. The phone booth, Susanne calls it. There is nothing inside but a crammed-in desk and a squarish black phone. I lay my hand on the receiver: What do I say? But the ringing stops. Still, I lift it, imagine my words passing in, and through. I unscrew the microphone and find two thin metal plates. I know carbon granules lie compressed between the plates, and I imagine the sound waves of my voice compressing and decompressing those granules.

"I feel obliged to make you aware, young miss, that you have an audience."

I turn. I see Rune. He stands just feet away. His long fingers are folded together; a clump of hair sticks behind one lens.

"The phone rang," I say. I hold the receiver in my right hand, the microphone cap in my left. I feel hot, bright. I try to screw the cap back on, but the threads won't align.

"I take it you didn't like what the caller had to say?" He lays his hands over mine, over the cap, the receiver. I know he's teasing—I've heard him tease Susanne this way. And yet he's not smiling. And his eyes rummage mine.

242

I slip my hands away, leave the receiver and cap in his hands.

"I just wanted to look inside," I say. "See how it works."

"How does it work?" He exposes the inner microphone. "Show me, and I'll keep this little tryst to myself."

And so I do, and I feel myself relax: this is a world I know. No men with exposed midriffs. No preachers with extraordinary powers. No divine incarnations of anything.

"Come with me," he says when I've finished explaining and screwed back on the cap. "I may not have any idea what you just said, but I do have some talents."

I walk with him across the nave, over to the table where he'd been working. "Mor and Sanne aren't here," he says, although I didn't ask. "They went to pick up a few things. For Wednesday night. There's a dedication then, for one of those babies who were wailing at the end of this morning's service. But you wouldn't remember that, would you? You were otherwise engaged."

I feel my skin again brighten.

"Don't be embarrassed," he says. "Mor's a force. She could mow over just about anyone." He reaches up and takes my hand in one of his hands, my forearm in his other, and he leads me to sit with him. There's a large piece of paper on the table before him, but it's blank. "What were you working on over there?" he says. He gestures toward Mother's vault.

"Some translations for Sanne. She really thinks it's possible I was born of a virgin birth. . . ." But as soon as I say this, I wish I hadn't: it sounds absurd.

"She's toying with you, Aslaug."

"No, really . . . ," I say. But then I wonder, Is she toying with me?

Rune still holds my hand, his skin warming. He looks into my eyes, his face so close I can feel his breath. Gold paint speckles his dark hair; he smells metallic. "You're shaking," he says; there's no teasing in his voice now. "Are you cold?"

I'd like to lie, but I shake my head.

"Who are you?" he says.

"Who's my father?" I think he believes somehow I know.

"God, Aslaug. You and Sanne have one-track minds. I was talking about you. I don't care who your father is any more than I care who mine is." But then he stops, reconsidering his words, it seems. Realizing that we may be talking about Mikkel either way.

"But you know who your father is," I say. "It's different."

"Is it? I mean, I know my father's name. That he cheated on my mother—"

"Maybe he didn't."

"He did," Rune says. "Mikkel had had more than one affair, long before Maren entered the picture. That's why their marriage was falling apart."

"But Sara said their marriage was difficult because they didn't share the same faith—"

"Classic chicken and egg. The faith issue became important because of Mikkel's infidelity. It didn't precede it."

"How do you know this?"

He shrugs. "Mikkel said he wanted to explain what happened between him and *Mor* 'man to man.' Give me a *fucking* break."

Mother was not averse to cussing. I'd looked *fuck* up in the dictionary years ago. When Sanne uses the word, it seems meant to shock, but I don't feel shocked by her; I'm used to Mother. But I do feel some shock now. "So you do think Mikkel is my father."

"I didn't say that," he says. "Christ."

"But you think he is."

"No. I don't. You don't look like him, all right? And you don't have syndactyly. But I don't think you were born of a virgin birth either, okay?" He takes his hand from my hand, cups my face like it's water in a creek. "Aslaug," he says, "it doesn't matter who fathered you. You are who you are. Quit wasting your life with this crap."

"It's not that easy," I say. But maybe it is that easy.

"Why isn't it?" He releases my face, lets his hands drop away. "Are you going to change who you are, how you act, what you do with your life, because of who your father is?"

"It's not that. I just want to have a context. I want to understand how I fit into the world—"

"But your context may become your prison."

"What does that mean?"

He cups his own face now. "I don't know what it means," he says. "I guess I feel I know what my limitations are, you know. These clinicians when I was a child describing what I was, what I wasn't, what I'd never be. I was just six when *Mor* took me out of school because of my so-called challenges. At six I was boxed in. Or out, as the case may be. And then knowing about Mikkel, what he is. Sometimes I see him in me, and then I'm sure I'm going to be just like him. Like I know my fate. And then there's *Mor*. . . .

245

"You know, Aslaug," he says then, "when we were growing up, Sanne and I used to talk about you in secret. I wasn't even sure you were real. I thought I remembered you, but maybe I just created the memories of you from Sanne's stories. But when Sanne read me that article about you, and then when you arrived, it was like this mythical goddess came to life." His fingers roam his mole, the frame of his glasses, the hollow of his neck. "Sanne would never admit it, but you stole her limelight. Before you came, she focused on the idea of you, and it was her thing. It was her way of being provocative. But now that you're here, well, it's the real thing that's provocative."

"I'm just Sanne's toy, remember? Nothing much provocative about that."

"Actually, you're my toy," he says, and he smiles, and his upper lip is gone. "Kidding. But honestly, about Sanne, she was always the perfect child. She was always what I wanted to be. So smart. No issues. And then she went ahead and created issues. God knows why. I swear, she spent hours and hours on the streets in Bethan studying the ragamuffins so she could mimic them. Then, when she got bored with that, she started in on Maren and you. I was relieved in a way. Her shenanigans took the spotlight off me. But now the spotlight is on you, and I don't think Sanne likes it. She wants to feel she's unique. Special. Not just part of the masses. It's not that *Mor* doesn't love her, it's just that *Mor* loves everyone. I think Sanne felt rejected by Mikkel, even though it's *Mor* who left Denmark. And then *Mor* took on a whole new family by starting this church."

"Sanne is special to Sara," I say. "You both are. It's

obvious." And I think of my mother. I was Aslaug Datter, my mother's daughter. I was special to her. But now I'm a ploy. A means to an end.

"What's obvious to me—and Sanne, too—is *Mor*'s interest in problems. My problems in particular. And how my problems reflect her failings. I mean, I love *Mor*. And I know she loves me. But she feels a lot of guilt about me. She feels responsible. It's hard to love someone who makes you feel so guilty. The people in the church, she has no baggage with them. They need her, and they're easier for her to love. I'd like for once to feel love without the guilt."

"Why does Sara feel so responsible? So guilty about you?"

"Because she is responsible, at some level. But that's another issue."

"It was hard for my mother to love me, too," I say. "I don't know why. I felt I failed her, a lot. But I also felt I'd fail her no matter what. Like I was tainted, you know."

"Yes, I know. The tainted seed. We're both tainted seeds. What was she like, though, your mother? What was Hartswell like?" He pauses, then says, "I already know everything about you, though, of course. Sanne filled me in." And he laughs.

So I tell him. I tell him of Mother and our house. I tell him of the area where we lived, where the flowers bloom like living jewels and the fog hangs heavy. I tell him of the nights, so close to here, and yet there the sky stretches to the oblivion in layers and layers of stars that can't live here. I tell him of the smells: of freshly baked bread and Mother's tea and pollen. And I realize I miss my home.

"Was she good to you?" he says.

"My mother?" I don't know how to answer this question. She was my mother; I was her Aslaug.

"I wanted to show you something, remember?" he says. He flips the paper spread before him. It's a drawing of me. "What do you think?"

I try to smile; I try to say, "I didn't know I had an audience." But I can't; I'm not sure what I feel.

"You don't like it," he says.

"No," I say. "I do." The picture shows me as I was an hour earlier, a book open before me, my hair loose around my face, a background of stained glass and dark wood. "I'm just surprised. I thought you were writing. I didn't even know you'd seen me there."

He stands, takes my hand again. "Come with me," he says.

Together we walk down the stairs that lead to the underbelly of the church, where the narrow bedrooms spread from the hall like insect legs. I've never seen inside Rune's room, although I've known where it is. The doors to each bedroom are short and rounded at the top, the tiny windows swing open and closed, and Rune's is closed and covered with dark cloth. He unlocks the door. I'm surprised by this, surprised it would be locked. We step inside. There are no windows to the outside in his room either, and the room is dark. He turns on the light.

Paintings and drawings of me hang everywhere. On the walls, the interior of the door, the foot of his bed. Pictures of me talking, reading, eating, writing, sleeping. They are beautiful, the paintings. Strange and beautiful. Like the purple passionflower—the crown-of-thorns flower. Bizarre; perfect.

My body is my body, and yet, how do I know? I'm both exaggerated and understated. And my face: I see myself in these pictures as I feel myself, not as I've seen myself. He's captured something in me I thought was mine only.

"I don't understand," I say. I'd grown up never seeing my face, wanting to see my face. Now I want to run from it, from them. I spent my childhood alone, unobserved except by Mother, and Grumset. It seems wrong someone could study me like this, capture me without my knowing. And yet, I'm touched. And relieved in a way: he feels something, too.

"Rune?" I hear Sanne call down the stairs. "Are you down here?"

"Coming," he calls. He lays his hands on my arms, turns me toward him. "I don't understand either," he says, then his arms slip from my arms to my ribs and he tickles me. I laugh, even though I don't feel like laughing. He stops the tickling; I see he's not laughing. "But they're good, don't you think? It's the first time in my life I actually feel good at something."

"Rune," Sanne calls again. "Where's Aslaug?"

"Resting," he says, and he nods toward my room. "She's not feeling well."

I step into the hall.

"Feel better," he says, and now he smiles.

I walk down the hall and into my room.

"Aslaug," he says. And I turn back. "Sanne and *Mor* don't know about this—the pictures, I mean."

I look into his eyes; I try to understand. Then I close my door.

* * *

As I climb into bed, the rigid springs of the mattress come alive; they squeal and moan, as if I'd sprawled atop Mother's aching hips or cancer-laden spine. The noise seems more pronounced on this night, more jarring. And the stiff knobs of old springs seem to have proliferated during the day. Finding a comfortable place to settle in, fall asleep, proves difficult. But I want sleep. I want some reprieve from what just happened with Rune; I want some reprieve from my mind.

Yet I lie here for what seems hours, and still I don't sleep. I slip from the bed, out of the room, into the bath, and I bathe. Then I return and lie down. The small bedroom is hot as usual. I turn on a light, open the Essene Gospel of Peace, and I read, until the preacher knocks on the door; I'd forgotten she'd be coming.

She inches open the door. "You're awake," she says, and she steps in. "Rune said you aren't well."

"I'm better."

"Hungry? I know you had no dinner. We ate late. You were resting. Sanne prepared this for you while I cleaned up." She hands me a tray of *rugbrød* with blue castello cheese, and a glass of homemade schnapps, as she's given me every night since I first came. "A Danish tradition," she told me that first night. In the short time I've lived with them, she's made me *aebleskiver* and *aeblekage* and *wienerbrød*. Mother made these dishes when I was a small child. Not often. And Mother made schnapps: she'd steep apple or dandelion or blackberry or elderberry in Danish aquavit, and sometimes she'd mix in some dried plant. But she never gave any to me. But Sara does each night. And twice she's sat with me, drunk with me, even though she says she doesn't

drink. That preachers don't drink. I find the schnapps relax-
ing and soporific. And the ritual of consuming the schnapps
feels soothing to me, nurturing. When Mother was alive, my
daily life was so predictable. Now little is: little but this
schnapps, and Sanne's white garb.

"Yes," I say. "I'm hungry. Thank you."

The telephone rings; I hear it through the ceiling.

"You're welcome, Aslaug. Sweet dreams. We'll start your
schooling at nine tomorrow, if you're feeling well enough."
The preacher plans to homeschool me, as she does Sanne
and Rune.

The ringing stops.

"Okay," I say, and I watch her walk out. "I'll be ready."
She shuts the door.

"*Mor?*" I hear Sanne's voice in the hall. "There's a call
for you. . . ."

I adjust the tray on my lap. The preacher is growing on
me, I think, as Sanne said she might. And I think of the
phrase "growing on me." I'd never heard it until Sanne said
it—I've never heard many of the phrases Sanne uses. But
this one I like. I'd like to think maybe I'm growing on the
preacher, too. I think it's possible I am, as if these services
today had a way of nourishing each of us with the other.
The way the church flutters to life when the preacher shakes
that tambourine. And her touch. When I walked to the
front of the church, felt her palm on my skin, I think
she could see there was more than a trickle in my spirit. Because I got it—I felt it—my spirit. And despite what Sanne
says, the preacher didn't push me. Although it felt like
something did.

I eat the cheese and bread quickly, almost without tasting it. Quaff the schnapps.

Then, as I've done many nights in this stale room, I strip off my nightgown before I lie back down. Although I've just bathed, I'm sweating, and the cotton fabric of the nightgown was clinging to my skin like it was blanketed there, like it was glue. I drop to the bed; the sensation of the worn sheets against my skin feels almost human.

Solomon's Seal

2007

—*A*re you going to cross-examine the witness, Counsel?

—Yes, Your Honor. Detective Hoder, you didn't find any evidence linking Ms. Hellig to the fire at 7 Kettil Street, did you?

—Other than she was standing there watching the place burn to the ground, watching those people burn up inside? Nope, not a thing.

—So you found no remnants on Aslaug's person of kerosene from those rags that started the fire, right?

—Nope. None.

—And you found no fibers from the kerosene-soaked rags on Aslaug's body either, right?

—Not a one.

—And nobody witnessed her starting the fire, correct?

—She was the only witness to the fire, as far as we know.

—So your answer is no?

—My answer is no.

—Thank you. Now, you said Aslaug was watching the building burn, not saying anything to anyone. Did it ever occur to you she may have been in shock?

—No.

—When she, in your words, "started going ballistic," did it ever occur to you she was overwhelmed by what was happening?

—She was pissed—excuse my French. That's different from being overwhelmed.

—That's your opinion, isn't it, Detective? You don't really know what Aslaug was feeling, do you?

—I know what I saw.

—But you don't know what Aslaug was feeling, do you?

—I agree I can't get inside the mind of that woman.

—A simple yes or no would be fine, Detective.

—My answer is no, I don't know what she was feeling.

—Thank you. Now, when you took her to the police station, you didn't tell her why the doctor was examining her, did you?

—I don't know what she was told.

—You didn't tell her why, isn't that right?

—I didn't tell her.

—And when you had the technician draw her blood, you didn't explain to her what was happening, did you? You just had the person head in there with the needle, isn't that right?

—I had a search warrant. I didn't need to get her permission.

—So your answer is that you didn't explain to her that the technician was going to draw her blood, right?

254

—Like I said, I don't know what she was told.

—But you didn't explain to her what was happening, did you?

—No.

—Detective, when you learned Aslaug tested positive for atropine and scopolamine, did it occur to you that maybe she was acting strangely because she'd been drugged?

—No.

—Why not?

—Some junior officers had just informed me about her prior arrest, about that situation with her mom—

—Objection, Your Honor. Move to strike. Nonresponsive. .

—Objection sustained.

—Detective, just so it's clear, you have absolutely no evidence linking Aslaug to the death of those two women or to the fire, other than the fact that she was at the scene, isn't that right?

—Given the circumstances, I'd say that may be enough.

—Objection. Move to strike. Speculation.

—Sustained.

—Please just answer the question with a yes or a no.

—No.

—Thank you, Detective. I have no further questions.

ASK AND EMBLA
2003

His lips and breath and tongue flood my neck, then trickle along the line of my jaw to the base of my ear, then in my ear, first swirling and then deep. Then deep and still. He is smelling me. I can hear the faint pull of his nostrils, my cleansed skin, my moist hair. Then he crushes my hair to his face, to his nose, to his mouth, and the pull of his breath is no longer faint. It is gulping my scent, holding it deep within, releasing it slowly, methodically, with reluctance. Then gulping again. And again and again and again. Then it doesn't release, and his mouth finds mine, and my scent becomes his breath in my mouth. And I forget who I am, what I am, and I don't care. The universe becomes his lips, his tongue, his teeth, and the weight of his body, and the tension in his body, and his scent.

He slips free the sheet that lies under him, over me, that presses into him, into me. His breath bursts into my mouth with

256

each tug. And with each tug his body becomes more than weight. It becomes skin and coarse hair and the undulating rigidity of muscle.

I remember myself only when his thighs press into mine, his torso pulls back from mine, and he collects me into his eyes. My face, my neck, my shoulders, my breasts, the plane of my stomach, my hairstreak. Then his fingers—the tips of his fingers—traverse the course of his eyes, gently, so gently, the sensation of funneled breeze. And I see I am beautiful and desirable and desired.

I try to reach for him, to bring him back to me, to give to him what he is giving to me, but I cannot move. Not my arms, my legs. So he falls to me, as if he understands.

Say yes, he says. Say yes.

And I do. Over and over. But he doesn't move, as if he's savoring my words. I again strain to move, but my limbs remain spread above and below like the wings of an angel of God. I call to him. Rune. Rune.

Aslaug. The name is muffled to my neck. Sweet Aslaug, dear Aslaug.

Then the pressure of him fills me, and I cry out, for I've never known—never imagined—this unity of bliss and pain. Then less pain, less pain. Then bliss. Only bliss. The tingling, quivering rhythm of bliss.

My sheets are cold and damp, below me and above me. And my skin and hair are wet. I've just woken, and for a moment, as I begin to climb from the sheets, my mind thinks of nothing but the moist chill of my body wrapped in the moist chill of the sheets. But then the dream slams into my brain. And I fall back to the sheets, back to the clinging discomfort of them, struck by the power of my mind.

I try to hold on to the dream—remember it. But I sense it slipping from me as if in mud; it seems little but an indentation of it will last.

The room is still dark. I explore the nightstand like braille for the paper and pen I know can hold the dream in a way I can't. But my arms, my hands and fingers, feel leaden. I flick the light switch, and the brightness blinds me more. I close my eyes: I feel I'm floating; I feel like laughing. I open my eyes again and now I see, but I see no paper, no pen.

I pull myself up—my body feels leaden, too—and I look down to the floor; I nearly plummet to the floor. The paper and pen lie there: the paper somewhat crumpled, the pen marring the stone. I collect them and lie back propped. I write; I try to record every memory. But how can I record what I experienced? The sensations of the dream seem otherworldly.

When I finish, I read the words I've written: the dream has all but faded, and my words seem to have been written by another. I read the piece twice, and then again, and each time I feel more confused. Is it normal to have such dreams? I know so little about sex. Mostly what I know I've derived from books. I understand biology, not passion.

Then I remember *The Scarlet Letter*. Maybe I was dreaming of Hester, and Dimmesdale. Not me. Not Rune.

I fold the paper until it's the size of a walnut and climb from the bed. I trip over nothing. Get up. I trip again before I find the old coat Sanne gave me; I zip the dream into the inner pocket. I know I must hide it from the preacher and Sanne. I know I must keep the dream from Rune.

In Norse mythology, the god Odin formed the first two humans from logs: the man from the log of an ash tree, the woman from the log of an elm. The man was called Ask, or "ash," and the woman Embla, or "elm." They lived in Midgard, in the middle of the great ash tree. Before this dream, I thought the Norse story was a beautiful one. I imagined the crevices of the dark bark stretching and curving, and forming; I imagined the woman emerging, her skin and hair the color of the elm. And the man, as the ash tree gave way, molding himself into limbs and shoulders and a torso, and a head and hair of ash. But now, the beauty of the story has faded some. The emerging woman seems lonely, to me, hollow; the man no longer seems strong and sturdy—having been born from the great ash—but fragile.

Something has shattered. I'm dressing and fumbling when I hear it. It slams, bursts, scatters. And then another slam, another burst, another scatter. The sound came from near, from one of the other bedrooms, I think. I lean against the bedroom door, peer out the window in the door, into the hall, down the hall.

At first I see only the hall's cold-stone floor, its cold-stone walls. And the closed doors that line it. But then I see the color of blood escape from the preacher's room, from under her door; it paints the pale crevices between the stones.

My hand is on the door's lever, but my breath is caught somewhere inside me. And I'm caught: I don't throw open the door; I don't burst into the hall; I don't launch into the preacher's bedroom to save her. I don't want to find my mother in the form of the preacher, but I do find her. I have found her, in my mind: I envision Mother on the hardwood floor in Hartswell, still folded into her package, still brittle beneath the hovering. But Mother has the preacher's face.

Or does the preacher have Mother's face? She's in the hall, suddenly, the preacher. But her face bulges red, like Mother in pain; and her eyes show red, like Mother's eyes steeped in madapple. But she's not bleeding, I think. She's not dead.

I watch the preacher lurch, halt, stagger, descend. And now I do throw open the door, I do burst into the hall, I do run to save her. But I slip, and I tumble onto her heap: she's warm, and her breasts rise and fall, and the trickling red has reached her; she wears the same clothes she wore the evening before, but they are creased with deep paths, and the red climbs one path.

"Sara?" I say, and I lift myself from her, sit on the stone beside her.

Her mouth falls open. She snores. The stench of sweet schnapps puffs with her breath. I realize the red on the floor is not blood: it's schnapps.

I remember seeing Mother inebriated, reeking with a new batch of elderberry wine, or schnapps. Her dry-ocean eyes would shine wet, and her pale skin would shine bright. And her rounded vowels would further round, her consonants would soften and blur. But Mother was still Mother: lording over, not lorded over.

I stand, leave the preacher on the floor and follow the trail of schnapps. The preacher's room is dark, but I see the broken bottles, the splinters of glass, the pool of schnapps. I see the unbroken bottles arranged about the room like pebbles tossed.

And I see Rune. He sits on the edge of the bed; he stares into the pool; his hands dance in a circle around one another.

"Rune?" I say, and he looks up, but without recognition, it seems.

Then suddenly there is recognition, and he springs from the bed into the schnapps pool. "She doesn't do this anymore. She did this because of me. Don't tell anyone, Aslaug. She'll lose her church. . . ." He also wears clothes from the day before, and his hair is a mess of coils and spikes.

"I'm not telling anyone . . . ," I say, but I don't understand. And I can't help but think of the dream of Rune, of how real it seemed, how real he seemed. Of how I wish he could hold me now.

And I can't help but think that I'd like to sit down. That I need to sit down. "She's out here, Rune," I say. "She fell."

"She fell?" He pushes past me, and the schnapps smears past me, and I catch myself on the frame of the door.

I watch as he cradles her head, as he dabs the drool with his sleeve. "I'm sorry, *Mor*," he says. "I'm so sorry." He lifts her chin, attempts to close her mouth, but it hangs again. His fingers explore the rays etched around her eyes and the wrinkles that slice the skin between her nose and lips. "She didn't sleep at all," he says. He's talking to me now—he must be. But he looks at the preacher's wide mouth and breathes the preacher's stale schnapps. "I heard her this morning. . . ." Then he does look at me. "My God," he says. "Oh my God."

"What?" I say. "What is it?" And I feel my backside slide, see the crook of my knees, feel the cold stone on my rear.

He looks at the doorway where I stood, not where I landed, not where I sit. And I realize there is a world here I'm not part of, where the laws are different, the meaning of words is different. And people are not what they seem.

The preacher opens her eyes, arranges her hands over her eyes.

"Come to bed, *Mor*," Rune says when he sees her stir. He lifts her like a root: his hands encase her torso, and he pulls her up, and straight. They walk together back through the schnapps tracks. Rune closes the door against me. And I'm left to the universe I think I know: where blood is blood and dreams are dreams.

And schnapps is schnapps. I sit here looking at the schnapps, knowing I should wipe up what I can. But I feel I can't stand. I'm sick, I think. Of course, I'm sick. How odd that Rune would pretend I'm sick and then I'd become sick. I feel like laughing. Again. But then I feel I'm going to get sick, and I do, onto the stone, into the schnapps. And I feel better. Better enough to gather rags, water. I mop what I can, wipe what I can, wash away what I can, but the stream of schnapps leads to the ocean of schnapps, and the ocean is beyond my reach, beyond the door. As are the glass shards that speckle the ocean, that speckle the room. As is Rune.

As was Rune.

He opens the door, sees me. "You were listening?" he says.

"No." I show him the rags, the pail. "I was cleaning up from the bottles. The broken bottles."

"The broken bottles are in *Mor*'s room," he says, and it feels a shard is embedding itself, prying us apart.

Sanne steps from her bedroom, her hands fists in her eyes. Then she stretches her lily arms high, and turns. She sees me squatting, Rune looming.

"*Mor*'s sick," Rune says.

"Is she . . . ?" Sanne looks from Rune to me and back. Her eyes speak a language I don't read.

"She got a call," Rune says. "She knows what I guess you already knew. I wish you would have told me."

"And I wish you would have told me," Sanne says.

"I didn't know," Rune says.

"You knew enough," Sanne says.

So the days pass, and the nights and the days, and my illness passes. But a coating covers the preacher and Rune. And Sanne, too. A kind of viscous weight that makes their days before seem frivolous, and too slick, too easy. I tiptoe around the stickiness, as life with Mother taught me: I pretend I didn't hear, didn't see, don't know even what I do know.

The preacher doesn't preach for a week, then two. And she doesn't begin my schooling. Rune avoids me, or this world, or himself; I'm not sure. He has a look that reminds me of Madapple Mother. There is a distance in his eyes, an awkwardness in his step. He seems transported, like Mother, to that other time and space: a time before me, a space without me. When our eyes meet, they don't meet; his pass through me, around me. I feel invisible to him.

Sanne does acknowledge me, but only to ask that I read and translate and translate and read. She doesn't speak of the preacher; she doesn't speak of Rune. She stares at the same page for an hour. She asks me to read the same book twice, and again. She forgets what I tell her. She forgets what she's doing. She forgets the day of the week.

And although I do read and translate, I forget, too: what I read, what I translate. I've also entered the fog. What's happened here? I wonder. What's changed? I can make no sense of this new world.

I walk into the kitchen now; it sits at the sanctuary's rear. The door swings open and closed and stirs the stench. I see the corroded dishes piled askew. And the tackiness that is everywhere. And bread with blue moss. I've barely eaten in days, but someone has, I see. And yet, maybe not. As I begin to clean, I see the piled dishes are piled with food. Someone had the idea to eat, it seems. Not the ability to eat. I pull out the garbage bin to scrape in the old food, and I see them.

I see me: Rune's pictures, his drawings.

I free one of them, try to salvage it. But my painted face is torn and muddied, my body creased and smeared.

Why did he do this? How could he do this, throw these away? He was so proud of them. And I feel a hurt that's deep. And strange. And I long for Mother, for Hartswell.

I leave the kitchen, the church. I walk into Bethan. It's the first time I've left the church since arriving, and I'm surprised by this now. Surprised it hadn't occurred to me to leave. I remember arriving here in the car, meeting the boy-man, losing my car. I remember the abundance of heat, the abundance of skin, the abundance of noise. And yet, I don't remember. I'm a different person now: a person with a place. I feel the Bethan air, see the Bethan skin, hear the Bethan noise, yet it doesn't seem any of these winds could just blow me away. As I walk back to the church, I long less for

Mother and Hartswell, more for the Rune who made me laugh. For the Sanne with zeal. For the preacher with the power to heal.

The preacher answers my prayer.

The day after my walk into Bethan, nearly three weeks after her fall, she resurfaces, and she's the eruption of spring, even though the weather has cooled and the leaves fall. She opens the church, preaches on the trials of Job, sings and laughs. And I feel my spirit lift again, and fill again. And when I see Sanne laugh, I have hope the preacher and Sanne and Rune have begun their journey from the parallel universe back to me.

Solomon's Seal

2007

—Please state your name for the record.

—Hagen Grass.

—How old are you, Hagen?

—Seventeen.

—You live in Bethan?

—Well, I did my whole life until three, four years ago. My sister got into some trouble, so we moved away. My sister stayed here, you know, with the church. But my parents and I moved away.

—What church are you referring to, Hagen?

—The Charisma Pentecostal Church.

—Do you know the defendant? The woman here, named Aslaug?

—She went to our church for a while. Before we moved.

—To the Charisma Church? The one that burned down?

—Yeah.

—How long did she attend the church?

—A couple of months.

—Did you get to know her during those months?

—Not really. She kind of gave me the creeps. She stared at everybody all the time.

—Objection. Move to strike. Relevance.

—Sustained.

—Hagen, I'm trying to establish how long Aslaug attended your church. You said she attended the church for a couple of months. Are you sure about this?

—Yeah. I remember Pastor Sara announcing Aslaug was visiting, you know. Aslaug was related to Pastor. And then a few months later, Pastor announced during church that Aslaug had moved back to wherever she'd come from. I remember it because my parents were talking about moving then. Like I said, my older sister had gotten into some trouble, and it was really hard on my parents. I remember wondering where Aslaug had moved to, you know, just because we were talking about moving, too.

—So you never saw her after that?

—No. Not until she got arrested. Then I saw pictures of her, you know, in the paper and stuff.

—Now, Hagen, you said you didn't get to know Aslaug well, but did you spend any time with her?

—Well, some. My sister, Rebekka, was good friends with Pastor's kids, so we all hung out some. And Rebekka, she tutored Pastor's son, Rune. I went with Rebekka when she tutored sometimes, when my parents were busy. But I was younger, you know, than all of them, so they didn't want me

267

around much. But I spent some time with them. Some time with Aslaug. I remember my sister telling me Aslaug was obsessed with Pastor's son, you know. With Rune. Like she really liked him. Rebekka said it was weird, because, you know, they're related.

—Objection. Hearsay. Relevance. Move to strike.

—Sustained.

—Hagen, you said earlier that your sister got into trouble and that's why you and your parents moved away. What kind of trouble?

—Objection. Relevance.

—Is this relevant, Counsel?

—It is, Your Honor, if you'll give me a minute.

—One minute, Counsel. Get to the point.

—Thank you, Your Honor. Go ahead and answer, Hagen.

—Well, she got pregnant, you know. Rebekka got pregnant, and she wasn't married. So she ended up staying at this home for pregnant girls for a while. And then Pastor Sara invited her to stay with them, in the church, you know. The church had been, like, a monastery, I guess. So it had bedrooms and a kitchen and stuff. Pastor and her kids lived there.

—Did your sister ever mention Aslaug to you when she was staying at the church, after you moved away?

—Objection. Hearsay.

—Overruled.

—No.

—She never told you Aslaug also was staying at the church then?

—Aslaug wasn't staying at the church then. She'd left by then.

—Objection. Move to strike. Hearsay. Speculation.

—Sustained.

—Hagen, do you have any reason to believe Aslaug was staying at the church during the period when your sister was staying there?

—No.

—Thank you. I have no further questions, Your Honor.

Golden Bough

2003

*T*ransparent clouds thread the sky, gray and cream, they stretch and cross. But beyond them, there are only more clouds, mountains of fleshy, cotton-filler white that seem to weigh against their gauzy cousins, and mock them.

This is a Hartswell afternoon; this sky, a Hartswell sky.

As I step onto the grass, the moisture seeps through my shoes. I kneel to the ground, collect a fistful of damp leaves, hold them to my nose.

It's been well over a month since my arrival at this church, and nearly that long since my dream of Rune, and since the preacher's fall, before the resurrection. Hartswell was fading away. But not today. Today the leaves' sweet-earth aroma transports me back to Hartswell, where Mother and I had worked beneath this sky, heaving mounds of wet leaves upon a coarse black tarp, which we dragged to the rear of the lot. Then we burned the leaves, charring their sweetness. That was years before Mother's illness crippled her. Before the cancer consumed her.

"It's supposed to snow. October snow. Only in Maine."

I hear Rune's voice; I touch my breast near where the folded dream still lies, and I feel it there, a small knot. I look up at him just before he tackles me in the leaves.

"Hey," I say, and I hear myself laugh, and I remember this gift Rune gave me. And I wonder, Is Rune back? Although the preacher is again the preacher and the flock has returned, and Sanne again fills my days with her version of Mother's mind, Rune has seemed caught, stretched between that other world and this one.

"Good morning," he says when we're both on our backs. He sits up and dribbles a handful of leaves on my head, in my face. "I love days like this. So cold your breath makes art in the air."

"How are you?" I say. The length of his body presses along the length of mine. This is the first time he's touched me since the day he showed me the portraits, the day before the dream; it's one of only a handful of times we've talked since then. We've moved around each other like strangers. And I've reminded myself to lessen the hurt: in many ways, we are strangers.

" 'There's a certain slant of light,' " he says, " 'winter afternoons, that oppresses, like the heft of cathedral tunes. Heavenly hurt, it gives us. We can find no scar, but internal difference, where the meanings are. None may teach it, any, 'tis the seal despair. An imperial affliction sent us of the air.' "

"Emily Dickinson?" I say.

271

Now he laughs, but it is a different laugh than I remember. "Yes," he says.

"You're still not okay," I say. "It's Sara? The drinking?"

"She's still drinking, yeah. But that's putting the cart before the horse. No, this is heavenly hurt. That slant of light. This is the sky." He takes my hand with his hand, tries to intertwine our fingers, but his webbed fingers set the twining off course. "You're not going to try to steal away, are you?"

"Steal away?" I say, but I'm thinking of the rough warmth of his callused hand, and the smell of paint from his clothes. Or his skin.

"I haven't scared you away, then?" he says. "I've been awful to you, I know. I've been an ass."

"You weren't awful," I say, but I think of the portraits. The garbage.

"You're a terrible liar." He points to the sky. "Look," he says. "Snow. The first snow. 'An imperial affliction sent us of the air.'"

I look up and see the swirling flakes. "I'd rather think of each flake as art in the air."

"I have an inkling you could tell me a lot about snow. No two snowflakes are alike, et cetera." He catches a flake on his palm.

"A stellar dendrite," I say.

"It has a name?"

"This crystal's treelike, see?" But he can't see; the flake's melted. "*Dendrite* means 'treelike.' A stellar dendrite has six symmetrical branches that hold asymmetrical side branches."

"And *Mor* is supposed to teach you?" he says, referring to

272

the homeschooling that has yet to happen. "How do you know all of this?"

"How do you know how to paint?" I say, and I'm carried back to his room, to me and me and me in his room.

"That's different. People don't intuit names of snowflakes. I've started to wonder whether Sanne's not crazy—maybe you are a gift from God." He leans up on one elbow, looks at me.

I want to tell him about the dream.

"I thought you said she didn't really believe that," I say.

"Who knows what Sanne believes? I don't even know what I believe in anymore. I've been ordered to put my head in that proverbial sand. I can't keep up with Sanne, too." He streams his fingers through my hair, pulls it out across the leaves. "Perhaps I should put my head in the clouds instead. You're an angel." He reaches over my head and stretches out my hair opposite him. "You have wings." He starts to stand, but I stop him, and when he looks back at me, his body suspended, the dream again comes alive. "What is it?" he says.

"Do you think we're brother and sister, Rune?" But when I see the expression on his face, I wish I could take the words back.

He pulls away from me and climbs to his feet, then reaches down and pulls me to mine. "'Much madness is divinest sense to a discerning eye,'" he says. "'Much sense, the starkest madness. . . .'"

"What does that mean?"

"Directly translated? It means 'Let's play in the snow.'"

*   *   *

273

"Pagans celebrated December twenty-fifth as the birthday of the sun god Deus Sol Invictus," Sanne says a few weeks after that first snow, "long before anyone celebrated the birthday of Jesus Christ. The fact is, Christ wasn't born anywhere near December twenty-fifth."

The preacher's fall from grace precipitated my fall from grace in Sanne's eyes. Or perhaps it's the reality of me—versus the idea of me—that precipitated my fall. It seems clear now Rune was right: I was an instrument of rebellion for Sanne; another streak of color in her hair. And a streak that turned out to be not as provocative as she hoped it would be. She still asks me to translate texts my mother read under the guise of their having some connection to my birth. And she still hoards Mother's notes, and pontificates: pagans, Gnostics, Essenes. But her interest lies in the ideas, not in me. I seem at best a tool—I can read texts she can't, translate them for her—but more often I'm a disappointment. A spoiler of her plans. Too unexceptional to be a "consecrated human being." Too unremarkable to be the divine on earth.

I never believed I was this—the divine on earth—yet I wanted to be something. Someone. And Sanne's theory of me gave me this: a theory of me. Without a theory of my past, my source, I seemed a nameless weed. But I've thought back again and again to Rune's words on that blueberry day so long ago. "Your context may become your prison." And I've wondered of the difference between a flower and a flowering weed. And I've wondered of a plucked plant submerged in water, which grows roots anew. Can living, changing, growing things ever really be defined as one thing or another? Am I or Sanne or Rune or the preacher one thing or another? I know Mother's mind imprisoned me even as it freed me, that it was never one thing or another. And I know I miss Mother's mind—that I long for those roots that both confine and unleash.

Sanne is now the gatekeeper to Mother's notes, to Mother's mind before me. But the gate Sanne holds open is narrow. The tiny fraction of the whole becomes the whole in my eyes. I look at the vein of a leaf, but I don't know its source of nourishment, or what it helps to nourish. I know only that it passes from somewhere to somewhere. I don't know the direction of the passing. I'm not sure it's part of a leaf at all.

As I listen to Sanne now, as I watch the sixth or seventh or eighth snow of the season splatter the stained windows, and mute them, I remember Mother comparing the Christmas tree to the pagan tradition of hanging apples from the evergreen tree at the time of the winter solstice. "The evergreen tree," Mother had said, "represents the sun god Balder. But the tree's also a symbol of fertility, since laurel, yew and fir are green throughout the year and therefore impart life into the barren months of winter."

Christmas was a strange and wonderful time in Hartswell—a time when Mother became the quirky evening star. I loved this time, and yet I feared it in a way, too, because Mother became more unpredictable. She bought spices in stores, and raisins, almonds, rice and black cherries. She made pudding with the rice, a sauce for the pudding with the cherries, and she hid an almond in the pudding for one of us to find. She refused to say whether it was good luck or bad luck to find the almond—so though I longed for the

275

almond, I dreaded it, too. And Mother mulled the spices she bought—orange peel, cardamom, cinnamon and cloves—with elderberry wine, muscatel and aquavit. Then she poured the hot *gløg* over plump raisins and blanched, skinned almonds, and we drank together.

After the *gløg* sent me to sleep, Mother stayed up late into the night—the evening star—and she hung strands of holly, ivy and mistletoe around the house. In the morning, she insisted mischievous elves she called *nisse* had hung the decorations, not her. She warned me the *nisse* could wreak havoc. And in later years, when Mother was more unwell, they did; she did. I woke some days to find the holly torn from the walls, the prickly mistletoe scattered about the floor, the ivy ripped to shreds and Mother reeking of *gløg*.

Yet even then she remained resolute about the existence of the *nisse*, and I started to wonder if she herself believed in them—part of me wanted her to believe in them, part of me feared for her mind. During these years, Mother prepared a special porridge and left it out for the *nisse*, "to appease them," she said. So they would wreak no more havoc. And as she prepared the porridge, she told me stories of the ancient Yuletide festival in Scandinavia, the celebration of the return of the sun, when a log was cut from the center of a tree—the Yule log—and hauled to an open fireplace, where it was kindled and left to burn for twelve days. "From this," Mother said, "came what is now known as the twelve days of Christmas." Mother also described the use of the holly, ivy and mistletoe as having non-Christian roots. "Holly, with its prickly leaves and blood-red berries," Mother said, "is a symbol of male sexuality, and the curling dark ivy, female fertility." Mother said mistletoe was considered to be life-giving, a sacred symbol of the sun. "Pagans believed mistletoe could protect them from poison and illness. They called it 'the golden bough,'" Mother said, "and gathered it on Midsummer Eve and the winter solstice."

"It makes sense the date of Christmas was derived from a pagan tradition," I say to Sanne now. "Mother said many of the Christmas traditions were built on pagan traditions." I feel proprietary about this information, and a sense of relief: I have something to add; Mother didn't keep all of this from me.

"It's not just Christmas, Aslaug," Sanne says, and her face takes on that high-browed, wide-eyed, soft-lipped look that conveys she's again unimpressed with me. "Many Christian traditions have pagan roots." The snow accosts the window behind Sanne's head in a loud, wet slap; the lights flicker, once and again, then go black.

"We lost power," I nearly say, but I stop myself: of course we lost power.

"The celebration of the birth of John the Baptist was a substitute for the pagan celebration of the summer solstice," Sanne says; she addresses the blackout in neither words nor tone. "And baptism was practiced by adherents of many mystery religions long before the time of Christ." Although her voice is unchanged, I hear it now in a different way: it's nasal and high-pitched and girlish. "And then there's the miracle of speaking in tongues," she says. "That happened before Christ lived, too."

"What exactly is speaking in tongues?" I say, but what I want to say is, "What about the lights? Didn't you notice they went out?" I feel a sort of frantic energy charge through me, like the electricity surged from the lights and infused it-self in me. And I realize I've become dependent in a way Mother never wanted to be: dependent on those zipping, bumping, heating electrons that tunnel their way through a hundredth of an inch and produce light.

But Sanne doesn't seem dependent on the light; she doesn't seem affected by the outage at all. And I start to wonder: maybe it's just me who's in the dark; maybe we didn't lose power. I wave my hand near her voice. Does she see it? Can she see me?

The lights flash on and off and on; my hand is inches from her face. "The lights went out," I say, as if that explains my hand.

"Really?" she says, but I see she's trying to make sense of my words, my hand. She swallows hard: her rail-like neck bulges and settles. She plumps her plump lips, wets them. And I see chaos behind those black-eyed-Susan eyes. "You've heard people during the services blathering, of course." Before her voice teetered high; now it's fallen, and sounds muffled. "The term that describes what they're doing is *glossolalia*."

"Derived from the Greek *glossa*, meaning 'tongue,' and *lalia*, 'to talk'?" I say.

"Probably," Sanne says, but the shield has cracked some, her armor has thinned: I've stumped her, without meaning to. She thought she understood me; she thought I was pre-dictable. But what was my hand doing in the air, ready to strike? I feel a rush of . . . Delight? Power? Something.

"Glossolalia is first mentioned in the Bible in the Book of Acts. Chapter two, I think," she says. "It describes the day of Pentecost, when the apostles supposedly were filled with the Holy Spirit and began speaking in languages they'd never learned."

I recall the first night I arrived at the church, when I peered through the door at the woman in army fatigues, her words spewing forth, messy as foam. And I remember the man next to her, seemingly interpreting her mess of words, honing them down to alleys of darkness and light, and snakes to the soul. "So you think that really happened? That it really happens? That people speak in languages they never learned?"

"Well, some form of glossolalia exists in many non-Christian traditions, too. Tibetan monks do it, and fetish priests in Africa. Shamans in Siberia and Greenland. It's widespread in Haiti. And among many aboriginal peoples, including some Native American tribes."

"Mother knew all of this?" I say, and I feel myself swelling with my mother, with the breadth of her.

"Maren knew way more than this. Many of the miracles attributed to Jesus were performed by other god-men long before Christ. Changing water into wine—we talked about that—stilling the sea, raising the dead, supernaturally catching fish. The story of Christ and his disciples catching the one hundred fifty-three fish is very similar to a story about Pythagoras. And the Pythagoreans believed one hundred fifty-three was a divine number, symbolized by the image of a fish.

"Why?" I say. Yet I can't shake that feeling I experienced when the lights flashed back on, when I saw her cracking, and thinning.

"Because when two circles intersect, and the edge of one meets the middle of the other, the resulting figure is known as the 'sign of the fish,' *vesica piscis*. This image is often associated with Christianity, right? But the ratio of the figure—that is, its height to its length—is 153:265."

"That's amazing," I say. It seems so right to me, this meshing of science and the sacred. But what did I miss? I think. When Mother was teaching me science, what did I miss?

"Yes and no," Sanne says. "It's not like it was an accident, the use of the number one hundred fifty-three. The Christians used many of the numbers pagans believed to be sacred. And they used them *because* pagans believed the numbers were sacred."

"Like what?" I say. "What besides the one-fifty-three?"

The window behind Sanne is fully snow-covered now, the stained colors hues of white. I can hear the wind ripping at branches, stripping them of the straggling leaves—just a handful left per tree, all iced and brittle-stiff.

"Well, the number twelve, for instance—Jesus's twelve disciples. The number was important in the pagan world. Pagans referred to the twelve signs of the zodiac repeatedly. And to the Pythagoreans, a formation of twelve circling one represented God. Then there's the name Jesus—that was no accident, that the Jewish god-man was named Jesus."

I hear footsteps; I hope they're not the preacher's. "What does the name Jesus have to do with numbers?" I say, but softly. The preacher knows I read what Sanne asks me to read, that I translate what she asks me to translate, but she doesn't know how interested I am in Sanne's words and Mother's mind. I don't want her to know this.

"In the ancient Greek alphabet, every letter represents both a sound and a number," Sanne says.

"Jesus was called *Iesous* in Greek?" I say, and I listen. Is the preacher coming?

"Right," Sanne says, with what seems a raised voice. "When you add up the numbers of the letters in *Iesous*, you get eight hundred eighty-eight, another sacred number. All the letters in the Greek alphabet, added together, equal eight hundred eighty-eight."

"But Jesus would have been *Yehoshua* in Hebrew. *Iesous* is just the Greek version of *Yehoshua*." I hope the preacher hears me now—hears my challenging Sanne. I want her to know: I don't believe everything Sanne tells me.

But Sanne says, "That's exactly my point. Early Christians referred to their god-man as *Iesous*, not because it was based in fact, but because the name was sacred according to pagan *gematria*, sacred math."

It's Rune, not the preacher, who walks into the sanctuary, into the vault where we're talking. "The lights went out," he says.

"Really?" Sanne says again, and I know she's needling him this time, but she looks at me.

It's a month shy of the winter solstice, the birthday of the sun god, or Christ; a time of holly and ivy and evergreen. And mistletoe. In my dream this night, Rune comes to me carrying mistletoe. He lays it around the bed and in my hair.

I wake early to a day that is not yet day, and to a wave of nausea that rolls through my middle, into my throat, then settles in my gut like too much water, before rolling anew:

281

I'm sick. I'm sick again. When Mother was alive, sickness was Mother, not me. But now it seems this part of her has seeded in me.

The air inside tastes stale; my breath tastes stale. I need to swap this air.

I dress and find my way through the dark hall, up the dark stairs, into the dark sanctuary. No light passes through the stained glass to bathe the sanctuary in bent rays. No sounds wave from the floor or bounce from the stone walls. I step onto the floor with my socked feet, and waves roll from me, and in me. I reach the door and slip on boots; I try to distract myself from myself with the promise of fresh air, and with hope of spotting a tree sparrow or cedar waxwing or hawk owl. In winter in Hartswell I'd sometimes see one of these birds in the early morning from the back porch while Mother slept, so delicate against the bitter backdrop of snow and ice. So delicate, yet so buoyant and able, undeterred, it seemed, by the harshness all around it. Like the mallards, I think, and the harlequin ducks and eiders, which I know still speckle the harbor, despite the cold. Perhaps I'll walk there, to the harbor. Breathe in the cold. Watch them.

But I can't open the door. The snowdrifts are so high, I can't open the door, and the first snow seems a dream. I push, hard, but the snow weighs against the door, and the waves roll and weigh against me. I retreat breathing the same stale air to my bedroom to breathe the same stale air. I'll sleep, I think. And I'll dream of the sparrows and owls and eiders.

My robe lies disheveled where I threw it, spilling from

the foot of the bed as if struggling against the bed's embrace. The paper and pen sit on the makeshift nightstand. My clothes from the prior day lie strewn across the floor. The glass still rests near the bed, the last drop of schnapps condensed in its basin, forming a small stone of sticky crimson.

Rune stands over me holding a rose in his teeth. It's not a wrinkled rose or a swamp rose or a dog rose. I wonder what kind of rose it is, and where he got it in winter. And then I think, No rose grows in winter, in snow; I'm dreaming. I dreamt of Rune last night decorating me in mistletoe, and now I'm napping, dreaming of him holding this rose. I'm molding him into the plants of Hartswell. Trying to make him more integral to my life than he is.

But when I sit up and look around the room, I see it is as it was before I lay down, and I realize he's real. The rose is real.

Rune removes the rose from his mouth with his webbed hand. "'If she had been the mistletoe,'" he says, "'and I had been the rose.'" He lays the flower on my belly; its petals are yellow, tipped with red.

"Why did you say that?" I say. "Why did you say that about the mistletoe?"

"It's from a Dickinson poem," he says, his eyes no longer smiling. "I was bringing you a rose. . . ." He sits down on the bed near me, and I feel gripped. "Mor said she checked on you when you didn't get up. That you were still sleeping. She thought you might be sick."

He folds his hand around my wrist. I want to tug my

arm away. How did he know about my dream, about the mistletoe?

"What's wrong, Aslaug?" he says.

I do pull my hand back. "I don't feel well."

Sanne steps into the doorway, a glass of water in one hand, a plate with bread in the other. "You don't feel well? Mor guessed right," she says, and she walks inside. "Did Rune wake you?"

"I brought her the flower," Rune says, but he takes it back in his webbed hand.

"Well, I brought you something useful. I've learned something from *Gudinden* about caring for the needy." Sanne sets the water and plate on the table, on top of the paper. She picks up the schnapps glass, smells its remains. "How can you drink that stuff?" She tries to set the glass back down, but she rests it askew; it tumbles to the floor and cracks in chunks. "Rune's been preparing your tray since—how shall I say?—since *Mor* took the bite of the apple."

Rune's moved from the bed to his knees to collect the chunks. "Shut up, Sanne," he says.

"It's probably Rune's fault you're sick. What did you give her, Rune?"

"Very funny, Sanne," he says. "Why don't you pick this mess up?" But he's already picked it up and holds the chunks against the rose. He sits, again, on the bed, but at its foot.

Sanne fakes a smile, turns back toward me. "Do you have a fever?" she says. She touches my forehead. Her hand feels moist and cold against my skin; her eyes look moist and cold. And a pinkish orange is making its way from the white of her collar to the white of her face; her words jerk out with what seems uncertainty. She's worried about something, I think. Is she worried about me?

"I'm tired," I say. "Nauseous."

"Nauseous?" she says. Her fingers find her hair, twirl a strand; she rocks her long body like a windblown reed; and the pink-orange further stretches itself into her milky face. "See. It was Rune. I told you."

Rune stands and walks out of the room, still embracing the chunks, embracing the rose.

"What's wrong with him?" Sanne says.

Peppermint flowers are lavender to pink, and whorled. In marshes and ditches and alongside brooks, and in wet meadows splattered with their pale color, the scent of peppermint is common in Maine, common in summer. Mother and I would gather the plant and boil its leaves to make tea. And sometimes we would add its flavor to baked goods and stews. The smell of peppermint reminds me of Mother, of her grip around a hot mug, the scent of peppermint wafting with the steam, and of her breath.

I smell the peppermint before the preacher steps into the room; I think I smell Mother. "Rune said you're nauseated," the preacher says when she enters; her fingers circle a mug and the steam circles the air. "*Fader* used to make Maren and me tea with peppermint oil for upset stomachs." It's only the second or third time she's mentioned Mother since telling me of my birth.

"Apparently you learned some things from *Bedstefar* despite yourself," Sanne says.

The preacher's mouth tightens into Mother's mouth, but

285

she doesn't address Sanne. She holds the mug to my lips. "I gathered some fresh peppermint this summer. Made the oil. Try to drink this tea, Aslaug. It should help."

But nothing helps. Certainly not the peppermint. I'm sick the rest of the day, and the next. I can't eat; I can barely hold down the tea, although the preacher brings it to me again and again. Rune doesn't return to visit me, but I see him in my mind as I lie in bed, as I try to drink the tea. I hear him recite the poem, and I see him spread the mistletoe in my dream.

SOLOMON'S SEAL

2007

—Cross-examination, Counsel?

—Yes, Your Honor. Hagen, given you'd moved away from Bethan and were no longer attending the Charisma Church, there's no way you could know for sure whether Aslaug was living at the church, is there?

—Well, like I said, my sister, you know, Rebekka, was living there. She would have told me if Aslaug was living there, too.

—But you didn't talk with your sister much during this time period, did you?

—Not a lot.

—In fact, your parents had prohibited you from talking to her at all, hadn't they?

—What Rebekka did was really hard on them. They were upset.

—Hagen, please just answer yes or no. It's true, isn't it,

that your parents prohibited you from speaking with Rebekka during the period when Rebekka was living at the Charisma Church?

—Yes.

—In fact, you've spoken with Rebekka only three times in the past four years, isn't that right?

—That's not right. Before we moved away, I spoke with her all the time.

—But after you and your parents moved from Bethan, during the years when Rebekka was supposedly living at the Charisma Church, you spoke with her only three times, isn't that right?

—Something like that.

—In fact, you don't even know where Rebekka is living now, do you?

—I know she left the church before it burned down. I know she moved away.

—But you don't know where she moved to, do you?

—No.

—So it sure seems possible Rebekka could have been living at the Charisma Church with Aslaug and not mentioned this to you. I mean, Rebekka didn't even tell you where she was moving to.

—Objection. Argumentative.

—Sustained.

—Hagen, it is possible, is it not, that Aslaug was living at the Charisma Church during the period when Rebekka was living there and Rebekka just didn't tell you?

—I guess so.

—Thank you. I have no further questions.

Bee Balm

2003

*T*he preacher leads me into a lobby, painted peach, so shiny the walls look wet. Like ripe cantaloupe, I think, and then wish I hadn't—I can't bear the thought of food. The carpet in the lobby is low shag, also peach, and the chairs are turquoise. I smell bleach. A middle-aged man sits behind a glass window, his hair thin, his jaw loose, his Adam's apple lifting and falling. I realize he's eating—peanuts, I think. And I try to back away, but the preacher presses her hand against the small of my back; the man wipes his palms against one another, slides open the window.

"Yes?" he says.

The preacher speaks. "We have an appointment."

"We?"

"Susanne does." I look at the preacher; I almost correct her. She shakes her head, barely.

The man peruses his schedule. "Susanne Lerner. Yes, here it is." He hands me a clipboard. "You can have a seat. Fill out the form. The doctor will be with you soon."

The preacher leads me to one of the turquoise chairs. "You're underage and I'm not your mother," she whispers. "I'm not sure the doctor would see you." She takes the clipboard from me, fills in Susanne's full name, hands the clipboard back.

I try to fill out the form, but I can't answer the questions; I don't understand most of the questions. The preacher takes the clipboard back, fills the information in.

A woman swings open the door near where the man sits. "Susanne?" she says. "The doctor is ready to see you."

I follow her through the door. Her shoes sigh as she walks and her braid tails her. I look back and see the preacher through the window, but her head is sliced from view.

I've never been to the doctor before—I've no idea what to expect. The hallway we walk through is beige, lined with paper versions of the mallards and harlequin ducks in the harbor. And the smell of bleach is stronger. The woman pushes open a door to a bathroom, hands me a vial. "We need a urine sample," she says.

"A what?"

"Read the instructions," she says. "Inside."

I step in the bathroom, see the instructions above the sink: wipe, urinate, seal. I'm not sure what to do with the vial after it's filled. I open the door: the woman with the braid stands there, hands gloved, and she scoops the vial from me and deposits it on a tray. Then she leads me into a small room that's white and bright. "Put this on," she says. And she hands me a large sheet of folded paper. "The doctor will be right in."

She shuts the door, and I unfold the paper and see it's some sort of gown. I'm not sure what I'm supposed to do with it: I put it on over my dress. I hear a knock; the door opens without my responding and another woman steps in.

She starts to laugh. "I'm sorry," she says, and she covers her mouth with her hand. "You're supposed to remove your clothes. Put the gown on then." But she doesn't leave to let me do this. "I'm Dr. Hoenir, Susanne." She looks younger than I expected she would. She reaches out her hand, shakes mine; her hand is small and light, like a chick in my grip. "Would you like your mother to join you in here?"

"My mother?" I say, and then, "No. No."

"Okay," she says, but I sense she noticed my confusion. She motions for me to sit down. "What's the problem to-day?" She has what I know is a stethoscope around her neck. She lifts it to her ears and pulls down the neck of my dress, puts the metal to my chest, near my breast. I can feel the in-strument's round weight, and its coolness.

"I'm feeling sick to my stomach."

"Deep breath," she says. "Good. Any other symptoms?"

"I'm tired. I've been tired."

She moves the stethoscope to my back. "Deep breath. How long have you been feeling like this?"

"Three, four days, maybe."

"Another breath. Good. Are you sexually active?"

She's behind me now—I can't see her face. "Am I what?"

She pulls the stethoscope from my dress. Pushes up my

sleeve. "I'm going to check your blood pressure," she says, and she wraps the cuff around my arm. "You'll feel some tightening here. Do you have a boyfriend, Susanne?"

I feel the squeeze. I shake my head.

"Have you ever had sex?"

"No," I say, but I think of the dream.

"When was your last period?"

"My what?" I say—I don't know what she means.

"Your period. Do you menstruate?"

"Yes," I say. "Yes. The last time was a couple of months ago. But that's not unusual for me. I only started menstruating last year. I don't menstruate every month."

She inserts the stethoscope into the cuff. Listens. "One twenty over seventy," she says. "Good." She removes the cuff, writes something on her chart, wraps her hand around my wrist, looks at her watch. "Seventy-two," she says. "Okay. Now, I'd like you to take your clothes off, put this gown back on. Leave it open in the front."

She steps out of the room and I pull off my dress. I wish the preacher were with me now. I wrap the paper around my shoulders, but I can't keep it closed. The doctor knocks and steps in.

"You'll have to remove your underwear," she says, but this time she doesn't laugh. "And your bra, so I can do a breast exam." She looks at me in a way that makes me want to turn away.

"Can Sara come in?" I say.

"Your mother?" she says, and I nod. "Are you sure you want that, Susanne?" I nod again. "Okay," she says. "That's your choice."

She exits the room, and I remove my underclothes, try again to hold the paper closed, but it seems a blossom seeking light. The doctor returns with the preacher. "You can sit over there," the doctor says to her; she points toward a chair in the rear of the room.

"I'll need you to sit here again on the examining table," she says to me. "I'm going to do what's called a pelvic exam. Your mother tells me you've never had this done before. It's a bit uncomfortable—but it's over quickly." She turns my body on the table until I face her. "Go ahead and lie back," she says. "Your feet go here, in the stirrups." She positions my feet—I can't believe what's happening. I feel I'll throw up. "You'll feel some pressure now," she says. I close my eyes—I want to disappear. And then I do disappear, to the dream, where, through some contortion of my mind, a version of what is happening to me now was beautiful. Then I feel hot tears run into the thumping in my ears; I've reappeared. The doctor stands. She presses her hand into my abdomen, into the home of the hairstreak, but the hairstreak has faded; it's gone. "Okay," she says, and she pulls off her gloves. She moves nearer my head, opens the gown on one side, scrambles her fingers around my breast and up into the pit of my arm. Then she walks around the table, scrambles the other side. "All right," she says. "You can get dressed." She looks at the preacher. "I'd like you to wait in the lobby."

"No," I say. I wipe the water from my ears. "I want her to stay."

"You're sure?" the doctor says, and suddenly I'm not sure. But I nod my head.

*　　*　　*

Hummingbirds are attracted to bee balm; they flutter around the showy red blossoms, darting in and out, lured by the bursting scarlet, and the perfume. They drink the bee balm's sweet nectar, and then they escape to find more bee balm, more sweet nectar, more intoxicating color and perfume. Mother would make tea from the leaves of the bee balm when peppermint was scarce. But bee balm was not her preference, and I imagined the hummingbirds were grateful for this. Mother never commented on the beauty of the bee balm, or its scent; she cared only about its dark green leaves, coarse and toothed—about the flavor of them when dried and steeped. As I sit here with the preacher, waiting for the doctor to return, I see those hummingbirds in my mind, and I remember the scent of the bee balm tea. Snow blows against the window, spots it in wet white. And I wonder where those hummingbirds are now. The bee balm flowers have long ago withered, their sweet nectar drunk or dried. And the leaves have dropped to the ground, now that Mother is gone. I look at the preacher sitting near me, and I wonder, Is she more the hummingbird, or more like Mother? And what of Sanne and Rune? As to the preacher and Sanne, I'm not sure I know the answer yet. But as to Rune, he is the hummingbird.

"You're pregnant," the doctor says when she returns to the room. "I'd say you're over two months."

"Pregnant?" I say.

"Pregnant?" I hear the preacher say.

"That's not possible," I say. "There's no way that's possible." I can't quite take in what the doctor is saying. I am not the hog peanut. I am not the daylily, which can produce vegetatively, without fertile seed. I am a human, and a virgin. I can't be pregnant.

"It is possible, Susanne. You are pregnant. I know this is upsetting for both of you—I can see you're surprised. I imagine you need to talk. I don't need this room for the next fifteen minutes. I'm going to give you some privacy, let you talk. Then I'll come back. We can talk about your options."

I see the doctor open the white door in the white wall; I see her step into the hall. And I see the white door shut. But it's not the white I see. It's the black of Mother's clothes: I see them in my mind. I see her in my mind. And I imagine those black clothes bulging with me.

"Who's the father?" the preacher says to my back.

I don't turn around. I don't know what to say, to think. Mother claimed I was born of a virgin birth, and now I'm pregnant, and I'm a virgin. The preacher didn't believe my mother. Why would the preacher believe me? I wouldn't believe, if it weren't happening to me.

"Don't tell me it's Rune, Aslaug," the preacher says. "Please don't tell me that."

"Rune?" I say. And now I do turn around, yet I can't look at her God's-eyes. "No. No." But there's a gnawing at me I can't free myself from: Rune the hummingbird, Rune the bearer of mistletoe.

"I found a picture he drew of you. I found it on the table one night after Sanne and I were out, when we got home. You and Rune were downstairs when we got home—"

"No," I say again. "It's not Rune."

She covers those eyes I can't look into with hands that

295

are shaking. And her breath, too, shakes in and out. She slides her fingers away, opens the windows of her eyes. "We need to keep this quiet. No one can know. I'll help you, but no one can know. And you have to tell me who the father is. I have to know that."

"You don't understand," I say. "I've never been with anyone in that way."

"No," she says, and I know Mother has come back to life in this room. "No."

I look at the preacher's eyes now because they can't look at mine, and I see hers are still and unblinking. "Get dressed," she says, and she unwinds my ball of clothes. "Right now." She rips the robe from my shoulders, down my back, then stuffs it in the trash. I feel her watching me as I pull on my underclothes. She yanks Sanne's dress over my head, hands me Sanne's coat, Sanne's boots. And we stream out, past the mallards, through the bleach, into the snow.

The preacher doesn't speak as we drive back to the church. Her hands grip the black wheel, and her knuckles show white. I hear her breathing, deep in, jerking out. She drives fast. Snow sprays the side of the car and splats against the windshield. The heat is off and I can see my breath, and hers quivering out. "Art in the air," I hear Rune say in my head. But I want him to stop.

The wind presses against the car, and I feel the wave as the car is pushed nearer the centerline, and then back. The evergreens we pass are so heavy with snow—I watch mounds of it drop in the wind—and the deciduous trees sparkle in ice and the rare ray of sun. I'm pregnant, I think. There's a baby growing inside of me. The sun passes back behind a cloud, the sparkles fade. And the thought of Rune drags at me more.

We pull into the drive. The witch hazel has lost its leaves and stands skeletal. The stone of the building is peppered with snow. The preacher's hands still grip the wheel; the engine still runs; the exhaust drapes the car. "Did you know?" she says.

"That I was pregnant?" I say. "No. How could I have known?"

"I can't do this again." Her hair has come loose; her lips are dry and chapped. "Tell me you know how you got pregnant, Aslaug. Tell me that." Her eyes show pale, like Mother's. And they glisten, unlike Mother's. She takes her hands from the wheel, drops her face into them. "Tell me that," she says, her voice broken by her hands. "Tell me that."

I can't, I think. But I wonder. Rune's face and his body and his touch were so real. They were real.

I remember the schnapps; I remember Sanne mentioning Rune's preparing the tray for me. Any plant could have been put into that schnapps. Did he drug me? Had he been drugging me?

He knew of the mistletoe.

And the pictures, I think. There were pictures of me sleeping. I'd seen them in his room, but it hadn't occurred to me at the time: when would he have seen me asleep?

"Rune raped me," I say. I don't mean to say it; I mean to think it. But I say it.

"What?"

"He raped me." And now I mean to say it; it all seems

clear suddenly. Neither the preacher nor I have moved; everything around us looks exactly the same. Yet everything has changed. "I thought it was a dream."

"No," she says. "Rune thinks he's in love with you. I've seen the way he looks at you. But he wouldn't do that."

"But he did," I say. "He did."

She rams her finger toward my face. "Shut up," she says. "Shut up." She's sweating despite the cold, and her left eye twitches, becomes Mother's eye. "Maren almost destroyed this family. I won't allow you . . ." She drops her hand, folds her fingers into a fist, turns her face from mine. "Your father isn't Mikkel, Aslaug." Her breath fogs the window, and now the fog spreads wide. "Your father is my father."

"That's a lie," I say.

But I'm not sure it is.

SOLOMON'S SEAL

2007

—Ms. Hellig, you claim you became pregnant approximately four years ago, isn't that right?

—Yes.

—But you claim, don't you, that you'd never before had intercourse at the time you became pregnant?

—That's right.

—You hadn't undergone any type of in vitro fertilization either, correct?

—Any what?

—You hadn't had any medical procedure in an attempt to get pregnant, right?

—I wasn't trying to get pregnant. I was a teenager.

—Ms. Hellig, you are aware, are you not, that in order for a woman to become pregnant, she has to either have intercourse with a male or undergo some sort of medical procedure, such as in vitro fertilization?

—Objection. Argumentative.

—I'm going to allow her to answer. I think it's important we understand her knowledge about these things.

—I understand that's what usually happens, but that's not what happened to me.

—Ms. Hellig, what you're saying, then, is that you became pregnant supernaturally?

—I don't know how I became pregnant.

—Ms. Hellig, please take a moment to review this document. I'd like to mark this document as Exhibit Y. Are you familiar with it?

—Yes.

—Ms. Hellig, investigators found this document zipped into the pocket of your jacket when you were arrested. Did you author this document?

—Yes.

—Ms. Hellig, the date on this document indicates it was written about the time you claim you became pregnant, isn't that right?

—Yes.

—This document basically is a record of two people having sexual intercourse, is it not?

—Yes, but it—

—And one of these people you wrote about is in fact you, correct?

—Yes, but—

—Thank you. And the other person is your cousin Rune Lerner, isn't that right?

—Yes.

—So this document describes you having sexual intercourse with your cousin Rune Lerner?

—Yes, but it was—

—Thank you, Ms. Hellig. But you still claim that you were—that you *are*—a virgin?

—Yes, I—

—Thank you. Now, did you see a doctor to confirm your supposed virgin pregnancy, Ms. Hellig?

—Objection. Argumentative.

—Sustained.

—Did you see a doctor about your supposed pregnancy, Ms. Hellig?

—Yes.

—Do you remember that doctor's name?

—Her name was Dr. Hoenir. She had a clinic in Bethan.

GOLDEN BUTTONS

2003–2004

I want to dream; I want this life to be a dream. I want to wake to find I'm that hairstreak, or a flower, or the oak tree come to life. For this life is transforming me, and the people around me; altering our forms, our composition, making us into something that seems but a slice of us, only harder: water frozen in motion, now an icicle knife. Is it the hairstreak's freedom I'm longing for, or the resourcefulness of the flower? Or the deep roots of the oak? Or is it that I long to be another? Any other. Anything but a slice of myself. Because I am pregnant, and Rune raped me, and my father and grandfather are one.

My father and grandfather are one. Or are they? Did Mother prevent my seeing my reflection because she didn't want me to know my face is her face, because her face is her father's? Or is the preacher trying to startle me: into not seeing what is possible, because she couldn't see what was possible those years ago, with Mother; or into not knowing what I know, that Rune raped me?

I wish I could see without the filter of me. I wish I could recall the preacher first describing *Bedstefar* to me those months ago, without the filter of me. I remember the preacher's tone as awash in awe at *Bedstefar*'s love for Mother, and some longing for this love. But was her tone disguised to conceal the disgust, horror, repulsion, she felt? When Rune showed me the picture of *Bedstefar* holding Mother, I saw in *Bedstefar* eyes of pride, and protection, not the voracious eyes of Grumset, not the greedy eyes of the boy-man in Bethan. But did I see what I wanted to see? Do I remember what I want to remember? *Bedstefar* wouldn't have harmed Mother, I tell myself now. She was his daughter; he loved her as a daughter. And yet I wonder, is love boxed in in this way? Or are my constructs just this, constructs that simplify the world as they distort it? Were my readings of the preacher and Mother and *Bedstefar* and Rune, and myself, such constructs? Have I imagined a world, only to miss the world?

In the world of my mind, I believed I was learning to see the preacher for what she was: human in her godliness; drunk in the spirit and on the earth. Capable of loving all sheep; therefore, capable of loving me.

But I saw today I am not one of her sheep; I will never be one of her sheep. I am Aslaug Datter, daughter of Maren. I am a reflection of who Mother was, and who Mother was is a reflection of her life before me. I am closing the circle, bringing the end back to the beginning, back to Sara, the sister of Maren, a person the preacher now must exhume.

I can hear them shouting—the preacher and Sanne and Rune. They are somewhere in this cavernous place—the beauty of which in this moment seems a gaudy wash. Their voices mingle the piercing with the leaden with the airiness of surprise. I hear wide gaps, broken-off chunks and the fading away. "How could you?" "She's lying." "Can't you see it makes sense?" I know these words are about me, about the baby growing in me.

And I know I have to leave.

I have no idea where I'll go or what I'll do, but I know I have to leave.

How could there be a baby growing in me if not for Rune? "She's lying," I hear him say again. "She's making it up." I wish this were true; I wish it weren't Rune. When the preacher mentioned Rune's love for me, I wanted to recant. I wanted to tell her instead: "I'm in love with him, too." But what do I know about love? I can imagine Mother mocking me, making fun of my adolescent feelings. "You're little more than a child," she'd have said. "Love is not responding to pheromones. Love is not feeling animal urges."

Is that all it was? I wonder. Pheromones? Hormones? Animal instinct? Was my attraction to Rune simply this? It felt deeper to me, like he was not only awakening my body but filling my spirit. The same spirit awakened by the preacher's touch. But now? Now I think, If it was love, then whom did I love? The Rune of my world would never have raped me. The Rune of this world did.

And then I stop myself from thinking about anything but leaving. I'll leave tonight after they've all gone to sleep. I'll slip out, and their lives will return to what they were before. And my life?

304

I'll find my life. There is a world I left Mother's world to find. A world I wanted to experience. I've been reading about God's creation, not living God's creation. Now I'll find it, live it. Like I found the suitcase in the outhouse in the carrion stench.

I'll have to find that suitcase, first, and again. I'll have to find Mother's notes, and the case of photos: these I can't leave. And with the money and Mother's mind as it was before me, and with Mother's paper smiles, and her paper eyes, I'll leave with more than when I came. And then I again think of the baby in me: I'll leave with more than when I came.

But when the lights go dim in the hallway, and the sounds all fade, I can't open my door. At first I press the handle quietly, try to push, but the door stays put. So I push harder, shove my shoulder against the door, but the door stays put. It's locked, I think, and I slam my body against the door, no longer worried I might wake someone. But the door stays put. I start pounding and shouting. I want someone to hear me now; I want them all to hear me. I want them to come. But no one comes.

In my world, the preacher and Sanne and Rune agreed on almost nothing; in this world, it seems, they agree on this: to keep the inside in.

I wake to the sound of the bedroom door being shut and locked. I sit up and see I'm still alone. A plastic tray sits on the floor, holding a bright purple plastic cup full of tea steaming near a forget-me-not blue plastic bowl of clumped porridge—Mother's porridge—and a peeled, graying banana. Next to the tray stands a paper bag, the same as the preacher used for the nails and wrappers and gum. But this bag is full of food: the sliced bread Sanne likes that tastes and feels, to me, like cardboard; the salty, sweetened peanut butter Sanne eats by the spoonful. *En skefuld lort*, I couldn't help but think each time I'd watch her mash it. I unpack green apples and red apples and yellow apples, and hairy carrots, and celery, and a block of too-orange cheese, and a heavy bag of nuts. And a spoon. Plastic. And another plastic cup. And a cloth napkin embroidered "Jesus Saves."

I sit down on the floor, circled by this rainbow of food, and plastic, and Jesus. How long are they planning to leave me in here? It hadn't occurred to me last night they had any intention of keeping me here. They had to talk, I assumed. They had to decide what to do, before they let me free. Yet what of this food? It is more than for a day. It may be more than for a week. And the irony of my escaping the cage of Mother's grand house, full of books and Mother's mind, to find myself in a cage a fraction of that size, full of plastic tableware and cardboard bread and a jar of shit, and a Jesus napkin to wipe away the shit, seems at once comical and horrible. And before my brain knows, my body knows: I have to get out of here. It feels every plane on my skin has an edge, every fine hair on my body has come alive. I stand and look out the small window on the door: no one is in the hall. I push the lever on the door. Locked.

Help me, Mother, I think. Help me figure out what to do. Urd, Skuld, Verdandi?

And then I realize: they've locked up my body; they haven't locked up my mind.

I lift the plastic mug of still-warm tea, hold it in my

palms. The smell of the tea is strong, and familiar. Distinctive. Not peppermint. I lift the mug to my lips, but I stop; I don't drink.

Golden buttons. The scent of the tea comes from common tansy, the plant Mother called golden buttons. "I should have taken the buttons when I was pregnant with you," Mother said to me once, waving a fistful of the orange-yellow tansy, mixing their scent into the wind. I'd been sloppy in my gathering, mistaking poisonous corn cockle for the garden phlox Mother used to treat her boils. But even Mother wasn't this cruel, and she retracted her comment. For the golden buttons cause miscarriage—I figured this out later that night as I scanned one of Mother's herb books, trying to understand Mother's comment, her regret.

Who would do this? I think now. Who would even know to give me this?

I long for my mother. She was vicious at times, but she was my Artemis.

I can't imagine Rune would do this—give me the tansy—and yet, I remember the morning only days after I'd arrived. He'd made me pancakes, served me them with the king's crown jam. He'd known to make the jam; maybe he'd know to make the tansy tea.

I set the tea back on the tray, sit down on the bed. I look at the tea. Maybe I should drink it; maybe I should drink the golden buttons, let this pregnancy wash from my torso, like the painted hairstreak and the painted touch-me-not washed from my torso. Over time would the pregnancy be as if it never was? Or is its touch forever? Less the touch-me-not, more the sprawling forget-me-not.

Forget me not.

I am Artemis now. I throw the cup against the door, and the golden buttons bathe the floor.

The parishioners filing into the church sound like mice in the attic. About to enter the trap. It is Sunday morning, two mornings after I was locked in this room, and I've seen no one, heard little. But now the music beats through the floor, and the muffle of the preacher's ranting rumbles through me.

I imagine the woman in army fatigues gyrating, and squealing laughter. My mind sees the preacher's tambourine glinting with paned light, and Sanne's smug expression, and Rune's fingers screeching across the strings. I hear Sanne and the angel girl singing, "I need thee, oh I need thee. Every hour I need thee. Bless me now, my Savior, I come to thee." But I don't hear Rune.

I listen to the activity above me for a half hour before I realize: I have an audience. If I can hear the sheep, they can hear me. I stand on the bed and, stretching, ram the hard heel of my clog into the low ceiling. It cracks into the plaster, and the plaster dusts my face. I pound again: the crack spreads; the dust spreads; the air around me jitters with dust. I stop, brush my face and shoulders and sleeves, shake my hair. And I listen, hoping to hear footsteps on the stairs, on the stone floor of the hallway. But I hear only the sound of a man's voice magnified, testifying, "It was a miracle." I climb from the bed and carry my clog to the door, and I smash it there, against the wood. Then I smash it against the small window, and I shatter the window, and I pass from this room, from my teenage self, to our yard in Hartswell, to my tiny self. And to Mother, and the hammer, and the splintered glass of our car's mirrors.

I don't hear the footsteps until the preacher rounds the corner, running. I see her face and body framed in broken glass: her hair sprays from its bun; a red modesty cloth flaps behind her like one futile wing. Then Sanne rounds the corner, enters the frame, and she is a white monster with a flaming face and flaming hair. They fill the room before I realize what's happening, and I'm on my stomach before I think to struggle. Sanne's pushed me to the ground, kneed my back. I feel lumps of apple beneath me; a plastic bowl or cup dents my shin. The opened bag of nuts is flung or struck, and nuts skitter across the stone floor and swat my face. Sanne wrenches my arms to my back; the preacher tightens the modesty cloth around my wrists. Then Sanne yanks my head backward; I feel my hair rip.

"Stuff it," Sanne says. "Stuff that."

The preacher balls the Jesus napkin and tries to shove it in my mouth, but I bite her. She rears back and slaps my face. I feel the hot imprint of that anointing palm, her long fingers. Sanne digs her knee deeper into the small of my back and wrenches me further.

"Why?" I say, but barely, and then the napkin slides in and stays in and my voice is caught in it.

"I'm sorry, Aslaug," the preacher says, and I smell the schnapps. "They'd put him in jail. He'd go to jail."

"Tape it," Sanne says. "There's tape in that drawer."

I kick toward Sanne's back, but she's stronger than I am, and it feels as though a pick jabs the base of my neck each time I move. And it's hard to breathe because of Jesus.

The preacher opens the drawer and finds the tape, then she finds the broken bulb, the bulb I broke months ago. "What is this?" She exhumes the bulb, the shards of sharp glass.

"It doesn't matter," Sanne says. "Just tape. Now."

The preacher stretches the tacky coverlet over my lips, but her hands shake; her eyes seem unfocused. She drops the tape and moves nearer the door. I kick again, then go still. Because I see, and I hope Sanne sees what I see: the preacher is retreating, at least in her mind.

"Rune didn't do anything, *Mor*," Sanne says, and her hold on me weakens. Her strength is now directed toward the preacher, it seems. Toward holding the preacher. "Aslaug's lying. Rune said so. Aslaug's scared, *Mor*. She's lying."

"Then how? Aslaug's pregnant. How is it that she's pregnant?" The preacher's words are rounded with schnapps. And disbelief, I think.

"*Mor* . . . I know it's God. It's like with Maren," Sanne says. "I didn't really believe before either. I wanted to believe, but I didn't, not really."

"No," the preacher says, and now her eyes focus and meet mine. "This has nothing to do with Maren."

"But it does," Sanne says. "I read her notes, *Mor*. It does."

The music starts again; I hear it through the floor.

"We should go," the preacher says, and she sways.

"We have to tie her," Sanne says. "We can't leave without tying her."

Tie me? I feel incredulous. And then I think of the preacher's skepticism; I have hope she'll resist Sanne.

"We'll tie you on the bed if you don't fight, Aslaug,"

310

Sanne says now to me. "Otherwise, it'll be the floor. I know you don't understand. I know you're scared. But I understand. I do. You have to trust me." She lets go of my hair and my face hits the floor. "All right?" she says, as if I can answer, as if any of this could be right. As if Sanne could be right: a virgin birth. As if I would trust her after this.

The preacher doesn't let me go. Neither she nor Sanne looks at my face as they flip me, lift me to the bed, roll me back on my belly, stretch my legs wide. "We need something to bind her," Sanne says, and I hear a confidence in her voice that seems newly born. The preacher walks from the room. Sanne sits on me; her white dress rides her calves, and I see the edge of the tattoo she claims is not there. When the preacher returns, she carries several more modesty cloths, and she and Sanne secure my legs to the bedposts with these.

This becomes the ritual. Before each service, I am cleared away, along with the crumpled papers in the pews and the stale gum. They arrive an hour or so before the service. Sanne binds my hands; the preacher gags me. And together they attach me to the bed. Then they return to the sanctuary to set out the tambourine, the glasses of water, the anointing oil. And I comply: I hold my wrists together, open my mouth wide, lie still as they tie me to the bed; for if I don't, I stay tied the remainder of the day, and through the night. And I remind myself: they can't bind my mind.

In my mind I scale the worlds of Yggdrasil. I imagine the great ash, its green the color of climbing, wet moss; its thousands of tangled branches become thousands of tangled stories, spun of gods and goddesses, elves and giants and

311

dwarves. And fire. And cold and ice. Hours became days and now days become weeks and weeks become months, and these stories of Yggdrasil grow in my mind. As my belly grows round, and my breasts full, as I feel the flutter of the baby within me, my mind flutters with these, these stories that carry me up and away to other worlds. And yet, inevitably, I fall back to the roots of Yggdrasil, deeper even than the world of Niflheim, the land of the Maine winter, the land of cold and ice. And I find I am still rooted to this room, to my body.

With this body. I've found the golden buttons upon waking on two more occasions now, each time steaming in a cup of tea. And each time I've slammed the cup against the door and splashed the buttons upon the stone. This body in me was rooted in me because of human desire, human need. And now? Does it stay rooted by choice? When I slam the buttons against the door, it feels like fate, not choice.

And I wonder if fate also roots me here, in this room. The bedroom door is sealed each night like Mother might seal a jar; I have nothing I could fashion as a tool to pry it free. And, absent the broken bulb, which Sara took, I've nothing I could fashion as a weapon. My freedom lies in the travels of my mind, and my words and hands must be my weapons.

Sanne and the preacher do take me outside several times a week into the slush and Maine fog. But my words they catch in the handkerchief, my hands in the modesty cloth. We go early in the morning, when the sun creeps in faint lines through the pines. The preacher stumbles along on one side, Sanne holds firmly to me on the other. They grip my arms and walk me about the back of the church near an old burial ground, its finger-like tombstones a Hartswell-sky gray. The church is shielded from the houses around. There is no Grumset here, no spying neighbor to call the police.

But there is Rebekka. She is here often. She hears me, she sees me. And yet she seems to not hear me, she seems to not see me. She wanders the hall outside my cage, humming to herself. I can hear the soft patter of her feet, so unlike Sanne's plodding, so unlike the preacher's. And at times I see her when Sanne or the preacher opens my door. Her belly is growing like mine, and it pulls me like a magnet. But she seems oblivious to my belly, oblivious to me. "Help me!" I call to her. "They've locked me up!" As if somehow she doesn't know. But she doesn't help me.

I ask Sanne and the preacher, before they stuff me with Jesus, why they are confining me. The preacher says, "I can't let you go to the police," or, "It would destroy Rune. It would destroy my church." But she says this through schnapps and slurring; it seems it is she who is self-destructing. I tell her I'd never do that—I'd never go to the police. But then my words get trapped. Still, I sense the preacher doubts. But does she doubt Sanne or Rune or me, or God?

Sanne repeats some version of "How can you not believe? It's a miracle, like with Maren. A virgin birth." She leaves me books of theology, marks pages about virgin births and prophets and messiahs. I'd like to tell her to shut up, throw her books back at her; sometimes I do. But other times I listen and take the books. I need other worlds for my traveling mind.

I rarely see Rune, but I do see him as we pass through the

sanctuary on the way outside: he slumps over a painting or listens to Rebekka read. Sometimes I see him through my opened door, standing far behind the preacher or Sanne at the end of the hall. But I never hear his laughter; I never hear his music.

I listen for him now as I lie on the bed, as I stare at the walls, at the ceiling, as I read Sanne's delusions, trying to stave off insanity. I tell myself I wouldn't long for Rune the way I do if I weren't trapped in this cell of a room. I tell myself my feelings for him are biological, hormonal, nothing more. But I don't really believe this. I hear the preacher in my head over and over telling me Rune was in love with me, and at times I think I'm in love with him. But then I hate him.

"Why did you say it?"

I open my eyes and see his face above mine; Rune's face hangs above mine. I'm not sure if he's real or if I'm dreaming. Even if I touch him, I think, I won't know if I'm dreaming.

"Why did you say it?" he says again.

I shake my head; I don't know what he means. I want to reach up, feel his hair. A kerosene lamp burns on the table— he must have carried it into the room—and its light wanders through his hair and down his face and neck.

"You said I raped you," he says, and his dark eyes close. He's not wearing his glasses and his face is moist, and then my face is moist and I know I'm not dreaming. He opens his eyes and looks at mine. "I can't stay in here—if *Mor* finds me here . . . But I need to know why, Aslaug. Why you said it."

"Didn't you?" I say.

"Didn't I what? Didn't I rape you? How can you ask me that?" He pushes himself up, jerks the kerosene lamp toward him.

"Wait," I say. I try to reach for him, but he backs away. "Did you leave the tansy? Did you leave me that tea?"

"What?" he says. "What are you talking about?" And I see he doesn't know.

"I'm in love with you," I say.

He backs up against the door and almost falls. "You're crazy," he says, and I think I see fear in his eyes. "You're completely nuts." He knocks the door open.

"Wait," I say again.

But the door shuts and I hear the lock snap.

Solomon's Seal

2007

—Please state your name for the record.

—Dr. Amelia Hoenir.

—What's your profession, Dr. Hoenir?

—I'm a physician. An internist. I've had an office in Bethan for thirteen years now.

—Are you aware of any other doctors with the last name Hoenir practicing in Bethan?

—As far as I know, I've been the only Dr. Hoenir in Bethan since I opened my practice.

—Dr. Hoenir, have you ever met the defendant, Aslaug Hellig?

—I don't remember meeting her. I meet a lot of people, though.

—Do you have any records of ever having treated Aslaug Hellig?

—No. We looked for any records regarding her. We found none. And we have an excellent record-keeping system. Lots of checks and balances. It's pretty rare we would misplace anything. But even if we had, we've scoured our system trying to find records regarding Aslaug Hellig. We've found none.

—So you feel confident you never treated Ms. Hellig?

—As confident as I can be.

—Thank you, Dr. Hoenir. No more questions, Your Honor.

RAGGED ROBIN

2004

If not Rune, then how?

Another month passes. And then two, and this question balloons within me. I want to tell Sanne I'm no longer sure how I became pregnant; I want to tell the preacher and Rune. But how can I tell them? What would I tell them? That I am a child of God? That I am carrying the child of God?

Sanne opens the door; she's holding two books. "You'll enjoy these," she says, and she waves the books. She's a ragged robin: her hair is almost completely pink now, and it flames every which way. A cuckoo flower, Mother called the ragged robin. "These books are different than others I've left for you," Sanne says. "Nothing about a messiah in here. But they're provocative. The Essenes would have loved them." She tosses copies of the *Tao-te Ching* and Chuang Tzu on the bed. "You can't keep your life on course if you don't let it flow. 'Those who flow as life flows know they need no other force.'"

"What does that mean?" I say, and I think as Mother would have thought: a cuckoo flower. I grab a handful of old food from a tray and fling it at her white front; it forms a sick-star blemish of bleeding orange.

"That's brilliant," Sanne says. She picks clumps from her dress. "You know, Aslaug, the one thing I just can't understand is why God picked you for this and not someone with more imagination."

"You mean you can't understand why God didn't pick you, isn't that right?"

I see recognition in her eyes, but she says, "Flow as life flows, Aslaug."

"What the hell does that mean?" I say again.

"Cussing doesn't become you." She still picks at the star. "The saying's from the *Tao-te Ching*."

I look at the book lying on the bed. "I didn't ask where it's from. I asked what it means." I have the urge to pick up the *Tao-te Ching*, hurl it at her, but I resist; I want to read it. "That I should let you and *Gudinden* keep me locked up? That I should just accept I'm pregnant, even though I don't know how I became pregnant? Is that what you mean by letting my life flow?"

Sanne has turned to walk out the door, but she stops in the doorway; she turns around. Her pink hair slips into her face, falls out of her face. She reaches up and knots it, just like Mother used to do. I recognize my mother again in her, in her gestures, the shape of her wrists, the tendons that rail

319

her neck. "You just said you don't know how you became pregnant," she says.

"I don't know."

"But you said it was Rune. . . ."

"It wasn't Rune. I was wrong." And I feel the weight of what I'd said about Rune lift.

"How could you make a mistake about something like that?"

"I dreamt it," I say, "that Rune raped me. I didn't realize it was a dream."

Sanne steps back into the room, wraps her arms around me. I feel my middle press into her, the baby enveloped between us. I let myself be tucked into her body, as if I could share this enveloped baby, share the burden of what I'm carrying. And I sense myself go still inside, like a torrent has passed through me, cleaned me out.

"Until you became pregnant, it was all sort of a game to me. I was intrigued by Maren, her ideas. But I didn't really believe you'd been born of a virgin birth—that you were any sort of 'consecrated human being.' But I wanted Mor to think you might be. I wanted Rune to think you might be. I wanted you to think you might be. One night I even steeped jimsonweed in that schnapps Mor would give you, so you'd hallucinate or something. So you'd seem unusual to Mor and Rune. So they'd wonder."

"You drugged me?" I say. "When did you do that? Why would you do that?"

"For entertainment? I don't know. I was mad at Mor. I was mad at the world. I was bored. It was a stupid thing to do. Mor ended up drinking a whole bottle of the schnapps

I'd doctored. It nearly killed her. And it made you sick, too. I could have killed you both. I mean, I couldn't have known *Mor* would get that call. I couldn't have known she'd start drinking again. . . . Don't look at me like that, Aslaug. It was wrong. I know that. I don't know if I could've lived with myself if *Mor* hadn't recovered. But she did recover, and then you got pregnant, and I realized it wasn't a game. It had never been a game. God really had directed me to Maren's notes. God really had directed you here. This was real. What happened to Maren was real. What's happening to you is real." She says this, and yet I wonder, Is she trying to convince herself? "*Mor* wants to believe, too, because she doesn't want to think that Rune . . . But now she'll have to believe. What other ex- planation is there?"

What other explanation is there?

"Have I told you the Essene prayer about the Virgin Mary?" Sanne says. "Remember I mentioned some scholars think Mary was an Essene? Well, there's this prayer that seems to be about Mary. 'Within the Most High your soul blossoms. It leaps for joy at the sight of the ascendant path. What is on high came to meet what is below, and the Most High has impregnated your soul through His radiant look. Out of all the generations, yours is blissful, for the Almighty does great things for you. He impregnated your soul.'"

My knees shake as she recites this prayer. Is it possible? I think. Is it possible God impregnated my soul?

After Sanne leaves, I pick up one of the books she left, Chuang Tzu. I open to a passage and I read:

"Once upon a time, I, Chuang Tzu, dreamt I was a butterfly, fluttering hither and thither, to all intents and purposes a butterfly. I was conscious only of following my fancies as a butterfly, and was unconscious of my individuality as a man. Suddenly, I awaked, and there I lay, myself again. Now I do not know whether I was then a man dreaming I was a butterfly, or whether I am now a butterfly dreaming I am a man."

I think of the hairstreak for the first time in so long. I remember taking the butterfly in my mouth that day when collecting plants with Mother; I remember thinking of it as a butterfly soul; I remember wanting it to find a new mother— wanting to be its mother.

Is that how I became pregnant? I think. Was the hairstreak really a butterfly soul? But then I stop myself. Maybe Rune was right: maybe I am going mad. Mother used to mock me, offer me watercress, claim it was used to treat insanity. She'd call the plant *nasus tortus*, "convulsed nose," because of its pungency. I wanted to tell her at the time it was she who needed the convulsed nose, not me—it was she who was not sane. Yet I'm beginning to wonder. I've spent so much time in this room, staring at these walls, thinking of gods and goddesses, of Rune and Mother, and now of an impregnating God and butterfly souls. I can't help but question what's real, what could be real. I'm not sure anymore if I know.

I pray as I fall asleep this night, but I'm not sure which god I'm seeking. So I retreat to the crones, and again I ask them for understanding; I ask them to show me a glimmer of my fate.

In the morning I begin reading all the books Sanne's left for me. Really reading them, expecting for the first time they truly may be the only way for me to understand what's happened to me—what's happening to me. The more I read, the more interested I become; the more I start to believe there may be an answer hidden somewhere in one of these books. And Sanne senses the change in me, and she and I start to discuss what I've read, what she's reading. And I find myself feeling almost excited. I find myself believing this baby I'm carrying may actually be a prophet, some sort of messiah. The Essenes' "custodian of the divine on earth." And as more months pass, I wonder almost daily whether this is what Mother felt when she was carrying me. Only to find I was a disappointment.

According to Mother's notes, the Essenes believed the human mind is incapable of understanding the divine in any rational way; they believed the world as humans perceive it is essentially what Hindus call maya, or illusion.

"In certain mystery faiths *ma* meant 'soul,'" Sanne says. "And woman symbolized the soul. Woman also symbolized the earth. And the earth was thought to mirror the universal soul."

Sanne sits across the bed from me; a plate of *rugbrød* and blue castello teeters between us. She and the preacher no longer tape my mouth when we walk outside, and sometimes Sanne leaves me alone with the door unlocked for several minutes at a time. "I remember Mother paraphrasing a passage from one of her books," I say. "She hardly ever shared what she was reading with me, but one day she said something like, 'Regard this phantom world as a star at dawn, a bubble in a stream, a flash of lightning in a summer cloud, a flickering lamp, a phantom and a dream.' It was beautiful, I remember. Poetic. But I didn't think much of it at the time. But now it seems it's like this concept of the Essenes'. Like she was speaking of maya."

"That passage comes from Buddha," Sanne says. "That's something Buddha said. But the Essenes studied Buddhism. They studied whatever they could get their hands on. And that's what Maren did. That's what we should do. Because many of these concepts, like maya, cross many religions. The Gnostics, for instance, also believed in a form of maya they called Docetism."

"Meaning illusionism," I say.

"In Gnosticism the idea is that each human being is divided into two essential parts. A physical being, the eidolon, that suffers and eventually dies, and a spiritual being, the Daemon, that is utterly free from suffering and understands that the world is ephemeral, illusory. The Gnostics believed that the story of Christ's crucifixion and resurrection was a symbolic story: it represents the death of the eidolon and the resurrection of the Daemon. Through this death and resurrection, Gnostics believed each person can become a Christ."

"The stories you told me of Dionysus, Attis, Mithra, Adonis—they all involved death and resurrection," I say.

"Those stories were symbolic, too, obviously. The physical dies in a sense, so the spirit can live."

And then it strikes me: if death and resurrection are

symbolic, is virgin birth as well? The doubt I'd managed to bury is again breaking ground. "Maybe the stories about virgin birth were just as symbolic?"

Sanne holds her arms out wide, mimicking my roundness. "So your pregnancy is symbolic?" she says. "An illusion?" I'm over eight months pregnant now, maybe close to nine; my whole body looks swollen. "I'd say that's wishful thinking, Aslaug." And she laughs.

But I don't laugh. These stories are myths. Like the story of Yggdrasil. They're meant to represent spiritual teachings. They're not meant to be taken literally.

She pushes the plate to the side and rolls across the bed toward me. I couldn't do that, I think. Roll my body that way. My stomach is so round, and hard as an apple; the sacklike dresses Sanne gives me barely stretch across. And when the baby moves, the apple deforms and my torso juts to one side, but then the baby settles in and the apple re-forms, as hard and firm as it was at the start.

Sanne rests her head in my lap—her hair is thick like Rune's. She positions her webbed fingers on my middle. "Is the baby moving?"

Although Sanne and the preacher have controlled my movements and my diet and what I could read and do, they haven't taken the baby from me. They couldn't. They couldn't feel the baby move; they couldn't sense its life.

"A little," I say. And I move her hand to the spot where one tiny limb forms a knot. We sit without speaking for a minute, then two. Sanne closes her eyes; I have the impulse to run my fingers through her hair the way Rune ran his fingers through mine—make her an angel.

"I can feel it," Sanne says. She opens her eyes, and her pale cheeks flush some; she raises her eyebrows, giggles like I expect a child would. It feels good to share this with her. I hadn't realized how good it would feel to share the baby. And I realize the baby seems more mine suddenly, now that I've shared it. I feel more connected to the baby, now that I've opened its life beyond mine.

"I knew something like this was going to come into my life," Sanne says. She sits up, lifts her hand from my dress. "I can't explain it, but I knew. Something exceptional was going to happen in my life. The life I was leading before, it just didn't fit. And now *Mor* believes it, too."

"Sara? What does she believe?" The preacher treats me like a caged animal, but an animal she cares for. She speaks to me only about practicalities, but, since I retracted my accusation of Rune, she's been far more gentle. She asks whether I'm too hot, too cold, hungry, thirsty. She even rubs my feet when they swell, and my lower back when she sees my discomfort. And she tries to be less rough when she ties my hands, stuffs in the cloth.

"When you accused Rune, it was terrible for *Mor*," Sanne says. "*Mor* didn't know what to believe. Rune denied he'd raped you, but she wasn't sure. She wanted to believe him, but . . . she had reasons not to believe him, obviously. I mean, you're pregnant, and Rune . . . well, let's just say impulse control is not his forte. And we both could see he was taken with you. And he doesn't always have the best judgment—he's proved that. So you can imagine how relieved *Mor* was when you said you lied about Rune. And now she's come around. She believes this is a virgin birth.

She thinks you became pregnant because she laid hands on you. Do you remember that? When you were slain in the spirit? *Mor* thinks God touched you, and you became pregnant then. Leave it to *Gudinden* to find a way to pay tribute to herself in all of this. It doesn't matter, though, what she believes. Let her believe it's about her. That you got pregnant because of her. Maybe it will sober her up."

I've barely thought of my being "slain in the spirit" since it happened. But I remember it now, the way I felt filled up. I'd never made any connection between the pregnancy and that experience. But maybe the preacher is right; maybe I got filled up with this baby.

"Sober her up?" I say. "You mean literally? From drinking?"

"No," Sanne says. "And yes. It's not what I thought I meant." She looks at me now with an expression similar to her expression when the lights went out, then back on, when she saw my hand propped in the air. "People in the congregation don't know about *Mor*'s drinking. Pentecostals don't drink, right? It's not something I'm used to talking about. You know, *Mor* had mostly stopped drinking. She'd started when I was little. I remember her stumbling around, passing out. According to Mikkel, she even drank when she was pregnant with Rune. And the drinking continued after Maren left. Then when Rune started school, it wasn't easy for him. He had difficulty learning. He was diagnosed with a whole slew of problems. *Mor* blamed herself. She took us both out of school, started homeschooling us. And she started her church, and things got better—in a sense, anyway. She became addicted to God. Got drunk on God. She

327

went from getting drunk on Mikkel to schnapps to God. She did fall back into drinking once in a while after she started the church—mostly when Mikkel would call, after he'd call, or when there was some new issue with Rune—but for the most part she had the drinking under control. But she's drinking now again. Dulling herself. Trying to drown all the guilt she feels about Maren, it seems. Trying to bury the shit with Rune."

"You mean his learning problems? He seems so bright—"

"I never said he's not bright. He has an amazing memory. But he processes the world differently. And he sure doesn't think he's smart. . . . And he's impulsive, like I said. It gets him in trouble. And when he screws up, *Mor*'s reminded of how she screwed up."

"But he didn't screw up this time. She knows that—"

"Oh, but he did."

"What are you talking about?"

"Listen, it's not that easy for *Mor* to stop once she gets started, okay? And there are always setbacks with Rune. And there's always Mikkel—that hurt never completely left. And she doesn't like keeping you locked up like this. But she knows we did what we had to do. You didn't understand—"

"No," I say. "I didn't." And I don't.

"And, of course," Sanne says, "*Mor* feels the burden of what lies ahead."

"Of raising the child, you mean? She doesn't have to feel the burden of that. I know I'm young, but I don't expect anything from her."

Sanne's forehead creases; she straightens her back. "You don't get it, do you?"

"Don't get what?"

"You think you're going to raise this baby once it's born?" She shakes her head, and the pink strands fly. "This baby's not yours, Aslaug. You're just the vessel. This baby belongs to God."

SOLOMON'S SEAL

2007

—Dr. Hoenir, you do have records of treating Aslaug's cousin Susanne Lerner, don't you?

—I'm not at liberty to reveal that.

—In fact, you have records of having diagnosed Susanne Lerner as pregnant right at the time Aslaug says she became pregnant, don't you?

—Like I said, I'm not at liberty to reveal that information.

—Dr. Hoenir, when a patient arrives at your office, you don't check the person's identification, do you?

—You mean, do we check IDs? No.

—So someone could come in claiming he or she was one person and in fact be someone else entirely, isn't that right?

—I don't know why anyone would do that, other than for insurance fraud, maybe.

—But someone could do that, couldn't she?

—I suppose.

—It's possible, then, isn't it, that when Aslaug came in and you diagnosed her as pregnant, you thought she was her cousin Susanne Lerner?

—I never said I diagnosed Aslaug as pregnant.

—But it's possible you believed Aslaug was her cousin Susanne Lerner when she arrived at your office. If Aslaug told you she was Susanne, you wouldn't have known otherwise, isn't that right?

—So what you're saying is Aslaug is a liar? That she lied to me?

—Dr. Hoenir, I'm asking you a simple question, and I would appreciate a simple yes or no answer. You believe patients are who they say they are, right?

—Yes.

—You don't question patients about their identities, do you?

—No.

—So if Aslaug told you her name was Susanne Lerner, you would assume her name was Susanne Lerner, right?

—Yes.

—Thank you. I have no further questions.

SNAKEROOT

2004

*T*his baby belongs to God.

But it doesn't, I think. This baby is part of me. No matter the father, I'm this baby's mother.

As I watch Sanne walk from the room, as I hear the door close and the lock snap, I realize I've allowed this baby's context to become its prison. The circumstances of my conception defined so much of my life; it seems the circumstances of Rune's defined much of his. And now I've allowed this baby's origin to define its life, even before its birth. And yet, the baby's origin hasn't changed the feeling of its life—its weight in my body, its prodding and flipping and pushing. It hasn't changed the sensation of running my hands across the pink mountain of baby after I've drunk a glass of juice and feel the kicking, this expression of joy in sweetness. It hasn't changed the intimacy, this sharing of life. It hasn't changed my desire to give this child what I didn't have: love without guilt; love without bounds.

Love without Sanne's bounds.

Yet I see now what I should have seen before: when this baby is born, I will lose control. The baby will pass from my body to Sanne's hands, or the preacher's hands. Not my hands. If I'm still here. If I'm still here . . .

I can't still be here.

But how can I not be here?

The thought of escaping began as a torrent, and yet it's trickled away. And now, it seems, the torrent is flowing upside down, mixing me up, making me think I want to stay. Despite the reality that I've been caged here, I've felt less caged during this past month than I've felt my whole life. It seemed I was finding my place in the world, as if this baby and Sanne and the research were being woven together to form a tapestry even more beautiful than freedom: a tapestry of roots and purpose and relationships; a tapestry of meaning.

There is a sadness that comes over me now, that seems to push out what felt like meaning, push in the meaningless. Where will I go? How will I raise this baby? Is it wrong to deprive it of family, as I was deprived of family?

I'm getting close to the time the baby will be born—I sense this. I'm experiencing this tightening, and releasing, and tightening around the baby—as if my body's preparing itself for labor, giving itself trial runs. If I'm going to leave, I don't have much time.

Rebekka is not pregnant.

"You have to leave," she says. I open my eyes. It's night, dark, and yet I see: her face inches from mine. And I hear: a voice I barely recognize. For a second I can't connect this faint voice with this faint face, but then I remember: these angel's tresses, and a voice magnified in the microphone, praising God.

Rebekka stands upright now, moves her face farther from mine. I see she grips a suitcase in one hand, a kerosene lamp in the other. The lamp rocks as she moves; the light jerks.

"Rebekka?"

"You have to leave," she says. "Get up. Hurry. Get up." She sets the suitcase down and tugs at my body with her body, and I remember being drawn to her body, to the baby in her body. My hand finds the baby in mine. And I realize I'm sitting up in bed—I don't remember pulling up. The light illuminates the ball of baby on my thighs; it illuminates Rebekka, flings her shadow to the wall. And I see her shadow: this large and dark mass, nondescript, and yet, something is wrong.

"Come on," she says, and she pulls harder. Her hand on my skin is tiny; she is tiny. My arm flails, slams into her middle, but the mound it strikes is not firm and round. She is deflated, fleshy.

"Where is your baby?" The large mass on the wall was not large enough. "You had your baby?"

"There's no baby," she says. The light from the lamp settles brighter on her face, and I see her eyes are smudged black and dark lines streak her cheeks. She tugs free her left hand, smears its back along her cheekbone and across one eye, and the black thins and spreads.

"What are you talking about? You were pregnant—"

"Stop," she says. "Shut up."

"Rebekka?"

"They told me I couldn't speak to you, even look at you. They said they'd send me away. My family left me. I had nowhere to go. I had to leave the program—"

"What are you talking about?"

"They took my baby," she says. "They made me give her away. They're evil, Aslaug. They're awful. They're going to take your baby. . . . There's this place. This home for girls. Pregnant girls. You can go there."

She turns from me; she yanks open the suitcase and the bureau drawer; she heaves clothes into the case.

And I realize: she's helping me escape.

"What happened to you?" I say. "Please. What happened to your baby?" I climb from the bed. The baby is silent within me. Can I trust Rebekka? Do I want to trust her?

Rebekka slams the suitcase shut. "Let's go," she says. She walks toward the door with her legs spread wide.

If only there were a tree of the knowledge of good and evil. I'd take a bite of the apple just to know the difference. Is it better to stay or go? Can I trust my own judgment on this? After I spoke with Sanne yesterday, I believed I should escape, for the baby; but now the door is opening, and I want to close it. For the baby? If I leave, I'll deprive the child of love and family and roots. If I walk out this door, will I close more doors than I open?

Rebekka opens the door. And when she collides with Sanne, I feel mostly relief.

"Bekka?" Sanne says. She looks at me, back at Rebekka. "You should be resting, Bekka. What are you doing here?"

"I heard her," Rebekka says. "I got up to get something to eat, and I heard noise in here, saw Aslaug's door was unlocked. I came in, and I found her. She'd packed a suit-case." She holds up the case. "She was going to leave."

"No," I say. "That's not what happened."

But Sanne shakes her head. "No one's leaving." She holds a tray with tea; the tray is wet from the collision. "Go to bed, Bekka."

"I was trying to help . . . ," Rebekka says.

"Go to bed, Bekka," Sanne says again.

After Rebekka's left, Sanne directs me to sit down. I set-tle my bulging body onto the bed, and sink into the bed. Sanne hands me a cup of the tea. "I couldn't sleep," she says. "I made myself some tea to help me sleep, brought it down-stairs, but then I heard commotion." She takes a drink. "You were going to leave."

"No," I say. My heart is beating too fast for the baby. I take a drink of the tea; I hope it will calm me.

But it's black cohosh tea; it doesn't calm me.

Mother referred to the black cohosh plant as snakeroot: its plumelike flowers fall away, exposing round seedpods that produce a sound like a rattlesnake. Mother would boil the black cohosh's gnarled roots whenever she had a sore throat, and sometimes she would take a dose for energy if she was tired. And she had other uses for it—uses she didn't discuss with me. When I was a child, I thought the snakeroot was magical; I convinced myself she was secretive about it be-cause it had magical power. But when I got older, I realized she took the snakeroot when she was menstruating, and that its power lay in its ability to make Mother less irritable at that time. But Mother never told me of the snakeroot's power to make babies. She didn't tell me of the isoflavone in snakeroot called formononetin; she didn't discuss phytoestrogen; she didn't tell me how the snakeroot can stimulate the uterus, how it can play God, hasten birth. It's Sanne who tells me these things after she's given me the snakeroot tea. And I've drunk the tea before she tells me of the formononetin and phytoestrogen, before she tells me my uterus is going to start cramping, before she tells me she's played God. "It was all in the notes Maren left," Sanne says. "The notes explained everything. Where to find the black cohosh, how it works."

"But why would you give me that?" I say. "Why would you want to force the baby to come?"

"It's time," she says.

It's not until after the birth that I realize what she means.

Solomon's Seal

2007

—Please state your name.

—Dr. Hilda Gunnlod.

—What is your profession, Dr. Gunnlod?

—I've worked as a psychiatrist for twenty-two years.

—Have you met the defendant, Aslaug Hellig?

—Yes, I conducted a psychiatric evaluation of the defendant.

—When?

—Two months ago.

—What, if anything, did you conclude about the defendant's psychological health when you conducted the examination?

—Well, her case is a challenging one, I have to admit. Her psychological profile doesn't clearly indicate she is suffering from any one particular disorder. She's intelligent.

Articulate. Very sensitive to others' emotions. And she was pretty broken up about her mother's death and the death of those two women in the fire. But the more we talked, the more obvious it became that her grip on reality is tenuous. I'm not saying she doesn't understand the difference between right and wrong—I think she clearly does. She seems to have a strong moral compass. But she has these notions about her own birth and her childhood that seem delusional. And she told me she'd given birth to a baby, even though she claims she's never had sex. And even though there's no evidence of any baby ever having existed.

—Is it your opinion she really believes these things she was telling you, or do you believe she was lying to you?

—Objection. Calls for speculation.

—Overruled.

—Again, she's smart—I think she has the ability to be fairly manipulative if she wants to—so it's difficult for me to be sure. But my conclusion after spending a great deal of time with her is she truly believes at least some of what she's saying. I think she thinks she did have a baby. My opinion is she had strong feelings for her cousin. Rune is his name, I believe. And I think she probably fantasized about having a child with him. And that fantasy became a reality for her.

—You said she understands the difference between right and wrong, though. Despite her having a somewhat tenuous understanding of some aspects of reality, is it your opinion she would or would not have understood killing to be wrong?

—She knows killing is wrong.

—So if she poisoned those women, she would have known it to be wrong?

—Objection. Argumentative.

—I'm going to allow the question, provided the jury understands the doctor is not testifying Ms. Hellig did in fact poison anyone.

—The defendant knows poisoning someone is wrong.

—So if she tried to poison her mother, she would have understood this to be wrong as well?

—Objection, Your Honor. Counsel is trying to mislead the jury here. This line of questioning is argumentative. And it's leading.

—I'm going to allow it, but it's important the jury understand the doctor is only testifying about whether Ms. Hellig grasps the difference between right and wrong. The doctor is not testifying as to whether Ms. Hellig did in fact do anything wrong.

—If the defendant were to have poisoned anyone, her mother included, she would have known that to be wrong. Her misconceptions about reality did not affect her understanding of right and wrong.

—Thank you. I have no further questions.

TWO-EYED BERRY
2004

I sleep; I dream of an island occupied only by robins and butterflies. The robins are unable to fly; their breasts bulge; the weight holds them to the ground. But the butterflies flit about in the air; the air jitters with them and seems alive. One robin cries out, then it bursts wide, as if its breast were too full, and the robin becomes a butterfly, and it flutters.

I wake to this dream, and I think of flying, and then I hear myself cry out, and I realize I'm this robin about to burst: I'm in pain.

The pain is the same as I'd had—the tightening—and yet it's different, too. It seems embedded deeper in me, it's pulling in more of me. I touch my mound of stomach; it's rock-hard, and I feel the rock reaching around me as if with limbs, gripping my low back, holding on. And then it passes.

The rock limbs drop away, the rock mound softens, and I think: Is this it? Is this labor?

Sanne is balled and sleeping on the end of the bed. Her hair fans her; her mouth pulls tight; her eyes flutter behind her lids, as if she's watching the same butterflies. Sanne gave me not only snakeroot but partridgeberry, too—the plant Mother called two-eyed berry. She'd been serving me the two-eyed berry in salads and soups for weeks—I'd no idea it was there. "Partridgeberry prepares the uterus to give birth," she explained before she slept. She spoke as if I should be grateful for this, her meddling. "Your mother used it, of course, when she gave birth to you," as if it were inevitable the two-eyed berry and I would become one.

My mother. Did she know this was my fate? Was my life leading to this, no matter? Did she know I would journey to the two-eyed berry?

Another contraction strikes, harder, faster. The two-eyed berry. I imagine the berry's eyes, one on either side of the plump berry flesh. If they had sight, these berry eyes, each would see so differently, looking, as they do, in opposite directions. Like me. It seems of my two eyes, one eye sees and feels, the other fails to see or forgets. Because the pain is the same that happened just minutes before, but in the moment of reprieve, part of me forgot. And this part of me again is surprised at this thickening and hardening and gripping all around, and another part of me thinks, *Yes, this I know.*

As the contractions come and go and come, this pattern of knowing and not knowing, seeing and not seeing, continues. And as I watch Sanne sleep, her eyes still aflutter, the eye of mine that forgets sees me leaving. I imagine myself unraveling from this bed, gathering the suitcase, slipping out the door while Sanne watches butterflies. But then another contraction grabs me, and it is the contraction that unravels me from the bed. I find myself on my knees on the floor, then on my hands and knees. I feel the pressure, that bursting robin. My back feels both spread and squeezed, and my knowing eye—my seeing eye—again says, *Yes, this I know,* and I know: I couldn't leave now even if I wanted to.

The rain comes then: it gushes down my thighs, streaks my calves, puddles beneath me.

"Your water," Sanne says. "My God, it's your water." Sanne is awake, I realize: she's passed from the birth of the dream butterflies to this birth. I wish her away; then I wish her near. Nearer. The pain seems to have washed from me with the rain, and I feel lucid in this moment. And I feel scared.

"*Mor,*" she says. "Sara. I'll get her?"

I see what seems surprise in Sanne's face. And I wonder: Did she think the snakeroot powerless? Is that why she's surprised? Did she doubt the might of the two-eyed berry? Or has this pregnancy continued to be a fantasy—a game— and now she must face the reality of what was until now unreal?

Sanne runs from the room, as much to get away, I think, as to get Sara.

"The baby's coming!" I hear. "The baby's coming!"

And I hear pounding, on the floor or in my head? Then my body starts to shake. I'm an emerald leaf quivering on

343

Mother's oak; I'm a windflower. I want to rest, but my body wants to shake. I want to float away in the wind, but my body wants to push to the earth, it wants to root itself here.

And then I hear a voice. "Your baby is wearing a mantle of snow," it says. "Your baby will have the hair of wisdom and will become the Word of God." I look around me, trying to see who spoke these words. Sanne? The preacher? But I am alone; it seems the voice has come from nowhere, and everywhere. It's in this moment I know: I have to push. And I do, I push. And now I hear people in the room. Sanne, yes. The preacher, yes. And someone else. A doctor, maybe. Or a midwife. They've brought someone to help.

But the woman is no doctor. She is no midwife. She's not here to protect the baby or ease my pain. She retreats into the background and seems to disappear, and I nearly forget she's there. But after the pain stops, the woman reappears, and she causes far more pain.

I feel the baby push through my bones; my body spreads and opens this door. I push again, and the baby passes from me, as simply as a pea from a pod. And as tortuously as a pod from a pea.

"It's a girl," the preacher says, but it sounds like a question.

I turn back and panic rushes over me, like that rain of water. I see the baby girl, and I forget the voice. The baby is small and still, and dead, I think. But the preacher scoops her finger through the baby's mouth, and it's as if she's scooped in life. The baby goes from limp to electric: her body jolts and her little fists flail and she opens her mouth and wails. Her voice should be familiar, it seems—I've carried her in me for so long—but it's not familiar.

"Let me hold her," I say, and I think, Will she seem a stranger when I hold her?

"The placenta still needs to come," the preacher says. "Lie down here on the bed."

I climb up to the bed, but my body trembles. And I see the red, the bright blood, so like that schnapps. It seems the Red Sea, and I carry it with me as I settle onto the bed. The bed becomes the Red Sea. And now my body jerks: a rhythmic beating; it no longer seems to know what it's doing. The placenta passes, I think. But I'm cold. I'm so cold. I close my eyes. I want the shaking to stop; I want to be warm.

"She should eat," I hear the preacher say. "Come, Rebekka, hold her. See if she'll nurse." But I don't know what she means. It seems my knowing eye can no longer see. Rebekka's baby. Is this Rebekka's baby? Yes, I think. That's why I didn't recognize the baby's voice. This is Rebekka's baby. And the nurse. Is there a nurse here? Why doesn't she help me, this nurse? I need her to stop this shaking. I need her to make me warm.

I wake to a room like the room I've come to know so well, and yet it is my room as it might exist in a dream. The same, and yet not the same. The bureau, the washbasin, the frame of the bed, all the same. But a different mirror hangs above the sink. A different makeshift nightstand sits to my left. And a chair sits in the corner, and the preacher sits in it,

345

sleeping. Her mouth hangs in a frown, and her face hangs. She makes no sound at all. And I think, I didn't go into labor; I didn't give birth. Then my hand finds my torso, and plunges.

"Where's my baby?" I say.

The preacher's body jerks, and I remember the baby, the way its body came to life. And its cry. That strange cry.

"Aslaug. Oh, thank God," the preacher says. "Thank God." And she rises from the chair as if from an egg or a chrysalis: all fits and starts.

"Where is my baby?" I say again.

"You scared us, Aslaug. You lost so much blood. I thought you might die."

And then I think, My baby died. It was Rebekka's baby I heard. Not mine. "She's dead?" I say.

"What?"

"The baby?"

"No," the preacher says. And she heaves, and my mind sees: the baby's first breath, when Sara scooped in life. "The baby's fine. She's healthy. She's lovely. She looks just like you. Like Maren."

I want to ask about the syndactyly. Does she have it? But then I think, Of course she doesn't have it; Rune's not her father.

"I was expecting a boy," Sara says, and I see the confusion that swims in her eyes, and the frown that remains.

"A boy?" Of course she was expecting a boy: she was expecting Jesus. And I want to laugh, and then I don't want to laugh: was I expecting Jesus? "I want to see her," I say.

Sanne opens the door, then, to this room that is my

room and not my room. "Aslaug," she says, and she walks in. "How are you? Thanks for scaring the shit out of us." Her whole body seems in motion; she's talking fast. "I knew you'd be okay, though. Thanks to Maren, I'd prepared the trillium tea."

Large-flowered trillium. Mother called it birthroot because, like *Sanguisorba*, it drinks up blood, but unlike *Sanguisorba*, it drinks up internal blood.

"How do you like your new digs? We had to move you to the guest room. We're cleaning your room. . . ."

The guest room. The green room. I think of finding my face there in the green room, and of longing for a different face, a different life. And now I have a different life with the same face. And now there is a baby with this face that is Mother's face. As I think this, I remember the voice—the voice with no source. Was I hallucinating because I'd bled so much? "I heard a voice," I say, almost without intending to. "Just before the baby was born. I must have imagined it."

"You heard a voice?" Sanne says.

"It said something about a mantle of snow and hair of wisdom and the Word of God."

"It's what Mary heard when she was about to give birth to Jesus," Sanne says, and her girlish voice becomes Mother's claws across a canning lid. "White snow is the Essenes. The hair of wisdom is God's wisdom. And the baby is a prophet—the Word of God. You heard the voice of God, Aslaug. That was the voice of God." Sanne grips her own hands, lets go, grips, lets go. Her feet jitter beneath her. Her eyes can't seem to focus.

"I have to go," the preacher says, and she stumbles, and I wonder if she stumbles from exhaustion or schnapps or awe at God's power. "You'll stay with Aslaug?" She doesn't wait for Sanne's answer. The door shuts.

And my mind swings wide, because I remember: I read this passage in one of the less convincing sources about the Essenes; I read that Mary heard this voice before Jesus's birth. But I'd come to believe this information was inaccurate— that the notion of Mary being an Essene was wishful thinking at best. As far as I could discern from the rest of my reading, the Essenes were all men. And yet, the voice. Why did I hear the voice? Maybe I just remembered what I'd read, imagined it was happening to me.

"I want to see her," I say. I try to sit up. Then I try again, and give up. "Where is she? I want to hold her. I need to nurse her."

"You're too weak," Sanne says. "You know that. We're taking care of her. She's being fed."

"Being fed? What are you feeding her? I should be nursing her." And I see in the film of my mind a memory I'd lost, and now find: a feral mother cat in a field of downy brome, and five kittens latched in a fan, like sun rays. And I sense the feeling I had then: a longing to be that feral mother.

"Mor hired Rebekka," Sanne says.

"Hired her?"

"She'll nurse the baby. Rebekka will."

"My baby?" And then I remember Rebekka's words: "They're evil. They're awful. They're going to take your baby."

"I want to see Rebekka," I say.

"She's nursing Sofie," Sanne says.

"Sofie?"

"The baby."

"Whose baby? Her baby?"

"No," Sanne says. "Her baby is gone."

"Gone? It died?"

"No. No," Sanne says. "Mor helped Bekka find the baby a home. A couple who couldn't have children—"

"You can't give my baby away—"

"Give Sofie away? Of course we wouldn't give her away."

"Then why are you calling her Sofie? And why isn't she here with me? Why would you ask that girl to nurse my baby?"

I see a tightening in the skin around Sanne's nose, and a flaring of her nose. "Because Sofie is not your baby," she says.

And I think, Why didn't I leave? I knew this was going to happen, that my baby would pass from my body to their hands. Why didn't I hurry like Rebekka prodded me? Why didn't I listen to her, and leave? If I'd moved more quickly, I could have escaped before Sanne arrived. "I can nurse the baby," I say. "I don't need Rebekka to nurse her. I'm not that weak."

"It's not up to you, Aslaug," she says. "It's not up to you who nurses Sofie. This has always been the plan. Even before you became sick. It's better this way. We'll all have our roles in raising Sofie. You, Bekka, Mor, me. And Rune? I don't know what Rune will do. First he'll have to get the stick out of his ass."

Split the baby, I think. But I say, "Wisdom," and I try to conceal the flood in me. This has always been their plan? And yet I know, as Mother would say, I made this bed: the

349

baby is in their hands now. "*Sophia* means 'wisdom.' You named her Wisdom."

"The Gnostic gospels characterize wisdom as a woman. The woman, Sophia," Sanne says. "And they refer to Sophia as the Mother of the *Logos*, the Word of God."

SOLOMON'S SEAL

2007

—Cross-examination?

—Dr. Gunnlod, you don't know for a fact whether Aslaug gave birth or not, do you?

—She said she'd never been intimate with a man—

—But you don't really know whether she ever had a baby? Please just answer yes or no.

—I know if she's never been with a man she couldn't have had a baby.

—Dr. Gunnlod, you're a psychiatrist, not a gynecologist. You didn't examine Aslaug physically to determine whether she'd ever been pregnant, did you?

—Of course not.

—So you don't know whether she did in fact have a baby, do you?

—No.

—Thank you. And you don't have any direct knowledge regarding Aslaug's childhood, do you?

—I know what she told me about her childhood, and I know the types of things she described as happening are unlikely to have happened.

—But you are not sure what happened to Aslaug when she was a child, are you, because you weren't there?

—I'm trained to be able to distinguish fact from fiction. That's part of my job. It's my expert opinion that Ms. Hellig fictionalized her childhood. I don't think she necessarily did this intentionally, but, nevertheless, I think her view of the past is a distorted one.

—But you can't be one hundred percent sure of that, can you?

—I can be ninety-nine percent sure. Ms. Hellig described outlandish events. People don't get pregnant supernaturally—that happens in books and myths. It doesn't happen in real life. She described having been caged up throughout her childhood, but her neighbor would see her running about their yard, climbing trees. Alone. She claims to have been caged up in this church that burned down. But people were attending church there at the time. And no one saw any sign of her being locked up. I could go on.

—Her neighbor was a drunk—

—Objection, Your Honor. Move to strike. Argumentative.

—Sustained. No more of that, Counsel.

—Dr. Gunnlod, you did not know Aslaug when she was a child, did you?

—No.

—And so you have no choice but to speculate regarding what did or did not happen to her when she was a child, correct?

—I'm trained—

—Please just answer by saying "correct" or "incorrect."

—Correct, I have to speculate, but I—

—Thank you. You said in your earlier testimony that Ms. Hellig was traumatized by the death of the two women in the fire and by the death of her mother, right?

—Yes, that's right.

—And you also described Aslaug as having, and I quote, "a strong moral compass," did you not?

—Yes.

—It's not your experience, is it, that a premeditated killer would have a so-called strong moral compass?

—It really depends on the situation.

—Does it?

—Yes. It's actually not all that unusual for a premeditated killer to have a strong sense of right and wrong. People who commit crimes like murder often know that what they're doing is wrong—

—But you have no evidence Aslaug actually killed or tried to kill anyone, do you?

—No, I don't.

—Thank you. I have no further questions.

MILKWORT

2004

"**P**urple milkwort is useless," Mother told me as we walked through the tiny rose-colored flowers. She grabbed a fistful and crushed them; I remember the escape of their odor, like wintergreen.

"Why is it called milkwort?" I asked. I loved hearing Mother's descriptions, her explanation for plants' names— and the names she herself would give to plants. Because she'd often plummet back into her child's mind—a mind that swirled in angels and devils and witches and kings. And snakes and robins and bees.

"People thought nursing mothers and cows that consumed it produced more milk, but that's hogwash," Mother said. "It doesn't work."

I remember wondering how she knew it didn't work. And now I wonder whether the milkwort could work, because I've not nursed my baby—and the milk's not come.

I've remained locked in this guest room that is not green, and in this body that lacks its guest. I hear the baby cry at night; the first few nights I heard the cry, I felt a tingling in my breasts I hoped would turn to milk. But it didn't. And now the tingling has stopped. I'm not that feral cat: no baby will find nourishment in me.

They named my baby Sofie, but that's not her name. No matter what Sanne says, no matter the voice, that's not her name.

Her name is *Gnaphalium*, like Mother. I think of her as Phalia. Although I can't remember what she looked like during those few minutes she was with me, Sara said she looks like me and Mother. And I see her in my mind's eye: I see the golden-petal hair of *Gnaphalium*. And I see the shimmering-pollen eyes. I see myself holding this child that is Mother, that is me. That is *Gnaphalium*, this life everlasting.

When they let me out, I will hold her close, I think. Mother never held me. I will tell her I love her. Mother never told me. I'll never hurt her. She will never be afraid of me. I will be for her the love Rune spoke of: this love without bounds. And she will grow with the security of knowing she will be cared for, protected and loved.

Rebekka needed money and a place to stay. Her parents had sent her to stay in a home for unwed mothers and moved away. But Rebekka kept running from the home, arriving at the church. Sara would return her, and she'd run again. Finally the home refused to take Rebekka back, and Sara agreed to take her in. "*Mor* told Rebekka she could live with us until she gave birth, and after if need be, if she agreed to give the baby up for adoption." Sanne explains this to me the tenth morning after Phalia's birth. She sits on the stone floor; she hugs her knees. The shoulder of her white blouse is splotched in creamy rings, and she smells like milk curdled by wild madder. "And then it occurred to me," she says, "Rebekka could nurse Sofie. It made so much sense. So after Rebekka delivered her baby, after the couple from Michigan arrived and took the baby, I gave you the snakeroot. It all just came together like it was destined."

I feel like strangling Sanne; I feel like wrapping my hands around that neck that looks so much like Mother's neck and squeezing until she can't talk anymore. I hate her in this moment, more than I've ever hated anything. And I feel, almost, that I could kill her. And not just in my mind.

"I'd like to see Sofie," I say, as I do every day, yet the name feels so wrong in my mouth. "Why are you keeping her from me?"

"You'll see her when you're ready."

"She is ready." I hear Rune's voice, then I see him in the doorway, and I see the bundle in his arms. And I feel again like the two-eyed berry: both the surprise of the new, of the not remembering; and the recognition of the old, of the remembering.

"You have no right, Rune," Sanne says.

"Shut the fuck up, Sanne," Rune says.

"Don't talk that way while you're holding Sofie."

"I'll talk any damn way I want to, Sanne. You may be able to manipulate everyone else around you, but I'm done letting you manipulate me. Now get the hell out of here. Let Aslaug have some peace with her baby."

"I'm not leaving," Sanne says. "You can't make me leave."

"Either get the hell out, or I'll go to the police, like I should have long ago. And leave the door unlocked. No one's locking this door again."

As I watch Sanne move past Rune and into the hall, I think, Rune still cares for me, despite what I did, what I said. I feel so much longing, for the baby or Rune; it's hard for me to separate the feelings.

Phalia doesn't have syndactyly. This is my first thought when Rune unravels the blanket and I see Phalia's small fists stretching to the sky. And I wonder, Why did I think that? And then I see her pink skin and bald head and her mouth open, and searching, and I know I'm feeling something neither the preacher nor Sanne nor Rune can feel.

"May I hold her?" I say.

He laughs. "Of course you can hold her. She's your baby."

She's my baby.

I don't take her from Rune's arms. I run my hands across the rings of her, on her legs and fat arms. I remember the picture of me and Rune with these same rings, separating the plump from the plump. And I feel that love without bounds, and yet I feel she is a stranger, too.

Rune moves her from his arms to my arms. It feels awkward to hold her. I feel I might drop her. She arches her small back; she cries out.

"What am I doing wrong?" I say.

"You're not doing anything wrong. I think she's hungry. Sit down. Try to nurse her."

"But I don't know how," I say. And I think what I can't say: I've squeezed my breasts in search of milk. And there's no milk. The milkwort, I think again. Perhaps the milkwort.

"Try," Rune says. "At first, no one knows how. Rebekka didn't. . . ." And then he stops, realizes what he's said.

Phalia starts to cry louder. My hands are slick on her body.

"Nurse her." Rune raises his voice above Phalia's raised voice.

And Phalia raises her voice further. And now she sounds like the squealing springs of the bed, but magnified, sharpened. And her pale skin is no longer pale, but purplish red; she looks near bursting. She pulls her plump thighs to her chest, arches her back more.

"I can't hold her," I say. "I'm going to drop her."

"You're going to drop her?"

I push her back into Rune's arms. "Take her. Please. I can't hold her. Take her to Rebekka."

"But you wanted to hold her—"

"I don't want to," I say.

Solomon's Seal

2007

—Ms. Hellig, during the period of time when you claim you became pregnant, you were infatuated with your cousin Rune Lerner, were you not?

—Objection. Relevance.

—I'll allow the question, but please get to the point, Counsel.

—I don't understand what you mean.

—I think you do, Ms. Hellig.

—Objection, Your Honor. Counsel is badgering the witness.

—Sustained.

—During the period of time when you claim you became pregnant, you were attracted to your cousin Rune, were you not?

—I don't know.

—You don't know?

—I'd never been around a teenage boy before.

—A simple yes or no answer, please.

—Yes, I was, but—

—But he was in love with another young woman, wasn't he?

—Objection. Speculation.

—Sustained.

—It's your belief Rune Lerner fathered another woman's child, isn't that right?

—Yes.

—You were jealous of this other woman, weren't you?

—I didn't know about her until later.

—Ms. Hellig, were you or were you not jealous when you learned Rune Lerner had fathered another woman's child?

—I was jealous.

—So jealous you made up some cockamamy story about having a baby yourself?

—No.

—Objection, Your Honor. Move to strike. Argumentative.

—Sustained.

—Ms. Hellig, it's true, isn't it, that you sometimes have difficulty distinguishing reality from fantasy?

—I'm not sure.

—You're not sure what is reality and what is fantasy?

—No, it's just that there have been times when I thought my dreams were real, but otherwise—

—So you'd agree, then, that you sometimes confuse fantasy with reality?

—Not about this, though. Not about being pregnant, having the baby. I mean, there's a child.

—But you have no idea where this supposed child is, isn't that right?

—I don't know where she is.

—So how can you be sure she is not just a figment of your imagination?

—She's not—

—How can you be sure you didn't dream you gave birth to a baby because you were so jealous of Rune's having a child with another woman?

—No, it wasn't a dream. Phalia was real.

—Phalia?

—The baby. But she's not a baby anymore. She's a little girl.

WATER LILY
2006

𝒮he looks just like me.

Phalia is over two years old now, and she looks just like me; she looks just like Mother. And yet, she is not like me; she is not like Mother. Phalia is the girl I was supposed to be; she's the girl Mother was longing for. Phalia is a child not of this earth; yet she is a child very much of this earth. As I've come to know her, I've come to realize Sanne was right: by some miracle I've not even begun to understand, God chose Mother, God chose me, to deliver this wonder into the world. The voice I heard when I was giving birth was not my imagination: it was the voice of God.

After Rune unlocked my door, Sanne told me I could stay or go. "But Sofie stays."

I thought of leaving; I thought of trying to steal Phalia away. But I knew I'd never leave. How could I leave? The responsibility of raising Phalia had become too real. I couldn't even meet her basic needs.

And over time I've come to see what Sanne saw from the start: Phalia is a gift from God. I realize now it truly was God's plan that Phalia be raised in this church, with Sanne and the preacher and Rune, and Rebekka, too. We all have something to offer her, something she needs. No one of us could nourish her alone.

I've had opportunity to read Mother's notes, and I've found Sanne was telling me the truth: Mother wrote of bloodroot and madapple and snakeroot, and the two-eyed berry; but she also wrote of Dionysus and Attis and Mithra and Adonis—of their virgin births, their miracles. And she wrote of the Essenes.

And I understand, now, why Mother was drawn to the Essenes. The Essenes' teachings must have felt to Mother as they do to me: like going home, to Hartswell, to Denmark, to *Bedstefar,* to Yggdrasil. The natural world, so central to Mother's understanding of life, was vital to the Essenes' understanding of the divine. And the Essene tree of life is Yggdrasil, slightly changed.

The lower branches of the tree of life contain earthly forces: the earthly mother, and the angels of sun, water, air, earth, life and joy. Its upper branches contain heavenly forces: the heavenly father, and the angels of eternal life, creativity, peace, power, love and wisdom. Humans live in the center of the tree, halfway between the angels of earth and heaven.

Mother's notes intimate the Essenes believed no one religion could embody the sacred—that all religious faiths seek to bridge the heavenly realm with the earthly. And, as Sanne said, Mother wrote of consecrated individuals, like Phalia: individuals sent to earth to help illuminate the commonalities among different faiths, to bridge this divide.

Phalia sits in my lap now, the soft and spongy leafstalk of the water lily in her grip. Sanne made a straw for her from the water lily's stalk, and Phalia sucks it now, dragging sweet liquid into her mouth that is my mouth, that is Mother's mouth. I think of the first time I saw that mouth as my mouth—that time so long ago when I was little more than a child, my childlike body stretching to see. It must have been torment for my mother to look at my face that was her face day after day. I wish she could be here now. I wish she could see that all was not for naught: God did have a plan.

"Aslaug?" Phalia says, and she plants her moist lips on mine, and I want to drink her in. And then I don't: as much as I love her, she makes me uneasy. It seems she should be knowable to me because she was part of me, because she looks so like me, because she is two. And yet, she is a mystery that only deepens as days pass.

Phalia peeks through the straw into my eye. "Your eye is a wantern," she says.

"A lantern?" I say. "How do you know what a lantern is?" But it is an inane question. How does she know half of what she knows? She imbibes the world around her as if through the water lily; she forgets nothing, it seems. Languages and stories and images and concepts race into her mind, take root, blossom. Yet it is less what she takes in, more what is just in her—what sprouts there without ever having been planted—that makes us all realize that little in the world is as we expected it to be. Including ourselves. For Phalia has changed everyone here: the preacher and Rebekka and Rune and Sanne. And me.

The preacher let her church pass away, let it fade back into the stone walls, let the stone walls come back to life. After my release, I'd see the preacher near the altar of the church, her hands gripping fistfuls of nothing, her mouth rambling in that language that is no language. Glossolalia. Pleading to her God for answers. Because Phalia didn't fit into the preacher's scheme of God, and even *Gudinden* couldn't discount what Phalia was, what she is. So the preacher ceased being Pastor Sara, and yet, in many ways, she is the preacher still. As Sanne would say, she's evolved from being drunk on Mikkel to schnapps to God to schnapps. And now she is drunk on Phalia. And yet, she still has a closeness with God, a spirituality. A sort of power. The angel of power in the Essene tree of life. And Phalia is drawn to this in her, and draws from this in her.

Rebekka remains living at the church, and she still nurses Phalia. I hated Rebekka for a time as I watched her nurse my baby. But I fell in love with her, too, as I saw her love my baby. Because she does love Phalia. She still refers to Phalia as Sofie, but she sings with her and reads to her, as she still does to Rune, and sometimes she falls asleep with Phalia across her breast. And she cooks for Phalia—for all of us—meals so different than Mother ever made, than I ever made. Mother and I ate what we could find when we could find it. We combined flavors and foods because we were forced, limited by the season, the weather, Mother's mind, Mother's health.

But Rebekka combines flavors and foods because they fit. She is an artist in this way; she has an innate sense of what fits. And I find pleasure in eating, in food, I never would have imagined. This is a gift Rebekka has given me; this is a gift she's given Phalia. Rebekka is the caretaker Mother never was. She's made this church into our home, adding sofas and comfortable chairs and beautiful bedding. When I think of Rebekka in the context of the Essene tree of life, I know she represents sustenance: she is the earthly mother. She is Phalia's earthly mother.

And Rune. He is Phalia's angel of creativity, and perhaps her angel of joy. He brings art and poetry to her life. And laughter. As he brought me. Not as he brings me. For Rune and I rarely speak, and when we do, it seems we speak in runes—everything he says, and I say, seems to have hidden meaning that neither of us understands. Although Rune still teases and jokes, it seems underlying his joviality is a harsh-ness, a coldness, as if he's sliding across the barely frozen wa-ter of the harbor, certain the ice will crack, certain he'll slip through. He doesn't trust me, I know. I hurt him, I know. Our relationship will never be what it was. And yet, when I see him cuddle Phalia, and tickle her, I can't help but re-member his touch in my dream. I can't help but wish he shared this memory.

Sanne. Although we've all learned a great deal about love from Phalia, it is Sanne who seems Phalia's angel of love. Phalia loves Sanne perhaps more than anyone. It seems Phalia knows, in some way, it was Sanne who believed in her all along. Sanne's frantic energy has waned; her hair is growing back to its natural color. She no longer seems driven by the need to be noticed or loved or wanted, because she is noticed and loved and wanted, by Phalia. She refers to Phalia as Sofie Phalia now; I know she does this to please me. And although she still insists we teach Phalia for hours and hours each day "to prepare her," she herself seems most content when she is listening to Phalia, not teaching her.

And I? In the Essene tree of life, I am Phalia's angels of sun, water, earth, air and life. Because I teach Phalia of snowflakes and lightbulbs. And of wartwort and bloodroot and devil's-bite and witch hazel—of all the plants that have shaped my life. Yet I also teach her of Yggdrasil, and of its three old crones. And of butterfly souls. And I hope these will help her on her way to bridging the gap between heaven and earth, as Mother in her own way helped me to bridge that gap. Maren Hellig: the angel of eternal life. She lives in me; she lives in Phalia.

As to the angels of wisdom and peace—those remaining angels in the tree of life—these angels have yet to arrive, it seems. Perhaps it is Phalia herself who will be these angels. Already she has taught us all so much: she came into the world knowing well how to laugh and love.

Rune sneaks up behind us, reaches around me, pulls the water lily stalk from Phalia's still-plump grip, hides it behind me.

"Hey," Phalia says, and she giggles. "It's Woon. He took the stwaw. He's playing hide-and-seek."

Rune peers from around my back. "You better hide, then," he says. "And hurry. I'm about to come seeking. You don't want to make it easy for me, do you?"

"No!" Phalia squirms from my lap, and I watch her feet, still in penguin mode, skitter across the stone and disappear.

"One, two, three. Come away with me," Rune says. "Four, five, six."

"Pick up sticks?" I've learned all these childhood games along with Phalia.

"Seven, eight, nine. I'm serious. We'll take Phalia. Ten, eleven. She shouldn't be here. She shouldn't have to endure this craziness."

"What craziness?"

"Twelve, thirteen. What craziness? You're not serious. Aslaug, I understand what you've done, what you're doing. I've done the same thing. It seemed I had to. I know you think you had to. But it's not fair to Phalia. And I know you love Phalia. I wasn't sure at first . . . but I can see you love her. Don't do this to her."

"Woon?" Phalia says. "You're not counting."

"Fourteen, fifteen."

"What am I doing?" I say.

"Sixteen. Aslaug, we can get out of here, with her. We don't have to do this."

"You're saying you want us to run away? Rune, we can't raise Phalia. We can't raise her on our own."

"Seventeen, eighteen. Why not? Is it better for her to be raised by a drunk, and a woman who's lost touch with reality?"

"Sara's not drinking that much—"

"Open your eyes, Aslaug."

"And who's lost touch? Who are you talking about?"

"Are you coming, Woon?" Phalia calls.

"Nineteen. Aslaug, Sanne really believes in the virgin birth bullshit. She's going to fuck Phalia up."

"It's not bullshit, Rune."

"Twenty," Rune says. "Ready or not. Here I come."

Solomon's Seal

2007

—Ms. Hellig, you started the fire at the church on Kettil Street, didn't you?

—Yes.

—Objection, Your Honor. Aslaug had jimsonweed in her system at the time. It affected her cognitive abilities. She's confused about what did and didn't happen.

—Objection overruled. What Ms. Hellig remembers is relevant, even if her memory is distorted. It's the jury's job to sort that out.

—And you started the fire in an attempt to kill your cousin Rune and the young woman, Rebekka, and their baby, isn't that right? You thought they were inside.

—Objection. Counsel is being argumentative. And his question was compound.

—They weren't inside. I knew they weren't inside.

—The objection is sustained. Please strike Ms. Hellig's answer from the record.

—You poisoned those two women with jimsonweed so they couldn't stop you from setting the fire, isn't that right?

—Objection—

—I didn't poison them, but it's my fault they're dead. I know it's my fault.

—Objection, Your Honor. Move to strike. Counsel is being argumentative.

—Objection sustained.

—Ms. Hellig, do you really expect us to believe your mother and your aunt and cousin all died with jimsonweed in their systems but you didn't poison them?

—Objection. Argumentative.

—Sustained. That's enough of that, Counsel.

—Ms. Hellig, you've admitted painting an image using bloodroot sap on your mother's torso after her death, correct?

—Objection. Asked and answered.

—Overruled.

—Yes.

—You are aware, are you not, Ms. Hellig, that remnants of bloodroot sap were also found on Susanne Lerner's body? Her dead body?

—Yes.

—But you're claiming, are you not, that you had nothing whatsoever to do with the bloodroot sap found on Susanne Lerner's body?

—I didn't do it.

—You didn't do what, Ms. Hellig?

—The image painted on Sanne, I didn't do it. I didn't paint it.

—What image, Ms. Hellig? No one's mentioned any image. How do you know there was an image painted on her torso?

—Objection, Your Honor. Argumentative.

—I'll withdraw the question. Ms. Hellig, just so we're clear on this, you would have the jury believe that these similarities between the death of Susanne and Sara Lerner and the death of your mother are mere coincidence, is that right?

—Yes. . . . I mean, no.

—Which is it, Ms. Hellig? Yes or no? Coincidence or no coincidence?

—Coincidence.

SWAMP LILY
2006

"She's gone."

It's the middle of the night. Sanne stands in the doorway to my bedroom, the same room where I dreamt of Rune, was caged, gave birth. The floral comforter Rebekka chose for my bed heaps around me; the flowers crease and hide as I pull myself up. Sanne turns on the light and the world flashes bright, then black.

"She's gone," Sanne says again.

I push my hair from my eyes, and the room filters in.

"What's wrong?" I say. Fear wells up in me; it locks my body, my mind. There is death in Sanne's face: doll's eyes.

"Sofie Phalia," she says. "She's gone." But her voice is too quiet for these words. I've misheard.

"I thought you said 'gone'?"

"I heard them leaving. I tried to stop them."

"What are you talking about?" I say. "Who do you mean?"

Sanne's body cascades to the floor, and she hugs herself, as if tucking her body into the package that enveloped Mother when she died. Sanne's eyes are open and quiescent. But her body rocks, like she's easing herself farther and farther in.

"Sanne?" I say. I feel the pull of the package; somehow I know what Sanne's failed to say.

"Bekka," she says then, as if not to me. "Rune. They took her. They took my baby."

"Why would they do that?" Rune wanted me to leave with him; not Rebekka. I lift myself from the bed, Sanne from the floor. Her arms feel brittle in my grip; she looks into my face. And I know.

"Do you really not know, Aslaug?" she says. "Do you really not know?"

"No," I say. But I do know. Suddenly I do know. How is it that I didn't know until now?

"Bekka's baby was Rune's."

Of course Rebekka's baby was Rune's. It's why Rebekka came to live at the church. It's why her parents left the church. It's why the preacher was so devastated by my accusation of Rune: if he had fathered my child, he would have fathered two, within weeks. But it had never occurred to me. Rune was in love with me; Rune couldn't also be in love with Rebekka.

"But why would they take Phalia?" I say. "Phalia's not their baby."

"No," Sanne says. "Sofie's my baby."

374

* * *

I walk past the table in the sanctuary where the jimsonweed dries; its kidney-like seeds grow gray, its leaves grow crisp. I put on my jacket, Sanne's jacket. I plan to go outside. But instead, I move toward the kitchen, where I know Sanne and Sara sit in a haze of rot, each inhaling a madapple cigarette, each imbibing a tumbler of schnapps.

They've been gone for two months now—Rune and Rebekka and Phalia. Day after day I've told myself they'll be back. But I know they won't be back. Rune and Rebekka have passed from this blueberry home, and they'll not return: they have their baby.

Sanne, too, knows they won't be back. And Sara knows. Their knowledge lives in dilated eyes and redberry-elder cheeks. Yet they don't know as I know, because of the eyes and cheeks: their brains are soaked in jimsonweed and schnapps. Sara began drinking morning till night after Phalia left, and Sanne smoked. And now Sara smokes, too. And Sanne drinks, too. They've escaped to Mother's madapple world, except I see now it's not a world where the windows are open wide, but a world where all desire to look out windows has wilted away.

I am alone in this pain.

I push open the door. I find Sanne and Sara with the schnapps, without the cigarettes.

"Sanne?" I say. She looks up at me, and I see her black-moon eyes are all black moon. "I want a cigarette."

"No more paper," she says. "I made stew. Schnapps."

A mush of potatoes and carrots and translucent onions bubbles in a pot on the stove. The jimsonweed's leaves snake through the mush; its seeds speckle the mush; and its steam is the haze of rot.

Sanne lifts herself. I think I recognize Mother in the unease of her movements, but then I realize it is the jimsonweed I recognize, not Mother. Sanne ladles the stew into bowls, hands me a bowl. Fills her tumbler, fills Sara's tumbler. Pours me a tumbler of the madapple schnapps.

My eyes trail the sodden path of jimsonweed; I imagine the crazy apple made invisible in the schnapps. And I know I can end this pain: I can pass to that place where desire is dead.

I watch the preacher take a spoonful, lift it to her mouth. I lift the spoon to my mouth; the madapple beckons me; I let it enter me. The taste of it rushes me back to Hartswell, back to myself in Hartswell as I lifted Mother's cold jimsonweed cigarette to my mouth, as I drew in the flavor. I remember wanting the madapple to carry me away, to take me to that place Mother had found. Now the madapple tempts me again. And I wonder, If I go, will I find Mother there?

Sanne eats a spoonful. And another. And another. And soon her bowl is empty. And the preacher's bowl is empty. Then the preacher drains her schnapps, and Sanne drains her schnapps.

I swallow the madapple. Then I swallow it again. But my body starts to heave. I run from the table, to the bathroom. And the crazy apple leaves me.

They are dead by morning. Sanne and the preacher are dead.

I fell asleep on the floor of the bathroom, and I wake to find them slumped on the stone. Sanne's white dress clings

376

to her splayed limbs, and her colorful mouth hangs wide. She is the swamp lily now: her limbs the stringy white petals, her mouth a red stamen. Her hair, dark at the roots, a menagerie at the ends, radiates around her head, forming a misshapen halo. I can see the tip of the tattoo she claimed didn't exist. I lift the white, and I find the painted roots, the painted trunk of the tree. I recognize the orange-red color of the bloodroot, and the layers of faded dye and fresh dye, and I know Sanne painted this image not once but many times. I lift the dress more, and I find the leaves and branches. I pull the dress over the halo, and I find the Essene tree of life. Or the tree of the knowledge of good and evil. Or Yggdrasil. Then I remember Mother's words: "One day the dragon Nidhogg gnaws its roots to shreds, and the entire universe comes crashing down."

Why didn't I stop them? I think. I knew the madapple was deadly—that it could kill them. I knew its strength.

The preacher's light eyes lie open; one hand stretches along the ground high over her head, as if she were reaching for God—as if she were slain in the spirit while reaching for God. I remember the feel of that hand on me; I remember the power that surged through it. I allowed the madapple to squelch that power. I watched as the preacher's hand gripped the spoon, lifted the madapple. And I said nothing.

The pain is more than I can bear. It is more than I can bear. I pull myself away from Sanne, away from the preacher. And yet everywhere I look, everything I see, gashes me.

I pick up the kerosene lamp that sits on the table near where Sanne's Yggdrasil body lies. And I smash it against the wall. And then I walk through the sanctuary, grabbing lamp after lamp, and I smash them. The kerosene puddles on the stone and streams between the stones, as did the preacher's schnapps, and the water of me.

I begin to take off the jacket to throw it into the kerosene. But then I see the red modesty cloths piled near the altar. I grab them and arrange a red road across the kerosene. I ignite one swatch, watch it burst to life.

SOLOMON'S SEAL

2007

—Please state your name for the record.

—Sergeant Ursula Silja.

—What's your profession, Sergeant?

—I'm a sergeant in the United States Army.

—Do you know the defendant?

—Well, I've met her. She came to Pastor Sara's church. I was a member there.

—The Charisma Pentecostal Church?

—Yeah. The church that burned.

—And when you say Pastor Sara, you mean Sara Lerner?

—Yes.

—Okay, Sergeant. You said Ms. Hellig went to the church. Do you know how many times?

—No. Not that many. She came while she was living with the Lerners. I'd say she stayed with them for a couple

379

months. She came to services during that time. She never came again after that.

—When was that?

—Let's see. It was right about the time this teenage girl in our church, Rebekka, got pregnant and went to live at the church, too. With the Lerners. I don't think they had room for both girls. So I guess Aslaug had to leave. That all happened about four years ago. A bit less, maybe.

—Objection. Move to strike. Speculation.

—I'll strike only the comment regarding why Aslaug may have left the church. Otherwise, the objection is overruled.

—Okay. So this girl named Rebekka went to live at the church because she was pregnant?

—Objection. Relevance.

—Overruled.

—Well, first she lived at this home for unwed mothers. I visited her there. Her parents arranged for Bekka to live there. They wanted Bekka to give the baby up.

—For adoption?

—Yes.

—When you say Bekka, you're referring to Rebekka Grass?

—Yes.

—Okay. Then what happened?

—Well, Bekka left the home and moved into the church. Bekka's parents had moved away, but they came back to the church one weekend. Confronted Pastor. Said they realized Pastor's son, Rune, had fathered the baby. Pastor had hired Bekka to tutor Rune. The two were alone a lot—

—Objection. Relevance. Hearsay. Speculation.

—Overruled. But please get to the point.

—Okay. And then?

—Pastor started drinking. The church fell apart.

—Did Bekka have her baby?

—Yeah. And Pastor was helping her raise the child.

—Were you or were you not attending the Charisma Church when Rebekka gave birth?

—I was attending. I attended until Pastor Sara closed the church. I loved that church.

—How old was the baby when the church closed?

—A few weeks.

—Do you know the baby's name?

—They named her Sofie.

—Did you ever see Aslaug at the church after Sofie was born?

—No. She wasn't ever there.

—Objection. The witness is speculating. She has no personal knowledge regarding whether Aslaug was ever at the church.

—I'll strike everything after the word *no*.

—I have no further questions, Your Honor.

GLASSWORT

2006

*T*he flames rise like slender glasswort, streaming orange and red and hot green. The jimsonweed has taken me someplace this time; the madapple has transported me. I watch the fire gulp the church, and I feel so far away.

The glasswort spikes shoot into the air; the plant grows before my eyes. I can't remember where I am. In a garden. A great garden, lush and warm.

And wet. Water gushes suddenly. Too much water. The glasswort wilts. People shout. They try to kill the glasswort. And then they do kill it; they drown it.

"Stop!" I scream, but my voice drowns, too.

I feel hands on my body, and on my arms, my neck. Hands on my leafless flower spikes, my stem. The hands rip me from the ground; they'll drown me. I am the glasswort, and they'll kill me. I ram my spikes into the pulling hands. I break free.

I wake in a ditch, in the taste of char, the smell of char. I see my scorched clothes, my burnt hands, and I remember the glasswort. Then I remember the madapple and igniting the modesty cloths. And I know which of these memories is real.

I want to dig myself back into this ditch, bury myself here. But then I remember: Phalia didn't die.

Somewhere Phalia is alive.

I'm on Irnan Street near the corner where I first parked my car, when I first came to Bethan. The circle I've made in returning here stretches high and low, in and out: this malformed circle has changed me.

I remember parking here, pulling the suitcase of money from the car.

The car.

I have to get the car in order to find Phalia.

And the money, the suitcase of money. Maybe it's still in the church; maybe it survived the fire.

SOLOMON'S SEAL

2007

—Sergeant Silja, there's really no way you could identify the biological parents of this baby, whom you call Sofie, could you?

—Well, I guess I couldn't know whether Pastor's son, Rune, is actually the baby's father, if that's what you mean.

—And you also don't know for sure who the baby's biological mother is, do you?

—Well, Rebekka was pregnant, then there was a baby.

—But you are making an assumption, aren't you?

—I guess so. But—

—You said Rebekka's parents wanted her to give her baby up for adoption. You don't really know whether she gave her baby up for adoption, do you?

—Of course I do. The baby was born. The baby was at

the church. She wasn't given up for adoption. I saw Rebekka nursing her—

—But the baby at the church could have been another woman's baby, couldn't she? Even if Rebekka nursed the child, she could have been another woman's baby.

—I'm sorry, but that seems pretty far-fetched.

—Please just answer yes or no, Sergeant.

—Yeah, I guess the baby could have been some other anonymous woman's baby—

—Not an anonymous woman. As far as you know, the baby could have been Aslaug's baby, isn't that right?

—Objection, Your Honor. Counsel is being argumentative.

—Overruled.

—Sure, why not?

FALSE SOLOMON'S SEAL

2007

*T*hey think I killed my mother.

They think I poisoned Sanne and the preacher.

They think I started the fire to kill Rune and Rebekka and Phalia.

They think I made up the story about having been pregnant.

When I failed to find the car, I went back to the church and the police arrested me. And I have spent the past months listening to the prosecutor's version of my life, my defense counsel's version of my life.

I sit in this courtroom now, and I hear the upheaval: the door shoved open, the startled guard, the shuffled bodies. I turn; I see Rune. But this Rune is too thin: his cheeks sink to deep vales and his eyes show prominent, more like black-eyed-Susan eyes than soft blackberry eyes. Yet for the first time in years, I recognize this person, as if that sticky weight that coated him has peeled away and left him raw. I see that beautiful power surging: I feel it slipping around me and in me. My body remembers his embrace. I've risen from my seat without realizing and moved toward him, as if he has embraced me, drawn me closer. But then my attorney's grip on my arm stops me; I see myself standing, and I sit back down.

"Aslaug!" someone says. But it's not Rune. And then she runs through the courtroom; Phalia runs through the court-room. "Aslaug!" She scales my knees, rides my thighs, presses herself into my stomach, my rib cage. But her body is too big, too bony. She nuzzles her nose and moist mouth into my neck. I smell her thin hair, her warm skin; I remember this buttered-toast smell. And the courtroom falls away. The world falls away. I feel suspended, and yet I feel submerged, too. As if buoyant in a saltwater sea.

I hear a woman's voice. "Sofie, come here!" But Phalia doesn't let go.

"Aslaug," Phalia says again. Her legs pinch my waist, her too-long arms squeeze. Her tiny chest expands and collapses against me. I want to say something, and yet it seems there is nothing I can say. Words can't encompass what I feel; no mold could hold this. I close my eyes. I feel and smell.

And when I open my eyes, I see Rebekka: her lighter hair, her darker skin, her eyes that seem deeper set. She kneels behind Phalia; she wears her hair bound caterpillar-like, tied at the base of her neck and again near its fraying tips. Her sweater is rose-purple, and fuzzy, and blanketed in pale pollen-like lint; its color clashes with her hair; her breath is stale.

"Sofie," Rebekka says. "Let go. Let her go."

387

"Rebekka?" I say. She doesn't respond. "Bekka?" Part of me wants to enfold her, too. To pull her into this circle of limbs, as if that could pull us all into the past, when Sanne lived and loved and Sara lived and loved and Phalia was the root that held us all together, not the strangling vine that divided us, kept us apart.

Keeps us apart. For I don't enfold Rebekka, even though I understand, now, the pain she must have felt when she lost her baby, the pain she must feel: that bottomless pit. Did she fool herself? I wonder. Trick herself into believing Phalia was genetically her own in a futile attempt to fill that pit of pain? She grips Phalia's taut arms and tugs. And I feel the strength in Phalia's small body. Never again, I think. Never again will you take my baby away.

"What's going on here?" the judge says. "Who are these people?"

Phalia doesn't move, but Rebekka does. She releases Phalia, rises, looks around. In this room of people dressed in blacks and blues and grays, she stands colorful and fuzzy. The garish purple passionflower that doesn't belong here.

Rune's gaze hovers, not on me, not on Phalia. On Rebekka. In this moment I see she is not garish to him; that, to him, she does belong here. I sense the caring he feels for her, how sorry he is. She came here because of him, I expect— because he wanted her to come, not because she wanted to come. And now she stands in the courtroom, a spectacle. And Phalia holds me, not her.

I reach out to Rebekka now. With one hand I hold Phalia; with one hand I reach. But she looks at it—my hand—as if it were the hand of a murderer, as if I did kill Sanne and Sara, as if she knows I killed them. She backs away.

388

"I apologize, Judge," Rune says. The judge's attention shifts from Rebekka to Rune. Rune walks through the gallery, toward Rebekka, toward the judge. I recall these elegant lines, this body. And his scent. "We learned of Aslaug's trial. In the paper. The newspaper." His voice is the voice I remember: the voice of many colors, the voice of my dream. And I feel myself wanting to run to him as Phalia ran to me. And I think of his asking me to run away with him, with Phalia. I wish we could run away—the three of us. Yet I don't want to run; I don't want to have to leave to grow free. I want the sunlight to shine here, in this place. "My mother died in the fire," he says. "And my sister."

"That's enough," the judge says, and he holds up his hand. "Please."

Rune stops, stands still; I feel he's trying not to look at me.

The judge turns to the jury, instructs them to step out of the courtroom.

"Your mother was Sara Lerner?" the judge says to Rune after the last of the jury members leaves.

Rune nods his head. "I'm Rune Lerner."

"I'm sorry for you, son." For the first time since the trial began, I see a softening, a sort of drooping, around the judge's keen eyes: he's imagining Rune's sadness, I think—the sadness of losing one's mother. And I realize: he's not looked at me that way; he thinks I'm guilty. "I expect these attorneys here may want a word with you." The judge looks at the prosecutor, my defense counsel. "I'm calling a recess to give you all some time to sort this out."

Rune turns toward me now, and his eyes meet mine. I feel this lightning. I feel this love. And I see his regret—that he left me—and I know why he couldn't look at me before. Yet I see his longing, too. To understand what neither of us may ever understand.

"I have something to say," Rebekka says.

"What?" Rune says.

"I need to testify," Rebekka says, "about what I saw at the church." The girl once so comfortable with her magnified voice now seems unsure of her voice. Her lower lip quivers; it seems she's trying not to cry. She rocks her body forward and back as if preparing to leap. "About Aslaug's behavior after I had my baby. Sofie. This little girl, here."

"Rebekka?" Rune says, and I think: Did I misread him again? See what I wanted to see, not what was real? Did they come not to help me but to ensure I'd be locked away, so they'd never have to worry about my trying to find Phalia, take her back?

"Whether you testify is up to the attorneys here," the judge says. "It's not up to me."

False Solomon's seal has an arching stem, its tip a pyramid of milky white flowers. It is this mass of flowers that betrays the plant, for true Solomon's seal has bell-shaped flowers that hang loose. I wish there were a sign like this for Rebekka, for me. I wish a mass of creamy white flowers could betray her, let the judge know, the attorneys know: this bundle of child still heaving in my arms is my baby.

Rebekka is the false Solomon's seal.

Solomon's Seal

2007

—Please state your name for the record.

—Rebekka Grass.

—Do you know the defendant, Aslaug Hellig?

—Yes.

—Under what circumstances did you come to know her?

—I used to attend the Charisma Pentecostal Church. I first met Aslaug when she came to visit the church about four years ago. She stayed at the church for a while, with Pastor Sara and her kids, Susanne and Rune.

—Okay. Did you spend time with Aslaug?

—Not a lot.

—Why?

—Because she was smitten with my boyfriend, Rune. Rune Lerner. Rune told me, and even Rune was grossed out by it, about her infatuation with him. They were cousins, Aslaug and Rune. Rune said they may even be siblings.

—Objection. Move to strike. Hearsay. Relevance. Speculation.

—Sustained.

—Ms. Grass, how well do you know Rune Lerner?

—We've been in a romantic relationship for over four years. We had a child together. The little girl who was in the courtroom earlier. Sofie.

—Aslaug Hellig seems to think that little girl is her child. Says her name is Phalia.

—That's a lie. But that's what I wanted to explain. Aslaug wanted Sofie to be her baby. She pretended like Sofie was her baby. But ask Sofie who nurses her. She'll tell you it's me. Sofie's three—I've been nursing her for three years. Aslaug's jealous I had Sofie, that Rune and I had a baby. She wanted Rune to be hers, too. I think she'd kill to get what she wants.

—Objection, Your Honor. Speculation. Move to strike.

—Objection sustained. The jury should disregard Ms. Grass's last statement.

VIRGIN'S BOWER

2007

*B*romegrass and canary grass and orchard grass and timothy all live in Maine. Which Grass is this now? I wonder. Which Rebekka is this?

I recall the first time I saw Rebekka, her heavenly voice praising the God who would later betray her. And I recall listening to that same voice humming and humming through the locked door, when she was pregnant, carrying her baby, before she knew God would betray her, not protect her from losing the child. Even now I can feel that magnet-pull, so strong, I felt drawing me to her, when my belly was round and her belly was round, before I knew her baby was Rune's and my baby was not. She seemed to have little interest in me then. Only later did I learn she was deprived of her interest, threatened with her interest: she wasn't to talk to me, look at me. But she did anyway, eventually. She tried to free me, to give me the gift of life that she herself had been denied: my baby. But now, now . . . Now she has deprived me herself: of experiencing my baby's life. And now she wants to deprive me of my own life: my freedom. The hurt she suffered has encircled her, it seems: it is the virgin's bower, that vine that cannot bear its own weight but lives by twining itself around another, making its host unrecognizable.

"She's lying." Rebekka sits in the witness box wetting her bottom lip, wetting her top lip, but Rune has risen to his feet and stepped into the well that separates the judge and Rebekka from the attorneys, from me. It takes a moment before I connect Rune's words to their meaning. "She's lying."

"Mr. Lerner, you'll have your chance to testify. Sit down. Please."

"But she's lying," Rune says. "Bekka's lying."

"Bailiff . . . ," the judge says. The judge's nose colors, his fist thumps the bench, and his eyes look at Rune no longer with the droopy kindness, the sympathy. I see the sharpness now in his eyes I saw before, each time he looked at me.

The bailiff seems stuck between the jury box and Rune. "Get them out . . . ," the judge says, and the bailiff jerks to face the jury box. The jury members scurry out then, but with reluctance, it seems. Several hesitate, look back as they leave.

"Aslaug would never . . . ," Rune says.

The bailiff moves now toward Rune. Don't take him away, I think. Please don't take him away. I remember the feeling I had the first time the preacher spoke of my father. And the feeling I had later, when she mentioned my father shortly after I learned I was pregnant. How I wanted to beg her to stop speaking, take back her words, not take my father away: for my father couldn't be my savior if my father was Mikkel, or her father. Now it is Rune who seems my savior. Our savior: mine and Phalia's. Rune did come here for me, to return Phalia to me, to help me save myself. But he can't be the redeemer if he's not allowed to stay.

"I didn't say Aslaug grossed me out," Rune says. "I never said that. Rebekka did. I was in love with Aslaug and Bekka knew it. She told me I was disgusting—that Aslaug was disgusting."

"Mr. Lerner, unless you sit down, you will be removed from this courtroom. . . ."

But Rune looks at me now, not the judge. I'm not sure he hears the judge; I barely hear the judge. Phalia no longer sits in my lap—the judge insisted she leave the courtroom—but I still feel her body, the memory of it. It seems as real as Rune's words: "I was in love with Aslaug." I used to imagine Phalia's body—the feel of it—in the months after they left, just as I imagined these words, Rune's love, when I was locked away. And now both her body and his words are real. And I realize how much of myself I locked up. It wasn't only Sanne and Sara who locked me from Rune, from Phalia; it wasn't only Rebekka and Rune who stole Phalia from me.

"The child's name isn't even Sofie," Rune says. "Her name is Phalia."

"Don't, Rune!" Rebekka says.

The bailiff grabs Rune: first one arm, then the other. But I see something new in the judge's eyes: not sympathy or kindness; not frustration or anger. Interest. I see interest.

Rune sits. The bailiff releases his grip. And I remember to breathe. "Any more outbursts, and you're done in here," the judge says, but I sense he's relieved Rune sat—that Rune can stay. "No more speaking out of turn from you either, Ms. Grass." And then: "What does the child say her name is?"

"Sofie Phalia," the prosecutor says.

The judge makes a sound I don't recognize: a sort of grunt, laugh, sigh, growl. He takes off his glasses, kneads his eyes, as if to merge the competing emotions packed in there. "Who does the child say her mother is?"

"First she said Susanne," my attorney says. "Then she said Aslaug."

"She changed her mind?" the judge says.

"But Rebekka does nurse her," the prosecutor says. "The child said so. Said Aslaug didn't nurse her. That Rebekka did. Does. Sure seems Rebekka's the mother—"

"Unbelievable," the judge says. He looks at his glasses, rocks them to and fro, puts them back on. "We need a blood test done on the child. Figure out who her mother is. We'll need one of Ms. Grass as well. We already have the information we need from Ms. Hellig, and from Susanne Lerner, the young woman who died." He looks at Rune then, but I can't see the emotion that filters through.

SOLOMON'S SEAL

2007

—Please state your name.

—Rune Lerner.

—Do you know the defendant, Aslaug Hellig?

—Yes.

—When did you first meet her?

—We were children together. I guess I met her when I was a baby, but I'm not sure I remember it. Maybe I do. Aslaug and her mother, Maren, lived with us until Aslaug was two or three, then they moved away. I never saw Aslaug again until she was nearly sixteen. But during the period when I didn't see Aslaug, my sister, Susanne, told me stories about Aslaug. It's hard for me to know which are my memories of Aslaug and which are Susanne's.

—Under what circumstances would Susanne tell you stories about Aslaug?

—Well, Aslaug was kind of a mythical creature to me and Susanne. My mother and Aslaug's mother, Maren, had had a falling-out, and Maren moved away with Aslaug. Aslaug was sort of the forbidden fruit to us—my sister and me. Susanne used to tell me these stories about Aslaug. Sometimes she'd tell me Aslaug was a goddess. Sometimes she'd say Aslaug was a witch or a magician. She'd make up stories about Aslaug's birth, too. Claim it was a miraculous birth, compare it to Jesus's birth. It wasn't until Maren died that I learned there was something to Susanne's stories. I guess Maren wouldn't tell my mother who Aslaug's father was. Maren intimated Aslaug's was a virgin birth. That's why Maren and my mother had their falling-out.

—Objection. Move to strike. What's the relevance of all this?

—Please get to the point, Counsel.

—So you said you saw Aslaug again when she was almost sixteen. What were the circumstances of your seeing her again?

—After Maren's death, Aslaug came to us. She found us somehow. I don't know if I ever learned how.

—And then what happened?

—She lived with us.

—Where?

—At the church.

—With your mother, Sara Lerner, and your sister?

—Yes. And Rebekka. Rebekka came to live with us, too.

—Why was Rebekka living with you?

—She was pregnant. We were kids, you know. We were fooling around and she got pregnant.

—You mean you and Rebekka were lovers?

398

—Yes.

—And the child—Sofie or Phalia?—is your daughter?

—Yes. I mean, she's my daughter. She's not Rebekka's daughter.

—I'm sorry. I'm not following this.

—Sofie. I mean Phalia. She's not Rebekka's daughter.

—But didn't you just say you and Rebekka were lovers and she became pregnant?

—We gave the baby up. For adoption.

—But you said you are Sofie's father.

—I am. When Aslaug came—when she moved in with us—I was so drawn to her. I broke off my relationship with Rebekka. But then I found out Rebekka was pregnant. I was only with Aslaug once, and then I found out about Rebekka—

—You mean you and Aslaug had sex?

—Yes. Just once. But Aslaug got pregnant. Phalia's our baby.

—Are you aware that Aslaug here claims the two of you were never lovers?

—Yes. At first when she became pregnant, she said I'd raped her. I couldn't believe it. Then later, she pretended Phalia was born of a virgin birth.

—Objection. Hearsay.

—Overruled.

—Did you rape her?

—No. God, no. It was totally consensual, our relation-ship. I mean, I was young, but I thought I was in love with her. I think she thought she was in love with me. I don't know why she said what she said.

—Objection. Move to strike. Relevance.

—Overruled. It goes to the defendant's credibility.

—Thank you. Mr. Lerner, you claim Aslaug is the child's mother, but why was the child with you and Rebekka, not Aslaug?

—Before Phalia was born, and even more afterward, they all got so strange. My sister and my mother, and Aslaug, too. They were pretending Sofie Phalia was born of a virgin birth. They said they were preparing her to be a prophet. It was really disturbing. I wanted to protect Phalia. That's why I left with her. And I felt guilty about Rebekka—about getting her pregnant, about my mother forcing her to give our baby up. So Rebekka and I decided to take Phalia and leave. We decided we would be a family, the three of us. That we'd raise Sofie Phalia as if she were our child.

—If that's true, Mr. Lerner, you've just admitted to committing a crime. It's illegal in this state for one parent to take a child without the other parent's consent—

—You know what? I don't really care. It was wrong of me to leave with Phalia. It was so wrong. I should never have taken Phalia from Aslaug. It hurt Phalia. I hurt Phalia. And Aslaug. And Rebekka. I hurt everyone. I knew what Phalia meant to my sister, and my mother. I knew it would devastate them if I took her away. I'm more responsible for their deaths than anyone. Aslaug isn't responsible. There's no way she is. Aslaug may have had some weird notions about Phalia's birth. Maybe she was pretending, I don't know. But she'd never kill anyone.

MADAPPLE

When I hear Rune's account of our relationship, I feel I've been told the world is flat. I am stunned, and yet, in a way, I feel redeemed. The world is as it seems: babies come from sex; the feelings I had for Rune were real; the sensations I experienced that seemed so real were real.

But how could I have mistaken real lovemaking for fantasy, a dream? Am I Mother's mad apple after all? Her crazy offspring? The tainted seed, as Rune once said?

Then I remember.

Madapple.

Sanne told me she'd once given me the jimsonweed stewed into schnapps to make me seem unusual, exceptional. I piece it all together in my mind, and I know: the dream of Rune was not a dream, but reality seen through the dilated eyes of madapple.

And now I feel I've died and been resurrected: a flower that's passed from winter to spring.

I climb with Phalia as if a schoolgirl; we skip into the Maine sky, high on the blueberry hill behind our house in Hartswell. But it is Phalia who is the schoolgirl: she darts ahead of me, then behind me; she stirs this summer-solstice day.

"What did *Bedstemor*—your mommy—call these?" she says as she spins around the mounds of diapensia flowers that wave in earthbound clouds above their sprawling tangle of green leaves. "What about these?" she says, stopped by the dwarf rhododendrons that seem to spurt their flashy magenta.

I tell her the names and a bit about each plant, and she repeats the names, and I see her scribbling away in her mind: recording, considering, wondering. And I know Mother's spirit lives on. But then Phalia chortles, cartwheels, and I recognize Rune in her angles, her grace, her joy. And I feel grateful: Phalia's ring of love is wide. It draws her into the past, to Mother and Sara and Sanne; it broadens her present to Rune—her father, my friend—and to me, and to Rebekka, too, and even to our neighbor, old Grumset, who loves her despite himself, and whom Phalia affectionately calls Grandpa Grumpy. And I know it will grow as she grows.

"They look cozy, Mommy," Phalia says, pointing to a low pink mat of alpine azalea. "Like my bed when the sun peeks in in the morning, when I don't want to get up!"

"They do look cozy, Love Bug," I say. "Do I need to tickle you, like I did in the morning before summer break, when

402

you wouldn't get up and I had to worry about the school bus honking, waking Grandpa Grumpy, making him grumpier?" I lift her in my arms and kiss her warm nose and moist eyes; her arms spread like butterfly wings, and we twirl and tumble, but not on top of the azalea. Although these flowers manage to grow in this harsh climate, where other flowers never could, they are tiny and delicate, and could not withstand our weight. Yet it is the smallness of these flowers— their delicate frame—that is also their saving grace. So diminutive are they, they need little in terms of food, and they can hide in low clusters from the brutal wind and cruel weather. And they've learned cunning: they are perennials, not annuals. For them, one season is never long enough.

When the blood tests came back, they proved what I now know: I am Phalia's earthly mother. And because of this, I was acquitted, set free. Yet I no longer feel the sepal blown about. Nor am I rooted in the way I thought I might be. Because living through the trial helped me realize we are all mad apples, but not in the way I feared.

The trial taught me that understanding a sequence of events, even down to the most minute detail, does not imply an understanding as to why those events took place. It seems we humans so want to divvy the world up into clean little packages that fit neatly together. But in reality, each package seeps into the next, affects the next. And the pile forever shifts. And, as far as I can tell, no one understands where the contents in the packages came from to begin with. I certainly don't. It seems to me now the point of living is less to understand, more to not become dulled to the miracles that are everywhere, Phalia being but one.

Because Phalia is a miracle to me—I realize that now—

403

as much as if she'd come from the hairstreak or the preacher's touch or some divine plan. Nothing can explain the why of Phalia's creation. Or anyone's. Why Avalon exists at all. And nothing can explain the intricacies of creation. The love. And the vast beauty and strangeness of it all.

It's time to open the curtains, let in the sun, let these mad apples grow.

Acknowledgments

First and foremost, I would like to thank the exceptional team at Alfred A. Knopf. In particular, I am grateful to my editor, Michelle Frey. She blessed *Madapple* and me with her faith, enthusiasm, sensitivity and intelligence. Because of her thoughtful editing, *Madapple* is the book it is. Many other amazing people from Knopf worked on *Madapple*— I am grateful to them all. I specifically would like to thank Associate Editor Michele Burke, who kept the ball rolling with enthusiasm and grace; Copy Editor Sue Cohan, who edited *Madapple* with great sensitivity and insight; Executive Art Director Isabel Warren-Lynch, whose creative vision beautifully represents both the content and tone of *Madapple*; Director of Publicity Christine Labov, for her reassuring openness and generosity of spirit; and Senior Publicist Kelly Galvin, for her creativity and energy.

Secondly, I would like to thank my literary agent, Laura Rennert, and Andrea Brown Literary Agency. Laura believed in *Madapple* early, and her faith never faltered. She was determined to find the perfect home for *Madapple*—and she did!

I also would like to thank Jonathan Barkat, the artist who created the cover art for this work. His thoughtful depiction of Aslaug and her world literally took my breath away.

I was fortunate to work with several other talented experts in the writing of *Madapple:* Dr. Janet Waner, PhD, a psychologist who also is my friend and sister-in-law and who was indispensable in guiding my development of the characters; Tina O'Neill Laurberg, a dear friend who advised me in the use of Danish terminology; Dan Smulow, Esq., a former prosecutor who counseled me on criminal law and procedure; Bowdoin College Assistant Professor Barry Logan, who assisted me in the areas of botany and plant pharmacology; Dr. Randall Shannon, MD, who advised me in pathology; and Patrick Hunt, PhD, who shared his expertise in mythology, religion and symbolism. I also relied on numerous research sources identified in the bibliography; I am grateful to the authors of these works. I specifically would like to acknowledge and thank authors Timothy Freke and Peter Gandy for their book *The Jesus Mysteries*. Their interesting research on early Christianity and paganism was extremely useful in my writing of this book. I also want to take this opportunity to thank my Web site designer, Madeira James from xuni.com, who is as brilliant as she is kind, and that is saying a lot.

In addition, my family and close friends have supported my writing of *Madapple* in what seems every way possible. I would like to thank my remarkable mother, Patricia Petrie, whose faith in me and in life has always been an inspiration. Two of my sisters, Amy Laughlin and Melissa Meldrum Aaberg, read the manuscript in its earliest stages and gave me invaluable feedback, and they each provided much-needed advice and support throughout the process. I also am grateful to my siblings Sarah Petrie, Daniel Meldrum and Elizabeth Bakeman for their excitement about this book and for their belief in me. The friends who have supported my writing of *Madapple* are many, and I am grateful to them all. A few of my close friends were readers for me, and to you I owe special gratitude: Liz Epstein, an amazing editor who greatly refined *Madapple*; Kim Oster, whose compassion and intelligence helped to give *Madapple* depth; Michael Bourne, whose honesty, know-how and humor kept me and *Madapple* on track; and Lynne Dewhurst and Renee Swindle, who gave me much-needed advice when *Madapple* was first being birthed. And to the brilliant and multitalented Julia Flynn Siler, who has guided me in endless ways, to photographer and friend extraordinaire Victor Hong, and to godmother goddess Betty McClennan: thank you!

Finally, but most importantly, I would like to thank my husband, Douglas Dexter, and my children, Jacob and Owen. They are the inspiration for my mind, heart and soul. *Madapple* could not have happened without them.

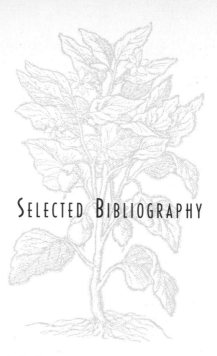

Selected Bibliography

Religion and Mythology

Bultmann, Rudolf. *Primitive Christianity in Its Contemporary Setting*. Cleveland: The World Publishing Company, 1970.

Chuang Tzu. *Chuang Tzu, Mystic, Moralist and Social Reformer*. Boston: Adamant Media, 2004. Facsimile reprint of an 1889 edition.

Enslin, Morton Scott. *Christian Beginnings*. New York: Harper Torchlight, 1956.

Freke, Timothy, and Peter Gandy. *The Jesus Mysteries: Was the "Original Jesus" a Pagan God?* New York: Three Rivers Press, 2001.

Hall, Manly P. *The Secret Teachings of All Ages*. New York: Tarcher, 2003.

Lao Tzu. *The Way of Life According to Lao Tzu*. Translated by Witter Bynner. New York: Perigee Books, 1944.

Massey, Gerald. *The Historical Jesus and the Mythical Christ*. Escondido, CA: The Book Tree, 2000.

Meyer, Marvin W., ed. *The Ancient Mysteries: A Sourcebook of Sacred Texts.* Philadelphia: University of Pennsylvania Press, 1999.

Pagels, Elaine. *The Gnostic Gospels.* New York: Vintage Books, 1989.

Pennick, Nigel. *Magical Alphabets.* York Beach, ME: Weiser Books, 1992.

S, Acharya. *The Christ Conspiracy: The Greatest Story Ever Sold.* Kempton, IL: Adventures Unlimited Press, 1999.

Vermes, Geza. *The Complete Dead Sea Scrolls in English.* New York: Penguin Classics, 2004.

www.bigpedia.com/encyclopedia/Norse_mythology

www.en.wikipedia.org/wiki/Norse_mythology

www.essenespirit.com

Science and Nature

Brock, Jim P., and Kenn Kaufman. *Butterflies of North America.* New York: Houghton Mifflin, 2006.

Bryson, Bill. *A Short History of Nearly Everything.* New York: Broadway Books, 2004.

Greene, Brian. *The Elegant Universe: Superstrings, Hidden Dimensions, and the Quest for the Ultimate Theory.* New York: W. W. Norton & Co., 1999.

Haines, Arthur, and Thomas F. Vining. *Flora of Maine: A Manual for Identification of Native and Naturalized Vascular Plants of Maine.* Bar Harbor, ME: V. F. Thomas Co., 1998.

National Audubon Society Field Guide to North American Trees, Eastern Region. New York: Knopf, 1980.

National Audubon Society Field Guide to North American Wildflowers, Eastern Region. New York: Knopf, 2001.

Pierson, Elizabeth C., Jan Erik Pierson, and Peter D. Vickery. *A Birder's Guide to Maine.* Camden, ME: Down East Books, 1996.

Russell, Sharman Apt. *An Obsession with Butterflies: Our Long Love Affair with a Singular Insect.* Cambridge, MA: Perseus Books, 2003.

Weber, Larry. *Butterflies of New England*. Duluth, MN: Kollath-Stensaas Publishing, 2002.

www.botanical.com

Locations and Culture

Calhoun, Charles C. *Maine*. Oakland, CA: Compass American Guides/Fodor's, 2000.

Doudera, Victoria. *Moving to Maine: The Essential Guide to Get You There*. Rockport, ME: Down East Books, 2000.

Karr, Paul, and Wayne Curtis. *Frommer's Portable Maine Coast*. New York: Wiley Publishing Inc., 2003.

Strange, Morten. *Culture Shock! Denmark*. Portland, OR: Graphic Arts Center Publishing Company, 1999.

Poetry

Dickinson, Emily. *The Complete Poems of Emily Dickinson*. Edited by Thomas H. Johnson. New York: Little, Brown and Company, 1960.

Sappho. *The Love Songs of Sappho*. Translated by Paul Roche. New York: Signet Classics, 1966.